WASHINGTON'S CHILD

Michael Dialessi

authorHOUSE®

AuthorHouse™
1663 Liberty Drive
Bloomington, IN 47403
www.authorhouse.com
Phone: 1-800-839-8640

First published by AuthorHouse   6/24/2010

ISBN: 978-1-4520-1638-2 (e)
ISBN: 978-1-4520-1639-9 (sc)
ISBN: 978-1-4520-1640-5 (hc)

Library of Congress Control Number: 2010905620

Printed in the United States of America
Bloomington, Indiana

This book is printed on acid-free paper.

I dedicate this book to my wife and children, who I love with all my heart.

Contents

Chapter 1:
The Dawn

A tiny ladybug slowly crawled down the brass barrel of the transit, as the dew-moistened grass swayed in the gentle breeze. The sun was just beginning to appear over the horizon, as the stern-faced youth surveyed the Virginia landscape. It was the beginning of a beautiful, early September morning.

He was no ordinary fourteen-year-old Virginian. He was a young man well beyond his years in wisdom, who arose every morning before dawn to earn his daily bread. As his small fingers adjusted the brass wheels to calculate the exact distance, his keen hearing detected movement in the woods. Soft footsteps were approaching with twigs snapping under foot. He believed it was a small party of travelers and not a cadre of men seeking evil, for they would be far more cautious. Never the less, he reached down with his right hand to check the secureness of the screw which clamped his perfectly napped flint in the lock.

From the corner of his eye, he saw them emerge. Not men of white, but natives of leathery skin with brown eyes. Slowly, not to startle the men, but unsure of their intensions, he lifted his flintlock, brought it to the ready and then clasped his right hand over the lock and drew back the hammer. Keeping part eye on the party, he lifted up the frizzen to check if the pan was properly charged.

Leading the group, there was a young Indian whose face he recognized. He was a young man he had not seen for almost a year. He grasped the hammer with his left hand and carefully lowered it, then counted six of them after the group had fully emerged from the woods. One of them wore colorful garments covered with symbols not of his knowing. He must have been an elder, from a tribe not yet discovered by the British or the French. Immediately, he was drawn to the eyes of the unknown elder. His left eye was brown, as were most Indians he had seen. His right eye, however, was a multi-layered blue; similar in pattern to what is seen when steel in quenched.

The familiar face gave him a nod and a greeting. He loosened his grip on his musket and carefully leaned it on the cherry tripod legs, which had the transit on the apex.

"Is it time?" he asked.

"Yes," the familiar face told him.

The seven walked toward the woods. Two braves were in front. The Indian friend and the strange elder followed. Next, was the young Virginian, followed by the last two in the group.

Before entering the woods, the young Virginian studied the pattern in beads on the back of the elder's garment. There were three colored beads which formed the shape of a triangle and a fourth dark bead in the center. Below it on the right, around the area of the kidney, there was a bright white star.

The group walked for many hours until they came upon the falls. The sun had started its trek toward the western horizon and a cool breeze began to blow. A small opening lay to the right of the falls and the seven entered, one by one; for the opening was narrow, and the footing treacherous. Once inside, all sat in a circle. The inner chamber was lit by five small torches set equidistantly apart, and the whistle of the wind could be heard along with the rushing water from the falls.

As the ceremony began, four of the torches were extinguished, which left a single torch to light the ritual. As the young Virginian closed his eyes, he could feel the room around him spin, and it seemed as if he was being bathed in very bright light. As the Indian elder spoke unfamiliar words, the young man fell into a strange state of hypnosis. Then all went black.

∽

The trek back began shortly after daybreak and he returned alone. He could see as he emerged from the wood that the cherry-legged tripod and shiny brass transit stood unmolested, along with the maple stocked musket.

A new passion has consumed the young man. He moved the equipment some fifty yards to the north and west. His nimble fingers adjusted the knobs. He trained the equipment east to the grassy hill, followed by south to the marsh. He then aimed the eyepiece to the west, where a light fog encased the long reeds growing in the damp soil. From where the transit was located, he walked about seven hundred yards to the south and slightly east. As he approached the water, he found a small, straight branch of a white oak, about three feet in length and then gently pushed it into the sand by the side of the bank. The transit was north of his current location and from the branch's shadow he knew that it was about half past two in the afternoon. The young man smiled and spun himself around while he looked in all four directions. It was at this moment that he realized this spot of ground was the ideal place for a great symbolic message to be constructed in stone.

The young Virginian then walked to his west, until the marsh dampened the bottom of his shoes. He squatted and looked straight ahead with firm countenance. "About an hour to the left," he said while turning his head slightly northeast. "There," he muttered while he pointed his small hand. "That is the place of the union."

He reached his hand into his pocket and withdrew a small compass. He assured himself that the measurements were true, while he observed both the current position of the sun and the compass needle. He then placed the compass back in his pocket and walked back to where his musket and surveying equipment rested.

Before packing up his equipment he said to himself, "38 degrees north, 77 degrees west. That will do." As the sun began to set, the young Virginian packed up his equipment and slung the tripod over his shoulder. He turned and glanced back at the open area he had just surveyed. "Someday, the great work will be completed for all to see. But will they understand what they are looking at, or its implications?"

Chapter 2
The Seven and Seven

"It is time to wake up Dayton." As the child opened his eyes, he saw the loving gaze of his father. "We have a date with an important lady, and we don't want to miss the first ferry."

The child arose from his bed and quickly caught himself from almost falling over. It was before sunrise. Today it felt earlier. It was a Saturday in the first week of June. He peeled off his pajamas and proceeded to put on the clothes that were neatly folded on the chair by the foot of his bed. After dressing, he slid on his black leather shoes and tied the laces in a double knot.

The young boy always loved car rides. Tunnels and roads full of big trucks and passenger cars always provided plenty for him to observe. After a few hours in the car, and a few donuts for breakfast, father and son arrived at their destination.

"Two tickets please. One adult, one for a child under twelve," the father said to the young woman behind the ticket counter.

"Okay, here you go." The tickets slid through the opening. "Just walk down the green path until you hit the docking area for the ferry," she said, pointing through the small rectangular cutout in the window. "I hope you and your son have a wonderful day."

Father and son boarded the ferry. It was white with black trim, and had plentiful seating, because it was the first ferry of the day out to her island. The motor hummed to life and the boat began its trek across the calm waters of the bay of New York.

In a short time, the figure of a green, robed woman could be seen in the distance, standing majestically on her small island with a golden-topped torch in her right hand. Her face gazed east at the place of the sunrise and she carried a tablet in her left hand with the date of America's birth.

The little boy couldn't contain himself. He pressed his face against the glass window of the ferry and squished his little nose flat.

"Are you excited Dayton?"

"Yes I am daddy. We were talking about her in history class, just before school got out yesterday."

"What do you know about her?" the father inquired.

"Well, I know a lot of immigrants knew they were in America when they first saw her. She's made of copper and was a gift from French school kids. And she has that poem on her by Emma...."

"Lazarus," piped in Mr. McCormick. "Give me your tired and poor."

"Yes daddy, THAT poem," said Dayton.

"The poem is correct, Dayton, but she wasn't a gift from French children. She was a gift from French Masons. She sits on Liberty Island, which was formerly called Bedloe's Island. The base of the pedestal she stands on was once Fort Wood and had cannons in it. They were used to protect New York City from naval invasions."

"Uh, Dad. What is a French Mason?" Dayton inquired.

Mr. McCormick loved his job as a history teacher, although he was frustrated with the common misconceptions taught to children in schools. But he never missed an opportunity to correct his son with the truth. "French means from France, so indeed, it was a gift from the French. Freemasons are a fraternal secret society----kind of like a men's only club," he explained. "Many things have been attributed to Freemasons that are both good and bad."

"Are they bad, Dad?" Dayton asked.

"I don't think so Dayton," his father explained. "Some of the great men who founded this nation were Freemasons. I think people like to believe what they want to believe, without looking up the facts. Human history is filled with that." He rubbed the top of his son's head. "There have always been scapegoats in every society, including ours."

The ferry made its way toward the dock. The swaying waters pitched the boat slightly to the left and right as it came to a complete stop. Dayton quickly ran toward the ramp with his father, Mr. McCormick, chasing right behind him.

"Come on Dad, hurry up!" Dayton yelled. The two, once they reached land, slowed from a run, to a brisk walk. "Dayton, wait up. We have all day," the father replied, while trying to catch his breath.

Mr. McCormick pulled out his 35mm camera from its case and used his thumb to forward the film. "Hey, son! Turn around and put your right hand in the air."

Dayton turned to face his father and put up his right hand, mimicking Lady Liberty.

Click. "I got it. Now you look like Liberty Enlightening the World," said Mr. McCormick, "which is her proper name."

"I am so glad we came after all that stuff they had around her was removed. And the new torch looks really nice, Dad."

"Yes, the restoration came out perfect. And it was a lot of work." He pointed up. "Dayton, she is ninety-three meters high from her base to the tip of her torch. It must have been difficult working under some pretty windy conditions on that scaffolding."

Father and son walked around and conversed together while discussing more about of the history of the Statue: from its designer Bartholdi, to the cornerstone being laid for it on August 5, 1884, to its completion, in 1886. Mr. McCormick, after he took a few more snapshots, sat down on a bench, took off his backpack and then removed the two brown bags containing sandwiches he made late the previous night.

Father and son sat and enjoyed an early lunch and both grinned ear to ear as they chewed.

After lunch, Mr. McCormick and Dayton walked around Liberty Island for a few more hours and continued to talk about the history of New York City and the Islands in the bay.

As their day-trip on Liberty Island came to a close, Mr. McCormick wanted to pose his son Dayton for one final snapshot.

"I'd like to get a shot of you with the Twin Towers and the rest of the Manhattan Skyline in the background," he said.

"Okay Dad," Dayton replied, as he put his right hand on the stone of Liberty's pedestal. Mr. McCormick forwarded to the next frame on his Canonet G3. As he looked through the rangefinder, he brought the two images of his son's face together in the dull yellow square in the center of the viewfinder by utilizing his thumb and index finger on his left hand. While waiting for his father to take the photo, Dayton was partially blinded by the sun's reflection off a passerby's mirror-style sunglasses. As Dayton wiped his eyes, the stranger turned his head and smiled. Click.

"You ok, son? Looks like I am going to have to take one more---- this time, without you wiping your eyes." Mr. McCormick used the thumb lever to forward the film, while he kept his eyes firmly on the passerby in the mirror shades. "It can't be," he muttered, as he squinted at the pedestrian. He shook his head and then recomposed the photograph.

"Are you ready? Okay." Dayton nodded. Click.

The McCormick's slowly began their walk back to the ferry dock, with the father's arm on his son's shoulder.

"I had a great day, Dad!" boasted Dayton, as he looked up at his father with a big smile on his face. The smile briefly reminded Mr. McCormick of Dayton's mother.

"I did too, son. I am glad you like history as much as I do." He smiled and began another monologue on the history of Lady Liberty. "You know, President Cleveland gave the acceptance statement for Lady Liberty. He told the crowd that, "We will not forget that Liberty here made her home; nor shall her chosen alter be neglected." That's a funny statement coming from a President who vetoed the funding for the building of the pedestal. History is full of interesting things like this, son."

"Why did the French Masons give her to us?" Dayton asked.

Mr. McCormick wondered for a moment how he could explain it in terms an eleven-year-old would accept. "Dayton, sometimes things are done for multiple reasons. It was a sign of friendship," Mr. McCormick continued, "And perhaps it could have to do symbolically with something much larger and more profound."

Dayton looked up at his father with a puzzled glance and shook his head. "What do you mean Dad?"

"I'm not quite sure Dayton. I am not quite sure. You know, when I look at that skyline over there, especially those two towers which stand out, I often wonder what it will look like fifteen or twenty years from now. Everything goes to dust eventually. People. Buildings. Everything."

Dayton put his hand over his eyes to get a better view of the Twin Towers. "Even those towers?" he asked.

"Even those towers. Yes. Everything. But remember this----my love for you, my son, is forever. It will last longer than the pyramids and the Sphinx in Egypt."

Mickey's statement made Dayton smile. He loved his father and his grandparents so much. He never knew his mother, who died in the middle of the night when he was still an infant. He had no brother or sister to fight with and spent most of his time with adults. At age eleven, he was a very thoughtful child well beyond his years in maturity and knowledge, and loved spending time with his father going on his history-related adventures. Dayton didn't want to think about the mother he didn't have, or the lack of friends his own age and instead hugged his father tight.

"Thanks for the great day, Dad."

Mr. McCormick smiled. "Well, it is time to head home."

The ferry came to dock back in New Jersey. Father and son walked slowly to the red minivan.

"If you are tired, you can sleep on the way home."

Dayton yawned, "I am not tired."

A few miles down the road, Mr. McCormick checked his rear-view mirror. Dayton was sound asleep. "The base of Liberty is a truncated pyramid," he said to himself. "Copper. Double-helix staircases. A woman with a torch. An eleven-point base. Seven rays on the headpiece. A woman facing east. Am I missing something?" he said, muttering under his breath. "I must be missing something----but the three are there in the woman. The fourth has been covered by a previous renovation."

He looked into his rear-view mirror and noticed his son was smiling in his sleep. He cleared his mind for the rest of the drive home and glanced numerous times through the rear-view mirror at his sleeping son. There was more to life than his research. Someday, he would write his book and inform the world, he thought to himself. But his son would only be eleven, once.

"Of all the trips I have taken him on, I hope he remembers this one the most." Mickey glanced again at Dayton. "And I hope to god the man I saw wasn't who I think it was."

Chapter 3
The Great Work

Dayton opened his eyes. The crackling sound and the strong aroma could only mean that his dad was cooking bacon. He slowly peeled off his Star Wars comforter and carefully tip-toed through his room, so not to disturb the celestial battle being waged by the plethora of action figures scattered across the floor.

Across the hall of the two-bedroom condo was his father's room. It was always neat as a pin, except for his desk where he did his research. On the wall, there was a tomahawk and a samurai sword, both of which he knew only to touch with his eyes. On his father's desk was a Brother word processor, a small stack of typed pages and a scattered pile of pictures, which the boy was unfamiliar. Next to the monitor was a small, framed photo of his dad and five other men in military uniforms.

"I know you're in my room Dayton. Don't touch anything on the desk," Mr. McCormick shouted from downstairs. "And why don't you come down? Breakfast is ready."

Dayton slowly crept down the stairs, hoping to sneak up on his father without him hearing him. His pajamas had built-in socks, so he believed that it would be easy to do on the carpeted stairs.

"I can hear you on the stairs. Come on down for breakfast."

"Coming, Dad," replied a frustrated Dayton.

As the two sat down to enjoy what was considered the favorite breakfast in the house, the phone rang. Mr. McCormick answered it on the second ring. Mickey looked uncomfortable as he listened to the caller.

12

"Talking on the phone is not a good idea. Do you understand?" Mr. McCormick said under his breath. After nodding his head a few times, he replied, "I need you to come over early this afternoon. I have to make a few arrangements first, but I need you here." Mickey placed his hand over the phone's microphone.

"Dayton," said his father, "Something has come up and I need to call your grandmother. You'll have to go over there today after breakfast. I'll have grandma bring you back tonight."

Dayton nodded his head as he sat chewing his pancake. A gentle stream of butter ran down his chin. He smiled at the thought of seeing his grandparents. They always took him somewhere fun and they had the greatest big white house on the edge of Richmond for a young boy to explore.

"Mom, something has come up. I really need you to come over and get Dayton for the day," said Mr. McCormick. "That's great. I'll have him dressed and ready to go within the hour. Thanks."

After breakfast, Dayton got dressed in his favorite jeans. He tied his shoes and then filled up a small backpack with some of his action figures and other boyhood essentials.

The doorbell rang at the McCormick's condo, and Dayton's grandparents came in the door. Grandma Martha was thin, with brown eyes and a pleasant demeanor. Gramps, or Grandpa George, stood a little over six-feet, and always wore a baseball cap to cover his thinning hair.

Mr. McCormick walked over to his son and got on his knees. He then gave the longest and tightest hug to Dayton that he had ever given him in his life.

"Son, I want you to behave for your grandparents and do whatever they tell you. I'll see you tonight."

"I will Dad. I love you."

"I love you too, son."

After they exchanged goodbyes, Grandpa George flung Dayton over his shoulder and walked out the condo door to the car.

"If you need anything, just give us a call," said Martha to her son Mickey. "We're going to take Dayton out to the park before lunch, then for supper and ice cream before we bring him home----if that is ok?"

"That's fine mom. Just take good care of him like you always do. But don't spoil him too much. He'll want to eat out all the time."

As the car pulled out of the driveway, Mickey McCormick headed upstairs to his bedroom where his work awaited him. He sat down in his chair and studied the aerial photographs intently.

"Absolutely incredible," he mumbled to himself. "Absolutely incredible. I have just about everything I need now."

He sat and began to type. He looked over at a previously typed sheet to his left. "Great preface. I am glad I made a copy. I only wish he would have helped me finish," he said sadly.

Mickey began to pack up various items in boxes. He then started filling his footlocker and placed a special small box safely at the bottom. "I know just where to put this." He loaded up his minivan and drove off, timing his special errand so that he'd be home when the caller was to arrive at his condo.

Chapter 4
The Note

Dayton was finishing his ice cream sundae and clanking his spoon against the glass. Gravity was pulling a small bubble of chocolate syrup down the left side of his chin.

"Whoa big guy! Let me get that," said George McCormick, who quickly swiped a napkin out of the holder and gently pressed it against his grandson's chin.

"It is 7:30 George. It is time to take Dayton home," said Martha McCormick. Being in their fifties, the McCormick's were still young enough to enjoy their sole grandchild. They paid their bill for the meal and desert, left the standard fifteen percent gratuity and then headed off with Dayton to their car that was parked four spaces from the restaurant door.

The drive back to their son's condo took only a few minutes and they parked to the right side of his red minivan.

George McCormick pulled out the key he had for his son's condo and unlocked the front door. Martha entered.

"Mickey, we're back with Dayton. Mickey," said his mother Martha.

Martha's inquiry was greeted by silence.

"That's unusual," said George. "His car is in the driveway."

"Maybe he is upstairs?" said Dayton, as he pulled his Grandfather's hand and towed him up the steps.

Dayton's father's bedroom light was on, but no one was inside.

The study desk with the Brother word processor was absent of any papers or photos. Dayton wondered where they went.

"Dad? Where are you? Dad?"

The monitor screen of the word processor was on and the elder McCormick could make out a faint reflection of words on the bedroom window.

"Dayton, wait here. Just a second," said his grandfather, motioning him to stay put.

George McCormick walked over to the monitor so he could read what was on the screen.

TAKE GOOD CARE OF DAYTON. HE IS A GOOD BOY. I'M SORRY.
MICKEY.

George McCormick's face turned white and for a minute he froze in place, as a very uneasy feeling came over him that only a parent could understand.

Keeping his composure, he walked over to his grandson and bent down. "Dayton. I want you to go downstairs and see your grandmother. I'll be down in a minute."

The boy, not knowing what was wrong, did so without question. Mr. McCormick slowly walked over to the bathroom door and noticed a trickle of light coming from the bottom. He hesitated, then pressed his palm to open the door, only to find it was locked. He then walked back into the bedroom to the desk, where in the middle drawer he found a few paperclips. He took the largest paperclip in the bunch, bent it straight and walked back to the bathroom door.

"No God, please no," he whispered as he pushed the paperclip through the small hole in the center of the doorknob. The lock made a clicking noise, indicating the mechanism had released. He pulled out the clip and again pressed his palm against the doorknob, clutching it with his fingers and turning it to the right. As the door slowly opened, he noticed a bloody hand lying limp outside the bathtub and pools of red smattered across the tile floor. He closed his eyes and prayed that it was his mind playing tricks on him and that he was really only imagining what he had witnessed.

"Martha!" yelled Dayton's grandfather, in a voice he hadn't used since the war. "Take Dayton outside!"

"Why?" she replied. "Is something wrong?"

"Just do it. Now!"

All the color in George McCormick's face had left him. He clutched the side of the wall as his legs lost their strength. He had seen plenty of death in the Korean War, but those men were not his son. He fought back the tears as he turned to walk back into the bedroom.

Clutching the phone, he tried to dial 9-1-1, but his index finger kept slipping out of the rotary dial. On his third try, he was successful.

The operator answered, "911. What is the nature of your call?"

Trying to compose himself, George stuttered in a broken voice as he breathed heavily. "Please come to 322 Sunset Parkway. My boy has killed himself. He was my only son."

He sat down in the chair at the desk, shaking uncontrollably, which caused him to drop the phone on the floor. The word processor's monitor stared back at him in silence.

TAKE GOOD CARE OF DAYTON. HE IS A GOOD BOY. I'M SORRY.
MICKEY.

"Damn you Mickey! Damn you!"

Chapter 5
Twenty-Two Years Later

The concrete-walled room was dimly lit and resembled the appearance of the city at dusk. Detective Dayton McCormick casually put on his hearing protection and covered his eyes with his amber-colored shooting glasses. At twenty paces, the man-shaped silhouette target dangled from a metal hanger.

He drew his weapon. It wasn't the standard department-issued sidearm. He wasn't officially on duty. His Ruger P345 felt better in his hands and had a longer and smoother double action trigger-pull than the Glock he carried while on official police business. He preferred the .45 caliber round over the .40 caliber S&W, especially with human predators.

Dayton brought the pistol up to chest level, then pressed it forward. The sight was aligned with the center of mass of the silhouette. He began to pull on the trigger and exhaled slowly.

Bam. Ba-bam. Three shots exited the barrel; two struck center-of-mass with the third hitting the head. He repeated the procedure a second time. Bam. Ba-bam. Then, pretending to flinch, he cycled two more rounds through the semi-automatic, which emptied the magazine.

He placed the gun down on the forward shelf and yelled, "Clear."

As the gun sat with the slide locked back, he thumbed the switch in the shooting booth; bringing the silhouette target home. Residual smoke slowly floated out the muzzle.

"Not bad Dayton. Except for the last shot only gave the perpetrator a Van Gough," teased Detective Mark Tilenda.

As Dayton turned, he saw his best friend and old beat partner. Mark grinned with his typical lady-killing smile. He stood at a hair over six feet tall and had a body presence more like a typical Marine than a metropolitan police detective. His hazel eyes peered at Dayton as he nodded his head. Dayton was glad to see him.

"What are you doing down here?" asked Mark. "Aren't you on leave?

"Just thought I would come down and collect my thoughts. Nothing better than a little range time," Dayton responded.

"You know it," he agreed. Mark then inquired about Dayton's partner.

"Considering he is having his gall bladder removed this week----I guess ok. I got the old guy, remember?" Dayton replied. "Mr. Ear hair."

"Yes---the old man. I remember when I was the older cop when you first started patrolling a beat." He rubbed Dayton on the head. "But you're no longer a green horn."

"Speaking of greenies, how's your new partner?" Mark pretended not to hear the question. "Oh come on Mark," Dayton prodded. "Don't tell me you haven't checked her out."

Mark rolled his eyes. "She's nice. And serious, like you. Good detective." Dayton stared at him while he tapped his foot. "She's not interested in me that way."

"Is it you already tried, or does she know you have been married twice already?" Dayton jabbed.

"Don't remind me Dayton." Mark looked over at Dayton's target, then back at him and cracked, "She's probably a lesbian."

"Oh, really?" Dayton replied.

"Yah---'Cause I think she's interested in you."

"You're an asshole Mark," Dayton retorted. He looked Mark straight in the eye, and then curiosity got the best of him. "How do you know?"

Mark explained that his new partner, Sarah, had been assigned to him only two weeks ago, and in that time, "She has asked me three times if you were single. I told her you were too busy with all your book stuff."

"What?" Dayton said, giving Mark the evil eye.

"Just kidding," Mark said with a big grin. "Speaking of your book, are you making a killing off it or what?"

Dayton explained to Mark that Triple E Books was a small publisher and also his status as a first time author. "I got five K signing up with them and I'll get a royalty of fifty cents per book."

"Cheap bastards," Mark responded while shaking his head. "You make more as a detective."

Dayton nodded. "I know. But since I was a kid, my father's dream was to write a book. He never got the chance. Besides," Dayton continued, "all my travel and hotel expenses for the next couple months are being paid for by the publisher."

"That ain't bad. You like to travel," Mark replied.

Dayton reminded Mark that his first book signing was in Richmond this evening. "Barnes and Noble on West Broad, 7 PM."

"If I can swing by, I will. But I'm on duty pal, and if something comes up---"

"It's not that big a deal," Dayton replied.

"I have to run," Mark replied, while motioning his head toward the door. "Good luck tonight. If I don't get tied up, I'll bring Sarah too."

Dayton smiled and turned to his empty gun. He placed it and the empty magazine into a small black case and then locked it.

"Hey Mark," Dayton yelled. Mark walked back over to him. "Could you do me a favor? My grandfather is really sick. I don't know how long he has. If you hear anything on the radio?"

"I'll call your cell right away," Mark said.

"And, if something happens while I am out of town?" Dayton's face began to frown. He thought about his grandfather and how tough the past year had been on him since his leukemia had come out of remission. He felt horrible guilt at the thought of abandoning him and his grandmother when he felt they needed him the most. Of course his grandparents would hear none of his complaints. They were so proud of his achievement and did not want to stand in the way of his future.

"Don't worry about it. I may not have the most fidelity when it comes to marriage, but I would never let my best friend down," Mark replied.

"You're a fine piece of work," he said. "Thanks Mark."

Dayton patted his friend on the back and smiled as he walked toward the door. He pulled the handle as the buzzer went off; signaling the electric lock had discharged. He headed up the stairwell toward the Chief's office.

"Well. It's time to go upstairs and thank the old man for granting me my time off," Dayton said to himself.

Detective Dayton McCormick had seen many gruesome sights while being a police detective, but nothing made him feel more uneasy than looking at the crowd of about twenty-five people who had gathered at the Barnes and Noble Bookstore to hear him pitch his book and get their signed copies. He took a deep breath, looked up, visualized himself making the sign of the cross and then slowly walked over to the podium, which was set up before the crowd.

He looked to the left and to the right. He could see all types of people: The young and old mixed in with the clean cut and the tattooed. He licked his lips once, pinched his lower lip between his top and bottom teeth, paused for a second and then began to speak.

"Thank you all for coming. I'll try not to stutter." The group sensed he was nervous and a few people in the crowd nodded their heads and lightly laughed.

Dayton continued, "I dislike the words "Conspiracy Theory." I much prefer the words fact and fiction. Ever since the assassination of John F. Kennedy, many authors around the world have presented a lot of accusations." Dayton paused to lick his lips again. "Accusations which, over time, have grown legs and created an entire industry." Dayton bowed his head as he thought of what he would say next. "My name is Dayton McCormick. I am a police detective here in Richmond." He continued to explain to the crowd about his role as a detective arresting bad guys and trying to keep them off the streets. "Only solid evidence presented in a Court of Law can keep the bad guys in jail. Evidence, which on careful inspection, is missing from most conspiracy theories."

A woman in the front looked at her friend and whispered, "He's the one who stopped the Birthday Murderer."

Dayton overheard what she said and recalled the incident, but quickly put it out of his mind to complete his task at hand.

"There are many people out there who think 911 was perpetrated by our own government. Seems plausible, doesn't it? I mean, the government has a lot of power, along with the means and the opportunity. After all, as many websites claim, there was "Operation North Woods," in the 1960's, which was a plan proposed to hijack or bomb American airliners and blame the Cubans, so our government could fire up the American people to support an invasion," Dayton said in a sarcastic tone.

Dayton smiled, "But folks, this is the same government that can't run a mass transit system properly or keep a stained blue dress secret." A gentleman laughed in the crowd, nodding his head in agreement. "Somebody would have talked, but nobody has."

Dayton squeezed his hands tightly against the small podium.

"I am here to answer questions and also to sign your books if you wish. Just to let you know, I have received "hate mail" already from those who think I am a sell-out to the powers-that-be, whoever they are? But I can assure you, especially if you read the book carefully, there are a lot of unanswered questions that I have concerning some events over the past sixty years. I am not looking for the truth, because truth is subjective." Dayton paused and licked his dry lips one more time. "I am looking for the facts, so a conviction can be made in a courtroom. Any questions?"

A young man with scraggly hair and a black tee-shirt raised his hand. He started to stand up and Dayton could clearly see the imprint on the front of his shirt, which had a circle with a slash through it containing the letters "NWO" for the New World Order.

"What about the New World Order?" he inquired.

Dayton replied, "What about it? The New World Order has been a phrase used by many in higher office. It was used by George H. W. Bush, of all days, on September 11th, but in 1990 or 1991." He continued to elaborate that the phrase New World Order was also used by his successor, President Clinton, as well as Bush's son, W. "Where is it? Many conspiracy websites tie this New World Order to the Club of Rome or the Committee of 500 and their desire to drastically reduce the population of the world. Well, prior to World War One, there was never more than a billion people on this planet, at least that we can recall. We are approaching seven billion. So it seems to me, if there is a plan to reduce the population, it has failed miserably."

The young man continued standing. "What about the plan for a socialist world government?"

"I don't think that is going to happen," Dayton replied. As he responded, his mouth and hands moved in unison. He explained to the crowd that most of the socialist world government nonsense came from the misinterpretations of speeches or laws and policy. "Senate document 7727 was supposed to disarm everybody. That was written when Kennedy was President. Presidents from Carter to Clinton were supposed to be the ones who would usher in global socialism. And George W. Bush, according to internet rumor, was supposed to declare Marshall Law. Has any of this happened? The answer is no." Dayton was becoming quite animated. "World Socialism?" Dayton exhaled, "I think Margaret Thatcher said it best----socialism only works when you have someone else left to steal from."

"What about Obama?" someone said from the crowd. "Maybe he will bring about World Socialism."

Dayton smirked, nodding his head. "Maybe he will, but I doubt it. More than likely, I think you'll see a continuation of his predecessor's policies----only he'll spin them differently."

Dayton took a few more questions from the crowd. After about ten minutes, the publisher's representative, a thin red-headed man named Steve, motioned Dayton that time was short and it was time to sit and sign books.

Dayton walked over to a long mahogany veneer table which contained stacks of his book in hard-cover. The color of the cover jacket was jet black, with bold, white lettering. He stopped for a moment to read the title, <u>Conspiracy Theory/Conspiracy Fact: Means, Motive & Opportunity</u>, and thought to himself, "I wish my father was here to see this. His son has just had his first book published."

He shook his head and grinned with a lopsided-smile on the right side of his face. Dayton sat down and began signing copies of his book. While signing the normal catch phrases on the inside first page for those in line, he noticed an older gentleman kept pacing in and out of the line. He walked away briefly to the rest room, then returned to the back of the line. Most people, Dayton thought, just wanted to pay for the book, meet the author, get it signed and get out. But this man, who was neatly dressed in a white golf shirt, navy pants and had an old London Fog raincoat draped over his arm, may have had something to ask him that he didn't want others to hear.

As the line dissipated and the ringing of the cash register at the other end of the table became intermittent, the neatly dressed gentleman got his apparent wish and was the last man standing.

He pushed the book in front of Dayton and the author opened the cover. The gentleman looked down at the detective with sad eyes and said nothing. Dayton looked up at him expecting a conspiracy question.

"What would you like me to write?" Dayton asked. The man took his right index finger and pointed it at the page, while he simultaneously placed another finger to his lips. Dayton looked down at the front page, normally reserved for kind words written from an author's pen, only to find that something had already been written there in pencil.

I was a friend of your dad's. He didn't commit suicide. He was murdered. Can we talk?

Dayton's eyes opened wide. He nodded his head and responded with the following words under those in pencil.

Any friend of my dad's deserves a free coffee and conversation. Wait outside. Respectfully, Dayton McCormick.

Dayton pushed cautiously on the door as he exited the Barnes and Noble. His first book signing had been a success, but instead of feeling jubilant, his thoughts focused solely on the mysterious stranger. He put his hand to his forehead to keep his eyes dry from the mist which was coating the city. The lamp posts appeared almost out of focus due to the heavy fog.

In the parking lot, he noticed the stranger was parked a few spaces down from his brown Jeep Cherokee and he was wearing the raincoat which had been folded under his arm while in the store.

"You pick the place. I'll buy," Dayton said.

Both men got into their respective vehicles. Dayton turned the key and the 4.0 liter high output six, roared to life. He turned on the wipers and proceeded to follow the stranger out of the parking lot. As the wipers waved back and forth, he glanced at the license plate on the blue Ford Taurus. He noticed right away, from the special markings on the rear plate, that it was a rental car. Either the man was from out of town, or maybe he suspected Dayton would run the numbers in the police computers and get his home address. Either way, Dayton waved any consideration that he might be in jeopardy. He had to know if this man was telling the truth or pulling his leg.

The stranger pulled into the small parking lot of an all-night diner located about four miles from West Broad. Dayton pulled into a spot a few spaces away, which mimicked the previous parking arrangements of himself and the stranger at the bookstore. A heavy downpour started, so both men quickly exited their vehicles and ran to the door of the diner.

"Let me get that," Dayton said, as he opened the door. They were quickly seated in the nearly empty diner and the dim lamps in the establishment provided a perfect atmosphere for a clandestine meeting.

The men faced each other uncomfortably while sitting in the booth. Dayton took a moment to size up his counterpart and record his features, in case they could be of future use. The stranger was nearly bald and had a long face. Age spots had formed on his forehead and his lips were thin. The eyes, his brown eyes, were what captivated his attention the most. They were sad, like the kind you see at funerals.

"Ok. You've got my attention," Dayton said sternly, but softly. "Who are you?"

"I'll tell you that and more, but you must promise not to react in any way which could draw attention," he whispered, while looking over his shoulders.

"Agreed."

"My name is Christopher Hartman."

"Okay, keep going," Dayton prodded.

"I served in the military with your father. I don't know if you knew he was in the service."

"Yes, my grandfather told me. He said he served in Vietnam," Dayton replied.

Christopher reached into his raincoat pocket and removed a small photograph which had six soldiers with arms over each other's shoulders. "This one is me," he said pointing with his right index finger. "The man next to me, you will recognize as your dad, Mickey."

Dayton's eyes opened wide at the sight. He recognized the face of his father. There was no mistaking it. As the waitress approached the table, Chris pulled the photo toward him to obscure it from view.

"One coffee, one Coke," Dayton told the waitress. Mr. Hartman pushed the photo back into view and handed it to Dayton.

Christopher twiddled his thumbs and repeatedly looked over his shoulders as he spoke. "We weren't really in 'Nam. That is just what we told our relatives. Our mission was in Cambodia and Laos. Your dad and I were part of a team, in 1970, which provided military reconnaissance----and did other things."

"I thought we weren't supposed to be there in 1970," Dayton questioned.

"We'll----let's put it this way." His voice softened. "If we were caught, the government would have denied our existence. There were no medals for what we did. Everything was hush-hush. I am surprised your dad was even able to keep this photo from our superiors, even though it was taken on base at Huachuca."

Dayton held back his amazement. He saw the waitress returning with their beverages and gave Mr. Hartman a forewarning nod. Dayton waited until after the waitress delivered their drinks and walked away.

"What were you doing there and what were these----other things?" Before the stranger could answer, Dayton popped another question, "What is that insignia?"

"That is the insignia of Army Intelligence. It is a lightning bolt, crossed by a key, with the Sphinx in the middle." Chris paused. "What were the other things? My job was locating potential uranium ore deposits. Your dad was doing something else. But we both were told specifically to interact with the native peoples to get intelligence on VC troop movements. I remember the day we arrived in a small village a few miles southeast of Angkor Wat. Your father and Mus," he paused as he pointed to Mussen in the photo, "befriended the town elder. We stayed there for a few days. The night before we left, Mussen and your dad disappeared with the little old guy. The rest of us feared that we'd all disappear soon too. Permanently----if you understand my meaning. So Hutch called for extraction on the radio the next morning." Chris breathed deeply and put his lips together. "However, Mickey, your dad, and Mus returned late in the morning. We waited for them. We couldn't leave without them. But both seemed like changed men. It was very weird."

Dayton looked puzzled and stared intently at the man across the table.

"Muss was white as a sheet. Your father, well, he had a look of new found determination----which is the best I can describe it. We told him about the extraction call and he was pissed. It was almost like he wasn't finished, or something like that. The six of us gathered our gear and headed to the extraction point," Chris said as he sighed deeply. He was clearly becoming upset. "About a mile from point, all hell broke loose."

Dayton knew little about his dad's life prior to his birth, because his father never discussed it. Everything Hartman was telling him was new and seemed so unreal.

Hartman continued. "We walked into a VC ambush. Gunfire was everywhere. We knew if we missed extraction, it was all over. So we ran like hell." Chris paused. "You never forget the sound of Ak47's on full-auto fire. The sound is very distinct. We ran so fast, most of us didn't realize when we were hit. I was hit in the leg and fell about twenty yards from the chopper. I think the others were aboard at that point, except your dad. He must have seen me fall, so he came back for me and dragged me with one arm while firing his M16 with the other. When his gun jammed, he threw it. By that time, I was hit again." Dayton could see the painful recollection of that day's events. It was written all over the stranger's face.

"I tried to act as a shield for your dad because I thought I was done. He picked me up and pushed me on to the chopper, right next to the side gunner. The noise was so deafening, I just sat there staring at the oncoming Viet Cong. I turned my head up and faced the top of the Huey's interior. Hutch was looking down at me and yelling at me to shut the fuck up. Then I saw him grab his face. The blood started trickling down from his hands and it dripped on my forehead and burned my eyes. That is when I blacked out."

Christopher Hartman looked down, almost in shame. His face began to distort as he fought back his tears. After a long silence, he recomposed himself and started to speak again.

"Your dad was a real hero. He saved my life and most likely the lives of all of us. And those pricks knew he deserved a medal, but didn't give him one because we weren't supposed to be there. So much for honor?"

Dayton was astounded. He inhaled a deep breath and held it while looking at the man across the table. But there was something he had to know.

"You mentioned my father was murdered----and that it wasn't suicide. How do you know that?"

Again, Hartman looked over his shoulders as if he was being watched. He looked back at Dayton and continued, "Because I saw your father the day he died and I feel partly responsible for it." Hartman looked down and continued. "No, I didn't kill him and I don't know who did. He gave me a few things to keep and send to the other members of our team for safe keeping." He paused. "It was part of the research he was doing, of which I had no knowledge of it. But I broke the first cardinal rule of intelligence. I used the phone. I was just trying to contact and old war buddy. I didn't know what he was doing. He told me he suspected it wouldn't be long. That is why he had your grandparents pick you up. He knew he was being monitored by someone----because of what he had in his possession."

Hartman closed his eyes briefly. He then reached into his coat and handed Dayton a small folded piece of paper and a wrapped box with a crinkled bow. It was about the size of a tie box and similar to the kind you see only at fancy men's clothing stores. The paper was worn and faded from being in storage for almost twenty-two years.

"This is what your dad gave me to keep. Now, I am giving it to you. I don't know what is in the box. I never opened it. The small piece of paper is the last available contact info for the others. I felt if any of this could help solve his murder and bring you peace, it was worth doing. Your dad was a good man and he never would have killed himself."

A tear started rolling down Hartman's face.

"It is time for me to go."

Hartman got up out of the booth and straightened his coat. He picked up his hat off the rack and placed it on his head. He turned one last time toward Dayton and then walked out the door into the rain.

Dayton stared at the faded paper on the gift box and sat dumbfounded. He twirled the straw in his glass of Coke between the melting ice cubes. After what seemed like an eternity, he arose from the booth, opened his wallet and left a few dollars on the table to pay for the beverages. He reached for the present, took it in his hand and placed it under his left arm and coat. The bow seemed to attach itself to his heart.

"My father was murdered," he thought to himself. "He didn't choose to leave me. He didn't commit suicide."

He looked down at the box in his coat and thought, "What an odd present on the night of my first book signing?"

He exited the restaurant and walked in the light rain toward his brown Cherokee. He sat down in the driver's seat and placed the box on the floor of the passenger side of the vehicle. He then reached back and pulled a blanket from the back seat and threw it over the box to cover it.

"Oh my god!" Dayton exclaimed as he started his vehicle, "My cell phone!"

Dayton reached down into his coat pocket and pulled it out. An uneasy feeling came over him. He remembered that just before his speech at the book signing, he turned it off. He held down the power button and the phone came to life.

"Two missed messages----shit!"

He looked to see who recently called on the received call menu on his phone. Both messages were from his friend Mark Tilenda. He was about to reply to caller, when his phone vibrated in his hand.

"Hey, Dayton. I have been trying to get a hold of you for about an hour. Your grandfather has been transported down to Johnston Willis." He emphasized to Dayton that it didn't look good for his grandfather and that he might not make the night.

"I'm coming right now," Dayton said, as his foot pushed down on the accelerator. He sped off toward the hospital. "I have to get there before he dies," Dayton said aloud. "He has to know the truth."

Chapter 6
The Gift

The Jeep Cherokee pulled into the parking lot at Johnston Willis' emergency room. Dayton quickly exited the vehicle and ran through the rain toward the doors. As he approached, he noticed Mark's partner standing under the overhang to keep dry. She looked more like a statue than a police detective. As her eyes met his, she spoke.

"He's up on the third floor. Mark is upstairs and he told me to wait here for you."

The two walked quickly down the hallway to the elevator. They entered through the doors and Dayton pressed "3". He turned and faced his friend Mark's new partner.

"Is he still alive?" Dayton asked as water dripped from his coat.

"Yes."

Dayton's mission of telling his grandfather the truth about his father's death was briefly interrupted as he gazed at her. Time almost seemed to stop. Her eyes were of a vivid blue, which matched her top. A few freckles dotted her nose and her face was pleasant to the eyes. She wasn't of a beauty in which most men would lose their minds, but there was something intoxicating about her. She smiled briefly and then looked down at the elevator's carpeted floor. Thoughts of guilt entered Dayton as he pulled out of his stupor. "You're such an asshole," he thought to himself. "Checking her out while your grandfather is dying. For god sakes Dayton!"

"Down the hall and to the left. Room 33B," she said.

He ran down the hall, leaving the female detective struggling to keep up. As he turned the corner, he noticed the "33" on the door, with the name McCormick underneath it.

Standing next to his grandmother Martha, was Mark. In the bed in front of them was Dayton's second father. He glanced at the clip chart on the wall and read the words "Do Not Resuscitate" in red letters located on the bottom of the paper.

He looked down at his grandfather. His skin was yellow and his breathing was labored. He did not look like the same man he saw only days earlier, or like the strong, proud man that he knew from childhood. Around his eyes, dark circles had formed and his upper cheeks were swollen and yellow.

George McCormick turned his head toward Dayton and opened his eyes.

"Dayton," he said as he reached out his hand. Dayton clasped his hand between his own. He became short of breath.

"I wish you didn't have to see me this way. I am sorry," he said in a raspy voice. His chest shuttered as his diaphragm tried to force air in and out of his lungs to keep him alive. He closed his eyes as he continued struggling to breathe.

Dayton bent down and kissed his Grandfather's forehead. He then moved to his left and put his lips close to his Grandfather's ear and began to whisper quietly.

"Grandpa----your son----my father----Mickey. He didn't kill himself. He was murdered." Dayton paused. He took his right hand and combed the hair on the front of his Grandfather's forehead. "And I promise you I will find out who did it," he whispered, so only George could hear.

George McCormick opened his eyes. With the last of his strength he pointed at the wall.

"Mickey."

His hand dropped to the hospital bed as his lip slightly curled; almost as if he was trying to smile. His chest jolted as he inhaled one last time. Dayton stood back and brought his Grandmother's hands over his Grandfather's left hand. He watched silently as the soul of George McCormick left his body through the exodus of his final breath and watched his skin turn gray as the air leaked from his lungs.

Dayton put his arms around his grandmother and gave her a light kiss on her temple. He left the room to allow her to have some final moments alone with her best friend and husband.

As he left the room, Dayton's eyes swelled up. He felt as if he was an eleven-year-old boy again, weeping in front of his father's casket. He felt the warm arms of a woman wrap around him tightly. He could feel her heartbeat on his back as a single tear dropped to the floor below. His friend Mark put his hand on his shoulder.

The three stood there in the hallway of the hospital for what seemed like hours. Dayton's grandmother then came out and put herself between Dayton and his friend Mark, and they all hugged together. The young McCormick opened his eyes and looked to the right at the nurses' station and noticed a toy stuffed lion on the counter. He thought for a moment and hoped it was a gift for a recovering child.

"A gift. Hopefully a gift," he thought to himself.

The sun glowed brightly and the sky was freckled with a few clouds. A small crowd had gathered in the cemetery to pay their respects. Dayton was the only child of an only child. Most of the siblings of his Grandparent's had passed and their children had moved away. The majority of the small gathering consisted of "cop" friends of Dayton's; with the two most significant being Mark and his new partner Sarah. There was also a small contingent of George's ex-coworkers, who he had kept in touch with since his retirement.

There were no military honors, even though George had served in Korea. He refused them. It was George McCormick's final wish that he be buried next to his only son. The priest said a few brief words, and then all those who had gathered gently placed red roses on top of the casket.

Dayton held his Grandmother's hand and walked her over to the car to drive her home. They were followed by Mark and Sarah.

"I don't know what to say. I am sorry about your husband, Mrs. McCormick, and your grandfather, Dayton." She turned to Mark and told him she would wait in the car.

"Sorry buddy. I know how much he meant to you," he said.

Mark put his right hand on Dayton's shoulder and gave him a nod. He then turned and lifted Mrs. McCormick's hand and kissed it. This wasn't the first time he had done so. He had enjoyed flirting with Dayton's grandmother for many years.

"If you need anything, Ma'am, just let me know."

Mrs. McCormick smiled back at him and turned to Dayton.

"He's a charmer," she said to her grandson. "Thanks for coming Mark----and please thank that young lady for me too. It meant a lot to us."

Mrs. McCormick got in the back seat of her car and waited for Dayton to drive her home.

Mark put his arm around Dayton. "Hey buddy. Your grandmother is one hot ticket and a good cook too," Mark said as he looked over at Martha who was now seated in the car. "I now know why your grandfather stayed married so long," he stated as he grinned from ear to ear. "Lot of love there."

"Get out of here," Dayton teased. "And thank you, both."

Dayton turned around and got into his Grandmother's car. He looked back as the cemetery workers began lowering his Grandfather's coffin into the ground. He put the key into the ignition.

"Bring me home, Dayton," Martha said softly. He nodded his head in silence as he started the car. Dayton fought back his tears. He had to remain strong for her.

Chapter 7
The Circle

Dayton spent a few days with his grandmother at her house. It was a lovely, large house painted in white. It was the house he spent his developing years in, until he became a man. As Dayton sat in his old bedroom, he recalled the day he moved in after his father's death. He walked over to the closet and found the box of old Star Wars figures he played with for hours as a child. As he sat on the bed holding the box, it creaked. "Oh, the memories," Dayton whispered. The bed's creak reminded him of the day he lost his virginity at age seventeen with the niece of his grandparent's next-door neighbor, while they were off visiting relatives in Florida. Looking around the room, he noticed everything was just as he had left it when he moved out eight years ago.

He picked up Luke Skywalker and Darth Vader and recalled his grandfather telling him that life was choices, both good and bad, and that they made us who we are. "I learned a lot from that man," Dayton whispered.

Dayton went downstairs and made two sandwiches for lunch, then sat and talked with the woman who was more of a mother to him than a grandmother. They reminisced about how angry George got when Dayton smashed his new car, and how he hated being disturbed when sitting in his chair reading the daily newspaper.

As Dayton took a bite of his ham and cheddar, he felt his cell vibrate in its belt case. He reached down and answered it. A familiar voice bellowed through the earpiece. "Dayton. Sorry to bother you----I know you're not officially on duty, and I know you want to be with Martha," Mark apologized, "but I would like you to come take a look at something."

"Where?" Dayton asked.

"Just come down to 93 Dwyer Road. Apartment 7-2."

Dayton looked up at his grandmother. She understood his life. "I'll be fine," she said.

"All right Mark. I'll be down in about thirty minutes," he said. "I'm just finishing my lunch."

"No," Dayton heard, sensing a change in his tone. "Come now!" Mark demanded, prior to hanging up.

Dayton pulled his Jeep into the parking lot of the small apartment complex. Mark's unmarked police car was just ahead and the front door of the apartment was ajar. Mark stood there waiting at the door.

"Sorry to call you----considering----but I think you might find this interesting. Besides, you have a better camera," Mark said as he greeted him outside. Dayton rolled his eyes. He walked to the rear passenger side of the Cherokee and opened the door. He retrieved his photo gear in the soft black camera bag on the floor behind the front seat.

The two walked into the kitchen.

"Where's Sarah?" Dayton asked.

"She's getting her car fixed, so she took the day off. There is a 10-56 in the bathroom. Something tells me this guy knew you."

Dayton walked into the bathroom. He saw the body of an older gentleman lying dead in the bathtub with his wrists slashed. His grey skin was in stark contrast to the dark red congealed water that just covered his private area. He took some Vick's Vaporub out of his camera bag and liberally dabbed his nose so the smell wouldn't make him vomit. He attached his flash to the camera and began to record the scene.

"Wait a second, paparazzi. I didn't really need photos. Come back out in the kitchen," Mark said waving his hand. He pointed toward the kitchen table.

On a cork board above the table, attached to the wall, were two newspaper clippings. The first, which was yellowed, was from the obituary section, dated 1987, with the words "Mickey McCormick." The second was from an article in the paper early last week about a book signing at the Barnes and Noble for a local policeman turned author. "Did this guy know you and your father?" Mark asked.

Dayton froze for a minute. He put his camera down on the table and walked back into the bathroom to get another look at the dead man. He then walked to the front door. He turned and looked at the mailbox, which had black letters typed in a white block: C. Hartman.

It felt like his heart stopped while looking at the name plate. He held his breath and recalled the meeting with the mysterious stranger a few days ago after his book signing.

"You okay pal? I have never seen you react this way before. Who was this guy?"

"Have forensics run a toxicology test on him."

"A toxicology test? What are you looking for----alcohol?" Mark questioned.

Dayton replied, "No," as he began walking around the apartment. He put on a pair of rubber gloves and began going through drawers, closets and cupboards.

"It is not here," Dayton whispered.

"What's not here?" Mark asked.

"My book." Dayton explained to Mark about the clandestine meeting he had with the mysterious gentleman, now laying dead in the bathroom. He told Mark about the inscription written in pencil by the recently deceased.

"I thought your father killed himself," said Mark. Realizing how cold his response must have sounded, he quickly added, "I'm sorry. I didn't mean it the way it sounded."

"I thought he did too, Mark. Up until a few days ago."

Mark looked curiously at his best friend. "How----"

Dayton interrupted him. "My Grandfather found him in the bathtub with his wrists slashed," motioning to the bathroom, "just like him."

Mark's faced turned white. He turned toward the window as he heard the motor of a diesel-fueled panel truck entering the complex.

"Coroner's here," he said.

Dayton replied, "Please stall them for a few minutes for me."

He went into the cupboard and took out the smallest Tupperware he could find. After pulling off the cover, he entered the bathroom and dipped the container in the bloody water. He tore off a piece of toilet tissue and wiped the outside of the container after he sealed it, then placed it inside a pocket in his camera bag.

Dayton then picked up his Canon 20d and began shooting all over the apartment. He then put his camera down and searched quickly around as Mark continued to delay the Coroner's entrance. After not finding anything of importance, he walked over to the corkboard by the table and removed his father's obituary and his newspaper article, then folded them neatly into his wallet. He then picked up Mark's camera and scrolled through the photographs and deleted all those which contained the kitchen table and the newsprint above it. He then re-shot the kitchen table scene without the evidence now contained in his wallet. Mark looked back and witnessed what he was doing, as he made small talk with the men from the coroner's office in the doorway. Dayton winked to let Mark know he was done.

The two detectives then led the coroner's men to the body so they could begin their work. Dayton packed up his camera and handed Mark's camera back to him. Then, the two walked out, as the coroners commented to each other about the horrid smell and ghastly appearance of the dead man in the bath tub.

"I saw what you did Dayton----with my camera. Why?"

"I'll explain later. Just make sure forensics does a toxicology test."

Dayton's thoughts returned to his grandmother. He removed his cell phone and dialed her number. After a few rings, she answered.

"Hello. "

"Just checking in with you Grandma," Dayton said. "I don't want to alarm you, but you might want to keep Suzy Weston handy until I come back."

"I'm fine Dayton, but I'll get her out. Just finish up what you are doing and don't worry about me," Martha replied.

"Ok."

Mark looked over at Dayton.

"Estimated time of death was around your Grandfather's funeral. If this man was murdered, I know you are innocent. Why remove the evidence?"

Dayton replied, "because if toxicology turns up something--- evidence was left by someone to try and frame me, regardless of where I was. I can't be a person of suspicion. There is something I need to do."

"Nuff said," replied Mark, uncomfortably.

"I will keep you in the loop with anything I turn up," Dayton replied.

"And I'll let you know what toxicology says," Mark said with a nod.

Dayton put his camera bag back on the rear floor of the Cherokee and drove off, leaving Mark to finish up his business with the Coroner's crew.

A few streets away from his condo, Dayton depressed the brake pedal and came to a complete stop. He looked over on the passenger side floor at the blanket covering the wrapped box. He lifted up the blanket with his right hand to check on it. The faded wrapped box and the crinkled bow were just where he left them. He reached into his coat pocket and removed the photo and folded sheet of paper, then placed them both on the passenger seat. He then picked up the photo and held it between his thumb and index finger to study the six young servicemen. He stopped at his father, who was in the middle.

"I'll find out who killed you Dad," Dayton said under his breath. He placed the photo back in his pocket and then picked up the list. On the list were five names. Four of them had home addresses. As he read the first name, he muttered, "Deceased."

Christopher Hartman
93 Dywer
Richmond Virginia.

Richard Andrew Mussen
Theology Professor-Georgetown

Henry Hutchinson
201 Big Sky Road
Bozeman, Montana.

John Windwalker
14 Sunrise Pl.
Tucson, Arizona

Peter Devine
14 Bridge Street
Lee, Massachusetts

He folded up the list and placed it in his jacket pocket, making sure the list covered the photo. He took his foot off the brake, switched it to the accelerator and pressed down.

He parked the Jeep in his assigned spot and walked toward the door of his condo. After unlocking the door, he reached around the door jam and flipped on the light switch.

"Life keeps getting better," he said aloud.

A sinking feeling came over him as he looked around his condo. Someone had gone through it like a tornado. The couch cushions were opened up; exposing the inner foam. Glassware was strewn about the kitchen floor. All the clothing in his hallway closet was thrown into various places down the hall. The mattresses in the bedroom had been torn apart and the drawers from his dresser and desk were overturned; leaving the contents to form a relief map on the floor.

In the spare bedroom, his keyboard was lying on the floor and the glass bookcase door was smashed. His books were piled like dead soldiers on the carpet. Nothing seemed unmolested. Dayton's phone vibrated. He took the phone off his belt clip and looked at the caller ID. It was a number he didn't recognize.

"What!" Dayton yelled as he answered the phone. He took a deep breath to recompose himself, as he listened to the caller on the other side of the line.

"Mr. McCormick. This is Steve----from the promotions office. I am sorry to disturb you and I must apologize."

"Go ahead," Dayton said in an apologetic tone.

"First, I'd like to express my condolences for the loss of your grandfather, George McCormick. It must have been very hard. And because you must be very busy, we have re-scheduled tomorrow's signing at the Baltimore Barnes and Noble, to this Friday. But the location has changed too, because of a schedule conflict."

"Where do you want me to go?"

"It will be at the Baltimore Library at 7:30PM----if that works for you?"

"Thanks Steve. I'll be there," Dayton replied.

"Once again, I apologize for both this call's lateness and for your loss."

Dayton, now calm, replied, "I'll see you Friday," and hung up.

On the wall in the living room, he read the word "Pig" mixed in with a number of obscenities in multi-colored spray paint. He reached for his cell and dialed.

"Mark, it's Dayton. Could you come over to my place?"

"Sure, bud. I can be over in twenty minutes. What's going on?"

He looked around at the mess. "I don't know."

❧

"Holy cow man----look at this place! I hope it was good for you too?" Mark said sarcastically. "Honestly though, who did this?"

Dayton looked up at his friend and smiled. He could always expect Mark to make an obviously asinine comment, followed by the seriousness of a true detective. "I don't know. Maybe it has something to do with the guy in tub?"

Mark looked at him skeptically. "Or it could have been some hoodlum who got your address after getting out of prison?"

"But this doesn't make sense. Someone went through everything." Dayton shook his head in disgust. "The one thing they didn't seem to break was my laptop," Dayton said, as he pointed at it. "Help me gather up some stuff and we'll take it to my grandmother's. I don't want her alone anyway----and it would be a good place to sort this all out."

Dayton retrieved his laptop and put it on the front seat of the Cherokee, as Mark sifted through the wreckage in his bedroom. The two then filled a couple trash bags full of Dayton's clothes and threw them in the back seat.

"Going to be a long night?" Mark asked as he looked at the graffiti in the living room.

"I think so. We should probably order some take-out, or a pizza," replied Dayton.

"Well, I know a great pizza joint near my partner's apartment. Why don't we call her and make it a threesome----studly?" Mark shook his head, did a little dance and raised his eyebrows a few times.

"You never give up----do you, Cupid?"

"Not for a minute," Mark smiled. "Besides, if it weren't for me, you'd have a real boring life. I'll call for the pizza and you call Sarah. Here's her number."

Dayton leaned up against the side of the Cherokee and looked up at the moon. It was incredibly milk-colored and full, and he waved his finger at it. "Something tells me life is about to change," he whispered.

"Full moon Dayton. AHHH OOOOOOOO," Mark howled. "Every crook, murderer and rapist is probably out tonight."

"Right," smiled Dayton.

❦

Dayton, Mark and Sarah congregated around the living room table at his grandmother's house. The pizza box wasn't the only box on the table. Dayton pulled out both the names list and the photograph Hartman had provided. Mark and Sarah's eyes lit up in astonishment as Dayton explained, in every detail, the story the stranger told him the night of the first book signing. It was the same stranger that was found dead in his apartment under the exact same circumstances as Dayton's father, Mickey.

"What could be so important in that damn box?" Mark asked as he pointed at the faded gift wrap.

"I don't know," Dayton replied.

"We'll are you going to open it?" Sarah inquired.

Dayton took the box in his hands. He briefly touched the crinkled bow on the top and rubbed his hand down the faded paper of the box, almost like a boat maker would while checking the finish of a hull on a small wooden boat. He took out his pocketknife and sliced holes in the corners of the gift wrap.

"It looks light----so it can't be a bomb," joked Mark.

Dayton removed the outer wrapping which revealed a simple, small corrugated cardboard box that was sealed with clear packing tape. He took his pocketknife and carefully sliced the tape adjoining the flaps.

Inside, he found papers carefully rolled into tubes and secured by rubber bands. The bands disintegrated as he touched them. He carefully unfurled the tubes, which revealed maps: Satellite maps. The maps were of Washington D.C., New York Harbor and the Giza Plateau. There was a one dollar bill wrapped within the D.C. map, along with a paper containing a series of codes.

Dayton looked puzzled. He knew these were only some of the clues his father had scattered to his former

Army friends before he died. However, he had a hard time comprehending how anyone would be killed over satellite maps of common locations.

Sarah picked up the dollar bill and flipped it to its reverse.

"Dayton, why is this circled?" she asked.

Dayton looked at the back of the dollar. The Roman numerals at the base of the pyramid roundel were circled in red pen. For a moment, Dayton became excited. He realized this might be the first clue among many to help him solve his father's murder.

Mark piped up, "It is 1776. Roman numerals----same year as the Declaration of Independence."

Both Dayton and Sarah looked at Mark with surprise.

"Don't you ever look at your money?" Mark jabbed. "And Dayton, you're the conspiracy buff. 1776, you know, the Illuminati," Mark said.

"Most of those groups are jokes, Mark. People believe what they want to believe," Dayton replied.

"Yeah, but do you really think your father was killed over maps you can see on Google Earth for free?"

Dayton thought for a moment. "Wait a second, Mark. I think you are on to something."

Dayton powered up his laptop. He had Google Earth installed and had used it before to find locations he was traveling to and the distances between them. He double clicked on the icon for Google Earth on his laptop's finger pad.

"Ok, Washington D.C."

As he typed in Washington D.C. in the location bar, Mark and Sarah crowded around the laptop. The picture of the earth soon rotated and zoomed in on the space between Virginia and Maryland. Dayton zoomed out enough so an area just above Capitol Hill and just below the Pentagon were visible; same as he'd seen on his father's aerials.

"Wait," said Sarah looking at the dollar. "The city is set up similar to the pyramid symbol in the first roundel on the back of the one dollar bill."

"Hey, that's interesting," commented Mark. "Washington D.C., and Washington on the dollar bill. Same symbols: The truncated pyramid and the triangle with the all-seeing eye."

Sarah pointed to the area above the Capitol, which formed a Star of David, just like the top of the Eagle Roundel on the right of the dollar's reverse. Then there was the Pyramid, running from 23rd street all the way up to Third Street. The Capstone Eye was the Grant Memorial and the triangle had for its apex, Capitol Hill. Excitement in the room was high, for they realized that symbols on the nation's currency were actually built into the Capital city itself in stone.

Dayton took the cursor pointer up to the ruler function for measurement with the sliding of his fingertip. "I wonder?" he said, as he set the first point of measure at Washington Circle on 23rd Street, NW and ran the ruler through 23rd street to an area across the Potomac, where the right side of the pyramid would have intersected, had Maryland Avenue continued all the way down to the base of the pyramid at 23rd Street.

"1.776 miles. Incredible! 1.776 miles. 1776 in Roman numerals at the base of the pyramid on the dollar," said Dayton.

"What if there is more than one pyramid," asked Sarah.

Mark replied, "Well, it couldn't be 1.776 miles. It would have to be something different----like yards or something."

"That's it," said Dayton. "D.C. was designed by Washington and L'Enfant, who was French. The French used the metric system. Where could 1.776 kilometers be?"

After a few minutes, two more 1776 measurements were found. The 1.776 kilometer measurement was found between the White House and the Jefferson Memorial, on what is called the Washington Meridian. Just as all roads lead to Rome, the same was true in the United States Capital, and a marker by the White House, the Zero Milestone, signifies its location today. Closer toward Capitol Hill, Dayton found the distance between bases of the Peace Monument and the Garfield Memorial were 17,760 centimeters apart.

"Three bases of 1776. Three pyramids. Giza has three main pyramids!" said Dayton excitedly. "My father was on to something."

"Dayton," Mark said, "It only proves that the city was designed with Egyptian and Roman styles that incorporated the year of the Declaration at their bases for measurement. There might be nothing else here."

"Perhaps," replied Dayton, brushing off Mark's skepticism. He felt there had to be something here of great significance. Otherwise, why would his father have left it?

He then moved the measuring tool with his finger and started from the center of the Capitol's Dome and moved west to the center of the Lincoln Memorial, where it meets at 23rd Street. He was still in metric measurement.

"3.56-3.58 kilometers," he said. Then he switched over to standard measurement. "2.22 miles. Holy cow! Two Twenty-Two. February twenty-second. That is Washington's Birthday."

"Makes sense, Dayton, considering it is Washington D.C.," said Sarah. "Why don't we see what we can find from any official government websites concerning this discovery?"

Dayton searched and searched with Mark and Sarah at his side. Not even the website for the Architect of the Capitol had any information about the measurements they had just made.

"It still doesn't prove anything buddy----not in a Court of Law," said Mark. Sarah looked up at the clock. It was half past midnight.

"We've got duty tomorrow Dayton. I think we're going to get going," said Mark.

Mark and Sarah said their farewells and left. Dayton sat in the chair for a few minutes wondering where all this was going?

Dayton walked back upstairs to check on his grandmother, who had long since fallen asleep in her bed. He walked down to his old bedroom and found an empty black three-ring binder. He brought it downstairs and took another look at Washington D.C. on both the Google Earth browser and his father's satellite map. He then took a blank piece of paper and laid out the city and the measurements that he had made, along with other facts and information he received from Hartman. He punched holes in the paper and set it in the binder.

"I'll look at this some more later," he said, as he shut off his laptop and collapsed on the couch. He reached over and picked up his binder again off the coffee table and looked at his sketch. "Where were you going with all this, dad?"

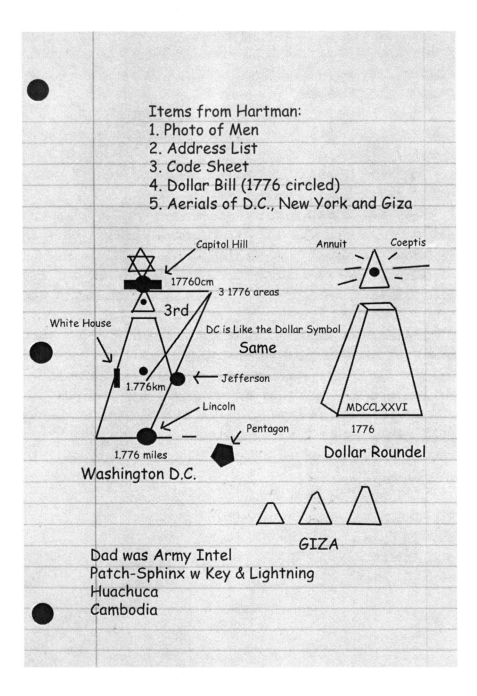

Items from Hartman:
1. Photo of Men
2. Address List
3. Code Sheet
4. Dollar Bill (1776 circled)
5. Aerials of D.C., New York and Giza

Capitol Hill

Annuit   Coeptis

17760cm

3 1776 areas

3rd

White House

DC is Like the Dollar Symbol

Same

Jefferson

1.776km

Lincoln

Pentagon

MDCCLXXVI

1776

1.776 miles

Dollar Roundel

Washington D.C.

GIZA

Dad was Army Intel
Patch-Sphinx w Key & Lightning
Huachuca
Cambodia

Dayton awoke about 8AM. His grandmother had already been up for an hour and had made them both breakfast. As he ate, he thought about his next book signing, which was in a couple days at the Enoch Pratt Free Library in Baltimore.

He pulled out the list of the names and last known locations of his father's war buddies from his coat pocket. Baltimore was only a few miles from Washington D.C, and he saw that Richard Mussen was a professor at Georgetown. He knew if he left today, he could spend a few hours in D.C. walking around and gathering research, as well as go to the northwest side of the city and hopefully locate the professor. He booted up his laptop to get the schedule for the rest of his book signings around the country. He noticed some of them were also close to the last known locations of the other individuals on the list given to him by Hartman. Dayton decided he would try and make contact with them during his free time between his book signings.

He searched online for a phone number to the Theology Department at Georgetown University. After a number of phone calls, he got in touch with a friendly secretary who knew Professor Mussen's schedule.

"Usually before class on Thursday, you can find him feeding the pigeons on a bench in Copley Lawn," she said.

"Thank you very much, Ma'am," Dayton replied.

Dayton helped his grandmother with the morning dishes and kissed her on the head. He told her he would be gone for a few days and not to worry. If she needed anything, she could always call him on his cell phone, or contact Mark or Sarah.

"Is Sarah single, Dayton?" his grandmother hinted as she raised her right eyebrow.

Dayton ignored the question as he walked up to his grandmother and gave her a big hug. He packed up his laptop and the black folder and put them into his Cherokee, then walked back into the house and looked at his grandmother sternly.

"Not right now Gram. There are a lot of things I have to do before I can think about that," Dayton replied. "And I don't like to date people I work with."

"If not now, then when?" she asked. "You're not getting any younger and you deserve a real relationship. Besides," Martha smiled, "I noticed you looking at her----and her at you."

"I was hoping you wouldn't notice," Dayton replied while looking down. "I have to get going."

"That's right. Change the subject," Martha replied. "Just be careful on your trip, dear."

As he got into his Jeep, he began to think of Sarah and the way she looked and smelled. There was something about her he couldn't put his finger on. He had dated other women, but none too seriously. They either all wanted something he didn't, or just weren't his type. It didn't matter anyway. "Sarah might be different," he thought, then shook his head. His father had been murdered and he was going to find out who did it and why. Sarah's face faded from his thoughts as he started his Jeep. He plotted out his course on the GPS for the ninety-three mile trip to Washington.

"Ninety-three." He remembered his trip to Liberty Island with his father the day before he was killed.

"She is ninety-three meters from her base to the tip of her torch. Synchronicity," he thought to himself. "All this ties together somehow."

Chapter 8
Perception

Traffic going north had been light. At both the morning and evening rushes, cars on the roads around D.C. move like snails going uphill, so leaving after the normal morning commute time was a smart move on Dayton's part. He crossed the Key Bridge and took a left on to M St. NW. Georgetown University was right there, so he turned into the parking lot of Lavinger Library. If he timed his trip right, he'd find Professor Mussen sitting on a bench feeding pigeons on the Copley Lawn of Georgetown.

As he walked up from the library, he could see what appeared to be an older gentleman wearing a tweed jacket with a brown hat. He was gently throwing stale breadcrumbs to a pack of hungry urban birds.

"Professor Richard Mussen?" Dayton inquired.

The older man turned around to look at his inquisitor. His bushy eyebrows, large nose and round faced stared back at the young detective.

"Yes."

"I was wondering if I might have a moment of your time?" Dayton asked.

The older gentleman turned his wrist and looked at his watch. "I have class to teach now. Could you ask your questions while we walk?" Mussen said, as he arose from the bench.

"Sir, I am sorry to bother you." Dayton said as he followed the professor and noticed the pronounced limp in his stride. "I believe you knew my father."

"And who was he?" Mussen replied as he walked.

"Mickey McCormick. You served with him in--"

Anticipating what the young man was going to say, Professor Mussen turned around and put his finger almost up to Dayton's mouth. His eyes had opened wide as saucers and the young detective could tell he had gotten his attention.

"I prefer to call it Southeast Asia," the man replied and then turned to continue toward the lecture hall. "Yes, I remember him very well. Tragic that he died at such a young age. I never believed what I read in the paper."

His response struck a chord inside him. Dayton looked over at his elder and stated, "That's why I am here. I am trying to find out what really happened."

"Well, if you want to talk, you'll have to wait until after I have my class. You are more than welcome to sit in if you like."

"I'd be happy to, Professor," Dayton lied. The thought of sitting in a classroom again was less than thrilling, especially one on theology. The older man sensed his feelings, like a literary critic reads books.

"Theology can be interesting, young man. It isn't really about god. It is more about human perception. Please, indulge yourself and come to my class." His large nose and bushy eyebrows browbeat Dayton into submission.

Professor Mussen opened the door to his classroom and Dayton followed. He sat in the back. The professor opened his briefcase on the lectern and then walked over to the large television sitting atop a wheeled cart. "Good afternoon class," Mussen said. "Today we deal with perception in theology. I will play a short segment for you to watch, which I hope you---ALL watched in the library over the weekend." Dayton watched his nose bob up and down as the professor engaged his class. "For those who have not---I preface to say it is from the fine <u>Sharpe Series</u> of movies produced by the

BBC through B.F.S. Video. In it you will see a scene where the main character, Richard Sharpe, shows his disgust about fighting and losing men while protecting a symbol cherished by the Spanish." Mussen played the clip showing the officer being angry about fighting for as he put it, "a rag-in-a-bag," which was an old Spanish flag dedicated to a saint. The flag, if flown above the chapel, was meant to incite the Spanish people to rise up against Napoleon. After Sharpe's comment, he was told that he also fought for a symbol, by a member of the British military intelligence. "So do you Sharpe. So do you," he said, referring to the British flag, known as the King's Colors.

At the conclusion of the clip, Mussen remarked, "Perception is everything. Richard felt fighting for the Colors of Britain was righteous and honorable. But fighting for an old Spanish flag was foolish." He then removed two photos from his briefcase and placed them on the chalkboard. One showed an American soldier on the left, and the other, a Muslim fighter on the right.

"The man on the left is a Christian American. He joined the Army after 911 to fight for his country and defeat the terrorists. He went over to Iraq, only to be killed by a roadside IED. The man on the right was educated in a strict Islamic school. He strapped explosives on himself and blew both himself and thirty others to kingdom come outside a market in Baghdad. Why? To protect his family and his religion from being destroyed. Both men prayed to a supreme god and both men ended up dead. Both men had families. Both men had nations. But neither man took the time to consider that they had anything in common with the other. Your assignment is to look at the big three religions of Christianity, Islam, and Judaism and write a short paper on the similarities of those three religions. You are also to read the chapter on Muslim controlled Spain in your textbook."

At the conclusion of the lecture, the young students left the classroom with books in hand; leaving Dayton and Professor Mussen alone. The professor motioned Dayton to follow him and they walked down the hall to his office.

Mussen sat down in an old oak chair which creaked as he reclined. Behind him was a bookcase full of theological texts. Dayton's eyes scanned the office, taking it all in. He noticed a futon with a small suitcase on it. Noticing, Mussen remarked, "I don't have a car, so I sleep here a few days a week."

"Sorry, I'm not trying to be nosey," Dayton apologized.

"Please sit," Mussen said as he pointed at the cushioned chair in front of his desk. Dayton sat down and looked curiously at the older man.

"Now where were we?----Your father and I met during our training at Fort Huachuca in Arizona. From there, we traveled with a small team to Asia on a fact finding and reconnaissance mission." Mussen paused. "One day, after stopping near Anghor Wat, we were ambushed by the Vietcong on our way to extraction, via helicopter. I took a bullet in the leg, as you can see from my limp. I was ten feet from the helicopter, laying in the muck, when your father grabbed my arm and dragged me on to the chopper. Needless to say, I wouldn't be here molding young minds if it weren't for his courage. What do you want to know, Mr. McCormick?"

"I ran into a fellow who was a serviceman in your company," Dayton said as he withdrew the photo from his jacket. "His name was Christopher Hartman. He told me my father was murdered. He gave me this photo along with a box containing satellite images of Washington D.C, New York and Giza, among other things. Hartman said my father was putting together information of great import, and that was why he was killed. A few days later, Hartman was found dead in his bathtub with his wrists slashed----the same way my father was killed twenty-two years ago."

Mussen raised his eyebrows. "Your father was into many things, as was I. The aerial photos, I believe have to do with his study of symbolism. Symbols----are very interesting. They allow a message to be told, and also to be concealed simultaneously. But for those who understand and have eyes to see the true meaning, the message becomes quite clear."

Dayton was curious. "A message huh? But why did my father use cities?"

"My young man, since ancient times, man has incorporated into his cities the symbols and measurement of cosmic significance. Giza, in many ways is just like the Capital, whose significance dates back to the Roman Empire, which had seven hills. Capitoline Hill, for instance, was dedicated to the god Jupiter and two lesser others. Washington was--in part--designed by Masons, who borrowed truth from all religions around the world. What you have to ask yourself is what truth there is in religion, or should I rephrase----there is universal truth in all religions----Have you read any Manley P. Hall?"

It began to click in Dayton's head. "As a matter of fact----yes, I have," he replied, remembering the research he did for his book. Dayton pulled out a dollar bill and showed him the sketch in his black binder. He pointed out the 1776 in the pyramid roundel, as well as in the measurements of the city. The professor responded and told him about the Aeneid, by Virgil, and the poem to the god Jupiter, which contained the phrase "Annuit Coeptis," and was above the pyramid.

Mussen looked at the dollar, then continued. "Time is a funny thing, young McCormick. We here in the west tend to think of time as being linear. Eastern and other cultures look at time as being circular, or cyclical. That is one thing I learned in Cambodia. It frightened me because I saw similarities which questioned my Jewish upbringing. Of course I saw other things which turned my stomach there too," Mussen paused. "You know, the Gregorian calendar was created because what was going on up in the sky was not coinciding with the feast, or celebratory days down here. Pope Gregory commissioned an Italian astronomer to come up with a calendar which was more accurate than the Julian one they had been using. That calendar we use today." Mussen continued his monologue. "Easter, in fact, is picked as the first Sunday after the first full moon after the Spring Equinox----which is quite interesting considering the Church has always told its faithful not to look at astrology or astronomy." Mussen smiled. "I think if you want to find what your father knew, you should ask yourself what certain symbols really stand for, and why they were placed where they are?"

Mussen looked out the window of his office and pointed at the tip of the giant obelisk at the center of the city, and muttered "Heliopolis." He then got up and turned to retrieve a book from his bookcase. He turned and handed a Bible to Dayton.

"Years ago, I received a package from Christopher. In it was this Bible. I found it ironic that someone would send it to me. It was your father's. Now it is yours. I'm sorry I have to cut off our discussion. I have a chair's meeting to attend. But if you are ever back in the District, please come see me." Mussen turned again to his bookcase and withdrew another book. "Here is another book of mine you can have. You might find it helpful."

Dayton opened the Bible, and written in the upper-right-hand corner was the name Mickey McCormick. He looked at the other book entitled <u>Picturesque Washington,</u> authored by Moore. He thanked the professor and bid him farewell.

Dayton packed both the books into his suitcase with care and drove off the Georgetown campus. He headed for D.C. center by driving up Pennsylvania Avenue. He noticed an open spot in a small lot across from an upscale hotel, next to Pershing Park. He parked his Jeep and got out. From where he stood, he could look down Pennsylvania Avenue and see the Dome of Capitol Hill. He grabbed the camera bag out from behind the passenger seat and removed his SLR.

He walked over toward the White House. Security was tight, and he watched guards searching vehicles; literally tearing them apart. He knew after 911, security in D.C. became extreme, and through his zoom lens, he could see the scope caps on the sniper rifles which were on the roof of the White House, along with a pair of shooters and spotters.

He walked over to the Zero Milestone, looked at the symbols on it and then photographed it from all four cardinal points. It was easy to do in D.C. for the city was laid out precisely from East to West: the White House was to the North and the Jefferson Memorial was to the South. He noticed at the Milestone, there was almost a line running straight from the White House to Jefferson Memorial. "Sixteenth Street," he muttered. The Washington Monument was a little to the east of the meridian line.

On the Milestone, there was a symbol for Mercury's helmet, along with a sun-styled direction symbol atop. A Fleur de Lys pointed toward the White House.

"1.776 kilometers," he whispered to himself. "And Jefferson wrote the Declaration. Hmm? Interesting. But why is the Fleur pointing north to the White House?"

He walked around the Capital for many hours and photographed all the main attractions of the city from different angles.

After taking hundreds of photos, he stopped on the way back to Pershing Park from Capitol Hill and sat briefly at the Zodiac Fountain on the corner of 6th and Pennsylvania Avenue. He looked at the various sky figures in stone around the fountain's side and thought about how many zodiacs he'd seen in the city that day. "Why all the zodiacs?" he muttered. "It must be because they are important."

Dayton trekked the remainder of the distance down Pennsylvania Ave, to his parked vehicle in Pershing Park. The exodus from the city had subsided about thirty minutes prior with the sunset, so he felt it would be an opportune time to make way for the hotel room awaiting him in the City of Baltimore.

At the hotel, Dayton called his grandmother in Richmond, told her he had taken some photos of the Capital and that he would show them to her when he returned. She mentioned that Mark and Sarah had stopped by to check on her and that they brought her an apple pie. Dayton's smile could be heard on the phone while he talked to her. "Good friends," he said to himself, after hanging up his phone.

He unpacked the Bible and the other book from the suitcase. Flipping open the Moore book, he noticed some writing in pencil on the inside front cover.

1m= 36.525

Dayton reached for his father's Bible, opened it and looked at his father's handwriting. "Similar," he mused. He thought for a moment and closed both the book and the Bible. His legs ached from all the walking around D.C. and he knew he needed a good night's rest before the signing at the Enoch Pratt tomorrow night. But there was something he had to do first.

Dayton took a few moments before bed to make a sketch in his black binder and list the evidence he received from Professor Mussen. He then placed the binder and books on the back of the table and turned off the light.

∽

Dayton awoke to the sound of two rings. The first ring was a wake-up call he asked for from the front desk. The second was from his cell phone in his jacket. He reached inside the coat pocket of his jacket, which hung on the chair and pulled it out.

"Hi Dayton, it's Mark."

"Hi Mark. What is going on?" Dayton sensed from the tone of his friend's voice that he was unhappy about something.

"Well bud, do you want the good news first or the bad news?" Mark replied in a sarcastic tone.

Dayton, still thinking about his findings the previous day, replied, "Surprise me."

"The good news----well----Sarah and I are coming up to your book signing in Baltimore. Chief gave us the time off to come see you. He said it would be good for us."

Dayton was taken aback by Mark's comment. The Chief had a poor sense of humor and was pissed as hell granting Dayton's leave to go promote his book. It also meant there were three less detectives out on the streets of Richmond. "Bullshit!"

After a short silence on the phone, Mark replied, "No, no really. I am not kidding. In fact, he told us to take a week."

Dayton knew there was more at hand here than meets the eye.

Mark continued, "Remember that guy in the tub, Hartman? The one you wanted a toxicology test done on?

"Yes."

"Well I ordered the test." Mark explained that yesterday, after Dayton left for Baltimore, a bunch of guys showed up down at the morgue flashing all sorts of federal credentials. They took the body as well as all the evidence. "I was pissed----so the Chief gave us time to cool down. Thank god you----"

Dayton interrupted Mark. "Mark----not another word. If they can send people that quickly, something is up and we are on the phone."

"What?"

"Can you and Sarah come up early? The signing is at 7pm at the Central Library located on Cathedral Street. We can grab dinner beforehand."

"Sounds good, I----We'll see you around four at your hotel," Mark replied.

Dayton turned off his cell. "Whatever was going on, goes pretty high," he thought. He sat in the chair and looked at the Bible and the other book on the table. The shadows caused by the light coming in from the window on the books resembled two tall pillars on the top of the desk. He picked them up and packed them in the suitcase. "Feds, confiscating all the evidence in a case? Smells like a cover up of some kind," Dayton thought. "But who had that kind of clout?"

Dayton sat in his hotel chair and typed on the laptop in front of him. He felt the first book signing went well, but really wanted to hammer home the rationale behind his book. His object was not to trash conspiracy theories, but to get people to think from his frame of reference. He was a cop who had to work within the guidelines of the legal system. There had to be evidence, or there was no case. Hear-say or loose-knit associations would not convict someone in a court of law. Evidence had to be iron tight, otherwise those who conspired would walk away as free men. People also had to realize when the Federal Government was involved in an investigation they might not always put forth all the information they have, because something could be classified. Dayton laughed when he remembered Hartman.

After composing what he felt was a decent opener for his signing, he considered exploring the historical district of Baltimore. He truly was his father's son and had a passion for anything historical or symbolic. After downloading the photos from the Hartman scene and making a flash drive copy for Mark, he turned off his laptop, got dressed and began his foot patrol of the city with his camera in hand.

Cathedral Ave. was appropriately named. After checking out the Enoch Pratt Free Central location, he began walking up and down the Avenue taking photos of the many churches in the area, along with admiring their architecture. Dayton had always found old church symbolism fascinating. He walked across the street to St. Mary's of the Assumption, and after he photographed the exterior, he walked up the steps and pulled on the door handle on the front door. He walked inside and paused, looking at a 16th century painting of Mary holding Jesus, with Joseph and another man on each side of her. Her head was elevated, so he took his finger and traced from Mary's head, to those of the holy men. "A triangle," he muttered. His stomach grumbled. "Time for lunch," he said quietly, as he turned away from the painting.

After his early lunch, he started walking toward the nation's first proposed monument to George Washington. The layout of the monument area was in the shape of a cross. It was aptly named Mount Vernon Way. In the center was the Doric column designed by Robert Mills, who also had influenced the design of the Capital named for the nation's first president under the Constitution. He took time to take it all in, and after shooting many photographs and admiring the six-pointed star-shaped ironwork surrounding the column, he took a break and sat on a bench nearby.

His cell vibrated on his hip. Before answering, he noticed that it was ten minutes to four.

"Hi, Dayton. We're entering Baltimore."

"Mark, I lost track of time. I am going to head down to the Basilica of the Assumption across from the Central Library. I'll meet you there." He looked again at the ironwork. The six sides reminded him of snowflakes, which by nature's design always have six sides.

Dayton packed up his camera and began walking at a brisk pace. It was only a few blocks away, but he knew how fast Mark drove and his light, early lunch left him feeling famished.

Mark was a man's man, so it was only fitting to his persona that he drove a large, red extended-cab pickup truck. He pulled up to where Dayton was standing and unlocked the doors. Dayton crawled in, sat down and gave Mark and Sarah a big grin.

"Okay Dayton. What do you want?" Mark said.

"What----you think I want something just because I am smiling?"

"Uh, yes," Mark replied sarcastically.

"Remember that girl six months ago you dated from the independent bio lab? Its name is Biohelix----I think," Dayton asked as he reached into his camera bag and removed the blood sample he had taken from Hartman's bathtub.

"Oh shit!" Mark said, "I can't believe you scoffed up a sample. I saw the extra pictures you took----but, oh man!" Mark exclaimed.

"And here is the other copy of the photos, for our own personal files," Dayton said, handing Sarah the flash drive. "So where are we going? I'm starving?" Dayton mentioned there was a great Italian restaurant a few block to the right.

At the restaurant, Sarah made eye contact with Dayton for a brief moment. "I've found something you might be interested in," she said.

The waiter took their orders and walked into the kitchen. Dayton asked how his grandmother was doing and both Mark and Sarah told him she was holding up fine. Mark had mowed her grass that morning and Sarah had helped her with the laundry. Dayton felt guilty about not being with her, but he was bound by contract to continue his appointments.

Sarah spoke. "I found something interesting. A few years ago, I read a book on the dollar by David Ovason. I recently found it, and re-read it. You know that star in the streets, just north of the White House?"

"Yes," replied Dayton.

"I think it stands for the star, Spica, in the Virgo Constellation."

Dayton was flattered that Sarah had taken such an interest in his investigation.

"That would make sense," he said as he continued on about the Masonic cornerstone ceremonies and the influence of French Masons on the country. "The Statue of Liberty is a woman, and I also noticed the feminine symbols on the Zero Milestone. The Fleur de Lys is pointed right at the White House. There has never been a woman President---so why?" Dayton smiled. "Perhaps it is for Virgo too."

Mark interrupted, "You mean all that symbolism isn't satanic, like it says on most of the websites?"

"Absolutely not," Dayton replied, shaking his head. "I don't believe the Masons are Satanists. A lot of people think they are because they are a secret society. Their main symbols are the G and the square and compass, not a pitchfork and horns. Where I think people get the satanic nonsense from Mark is the misinterpretation of <u>Morals and Dogma, the Ancient and Accepted Scottish Rite of Freemasonry</u>, one of the major works of Albert Pike, because of his positive use of the word "Lucifer." The other thing to consider is people's politics. Catholics hate Masons because they allow members from all faiths as long as they believe in a supreme being. Doesn't matter if you call him God, Allah, or something else. Many of the Founding Founder's were Masons and deists too. They believed that there was an order in the universe created by god, but that man made his own choices." Dayton remembered the words his father told him on Liberty Island. "Masons are often the focal point of many conspiracy theories----most of which are just bullshit."

The waiter delivered their meals, and the conversation turned to lighter topics as they ate. Mark reminded Dayton that it had been a while since they played pool, or went out on his boat, and Sarah opted to challenge them both to a night out playing pool, if they could find another woman for her to partner with. Dayton, looking at his watch, scooped up the last of his pasta. "We have to get going lady and gentleman. I have to go play author in about fifteen minutes."

Steve, the pale red-head, greeted Dayton and his friend's at the door of the Enoch Pratt Free Central Library. He quickly led Dayton to the special events room where the signing was being held. In the room was a chair for Dayton, surrounded by about thirty chairs arranged in a semi-circle. Dayton sat down and watched as the crowd grew larger and filled the half-circle of chairs.

He opened up with the speech he wrote on his laptop that morning, which explained the perspective of his book. He reiterated that he wasn't trying to dispense with all conspiracy theories and dismiss them, but claims made by those questioning the official explanation of events had to be verifiable. He answered a number of questions from curious book buyers wanting to go a little more in-depth before making the purchase of his hardcover book.

Someone from the group yelled, "911 was a controlled demolition." Steve looked irritated and glanced around to find the rude patron. Dayton stood up.

"It's ok," he said as he motioned Steve to relax. "It sure looked that way----didn't it? But was it? Most people don't realize the stress skyscrapers are under. If you are in them, you can feel them sway. After thirty years of stress, I am not surprised that they fell down after being hit by large jets going 600 miles per-hour. Yes, I am a cop, not a structural engineer. But I would like to know when some group could have gone in those buildings and set up this alleged controlled demolition without being seen. There are no reports confirming this."

"Any more questions?" Dayton asked.

A young woman stood up and began to speak. "Is there a Zionist conspiracy to take over the world? It seems most of the conspiracy theories I have read, whether it be 911 conspiracies, or those in banking, always involve Masons, Nazi's or Zionists."

Dayton looked over at Sarah and caught her looking at him. He smiled briefly, then opened his wallet and pulled out a one dollar bill. "See this," Dayton said addressing the crowd while pointing at the left roundel. "I'm sure you're familiar with the all-seeing eye. Many people believe that there is some Zionist, or Nazi, or Masonic plan to take over the world. I had a similar question back at my Richmond signing. The only problem is," pointing at the eye, "the eye is Masonic, but not in the triangle. As far as conspiracy theories go, every one involves some secret cabal made up of powerful and evil people. Truth is, everyone has their favorite dog to kick."

Dayton continued, explaining the inverted triangle Nazi's used on their Freemason political prisoners. He discussed books and popular fiction, like the <u>Protocols of Zion,</u> and movies, like <u>National Treasure</u>, or <u>The DaVinci Code</u>. "They are all interesting reading, or great films to watch. But unfortunately," Dayton smiled, "Fiction, if it contains some partial truths, has a habit of growing legs." He stood there and continued speaking. "Some people hate or distrust the Jews. Other people hate the Catholic Church. And others, just have vivid imaginations." Dayton began naming off groups and counting them on his fingers. "Masons, Jews, Knights of Columbus, The Vatican, the Bilderbergers, the Club of Rome, The Committee of 300, Opus Dei, the Illuminati, Bohemian Grove, The Council on Foreign Relations, People for a New American Century. I could keep going and going."

A member of the crowd stated, "You forgot the Tri-lateral Commission."

Dayton nodded his head. "Well, at least they have a triangle in their logo---yes----thank you for reminding me." He looked up at the crowd and turned his head slowly from left to right while still holding the one dollar bill. "So who is it? Which one is the evil cabal?" The crowd was silent. "Just because a group is secretive, powerful or wealthy doesn't mean they are plotting death and destruction." His point was well taken.

Dayton sat and signed books for about twenty minutes. At the end of the line were Sarah and Mark, who both held books for him to sign.

"To my best friend Mark, you're going to lose our next pool game, so you're going to buy the beer," Dayton said as he wrote.

"To Sarah," Dayton smiled. "Thanks for helping my grandmother. I hope to get to know you better."

Dayton wished his friends a safe ride home to Richmond. He packed up his things and walked out the front door of Enoch Pratt and on to Cathedral Ave. He knew it was a bit of a walk back to his hotel, but he didn't mind. The night air was getting cooler and the street was well lit. A long walk was perfect for gathering his thoughts.

As he walked out on to the sidewalk, he again gazed on the Basilica of the Assumption. "Mary's triangle," he whispered. "So much for the Illuminati?" He continued the walk back to his hotel and he considered everything which had recently transpired. He mourned the loss of his grandfather and worried about his grandmother. He met a man who turned his life upside-down by telling him his father was really murdered, which put him on a new course to find his killer and also to figure out why. That man, Christopher Hartman, turned up dead only days later. Then there was Richard Mussen, the wise old professor who seemed to be holding his tongue, even as he spoke. As he approached the Washington Monument in Baltimore, he looked up. He remembered the discoveries about the Capital City of his namesake and thought, "What secrets can a dead man tell?" He shook his head and finished walking back to his hotel.

He entered his room. It was just as he left it, sans clean sheets and towels placed by the housekeeping crew. The chair at the desk called him, so he sat down and opened his black binder. The aerials were tucked in the rear pocket, but the sketch he made of Washington D.C. lay in front of him. He took out a pencil and sketched the five-pointed star which was laid out in the streets north of the White House. In the middle of the star, he wrote the name "Sarah." He quickly realized his mistake, so he turned the pencil over and erased, "Sarah," then wrote the word "Spica" in its place. "Freudian slip," he laughed.

☙

"I know he is not married," Sarah said. "He's not----?"

"Absolutely not," Mark said as he turned his truck onto the highway. "Dayton likes a good-looking pair of---" Mark paused; almost forgetting his partner was female. He grinned for a moment, then continued. "Dayton is the kind of guy who is really focused. And he would take a bullet for you without even thinking about it. I spent two years patrolling the city with him. We both moved up to detective around the same time. His promotion was on pure talent and dedication, and he's known as the best detective on the police force. He's just got a lot of shit going on right now. We'll take him out when he comes home. Give him a couple beers----you'll see----he'll loosen right up." Mark looked over at her. "And I think he likes you."

"How so?" Sarah asked. Mark repeated that he had known him a long time, and most women don't keep his attention for more than a few minutes because they're not his type.

"What's his type?" Sarah asked.

"Someone, like you." Mark smiled at her. "If he can get over his prime directive not to date someone in the department." Seeing her cringe, he changed the subject. "That research you did. That was pretty interesting. And I bet Dayton is thinking about what we all discussed at dinner right now. And knowing him the way I do, he's probably putting it in his notebook."

Chapter 9
Return to Richmond

Dayton awoke to the sound of rain. He looked out the window and saw streams of water pounding the street below. He walked over to the closet, got out the suitcase, brought it over to the bed and opened it. He reached in and pulled out both his father's Bible and the book on Washington D.C.'s history given to him by the professor. He again opened the front cover and looked at the writing in pencil.

1m=36.525

"Strange," he muttered. He closed the book and studied it. It was a brown hardcover of medium size. At the bottom of the cover, there appeared to be three suns. The center areas of the suns were divided up into eight orange segments. There were two suns at the top of the cover. In gold inlay, there was what appeared to be the Statue of "Freedom" with three stars on her headpiece. There were also inlays of oak leaves and acorns. The back was plain. He opened it just before the index and found a map. He noticed how much had been added to the Capital, after comparing it with the more recent aerial photos, since the book was published in 1884. By chance, he opened to page eighteen and began to read the second paragraph.

There is a tradition that George Washington, when a mere youth, surveying the Virginia lands of the opulent Lord Fairfax, and little dreaming of the remarkable career fate had in store for him, predicted that someday a great city would be located on the territory now known as the District of Columbia, and the site was so admirably adapted for that purpose.... that when he had

reached the summit of human greatness, and had been proclaimed the Father of his Country, he should have exercised his authority to have the National Capital located on the spot he had been familiar with and admired from boyhood.
Picturesque Washington, 1884, P. 18

"Wow," whispered Dayton. He closed the book and took a moment to reflect on what he read. Then he opened the back cover. Written in pen was the name, R. Mussen and a Maryland address.

Dayton wrote down the address on the paper he had containing the addresses of his father's former military group. "I think on the way back to Richmond, I should pay Mr. Mussen another visit," Dayton said aloud. He was just about to leave the room, when he noticed that he had left his father's Bible on the table. Looking at it more closely, he noticed one page seemed to be thicker than the others. He opened it and found an odd picture, depicting a sacrifice on what appeared to be a Central American pyramid. He closed the Bible and with a puzzled look, started to wonder what was his father's intent? He added the photo as inventory on the sketch sheet he made from the evidence he acquired from Richard Mussen.

Items From Mussen:
1. Dad's Bible
2. Picturesque Washington Book

Class Schedule: Tuesday/Thursday
Georgetown--Theology Professor

Lecture--We are all the Same

Interested in Symbolism

Dad saved his life
Visited Cambodian Man
Secretive--What is he hiding?

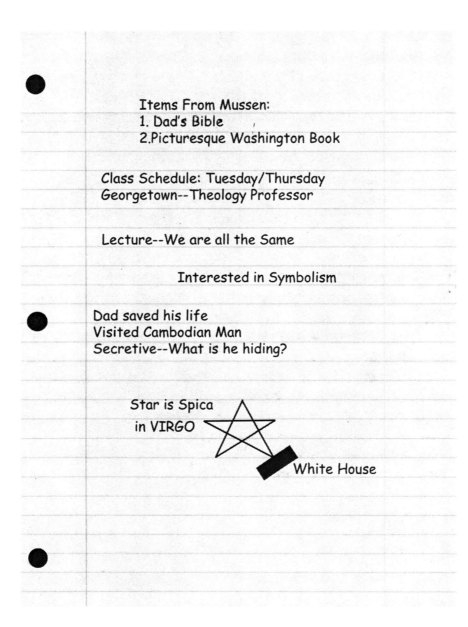

Star is Spica
in VIRGO

White House

Mark was uneasy asking Leslie for a favor. She was an attractive woman with skin as soft as milk. She was different. He had never met a woman who was serious about chemistry and biology outside the bedroom doors. As he walked toward the front door of Biohelix labs, he had to think of a way to charm her.

"May I speak to Leslie Stoddard please?" he told the secretary at the front desk. A few minutes later she appeared, wearing goggles, a facemask and lab coat. She looked at him sternly and asked him why he was bothering her on a Saturday morning.

He began to smile and look at her with the eyes of a puppy dog.

"I'm in a bind, and I didn't know who to turn to. Then I remembered the best biochemist in Virginia." She cracked a half smile under the mask and goggles. She tipped her head down and removed them.

"Okay. Flattery will get you everywhere. What is it?" she asked.

"Could you run an off-the-record test on this sample?" He lifted up his hand, almost as if hiding a diamond, to show her the sample of blood Dayton had absconded from the Hartman crime scene.

"I have half a mind to say no---but if you promise to take me out to dinner----wherever I want to go," she paused. Then she rolled her eyes and took the sample from him. "I'll do it."

Mark looked relieved, but he knew this was going to cost him. "I promise. When you get the results back, call me. And then plan out where you want to go for dinner."

Mark turned and walked toward the door. Before he could exit the building, he heard Leslie continue, "And a full night out on the town." The detective turned. He then scanned his eyes from the floor, all the way up her torso to her head.

"You got it."

Dayton pulled up his Cherokee to the curb in front of the address which was written on the <u>Picturesque Washington</u> book's rear cover. It was an older home in an established neighborhood and the streets surrounding Mussen's house were well-kept. He walked up the front steps on to the porch and rang the doorbell.

A hand swept back the curtain behind the door to reveal an interested face.

"Oh, young McCormick. Come in."

As Dayton entered, he noticed a small .38 caliber Smith and Wesson in Mussen's right hand. He walked over to the kitchen table and put it down on the lazy Susan. Mussen looked up at Dayton. "It is a nice neighborhood, but you can't be too careful these days."

Dayton replied, "I hope I am not bothering you----but considering what has happened over these past few weeks, I have so many questions. And my father never discussed this stuff in my presence."

Mussen motioned Dayton to sit at the table. He then turned the lazy Susan so the muzzle of the revolver was not pointing in Dayton's direction. Dayton placed the Bible and the Washington book on the table. He opened the Bible and removed the sacrificial picture.

"Could you tell me about this?" he asked.

Mussen picked up the picture. "Central American. Aztec----from the Florentine Codex. Common picture actually."

"But why was it in my father's Bible?" Dayton asked.

"I do not know," Mussen replied. "One thing I do know is that art in all cultures often coveys multiple meanings." Mussen look up at Dayton. "I look at this and see no difference from today. Instead of sacrificing people on pyramids for the sun god, we have wars and abortion."

"But what about another meaning?" Dayton inquired.

Mussen studied the depiction. "You mean the root meaning which is inherent in all cultures? Well----a messiah, or should I say the word messiah, has at its roots the word mesa, or flat-topped mountain." He pointed to the top. "No peak. Flat topped mountain of god---where the stars and heavenly bodies were observed."

"Okay. Please continue," prodded Dayton.

"There are seven men," continued Mussen. "There are many seven and sevens in the Bible. Cain. Job. The Apocalypse----or Revelations. What is the Apocalypse, but the peak----or in the case of the pyramids, the cornerstone?"

Dayton nodded his head as he took in what the professor had said. "When the Spanish came to the "New World" they found many depictions of a Madonna and child." Mussen continued, "But these were godless savages, not Christians. Yet, there are also the statues in Egypt with Isis and Horus----very similar----differing only in the appearance of the artistic styles. And the Church of Rome has its Mary and Jesus. I have often looked at symbols, including those of the faith of my upbringing, Judaism, and wondered about multiple meanings. Take the star of David, for example." Mussen got up from the table and brought back a pencil and a piece of paper and then drew a star of David. "Do you know what this symbol can also represent?"

"Besides Israel, or Judaism? No."

Mussen continued. "David's Star, or the Star of Solomon, actually pre-dates the tribes of Israel. It's not in the Bible. The Hebrews adopted it from the Egyptians, who no doubt adopted it from an earlier source." He drew a circle inside the star. He then drew smaller dots at the points and center points of the triangles. "Every twenty years Jupiter and Saturn conjunct with the earth. Saturn, of course, is the Greek Kronos, meaning timekeeper. Around those times, Jupiter and Saturn, also conjunct with the Sun. About every half interval, or ten years, they oppose each other, with the sun in the middle. If you trace Jupiter to Jupiter, Saturn to Saturn from these points in the solar system, from a heliocentric point of view, you get David's Star." Mussen then wrote the word snowflake on the paper.

Dayton smiled. "And do you know what this symbol stands for?" Mussen said, as he drew out a five-pointed star. Before Dayton could answer, Mussen continued, "It is not Satanic, it is the cycles of the earth, Venus and sun conjunctions, which occur every five hundred eighty-four days. Give or take a day. All cultures around the world followed astronomy. So quite possibly, that picture is representative of a cycle of some sort, just as the five pointed star, or David's six-pointed star. Do you understand, Young McCormick?"

Dayton sat motionless and deep in thought. He was trying to make connections between what Mussen was telling him and the evidence his father had left. "Yes. I have another question. In the Washington book, inside the front cover, there is a code. 1m=36.525. Do you know what that means?"

Mussen replied, "Well, I didn't write it, if that is what you are asking. I bought the book at a yard sale for a dollar many years ago, and when you showed me the aerial photo of the District, I simply thought you'd find it helpful." Mussen looked it over and replied. "A year is 365 and one quarter days. That is my best guess."

"Hmm?" Dayton mumbled, then closed the book. "I really thank you for your time, Professor. Could I ask one more question?"

"Of course. And as you can see, I live alone. I am always open for company, especially from the offspring of an old friend. I look at you and I see your father. Even though we were together in an unpleasant place, he was happy memory of mine."

Mussen's eyes were mesmerizing, and his voice almost hypnotic. Dayton shook his head; trying to remember his question. "Yes. Why would my father have been killed over symbols? I don't know if I asked you that before."

"Young McCormick. People have been killing each other over symbols for millennium. Do you remember the lecture I gave?"

"Yes."

"Maybe your father had deciphered a special meaning----one which could jeopardize the status quo. Something Biblical?" Mussen pointed his finger in the air. "Perhaps involving those aerial photos?"

"Or?" inquired Dayton.

"Perhaps he found something which could jeopardize someone's fame and fortune. There were a lot of funny things going on in Vietnam." Mussen closed his eyes. "I am one of three children. I have a sister in New Jersey." He paused, giving a long sigh. "My brother Jacob was killed in Vietnam. His body was never recovered."

"I am sorry to hear about that, Professor," Dayton replied.

Mussen arose from his chair and walked over to the window and then used his hand to move the curtains which obstructed his view. "I've never had closure. Until I do, I won't look for his name on the Wall."

"You will someday," Dayton assured him. He arose from his chair and walked over to Mussen, who was still staring out the window.

"I'm sorry I'm not good company at times, young McCormick. Please don't take it personally."

"I don't," said Dayton. "I left my number and address on the table for you, in case you want to use it."

"Please come again." Mussen let out a soft laugh. "I forgot I left my address on the back of that book. You are a good investigator young man."

Dayton smiled as he walked toward the door. "I'm sure I'll come back here again." He walked out the door and into his Cherokee. Dayton looked back at the house and started the engine. "He's still holding back on me. But he is leading me somewhere. Why?"

♋

A familiar, smiling face greeted him at the door. "Dayton, you're back."

Holding a bag, he gave her a big hug and walked into the house. "I brought your favorite----powdered donuts," Dayton said. The two sat down at the table and began to eat.

"So how have your signings been going?" Martha asked.

Dayton put up his finger as he finished chewing. He told her that overall, things had been going well, but he missed her and was tired. "I actually can't wait until this is all over," he stated.

"Why?"

"Grandma, I didn't realize what I was getting involved with writing this book and going on these signings." He swallowed some milk. "And some of the things people believe are quite interesting."

"How so?" she asked.

He laughed. "Grandma, the crux of the matter is that so many people don't trust their government at all----which isn't necessarily bad. But so many people believe that there is a secret group, within a secret group, controlling everything. And they are planning on enslaving them--or worse--killing them." Dayton took another bite from his donut. In a muffled voice, he continued. "I could go on and on. What bothers me is that people are so focused on the really bizarre, that when something does come around that is real, they don't even see it."

Martha nodded her head. "Dayton. We're all going to die one day. Nobody gets out of this life alive. And in a way, we're all slaves to a material world." She put her hands across the table on top of his. "We just have to make the best of the time we have here." Her tone changed. "So when are you going to take the time to find a nice girl and start a family? You're not getting any younger."

Dayton rolled his eyes and changed the subject. "If you don't mind, Grandma, I am going to crash upstairs. Someone broke into my condo right after," he paused, not wanting to mention the funeral, "and I still haven't cleaned up the mess yet."

"You are always welcome in this house Dayton. You could even move back in if you like." The old woman's eyes stared lovingly at him. He was all she had, since losing George a few weeks prior.

He walked upstairs and looked at the photographs framed on the walls. "There are a lot of good memories in this house," he said to himself. After grabbing the Bible out of his camera bag, he sat down in his bed and began to read the Book of Job.

"Hi Mark," Dayton said. "I was wondering if you were busy today?"

"Nope, still on paid leave. What ya need?"

"How do you know I need something?" Dayton asked.

"I don't know. It is 9AM on a Sunday morning. People only call at that time when they need something."

Dayton paused. "Come to think of it----could you meet me at my condo with your truck? I've decided to move back in with my grandmother, and the place is still trashed, so I was wondering----"

"I'll be over with my truck. Just let me throw some clothes on."

Mark pulled up in front of Dayton's condo in his large, red pickup. Dayton was talking to his realtor: a mid-fiftyish woman with bleached hair in a smart outfit. He told her he was cleaning out the place, he wasn't concerned about top dollar for it and if she felt anything needed doing before the sale, to settle the costs with him on closing.

The two entered the condo and began packing things into boxes.

"I'm only keeping my clothes, memory stuff, the keyboard in the spare room and maybe a few pots and pans. If there is anything you want, just take it."

"Does that include the Bose?" Mark asked, referring to the stereo in the living room.

"Mark, there isn't anything I have I wouldn't give to you. And like I said, if there is anything else you want, just throw it in your truck."

Dayton carefully packed up a box with his father's sword and tomahawk, along with the album of family photos. Mark and Dayton loaded up the Cherokee and the truck with what was being kept and stacked all the rest, including the torn up couch and other items on the curb, with a giant "free" sign on them. He went back in to the mostly empty condo and remembered what Mussen had said to him about multiple interests and whether or not things were related. Then his thoughts returned to his vandalized condo and he weighed that maybe the act wasn't related to the investigation into his father's death, and that perhaps, it was just a creep he had arrested who had a grudge, or possibly some kids out getting their kicks. "I don't know," he said softly. "I just don't know."

Mark overheard Dayton talking to himself. "Know what? I know something. You know this is going kill your love life," Mark said. "Living with your grandmother isn't exactly female-friendly."

"I don't care," Dayton replied. "My love life hasn't been active lately anyway. Besides, my grandmother could use the company."

Mark had the look on his face of a man with an agenda. "Speaking of love life----I brought that sample to Leslie over at Biohelix." Mark smiled. "I have a date tomorrow with a very interesting woman. I don't know how to take her. She is so serious----kind of like you----when you get to thinking." Mark looked down at Dayton with the same look on his face a criminal does while making a plea bargain. "Maybe we could make it a double?"

"I don't have a date, Mark. Would you like me to bring my grandmother?"

"Hey, your grandma is a hot ticket. But I had someone else in mind." Mark's face went from plea-bargain to Cheshire cat. "Why don't we make it me, you, Leslie and-----Sarah?"

"You think she'd go?"

"I'm not worried about her going. I'm more worried about you." He put his arm around his best friend. "And if you don't go, I'll tell her you like farm animals."

Dayton rolled his eyes. "Okay. It's a double."

Dayton went upstairs to the other spare bedroom his grandfather made into a study. In the corner was a large safe, which his grandfather used to store his firearms and other valuables. He reached into the desk drawer and pulled out the folded piece of paper containing the combination. He knew it by heart, but he wanted to see his grandfather's handwriting. After turning the combination, Dayton pulled the lever. The internal bolts released. He reached inside and pulled all the weapons out and placed them on the carpet. His grandfather had quite a collection: two Springfield 1903's, a number 1 Mark 3 Enfield and No 4 Mark 1 Enfield, a 1917 Enfield made by Remington for the First World War, an IBM M1 Carbine, a 1911A1 Colt .45 cal. a German K98, a Swedish Mauser in 6.5x55, an Ithaca pump shotgun and his grandfather's favorite, a H&R M1 Garand, similar to the one he carried in the Korean conflict. Dayton grabbed a silicon cloth and rubbed down each weapon after he inspected the bore and operating mechanisms.

She appeared without a sound. "You didn't have to move back in with me," Martha McCormick said while standing in the doorway of the study.

"You offered. I accepted," replied Dayton, smiling.

"Dayton," Martha said while looking over her late husband's collection, "everything George and I have is yours, you know. You're all we had after Mickey died. You're all I have now. I am so proud of how you turned out and I want you to enjoy these things."

"Grandma, you're not dead. This stuff is all yours," Dayton replied, looking sad.

"No, I want you to have it----and the house too. I know I am not dead, but someday I will be. I just hope you find someone to have a family with to pass it on," she replied, looking like a concerned mother more than a grandmother. "Your signings look like they have been taking a toll on you. You look very tired. Why don't you go out sometime and have some fun?" She walked up to him and gave him a big hug. "I'm going to bed. Get some sleep Dayton."

Dayton returned the guns to the safe. He reached into the drawer and removed his Ruger p345 and placed it in the safe with the rest of the collection. He then unpacked his camera bag and his suitcase; placing the black binder, the book, the Bible, his Father's military photo and the code page on the desk. He thought to himself that he was going to make sense of all this. Then his cell phone vibrated.

"Hello? Dayton. It's Steve from the publishing company. I came by your condo today, but the only one there was a realtor."

"Oh---shit. Steve I am sorry. I am selling it so I could spend more time with my grandmother."

"It must be difficult now, especially with all the upcoming travel. And that is why I called. I came to see you today with your plane tickets for Philly, New York and Boston----for the signings this week, and with your tickets to Chicago, Bozeman, Seattle, LA, Tucson and Dallas."

"Steve, you can return the first three. I think I'm going to drive. Sorry about that," Dayton replied. "I hope you don't mind. Um, you can send the others to this address----519 Coopers Way, Richmond, VA."

"That's okay, Dayton. I'll do that then," he said trying not to sound irritated because the tickets were nonreturnable. "I'll find someone in the building who wants to take a quick trip or something."

"I really am sorry, Steve. It is just---there are a few stops I want to make," Dayton replied.

"No problem," Steve sighed. "I'll see you in Philly on Wednesday. Do you have the addresses?"

"Barnes and Noble, 1805 Walnut St, near Rittenhouse Square. I'll see you before 7pm."

"Fantastic Dayton. I am sorry I called you so late."

Dayton closed his cell and put it on the table. He looked over at the list of last known addresses for his father's team.

Peter Devine--14 Bridge Street, Lee Massachusetts.

"Hmmm," Dayton muttered. "Peter Devine. What am I going to get from you?" He retrieved the Bible from the study desk and reclined on the bed. He looked at its tattered cover and yellowed pages. "I've never read it all," he said to himself.

He read the Book of Job the previous night, but tonight, he decided to start back at the beginning with Genesis. "What was my father trying to tell me with this?" he whispered. "And why did he send it to Mussen? What was the purpose?" he asked aloud, while remembering his father always did things for a reason.

"There is a methodology to all this----I just don't know what it is yet, or where it is going to lead me."

Chapter 10
Circle in a Square

Dayton awoke around 7AM the next morning. It was his first official night back in his old home. He quickly got dressed and met his grandmother downstairs, who had just returned from her morning walk. He felt refreshed after a good night's sleep in safe and familiar surroundings.

The two went out for breakfast. They sat across from each other in the booth; reminiscing both about Dayton's teenage years, and about Grandpa George's way of handling a curious and mischievous boy.

After breakfast, the two went shopping for various things around town. Dayton purchased a few items at the hardware store for fixing up the house. In the past few years, since the onset of George's illness, some simple repairs went undone, which Dayton wanted to take care of. To fill the cupboards and refrigerator, the two stopped at both the supermarket and Costco's.

Dayton helped his grandmother unpack the car and load the items into the house. He stood briefly in front of his Jeep, watching her carry items that normally people in their seventies wouldn't attempt. But she was strong. He attributed her good health to her morning walks, eating properly and letting the day's troubles pass before retiring for her evening rest. She certainly was older and had more grey hair than in the years of his upbringing, but with good health and a sharp mind, he knew she was going to see him through, until she felt her job on earth was finished.

Dayton reached into his coat pocket for his cell phone. "You almost ready?" Mark said on the other end.

"Oh shit!" Dayton replied. He had forgotten Mark's invitation for a night out on the town with Leslie and Sarah. "Give me about twenty minutes." Dayton ran upstairs to the bathroom and showered faster than a New York minute. He shaved quickly and nicked the right edge of his chin. He searched through the closet for the right clothes to wear, while he stood in his underwear.

After finding the only decent pants and a button down shirt which didn't require ironing, he put them on and faced the mirror in the bathroom; looking at himself while he adjusted his tie.

"Thirty-three years old," Dayton muttered under his breath, "and what do you got?" He stood there staring at himself. He had his father's dark hair, with the beginnings of grey making itself known. His brown eyes were deep and kind. His skin was darker than that of his father, who had the typical Irish cream and freckles, but he still had the same unattached earlobes and pointed chin. He had never seen his mother, so he had to imagine what she may have looked like.

He put his hands on his chest. It was pretty firm. His waist, however, needed a little more attention. He was no slouch, but he didn't have the athletic drive that his friend Mark had. Unfortunately, he did have the love for a good donut. "Why am I so nervous?" he thought. "Mark says she likes me----but I don't know."

A firm hand touched his shoulder, followed by a pair of kind eyes. He didn't jump, because for years, she had snuck up on him. She was almost like a ghost floating through the house and never making a noise. "You look handsome, Dayton," she said. "And Mark just came. He is downstairs." He turned toward her and gave her a hug. Sensing he was nervous, she asked, "Are you ok? You don't seem yourself."

Dayton stopped hugging her and put his hands on her shoulders. Looking down at her, he said, "I have got a date."

"That's wonderful. With whom?" she inquired.

"Sarah." Dayton paused. "You know----she is Mark's partner and has come by a few times." He shook his head. "But I never felt right about going on a date with someone who was also on the force." Dayton frowned. "But I do like her."

Grandma Martha put her hands on his face and smiled. "She is a nice girl Dayton and I think she likes you. Put aside your responsibilities and unwavering standards----and just go have fun. Besides, it is a double date, so isn't there less pressure?"

"You're right," Dayton replied. He kissed her on the forehead and walked downstairs to greet Mark, who was sitting on the couch.

"Come on guy. They're waiting for us in the truck," Mark said as he patted Dayton on the back. Dayton took a deep breath and walked out with Mark. "I have never seen you like this. Usually, you are a little more together."

Dayton walked over to the truck and opened the rear door of the extended cab. He looked in the front seat and saw Leslie, with her long, blonde hair riding past her shoulders. In the back was Sarah. He climbed in and became weak-kneed when he saw her smile and almost fell out of the truck. From the dome lamp, he could see she was dressed in a pair of black pants with a flowing white shirt, which he could faintly make out her bra line. Her auburn hair had a slight curl and fell down to her shoulders. Light freckles dotted her nose and her blue eyes were captivating. He sat down next to her and buckled his safety belt. He turned to her and said, "Hi Sarah." He wasn't as nervous around her before at previous encounters, because he looked at her as just Mark's partner, and not his date. But he did like the way she looked and smelled, and she obviously took time to look nice for this evening. He breathed deeply through his nose and looked forward, only to see Mark's eyes rolling in the rear-view mirror, telling him to calm down and be cool. This forced him to relax almost immediately. Mark always had a way of loosening him up, just as Dayton had a way of keeping Mark focused.

"So where are we heading?" asked Dayton.

Mark glanced briefly at Leslie, then turned his head to face his best friend. "I thought we'd begin our evening at Fleming's. Man needs meat." He placed his hand on the shifter, which was soon covered by Leslie's. He moved the shifter into drive and gave her a wink.

Fleming's was known as one of the best steak houses in Richmond, and the two couples stared at the plates of sizzling red meat as the waitresses walked by their table. After a few minutes, the bottle of red wine Mark ordered was un-corked and then began to flow, along with the conversation.

Leslie looked over at Dayton and Sarah. She sipped her wine, which matched her lips, then asked the big question. "So how long have you two been dating?"

Mark nearly spit his wine back into the glass. He couldn't believe Leslie was so upfront. "They----"

"We've been together for a while now," Dayton interrupted; looking over at Sarah as he wrapped his hand around hers and made eyes at her. She looked pleasantly surprised.

"Oh, thank god! When you first got in the car, I thought this was going to be one of THOSE double dates. You know, the ones where one couple tries to enjoy themselves, while the other is quietly at war, or don't click because it is a blind date."

Dayton and Sarah laughed. They understood exactly where Leslie was coming from, as well as enjoyed hiding their secret by leading her on. Mark didn't know what to think, but he was glad to see Dayton being uplifted out of his dour mood.

After they ate, Dayton asked Mark what he had planned next for the foursome. Mark put his left two fingers in the air and lifted up his right elbow while moving his wrist back and forth. Leslie became excited. She hadn't been out to a pool hall in a long time. She turned again to Dayton and said, "Mark tells me you wrote a book debunking conspiracies."

"Not exactly," Dayton replied while shaking his head. "I wrote a book which explores conspiracies from the perspective of a cop. A lot of people make claims they can't substantiate, or associations which at first seem plausible, but don't hold water." Dayton continued, "I didn't expect this book to go anywhere, but sometimes you get surprised in life."

"I thought about writing a book too. I have been published in chemistry journals. But you can probably understand that is for a limited audience," Leslie replied as she squinted her eyes and wrinkled her nose. She knew that "science" people were often looked at as odd or boring, but she was secure and comfortable with herself and her career choice and it showed.

Dayton talked about his upcoming signings as the four walked to Mark's truck. As they drove to the pool hall, Dayton realized which establishment they were going to: Diamond's Billiards. Mark looked in the rear view mirror and saw his buddy's face frown. "Oh shit!" he thought. He realized as he took the u-turn that he was in eyesight of Johnston Willis Hospital. He lipped the words "sorry" in the rear view, which Dayton responded by winking his right eye to reassure him everything was all right. And it was. Sarah was still holding his hand.

The parking lot was pretty full at Diamonds, and they were lucky to get a table after only a short wait. Mark got the beer orders from everyone and Leslie joined him, as he walked over to the bar.

Sarah turned toward Dayton and put her arm around him. "They make a nice couple," Sarah said, pointing over at Mark and Leslie. "Polar opposites----but I think she can hold his attention and keep him in line."

Dayton laughed as he agreed. When he regained his composure, he began to speak. "I never got to thank you for being there when my grandfather died. Thanks. And I am sorry it was such a horrible first date." His faced turned from a frown to a grin.

"Mark said you were an interesting guy. He was right. So what number date is this?" They both smiled and didn't notice Mark and Leslie had returned with beers in hand. The foursome began to play pool.

As Leslie was just about to take her final shot, Mark commented about its difficulty. She had finished putting in all the highballs; leaving the eight-ball in the center between the two-ball, three-ball and the six ball. The yellow, one ball, was in front of the side pocket, as she gently swung her cue stick back and forth; carefully measuring the shot from the cue ball, just to the right of the triangle of low balls.

"It's all geometry and math, nothing more," Leslie said grinning.

Dayton looked curiously at the table. His head was buzzing mildly from the beer, and for a brief moment, he stared at the green felt and the balls. The country music in the background became inaudible while a waitress, wearing tight black pants and a tiger skin top, walked by with a tray in her left hand. She grabbed a bottle with her right hand, raising it above a player at the adjoining table, to avoid connecting with his cue stick.

Sarah put her hand on Dayton's shoulder. "Are you checking her out?"

"Huh?" Dayton replied as the cue ball connected with the eight from Leslies shot and interrupted his concentration. It bounced off the side rail and rolled across the table into the opposite side pocket. Turning to Sarah, he asked, "Checking who out?"

"That waitress," she replied, while pointing at the women in the tiger skin top.

"No, I wasn't," Dayton said sincerely. "I just had a weird feeling."

Mark opened his mouth to cover for his friend. "Sarah, he get's like that sometimes. And the beer doesn't help."

"Hey guys! Game over," Leslie shouted, not aware of the conversation at hand.

Mark looked down at the felt. "Wow, she angled that right through the pyramid," said Mark in amazement.

"All a pyramid is----is a square circle," Leslie said after blowing over the tip of her cue stick. "Just cruise it right through. Next time, we should play for money," said Leslie after licking her lips.

Mark looked over at Leslie and eyeballed her up and down, as only a man can do, then responded, "You are one good-looking, pool playing biochemist."

The foursome got into Mark's truck. Leslie looked at Mark and asked if it would be ok to talk about the chemical testing of the blood sample he had given her, and he nodded his head yes. Dayton's eyes widened like saucers in anticipation of her response.

"At first, I thought it might have been a date-rape case." Leslie paused. "But then I noticed it had to be a man's blood due to the testosterone level and the fact that you really can't rape the willing," sending her carefully crafted sarcasm in Mark's direction. "But then

I noticed something else. There were trace amounts of Pancuronium."

Mark's eyes left the road to look at Leslie. "They use that in lethal injection."

"Yes," she replied. "But the level of it was not sufficient to paralyze the diaphragm and halt breathing."

"What was the other drug present?" inquired Sarah, as she felt Dayton's hand gradually tightening on her own.

"Flunitrazepan. And that stuff is highly illegal in the US. It's the date-rape drug. In other words, the man who had this in him was both limp, and in a semi-hypnotic state."

Dayton closed his eyes and took a deep breath. This was the confirmation he needed that both Hartman's story was true, and more importantly, that his father didn't voluntarily leave him twenty-two years ago. It also made something else possible; that his father's killer, or at least someone involved with his death, was still alive. He glanced over at Sarah with a look of uneasy satisfaction which was returned by one of curiosity.

Leslie opened up her large black handbag and removed a small rubber-stopped vile filled with congealed red liquid and an analytical printout of the testing she performed. She handed them to Mark, smiling, and said, "I think this is good for at least another good meal and a night of pool." She inched her neck forward and planted a kiss on Mark's lips, then pulled open her door and walked to her apartment. Mark sat motionless in the driver's seat, then got out and ran over to her; escorting her the rest of the way to her front door.

"I'll call you. Promise." He returned to the truck, smiling. "Holy shit you two, isn't she something?" He leaned over, which deformed the top cover of the seat, to look Dayton square in the eye. "And what the hell have you gotten yourself into?"

Dayton grinned, almost like a kid being caught sneaking in past curfew. "I don't know, Mark. I don't know."

"And what was that back in the restaurant about you two dating for a while?" he said, as he glanced at his partner.

"Seemed like the right thing to say," Dayton replied, as he looked over at Sarah.

Mark looked back at Sarah, almost like a concerned father. "It is fine with me," Sarah responded, "As long as there is another meal and a night of pool." The truck was immediately filled with a chorus of laughter, which lasted until they reached Sarah's apartment.

Dayton walked Sarah to her door while holding her hand tightly in his. He turned to look at her. Before she spoke, he noticed how the light reflected from the half-moon, accented her beauty. "You can have more than a night of pool and a meal, if you want to?" She looked at him, and gently twisted her hand free so she could touch the side of his face. She lengthened her neck, brought her lips close to his and shut her eyes. Dayton pushed his lips forward and pressed them against hers. As their first kiss ended, Dayton could feel a tingle going through his temples. "I'll see you soon. Goodnight," Sarah said softly.

Dayton climbed in the front seat of Mark's truck. "So what do you think of her?" Mark asked, as he raised his eyebrows.

"I like Sarah a lot," Dayton responded.

"No kidding, Dayton. I am talking about Leslie. Is she something or what? No flies on her either."

"She seems nice Mark. Good looking. Smart. Has a job. You're total opposites, but it might work."

"Yeah, and it looks like you are ignoring your prime directive number one by now dating someone in the department."

Dayton chuckled. "Yes, I know. But sometimes you have to put things aside and just have some fun."

Mark's tone became more serious as he changed topics. "So what are you going to do with the information Leslie gave us?"

Dayton responded. "I don't know yet. I still have a long way to go in figuring this whole thing out. But I do think we just got a very big piece of this puzzle. Whoever killed my father is still out there----somewhere."

Mark pulled in to Martha's driveway. "Well, I guess you're home. Judging from the light being on, I think she waited up for you," Mark joked as he lightly punched Dayton in the arm. "Say hi for me."

"I will." responded Dayton. "We'll have to do this again Mark." Dayton got out of the truck and walked toward the front door. He turned and waved to Mark as he drove away, then proceeded to look up at the moon above. "Square circle?"

As he came through the front door, he was greeted by Martha. The two engaged in small talk for a while in the living room. Her eyes lit up as Dayton told her about his evening and how he would most likely being seeing Sarah again. "She is a nice girl and I like her," she said with a smile.

"I do too." Dayton looked over at the television. "Are you watching C-span?"

"Yes. I have been listening to a Senator Cudman from Louisiana talk about how more Federal funding is needed to rebuild New Orleans."

Dayton rolled his eyes. "Don't you find it incredible how cities like San Francisco and Chicago can burn to the ground, or Nagasaki gets nuked, but are now bustling cities? But we can't find a way to rebuild after a hurricane without spending $140,000 per resident?"

"Times have changed. People are looking for someone else to save them. We really have lost our independent spirit in this country." Martha turned off the television. "It's time for bed."

"You didn't have to wait up for me," Dayton said as he kissed Martha's forehead. "But I am flattered. Goodnight."

Dayton walked up the stairs into the study and spread out the materials he had obtained. He copied everything, from the aerial photos to the names list. He placed the originals in the safe on a shelf above the rifles, along with the toxicology report and the blood sample. The copies of the others, he laid out on the table and punched holes in them, then locked them into his three-ring binder. He inserted blank CD's and made copies of all the pictures. Dayton then scrolled through the photos on his laptop of his recent stop in Washington D.C., until he found the one he was looking for. "Square circle," he whispered as he pulled out a photo of 555 Columbia Square, located just off Pennsylvania Ave. "Hmm? Why three? Different sizes---A triangle has three sides," he thought. "A pyramid has four." He scrolled across the table to pick up the aerials of Washington and Giza. "Three pyramids, different sizes. Three squares in the window----different sizes." He thought back to his high school social studies and history classes. "The pyramids were built supposedly by slaves. D.C. was constructed by slave labor. Giza was in the middle of the land of Egypt. D.C. was in the middle of the New Republic. Both united North and South." He focused the table lamp on the two aerials. "Besides geometry and history repeating itself, how are these two tied together? What did my father find?" He looked at the aerial for New York. "And how does New York City fit into this?"

Symbolism: Circle in a Square:

555 Columbia PLace--Windows are 3 squares
inside one another

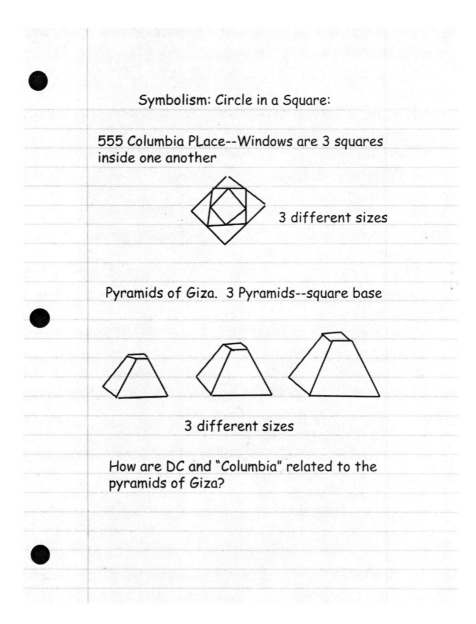

3 different sizes

Pyramids of Giza. 3 Pyramids--square base

3 different sizes

How are DC and "Columbia" related to the
pyramids of Giza?

Dayton awoke and packed his black suitcase with the clothes he needed for the next five days. He placed both the laptop and the black binder in the suitcase, but not the address list, which he folded into his wallet. His nicer clothes he reserved only for the signings, so he zipped them up into a pair of garment bags with hangers.

"Dayton," Martha yelled upstairs. "There is a young lady here to see you."

Sarah walked upstairs and smiled at him. "I just thought I'd come by and see you off." She walked up to him and gave him a big hug.

"So does this mean we're dating?" Dayton asked. "I'd kind of like to think last night wasn't just a fluke." Sarah looked him in the eye and gave him a slow kiss.

"I just wanted to make sure you were all right from last night, considering the information you got from Leslie."

"Do you have a minute?" Dayton asked. She answered yes. He took her hand and brought her into the study. He showed her the evidence he had collected, including his father's Bible and the Washington book on the desk, given to him by Mussen.

Sarah picked up the paper containing the codes. "Well, looks like we're continuing this investigation. You don't mind if I take a look?"

"Not at all. I've found some interesting things, but this page alludes me. I think they are codes of some kind, made by my father."

Sarah looked at the codes containing both letters and numbers. She thought for a moment, then let the page drop while she scanned the table, like a bargain hunter does at a tag sale, and inspected each item. She then placed her hand on the ragged cover of Dayton's father's Bible and rolled her eyes. "I am not sure about all of them, especially the last two here," she said pointing at the page. "But I don't think these are codes. I think these are passages in the Bible." She read aloud the first code. "GE114." She flipped open to the first page in the Book of Genesis. "Genesis 1:14 And God said: Let there be lights made in the firmament of Heaven, to divide the day and the night, and let them be for signs and seasons, and for days and years."

Dayton whispered, "Bible passages. How did you figure that out so fast?"

Sarah replied, "Back in Michigan, I have an uncle who is a Baptist minister. He is the kind that can cite chapter and verse by memory. If you want, while you're gone, I can pull all these out for you."

"If you want to, that's fine. Two heads are better than one." Dayton looked down at his watch. "Damn, I have to get going." He was very disappointed in having to leave her. It was rare that he could be around someone that shared his passion for a mystery, and when he looked at Sarah, he also felt as if he was leaving a piece of himself behind, even though he barely knew her.

"That's all right. I'll stick around here and take a look at this stuff----then maybe ask Martha to go to lunch." Sarah winked.

"She likes you, you know," Dayton said.

Sarah looked up at Dayton. "She loves you. And god help anyone who tries to hurt you."

"You're not going to hurt me, are you?" Dayton asked playfully.

Sarah gently shook her head no. "It is not my plan."

Dayton smiled. "So you have a plan?"

"Yes. After all, we've been dating for a while now."

Dayton had planned his departure to avoid the D.C. rush. The sound of his engine, as he drove up the Interstate, put him in a good mood. He loved the growl of his 4.0 liter straight-six. It was the perfect compromise of power, reliability and fuel efficiency, and the hum was more exciting to Dayton's ear than the political talk shows which permeated the airwaves around Washington.

Dayton smiled as he thought about how much he was like his father. Both shared a love of history. He recalled the many trips his father took him on as a young boy, and also how jealous his father would be of him right now. Because of the book signings, he was getting his hotel accommodations taken care of by the publisher, as well as his airfare, except on this batch, where he elected to drive.

Boston, he thought, was where the American Experiment began with the criminal and heroic acts of the Boston Tea Party and the stand at Lexington and Concord. The Declaration of Independence, cemented the path to revolution in Philadelphia. And New York City was where the future for America solidified. As he left Virginia, he felt alone as he began to think of both his grandmother Martha, and his new girl, Sarah, and how much he wished he could take them both with him. "Leaving Virginia," he muttered as he drove past the sign. "Come back soon."

A few miles up the road, the sign stating he was entering Maryland came into view. He began to recall the compromise of the placement of the Nation's capital, along with what he read in the book given to him by Mussen, the professor. And then it hit him. "The national capital was formed from ceded territory of Maryland and Virginia. "Wait a second!" Dayton exclaimed. He lifted the latch on his glove box to try and get out the pen and notepad he kept with his auto registration and other car essentials. "Birth of a nation. Birth! How come I didn't see this before?"

His eyes opened wide in his revelation. He didn't want to cause an accident while writing, so he exited off the first ramp on the highway. He pulled into a gas station and parked the Cherokee next to an air service pump. He took the pad in his left and grabbed the pencil with his right. He wrote down the names of the states of Virginia and Maryland in succession on the same thin blue line. He then proceeded to erase the last two letters from Virginia, and then the last four from Maryland.

"VIRGIN MARY," appeared on the notepad. "Formed from the womb. The Capital was formed from the womb," he repeated. He sat there for a moment and listened to the Cherokee's idling engine. Thoughts were dashing about like ping-pong balls in his head. "Was this planned? Was this coincidence? Was this a Masonic insult to the Church of Rome? What could this mean?" He then recalled the Masonic cornerstone ceremonies of both the White House and Capitol Hill, and how they were in October and September, respectively. "Virgo. Virgo is the virgin and Mary was a virgin when she conceived Jesus. The symbol----the five-pointed star of Spica that lies to the north of the White House. It's Virgo," he said aloud.

He considered the potential implications, until he pulled off the exit into the "City of Brotherly Love."

After he unpacked his suitcase, he placed his laptop on the desk and turned it on. He did a search for symbols of both the Virgin Mary and for the Constellation of Virgo. He noticed the symbol for Virgo was very similar to the letter M. "Mary," he whispered. "M is for Mary." After searching a few more minutes, he found a symbol for the Virgin Mary, which contained the "M," but had a royal crown above it. Dayton made a sketch and placed it in his notebook, along with other information he had collected. "What were you thinking, dad? What were you thinking? Is it Royal? Or does the crown simply signify the head?"

He shut down the laptop after looking at his watch. The signing was going to take place early this evening, and he remembered he wanted to photograph the historical highlights of Philly beforehand. The Barnes and Noble was at 1805 Walnut Street, just across from Rittenhouse Square, and just down the street from Independence Hall and the Liberty Bell Center. He grabbed his camera bag, exited the hotel and made a bee-line for Walnut Street.

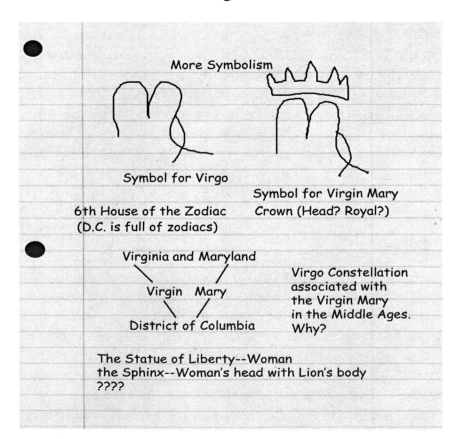

More Symbolism

Symbol for Virgo
6th House of the Zodiac
(D.C. is full of zodiacs)

Symbol for Virgin Mary
Crown (Head? Royal?)

Virginia and Maryland
Virgin   Mary
District of Columbia

Virgo Constellation
associated with
the Virgin Mary
in the Middle Ages.
Why?

The Statue of Liberty--Woman
the Sphinx--Woman's head with Lion's body
????

Sarah pulled her car up to the curb next to the meter. She got out, walked around the car and inserted three quarters. She walked over to the passenger side to open the door, but prior to her grabbing the handle, Martha McCormick opened it herself. "I've got it," she said with an air of independence. The two walked down the red brick sidewalk of East Main Street and stopped in front of Stan's. "I'll be right back, I just have to drop off these shoes."

"I'll wait right here," replied Sarah.

Martha emerged, the two waited for the light to change and then they crossed the street. It wasn't particularly busy at the Courthouse today, so there were plenty of seat's at Padow's Deli. Both women sat down and looked at each other.

"The ham here is wonderful, Sarah. You might want to try it."

"Okay. I think I will," replied Sarah. After the waitress took their order, Mrs. McCormick began her interrogation.

She started looking at Sarah more like a caring mother than someone whom she just met only a few weeks prior. "You know, my Dayton is a very nice young man. How was your date last night?"

"It went fine." Sarah paused. "I wasn't quite sure if Dayton was interested in me. I think the first time I spoke to him----"

"Was when George was dying in the hospital," Martha interrupted. "Don't feel guilty my dear. I had many good years with him. He was my high school sweetheart. We got married just before he joined the army. Shortly thereafter, I was pregnant and he was fighting in Korea." Martha paused. "Like most men who return from war, he changed a bit, but his love for me never strayed. We rarely ever fought. And he was such a good father to Mickey----and Dayton." Martha took a sip of her coffee. "Dayton is very focused. Sometimes it looks like he is off somewhere else. His father was the same way." She put her index finger to her lip. Sarah listened intently as Martha continued. "I don't know what Dayton has told you. I guess it doesn't matter. His father Mickey was a thoughtful boy. What George and I thought was daydreaming, was really his way of concentrating on something he was working on. So it wasn't a surprise to us when we saw our grandson behaving in the same manner." Martha looked up as the waitress delivered the two ham sandwiches with chips and pickle spears. "Thank you dear," Martha told the waitress.

"Sometimes I notice him staring off. He did that at the pool hall last night," Sarah replied. "I thought he was checking out the waitress." Martha raised an eyebrow and lifted her sandwich.

Martha then smiled and took her first bite. "It's his intuition," she mumbled. "He is incredibly gifted and intelligent. It is like he knows things, but doesn't understand them right away. His father was the same." Martha paused to chew her sandwich, then looked directly at Sarah. "My Mickey was an angry young man after the Vietnam war. He went out to live in the Southwest, where he received his training, and he stayed with his friends Peter and John." Sarah nodded her head and asked her to continue. "Mickey fell in love with a local girl, and she got pregnant. After Dayton was born, my son straightened himself out. I guess when a man looks into the eyes of his child, he changes." Martha put down her sandwich. "When Dayton was still in diapers, his mother died after she crashed her car driving home drunk. A week later, Mickey and Dayton were at my doorstep. The money for the train fare was borrowed from John. We took them in, and Mickey attended U of R and got a teaching degree. Then he went to work for the Thomas Jefferson High School as a history teacher. He loved his job. It gave him his summers off so he could take Dayton to historical places he was researching. He said he was gathering information for a book." Martha brought her cup to her lips and took another sip, then continued rattling on about her family's history. "Dayton's crib used to be in the study. When Mickey died, he lived in the bedroom down the hall from us. We were the only next of kin." Martha continued, "Before my Mickey's death, Dayton was a fun and playful boy. After he died, he sat around a lot. He didn't talk much. It wasn't until George bought him a BB gun and took him out shooting, that, he began to open up to us. I don't think he ever got over what happened to his father. What young boy would? Most children in that situation blame themselves----as do the parents." Martha eyes began to tear up, so Sarah placed her hand over Martha's.

Sarah and Martha finished their lunches. "Thanks for telling me about your family," Sarah said as she wiped a spot of mustard off her cheek. "I like your grandson very much, Martha. I'd like to know him better. He seems like a good, genuine man----and there aren't many of those around."

"You could do worse than my Dayton," Martha teased. "George and I raised him the best we could. I hope he has as much fun with you as I have had today." The two ladies smiled at each other and ordered dessert. "And we need to do this again. I hope you didn't mind all my talking?"

"Not at all. Anytime you want to talk or go out, just let me know," replied Sarah.

Martha looked at Sarah and knew after studying her reactions, that she was a good catch for her grandson. But there was something Sarah was hiding. The two left the deli and headed out to do a few more errands.

Chapter 11
The Keys:

Dayton pulled his camera out of the camera bag and walked down Walnut Street in Philadelphia. He remembered being there before as a child, walking around with his father, on one of his historical vacations.

In the Liberty Bell Center, he photographed the Liberty Bell with a telephoto lens, to get a better close up shot of the crack and the repair pin. Then, he walked to Independence Hall, where the Declaration of Independence was signed. He recalled it wasn't signed by all of the Founders there, nor all on July 4th, from the extra history lessons provided to him by his father. "Oh Dad, you are forever with me," he whispered. He sat down on a bench and glanced at his watch.

Dayton then trained his camera on the clock tower. "Time is so important. I wish I had more with my father," he thought to himself. After taking about twenty shots with his camera, he put it away into the open camera bag and placed it on the ground. Then it hit him. "Time. Washington's Birthday." He pulled the black leather wallet from his pocket, removed a Ben Franklin and flipped it over. While inspecting the clock tower on the reverse, he squinted as if he were evaluating fine jewelry. "I'll be damned. The time is 2:22 on the clock." He pondered, "Didn't the Liberty Bell crack on the day Washington died? So why use the month and day of his birth, for the time on the hundred dollar bill? It must be important."

He looked down at his watch again and realized it was getting late. It was time to return to his hotel room, shower and change for the book signing. He didn't want to be walking in just-in-time, like he did in Baltimore.

Steve greeted Dayton at the door of the Barnes and Noble on Walnut Street, just up the pavement from Independence Hall. The floors had been polished and the chairs were arranged neatly, as if some foreign dignitary was arriving for a conference. Dayton felt humbled as he passed a table with multiple stacks of his book for sale. He remembered researching and writing it, but it all still felt so unreal. Steve escorted him to the podium, where he was to address the crowd in twenty minutes. After acclimating himself, Dayton walked over to the beverage center and bought himself a bottled water, then walked around the bookstore and perused the titles of other authors until he had to start.

Dayton walked back to the podium. On the way, his legs nearly gave out, as the butterflies in his stomach affected his balance. It was his third book signing, but he was still nervous. His mouth edged toward the microphone, and he positioned his bottom lip just above the curved top of the device, like a properly trained public speaker would.

"Good evening. How is everyone here doing tonight at the Philly Barnes and Noble?" After his brief introduction, the small audience clapped and his butterflies subsided. Dayton continued. "My name is Dayton McCormick, and I am a police officer from Richmond Virginia. My job is to gather evidence and arrest criminals, so they can be put behind bars." Dayton paused to take a sip from his water bottle. "Everyday someone reads a book, or goes to a website where some conspiracy is being peddled. It has become quite an industry." He told them the reason he wrote <u>Means, Motive and Opportunity</u> was to give people a realistic assessment of what is being sold as truth, through the perspective of an investigating law enforcement officer. Dayton took another sip from his water bottle. "Are there any questions?"

"Yes. What is your question?" A young Latina with a thick Spanish accent began to speak.

"Mr. McCormick. Is there a conspiracy by the government to import drugs into the inner cities to harm minorities?"

Dayton took a big gulp of his water, which was loud enough to be picked up by the microphone. "Not that I know of. We have all seen movies about the CIA or some rogue government agency being involved in narcotics trafficking. I can tell you this, there are bad law enforcement officials. I busted one last year in Richmond. He was a beat cop who was enticed by the money he could make. But I don't have any evidence, or have seen any, that drug distribution is official US government policy."

Dayton frowned. "A man named Terry Woods wrote a book a few years ago about alleged involvement by Bush and Clinton in Iran-Contra and drug running. It's called <u>Compromised, Clinton, Bush and the CIA.</u> But considering both men are still walking around free, I don't know if there was any evidence to it, other than hearsay."

"But did they do those things?"

"Ma'am, no one has proved any of it. But let's say they did, just to speculate, which I don't like to do. Does anyone force someone to do drugs?"

She replied, "no sir," then sat down. She stood up again. "I have another question, Mr. McCormick." Dayton waved his hands, prodding her to proceed. "What about the use of fluoride in the water to make people docile or sick?"

"That's a nice follow-up, and an often asked question," Dayton replied. "Many people don't know this, but the Nazi Germans were the first to implement the fluoridation of water, supposedly as a way to control the minds of the German people and make them docile. Now, I can't speak as to the positive or negative effects of trace amounts of fluoride on the body. I am not a doctor or dentist. I am also not worried about my teeth, because I think I get enough of it in my toothpaste." Dayton grinned, showing his teeth. "But back to the supposed docility that fluoride is supposed to cause." Dayton put a half a smile on his face and shook his head. "Where are violent crime rates the highest? They are in the cities. Right?" The crowd nodded their heads in agreement. "I don't see lower crime rates in cities that fluoridate verses cities that don't. And I have looked at statistics for both. But you know what I do see?" Dayton asked. "I see a lot of criminals with bad teeth." The crowd laughed loudly as Dayton took another swig of his water.

After the signing was over, Dayton started walking to his hotel. He preferred the walk over driving to clear his thoughts, and because it was still early in the evening, he wasn't worried about his personal safety in the city.

He sat down in his bed and put up his feet. He reached into his jacket to pull out his cell phone to call his grandmother and Sarah. A look of frustration came over his face when he realized his cell battery was dead and that he had left his charger on the table in the study back in Richmond.

He felt tired and wanted to get a good night's sleep before his New York signing, so he pulled off his shoes and traded the casual dress clothes for some comfortable ones. He decided he would call his grandmother collect in the morning.

Dayton looked over at the complimentary alarm clock the hotel provided on the nightstand. He got up, walked over to the suitcase and removed his black evidence binder. He wrote "2:22" for the time on one of his evidence pages.

ℰ

Earlier in the day, while Dayton was strolling up and down Walnut Street taking photographs, Sarah had brought Martha back home after their outing. Together, they walked through the front door, entered the house and sat down at the kitchen table.

"It was very kind of you to spend the day with me. Other than Dayton, not many people your age would," Martha commented. "I told you a lot about my family. What about yours?"

Sarah looked down at the wood grain of the table, then looked up uncomfortably at Mrs. McCormick. "There is really not that much to tell."

"Nonsense," Martha replied. "Of course there is."

Sarah took a moment to consider how she would tell her story. "I became a detective a year ago in Flint, Michigan. I looked for an opportunity to travel, and when the detective position was offered in Richmond, I applied for it."

"Do you have any family around here?"

"No. My family lives back in Michigan. I am the youngest of three daughters."

"What do they do?" inquired Martha.

"My older sisters did the traditional thing. They got married and had kids. I didn't follow in their footsteps. I became a cop." Sarah became more uncomfortable. "My uncles were all ministers, so we were all cited Biblical chapter and verse all the time. Instead of raising a good, God-fearing family, I spent my days on the streets arresting criminals and furthering my education."

Like a good investigator, Martha prodded. "I know there is more."

Sarah nodded in agreement. She knew she wasn't going to get out of telling her story. "One of my uncles abused his wife and kids. After seeing my aunt with a big black eye, I arrested him."

"And?"

"When it came to going to court, my aunt refused to testify. She said she fell down the stairs. So, my family disowned me. Nobody offered to help me move, and I was told----in no uncertain terms, not to come back."

"That's terrible!" Martha exclaimed. "Family shouldn't do that to each other."

"You're right. Family shouldn't be like that. But mine was," Sarah replied. "I have nothing against religion and I believe in God. But when you see people preach one thing----then do another----I just couldn't take the hypocrisy anymore. At least on the streets, you know where the criminals are coming from," Sarah stated. "It is sad that sometimes criminals can be more honest."

"What about your parents? They wouldn't stand up for you?" Martha was deeply troubled.

"No." Sarah paused. "You know, I have had a really good time with you today. And except for you, I haven't told anyone here in Richmond about my family." She exhaled. "It was good to get it out."

Martha smiled and placed her hands over Sarah's on the table. "I had a good time with you today. It was nice to go out and do girl things."

"Yes, it was," Sarah replied.

Martha knew what Sarah needed. "You are welcome to stay as long as you like. We could play cards or watch television. Dayton and I enjoy discussing politics. As he puts it," she said, pointing her finger in the air, "I am not interested in what they are doing for me. I want to know what they are trying to do to me." Martha and

Sarah laughed. "When George died a few weeks ago, I thought I would be alone. But I'm not. I have Dayton and I am here now with you." Martha peered deeply into Sarah's soul with her soft eyes. "You want to know something? People think the darkest time of day is midnight. I disagree. I think that the darkest time is before dawn, because when things change in life, when the chapter of a book is completed, we are unsure of what comes next. It is the fear of the unknown, which is sometimes worse than what actually happens. But after the darkness comes light." Martha sipped her ice water and got up from the chair. "There are new sheets on the bed in Dayton's room if you care to stay."

The two talked and watched TV until it was time for Martha to retire for the evening. Sarah remembered that she had told Dayton she would decipher the codes, so she walked up to the study and clicked on the light. Everything was as Dayton had left it on the table. She stroked her finger across the tattered cover of Dayton's father's Bible, a Douay version, and opened it to the passages indicated by the codes, in the order they were written. She found a pen and piece of paper and wrote the code first, then the correct passage number, followed by what was written in the Bible passage.

GE114 GENESIS-1:14

And God said: Let there be lights made in the firmament of Heaven, to divide the day and the night, and let them be for signs and seasons, and for days and years.

MA161819 MATTHEW 16: 18-19

...Thou art Peter; and upon this rock I will build my church; and the gates of hell shall not prevail against it.

And I will give to thee the keys of the kingdom of heaven. And whatsoever thou shalt bind upon earth, it shall be bound also in heaven; and whatsoever thou shalt loose on earth, it shall be loosed in heaven.

MA2142 MATTHEW 21:42

...The stone which the builders rejected, the same has become the head of the corner?

LU2017 LUKE 20:17

...The stone which the builders rejected, the same has become the head of the corner.

IS2816 ISAIAS-28:16

...Behold, I will lay a stone in the foundations in Sion, a tried stone, a corner stone...

EC2424 ECCLESIASTES 24:24

I am the mother of fair love, and of fear, and of knowledge, and of holy hope.

LU2 21 Luke 2:21

And after eight days were accomplished, that the child should be circumcised, his name was called Jesus, which was called by the angel before he was conceived in the womb.

A34723 SS

O23672 SS

Sarah looked at the last two codes. They looked unfamiliar and she couldn't find a match anywhere in the Bible. She picked up the bible and closed it, then carefully placed it and the list of passages on the corner of the table in the study. "Where the hell was Dayton's father going with all this?" she whispered. Her thoughts turned to him, and she wondered why he hadn't called Martha today.

She switched off the light on the table and walked down to his bedroom. She pulled up the sheets and covers and crawled in. As she lay in the bed, she gently sniffed the pillow. The sheets may have been washed, but they still had his scent, and that comforted her as she began to fall asleep.

The next morning Sarah picked up the phone, and a mechanical voice spoke. "Call, from, Dayton McCormick. If--you--except--the-- charges, please press 1 now." Sarah pressed one on the phone's keypad.

"Hello, Grandma," said Dayton.

"Hi Dayton, it's Sarah."

"Hi Sarah. Did I dial the wrong number?"

"No. I am here at Martha's."

"Oh, good. For a minute there, I thought I was losing it. How are you?"

"Fine. How are the signing's going?"

"I just finished Philly last night, and I am heading out to New York within the hour. I wanted to call you both, but my cell battery is dead. I think I left the charger---"

Sarah interrupted, "On the top of the desk. I have it here." Sarah picked it up and placed it back in the drawer. "Will you be back Sunday?"

"Yes. New York is tonight. Tomorrow, I'll be in Western Massachusetts, and the following day is Boston." Dayton stopped for a second and took a breath. "Did you want to do dinner when I get back?"

Sarah responded, "I'd love to. Dayton, Martha is out on her walk. I'll let her know you're ok. And I'll call Mark too."

"Thanks, 'uh I uhmm----I'll see you soon." Dayton hung up the hotel phone. Sarah sat and wondered what he was going to say. She didn't recall ever hearing Dayton stutter in the short time she had known him.

Dayton looked at the phone. "It's nice calling home and talking to her. I could get used to that."

Philly was a little difficult to get out of, due to the traffic and road construction. But the remainder of the ride up to Manhattan was trouble free. Dayton felt that he had to really brush up on his responses for tonight, considering the Barnes and Noble was a stone's throw away from the worst terror incident in American history.

He planned to get a few photos of lower Manhattan, especially Ground Zero and the Financial District, to add to his portfolio before the signing.

He parked the Cherokee in the hotel lot, and after checking in, he walked out front and hailed for a taxi. He got in it and checked the equipment in his camera bag. "Ground Zero, please," he told the driver.

Ground Zero. It was still shocking to look at expensive real estate that was only partially re-built. Freedom Tower had been proposed and designed, but had not been started, and there was fencing everywhere.

He stared across the bay and looked at the small green woman holding the torch. Dayton remembered how beautiful she looked up close on the last trip he and his father took together before he was murdered. "He must have been trying to figure out what she really stood for symbolically," he thought to himself.

He reached into his coat pocket, where he had placed the list, and read the name Peter Devine and his address in Massachusetts. He hoped he would find him on his way to Boston.

He turned to step off the curb into the street, but stopped abruptly when he heard a loud horn. The driver stopped quickly before hitting him and yelled obscenities out the window, in a strong New York accent. Dayton brushed it off and walked toward the bookstore.

Steve was there to greet him as he entered the B&N on Warren Street. "Dayton. Great, you're here. Are you all set?" Dayton followed the pale red-head to the signing area. There was no microphone or podium, like in Philly. The setup was similar to the one he had at the library in Baltimore.

Dayton spoke to the crowd and gave his perspective on various conspiracy theories. Many hands quickly raised and the questions came in like the assault on Omaha Beach during the invasion of Normandy on D-Day.

"Are you aware that there is news footage showing live video of Building 7 standing up, as the newscasters said it was coming down?" asked one of the attendees.

"Yes. That is a common point raised by conspiracy theorists." Dayton sipped his water. "I have seen the footage myself. Did you notice the scenes behind the anchor people in newsrooms all around the world looked the same?"

"I guess," answered the questioner.

"It is because news organizations around the world were all being fed from the same camera. Due to the amount of traffic on communication lines that day, the feed was most likely cut off temporarily. So even though it said it was live, in reality, it wasn't. It was a live icon from a video character generator, nothing more."

Another hand went up. "Yes," Dayton responded.

A young man with brown hair stood up. "Are you aware, Mr. McCormick that Mr. Silverstein said that Building 7 was pulled, meaning, brought down by explosives?"

Dayton responded, "I think it was probably a poor choice of words." Dayton pushed his lips tightly then continued. "This is why many people feel 911 was an inside job." Dayton explained to the crowd that a proper demolition in a metropolitan area would take weeks to plan and execute. Building 7 was on fire, so there was no way demolition crews could have properly set the charges in place in the time allotted and during the chaos which was ongoing. "Many people would then ask me----well it could have been planned ahead of time. My response is---how do you place explosives in a building without anyone noticing? And Building 7 especially, because it had some very high stakes offices, like the FBI, the Securities and Exchange Commission and the Emergency Management Office for the City of New York."

"But what about reports saying the Port Authority cut the power to the upper levels of the Twin Towers for computer wiring upgrades the weekend prior to 911?"

"I can't confirm or deny that," responded Dayton. "But then the conspiracy gets so much larger. Too many people. And, no one talking."

Another questioner raised his hand. "Yes," pointed Dayton.

"Mr. Silverstein insured the complex for a lot of money against terrorism, and didn't he pay 3.22 billion for the WTC, after the higher bid fell through?"

Dayton responded. "That is correct. He did insure the complex against terror and did pay 3.22 billion originally for it. I know what some people believe because of the number 322. If you think that Bush was somehow involved, because this was some sort of a Skull and Bones operation, I have a hard time with that. You mean to tell me there aren't any patriotic Americans who went to Yale who would have broken their silence, especially over the death of 3,000 Americans?" Dayton shrugged his shoulders. "As far as insurance goes, the complex was attacked in 1993. I'd insure it too." Dayton looked up and took a moment to gather his thoughts. "Many conspiracy theorists have said Bush used 911 to launch two wars and was going to institute Marshall Law in America. Guess what? He is no longer President and Marshall Law hasn't happened."

Steve stood up and clasped his hands together as he looked around at the crowd. Then he picked up a hardcover of Dayton's book and held it high. "I hope you all have found this enlightening and hope you purchase the book Conspiracy Theory, Conspiracy Fact, to answer all those nagging questions so many Americans have." He smiled and brought the book down to his side. Dayton looked at Steve with his pale skin and red hair and thought of the resemblance Steve had to a Jim Henson Muppet he saw on television as a child. "We have time for one more question," Steve announced. He pointed toward a blonde woman sporting retro look glasses and wearing a shirt with a big peace symbol on it.

"What is your opinion of the Patriot Act----Detective?"

Dayton wasn't expecting that question. He took a deep breath and regained his composure. "My grandmother and I love to talk about politics," Dayton responded. He then stood up and continued his answer. "I think bills, especially big or controversial ones, sit on shelves waiting for when opportunity knocks." He started pacing back and forth while moving his hands as if he continued opining about his beliefs to a deaf man. "The Patriot Act contains many things which I find objectionable. But there have been no mass arrests. The internet is not being censored by the government. People can still come and go as they please, with the exception of being harassed at the airports. Martial Law has not been declared. Nor have the courts been dissolved." He watched as heads in the crowd began nodding in agreement. "I think no matter what bills are passed or proposed, eternal vigilance is required in order for a people to remain free." Dayton looked over at the blonde woman and nodded. "Thank you for that question."

Steve stood up again and was about to speak. Dayton put out his hand, gesturing for just another minute to talk.

"I just want to make one more point about conspiracies. Most of them are baloney. But they do one good thing. They cause people to watch what their government does. So in a way, that is good for America." Dayton smiled. "I have to tell you----people say New Yorkers are a tough bunch. And you were. Thank you everyone for coming here tonight."

৯

Lee, Massachusetts was a beautiful town, Dayton thought. The former Massachusetts mill town had transformed itself over the years into a quaint marketplace, by both hard work and having an ideal location off the highway. Dayton had the privilege of witnessing the foliage show its fall colors as he drove through.

He turned on to Bridge Street and depressed the brake to reduce the speed of his Cherokee, so he could read the numbers on the houses. He looked back at the list sitting in his passenger seat. "That's it," he said, pulling up to a dilapidated white two-story home.

He opened the Jeep door, walked up to the porch and proceeded to knock on the front door. He hoped that Peter Devine was still at the address in his hand.

About a minute later, a woman used her hand to pull the small curtain, which blocked a visitor from looking through the door's center window. Feeling secure, she opened the door for Dayton.

"Who are you?" the woman asked in a snide tone. She had obviously slept in late. Her nightgown was terribly wrinkled and judging by the bags around her eyes and her drooping cheeks, she was probably hung over. Her long and colored blonde hair was matted to the left side of her head, and judging from her pronounced crow's feet, Dayton estimated her to be around sixty years of age.

"Ma'am. My name is detective Dayton McCormick." Dayton paused as he remembered he was out of his jurist diction.

"You wait right here. Don't go away!" she yelled. About thirty seconds later, she returned with a slip of paper written in poor handwriting and handed it to Dayton. "I had to hire an investigator to find that bastard, because you people wouldn't do your job."

Dayton's eyebrows rose as he stepped back, taken by surprise. "Ma'am, I am looking for a Peter Devine."

"Yah, I know!" the woman exclaimed. "He is my ex-husband."

"But what I see here is an address with the word BASTARD above it," Dayton responded in a calm deep voice.

"That's him and that's where he is!" Her face began to turn red as an apple; displaying a high degree of animosity toward her ex-husband. "And when you find that fucking drunk, you tell him if he doesn't start paying me my alimony, I am going to go up there and rip his God-damn balls off!" she exclaimed prior to slamming the door in Dayton's face.

Dayton calmly turned around and walked off the porch. He glanced at the words on the sheet and wondered what kind of a man he was going to find.

BASTARD
1272 JAMES MORRISON RD, HUNTINGTON, MA

He stopped at a package store on the way to the turnpike and picked up two large bottles of liquor. Jack Daniels and Southern Comfort were his favorites, so he put them in a brown paper bag. Dayton felt, based on what had occurred earlier at the house with his ex-wife that they would be a wise investment in case Mr. Devine needed some liquid persuasion.

"Where the hell is it?" Dayton said, almost yelling at his GPS. "It has to be around here somewhere." He had turned on to James Morrison Road and had gone up and down it five times. After shaking his head, he started back to where he had first turned on to the road and drove very slowly, while inspecting every opening and looking at every tree.

He continued down the road for about a half a mile, going even more slowly, while looking for Devine's address. He spotted a man walking toward him on the side of the road, carrying bags in both arms while sporting a backpack over his shoulders. Dayton looked at the older man, who resembled a sixties throwback and wondered if he knew who Peter Devine was and where he lived. "I wonder if this hippie knows him," he said to himself. He was about to stop and ask, when he noticed "1272" faintly sprayed in red paint on a tree, in front of an almost hidden dirt driveway.

He turned in and followed the winding path until he saw the abode. It was a tiny rickety house made of grey barn board with a small black metal chimney coming out the side. He parked the Jeep and got out, carrying his black binder and the bag from the liquor store.

Dayton knocked on the door, but nobody answered. He sighed. "This might be my only chance for at least a month. Damn it!"

He turned to walk back to the Jeep. Someone was walking down the driveway. He recognized it was the hippie he had passed on the road.

"Hawoh," said the man. "Wet me put ma teet in."

Dayton watched as the man entered the house and put down his bags while leaving the front door wide open. He grabbed what appeared to be a small case off the counter and walked toward him. With his left hand, he opened the lid and pulled out a set of false teeth and snapped them into place.

"I didn't quite catch what you said," said Dayton.

"I said hello and let me put my teeth in," the man replied, "and who are you?"

Remembering this time that he was out of his jurist diction, Dayton replied, "My name is Dayton. I was wondering if I could have a word with you?"

The man took off his hat, which revealed a very shiny top surrounded by long, stringy hair around the perimeter of his bald head. His face was thin and his complexion pale. Dayton recognized right away he was an alcoholic. "So I guess the bitch found me," he said, putting out his hands as if waiting to be handcuffed. Dayton then realized the man knew he was a police officer.

"I'm not here about that," said Dayton, noticing the look on the man's face. "I'm here to talk about my dad."

"Well, I'm not your father kid. I'm not, right?" he said uncomfortably.

"No. You are not," Dayton snickered.

"So who are we talking about?" the man asked, showing off his dentures.

"You served with my father in," Dayton paused, remembering Mussen's preference, "Southeast Asia, during Vietnam."

The man looked at Dayton from top to bottom, almost like someone sizing up a prize fighter. He squinted one eye and walked up to Dayton, curling a half smile on the left side of his face. "Are you Mickey's boy?"

"Yes, my dad was Mickey McCormick. Are you Peter Devine?"

"Live and in the flesh," Peter smiled while looking at what Dayton was carrying. "Whacha got in that bag?"

"A present. Two bottles. Soco and Jack," Dayton responded.

Peter waved his hand in front of Dayton pointing toward the door. "Don't just stand there!" Peter said enthusiastically. "Come on in. My god, I haven't seen you for at least thirty years. You were just a little shit, about three years old. I came and saw your dad down in Virginia prior to settling up here." He placed his hand over Dayton's shoulder and walked him into the house.

The inside was much neater than Dayton had anticipated. There was a desk, and next to it, a bookcase filled with astronomy books. On nearly every surface, there were oil lamps or candles. Dayton noticed there weren't any light switches on the walls.

"I have very limited electricity. Use it only for refrigeration through my generator out back. All my cooking is done on wood or gas." Peter sat down on the couch, which was covered with a sheet to hide the rips. He opened the brown bag and placed the two bottles on the milk crates and sheet of plywood, which served as a coffee table.

Dayton sat down and they began to talk. "So you met my Ex?" Peter asked.

"You could say that," responded Dayton. Peter got up.

"You hungry?" Peter asked as he grabbed a cast iron skillet from the cupboard.

"Actually, yes."

Peter walked the skillet over to the wood stove and placed it on top. He then adjusted the airflow slider to increase the stove's heat output. He walked over to the small fridge and pulled out some hamburger meat wrapped in tin foil and formed two large patties, then placed them on the skillet. As they started sizzling, Dayton noticed Peter was missing the pinky finger on his left hand.

"Oh that. Huh, million dollar wound. When we were being extracted, I was shot in the ass on the way to the chopper. Hurt like hell, so I grabbed my can," recalled Peter, "and another round quickly followed and hacked the little bugger off. Kind of miss it." Peter made a sawing motion with his right hand over his left. "But you get used to it. I was lucky. Big Johnny took multiple hits in the back. But he still managed to climb aboard the chopper. Your father was a lucky son-of-a-bitch, only lost his Petri camera, as he pulled Dicky Mussen onto the Huey. Shattered the lens as I recall. Hutch got a scar only a mother could love. Bullet got him in the face." Peter shook his head and laughed.

"What about Hartman?" Dayton inquired.

"Hartman was lying unconscious on the floor. It was the last I saw or heard from him until I got a package a number of years ago."

Dayton's eyes lit up. "Do you still have it?

Dayton took the black binder he had placed between him and the couch arm and opened it. He placed it on the table and explained the situation. "I met Hartman a few weeks ago. He told me he knew my dad, and he gave me a box with these aerial photos in it, along with this picture." Dayton held up the photo of the six soldiers. "There was also an address list, and a list of codes." Dayton paused. "He said my dad was working on something and he mailed other items to all his buddies from this photo. Later that day, my dad was murdered."

Peter didn't blink an eye. "I didn't think he had killed himself," he said. "Guess you can't believe what you hear on the news."

Dayton continued. "I found Richard Mussen. He is a professor of theology at Georgetown."

"Yah, that would figure," Peter replied making a face. "He and your dad used to discuss religion all the time."

"Well, my father sent his Bible with a photo inside." He took a breath. "I think all this information is connected in some way I haven't figured out yet. When I do, I hope to find his killer."

"Good luck. So how is Hartman?" inquired Peter.

Dayton tipped his head down, facing the floor. "He's dead. He was killed the same way my father was the day after I met him." Dayton frowned. "I hope I'm not putting you in any danger by being here."

"Oh don't worry about that. They can't be any scarier than my ex-wife. Besides," Peter said, reaching under the couch and pulling out a pump shotgun, "there are ways to deal with unfriendly people."

The two ate their hamburgers and washed them down with cold beers. Peter began flipping through the few pages of the black binder. "These are Bible passages," said Peter pointing to the codes. "Well, most of them. Not sure about these two."

"That's what a---friend of mine told me," replied Dayton. "That might explain why Mussen had his Bible----being into religion and all."

Peter continued to flip pages, stopping at the sketch of Washington D.C. "There is something there. Your father knew that." He looked at the Giza aerial and then the one for New York. "Poor bastards," Peter commented while pointing to the area of the World Trade Center. "Getting mixed-up in some creepy ceremony."

"What did you just say?" asked Dayton.

"A ceremony. The terrorists were enacting the destruction of the temple. That is why they chose symbolic targets, and not something more potent, like the Indian Point Nuclear facility."

Dayton had a puzzled look on his face. "What, don't you see it?" Peter continued. "The Babylonians destroyed King Solomon's temple. It was re-built and then destroyed again by the Romans around 70AD." Dayton focused his attention on the aerials along with the sound of Peter's voice. "The Rockefeller boys did what all good Christians thought would be done in Jerusalem. I don't know if it was intentional. They re-built the temple in Lower Manhattan. The Twin Towers were Joachim and Boaz, the two pillars in front of the temple. Building 7, was Saloman Brother's Building. Sound a lot like Solomon, my boy? And Jesus said to his disciples that no rock would be left unturned and as I recall, those buildings became dust."

Peter's words struck a chord with Dayton. He explained to Peter that his father told him the day before he died on Liberty Island that everything goes to dust, which included the Twin Towers.

"Did he mention the statement by President Cleveland?"

Dayton responded, "Yes. He said something about Liberty's altar." A chill went down his spine. "An altar is a place of sacrifice."

"Yup, every ceremony needs an altar, right?" Peter responded.

"But why do it? And why was Washington D.C. attacked?" Dayton asked.

"I am not totally sure, Dayton. My last discussion with your father had something to do with history repeating itself."

"Really?"

"Yes. Your father told me he was studying architecture in cities. He told me many of them contain a message of some sort. He didn't go into details, other than to say Washington was the big one." Peter sighed. "Just after he told me, I got in my car with my wife to be, and drove up here. That was about thirty years ago." Peter picked up their plates and walked them into the kitchen. He returned to the couch with a couple more beers.

"So why are you living here?" inquired Dayton.

Peter smirked. "A number of reasons. A friend of mine owns this property, so the rent is cheap. You met my ex-wife. Can't say as I blame her for divorcing me. My eyes and hands have tended to wander a bit over the years." Dayton smiled, thinking about his friend Mark.

"What was your specialty in the military?" Dayton asked.

"Didn't really have one, except trying to gather intelligence from the locals about VC troop movements," Peter replied. "But that was another time---almost another life."

Dayton looked at Peter. "I hope you don't mind all the questions I am asking?"

"Not at all." Peter then explained that after he came home from the war, he learned a lot while recuperating in the army hospital.

"I had this guy in the bed next to me named Ralph Stevens. Poor bastard lost his foot to a booby trap. Me being me, I asked him how he was going to get the girls

131

when he got out. He told me women loved astrology and numerology. It mesmerized them. He had a number of old books, so he let me read them. And god damn it, he was right," Peter boasted. "Worked like a charm." Peter slugged down half his beer. "You're father and I used to talk about astrology and astronomy all the time when we were out in Arizona. We didn't see eye to eye on everything, but both of us came to the realization that what went on down here on earth had a lot to do with what goes on upstairs in space." Dayton looked over at all the astronomy books in Peter's bookcase. Peter looked over at the aerials in Dayton's black binder. "Let me explain a few things."

"I'm all ears," replied Dayton.

"Dayton, when you understand astronomy and numerology, 911 makes perfect sense. DC is one big observatory. Where the Kennedy center is now, was once called Foggy Bottom." Peter flipped to the D.C. aerial. "Right here. It is where the first US Naval Observatory was built. Now, let's go back to New York." Dayton leaned forward, giving Peter his undivided attention. Peter continued. "Solomon's Temple was a symbolic architectural construction of the Solar System: God's Creation. Both the structure and measurement of the World Trade complex represented the universe's attributes." Peter got up and walked over to the bookcase. He opened a folder and removed a circular depiction of the Constellations. He placed it next to the aerial of New York. "See this," he asked Dayton as he pointed to Governor's Island. "This building does what?" Before Dayton could respond, Peter answered. "It points north. And what is north?"

"The Twin Towers and the WTC." Dayton replied.

"Exactly." Peter smiled. "But do you know what those Two Towers represent in space?" Dayton gave a brief head wag, indicating no. "Joachim and Boaz are the twin pillars. The Constellation Gemini has two main stars----Castor and Pollux. Now," Peter said as he moved his index finger counter-clockwise, "Look where the Statue of Liberty is. It is a woman, with a torch." Then he pointed back to the Constellation sheet.

"Exactly where Virgo is." Dayton interrupted.

Peter nodded his head. "And the sun was rising in Virgo at the tail end of Leo on September 11th, and, Jupiter was right in the middle of Gemini." he added. "All astronomical." Peter looked at the measurement for Washington. "3.56 kilometers. Dayton, have you ever added up those planes?"

Dayton looked at Peter inquisitively. "The four flights from September 11th?" Peter smiled as Dayton grabbed his pen and paper, adding up 11, 175, 77 and 93. "I'll be damned. 356."

Peter was still smiling. "Everything is related boy. When Lincoln and Kennedy were killed, both had a VP named Johnson."

Dayton interrupted, "I have read about those coincidences."

"Really," Peter responded, changing his tone. "I bet you've never seen this." He began to write numbers on Dayton's paper. "Everything is related astronomically and numerically. Everything." He wrote down the flight numbers which hit the towers. "Kennedy was killed on November 22nd." He pointed the pen at the eleven, the number of the plane that hit the North Tower. Then he pointed at the 175. He wrote 17+5=22. "Eleven twenty-two. November 22nd."

Dayton looked at Peter skeptically. He then wrote down the year 1963. He took the 19 and added it to the 63. "Eighty-two," he said.

"So?" questioned Dayton.

Peter then wrote down 77, the number of the plane that hit the Pentagon. "Add five, because it is a five-sided building."

"Eighty-two," Dayton whispered.

"Correct," responded Peter. "Correct. Both sacrifices of some kind. Some weird connection. They are related in some way."

Dayton's thoughts turned to the Aztec sacrifice photo he found in his father's bible and the seven men in it.

"311, 77, 711----heck Sept. is the prefix for seven. Weren't those attacks in Madrid, London and India on those days?" Peter laughed. "I don't know how this all works, my boy---it just does. Want to see some more?"

Peter was opening up a whole new line of thought for Dayton. Although he was still skeptical, he asked Peter to continue.

"Kennedy and 911 are related in other ways. Where was he heading after his ride through Dallas?"

"The World Trade Mart." Dayton's hands felt cold.

Peter replied, "Yes, the WORLD TRADE mart. He was shot on Elm Street, in between North and South Houston Streets."

Dayton's eyes lit up. "That's true." He watched Peter's lips as they began their reply. "North and South Towers." Dayton was mesmerized. "Got another for you."

"Please----continue," he replied, eager to hear more.

"Your father told me once, he thought the Statue of Liberty was a symbol for a trinity. I didn't understand what he meant then, or now. But here is an interesting parallel. You've heard of the Manhattan Project, right?"

"Yes."

Peter explained the whole scenario. "The Manhattan project brought forth the Trinity Test, where man witnessed the destructive power of God. The atom."

Dayton interrupted. "And on September 11th, the symbol for the Trinity," he said, pointing at Lady Liberty, "witnessed God's destructive power in Lower Manhattan. Liberty's altar."

Peter stared at the two bottles of liquor on the table. "You're a pretty sharp kid. Your father and Dicky Mussen were the real symbolism nuts, you know. I took another direction---but one your father found interesting. I looked for cause and effect." Peter got up from his chair and went into the kitchen to fetch two glasses. He opened the bottle of Southern Comfort and poured two glasses and handed one to Dayton. "I think it's time we drink."

The two clanked glasses as if they were at a wedding. "We could be in a bit of trouble over the next few years," Peter stated, before downing the whole glass of Southern Comfort. He started to grin, showing off his yellow stained false teeth. Dayton raised his glass and took another gulp. Before he could put it down on the table, Peter was filling it up.

Dayton raised his glass to his lips and took a swig. "You've got my attention," he said.

"Good, because life, or I should say, society as we know it, is possibly about to change drastically. Cheers," Peter boasted. "Let me show you."

Dayton dribbled some of the flammable brown liquid on his shirt.

"Forget all the bullshit you've heard about the stages of societies." Peter took another gulp from his cup. "Only one thing matters." Peter pointed up. "Yes, simple demographics can show that we are entering a period that is unsustainable----especially financially.

But it is what goes on in space that determines the fate of both man and society."

Peter reached over and poured himself another glass of liquor. He looked at Dayton's half empty glass, then filled it to the top, forcing Dayton to sip some quickly, or stain his shirt again.

Peter continued. "While me, your dad and Johnny Wind all lived in Arizona, we used to go up in the mountains. Great stuff to see there. Johnny still lives there, so if you see him, ask for a tour of the cave." Peter smiled and chuckled. "Me and your dad used to take a telescope up there and watch the skies," Peter continued. "Why? Because, we were figuring out how this all works." He took his right hand, extended his finger, and pointed up. "And it ain't what NASA tells you. What I am about to show you has been my passion for my whole adult life. I only wish I could have told your father what I learned over the past thirty years. Wish I called him--but I knew I couldn't." Dayton held a poker face upon hearing the comment.

Peter got off the couch and walked to the kitchen. He removed a plate and a number of shot glasses from the cupboard, then brought them back to the coffee table. He placed the plate in the center of the table and picked up a candle, put it in the center of the plate and lit it. "The candle is the sun and the plate is the ecliptic---the flat plane the planets move in to travel around the sun." He placed the five shot glasses around the outer edge of the plate at varying distances. "This is Jupiter, Saturn, Uranus, Neptune and Pluto," he said. Then he removed some change, put five coins at various distance, but this time, on the plate. "Here are Mercury, Venus, Earth and Moon, and Mars." Dayton was wondering where he was going with all this. His head was starting to feel the effects of drink. Peter twirled his right index finger in a counter-clockwise direction and said, "All the planets travel around the sun in the same direction, at different rates. What make 'um go?"

"Gravity?" Dayton replied.

Peter looked at Dayton with sarcasm. "Son, were floating around in a windy river of soupy energy. The center of the sun rotates with a twenty-five day cycle, while its poles rotate at twenty eight. Every eleven years or so, the sun goes through solar minimums and maximums. It is like a giant synchronized machine." Peter continued. "Energy is going out from the sun and energy is being pushed into the solar system from most of the Constellations----and some is sucked out toward the galactic center." Peter took another swig and pointed at the plate. "The earth is just like the sun, only covered with dirt and an atmosphere. The sun is way bigger and has more mass, so it ignites, and the earth core spins, producing a magnetic field. The orchestra out there is what controls the sun and the weather on earth."

"So I guess you don't believe in man-made climate change?" Dayton asked sarcastically.

"Not at all. And most of those who promote that nonsense do so only to line their pockets. Cheers." Peter raised his glass to Dayton's and they both took another swig.

"Big weather events, like tornado and storm outbreaks, earthquakes, drought, unseasonable changes in temperature are all caused by planetary arrangements, as are sunspot activity and coronal mass ejections," Peter continued. "Let me show you." Peter arose from the couch and went over to the bookcase and withdrew a large binder stuffed with printouts and sketches. He brought them over to Dayton, and plopped them next to the makeshift solar system on top of the plywood.

"Yes, the earth tilts plus or minus twenty-three degrees as it goes around the sun. Yes, small earthquakes happen all the time, because we are moving at a thousand miles an hour and millions of miles in space per day. That is a lot of stress, my boy," said Peter. "But when the planets align, all is not fine, both with earth, and the sun. And this isn't just some horseshit. Our ancestors were quite aware of all this---and more."

Dayton could feel his head begin to spin, and his temples pulse. He took another swig and continued listening, as Peter withdrew a list from his binder.

"Here is a list of the most powerful solar storms over the past thirty years. I am going to arrange the planets as they were on those dates, and you are going to tell me what alignment caused them." He arranged the first, which was an X-class from December 6, of 2006.

"Pluto and Venus?" Dayton answered.

"Correct," replied Peter. He did a few more from various dates. Dayton began to notice a pattern.

"Most of these occur from alignments between outer planets, primarily Saturn, Pluto and Neptune, aligning with Venus and Mercury."

"Yes," replied Peter.

"But if that is the case, how come we don't get these large flares every time theses planets go around," said Dayton, pointing to the inner coins representing the inner planets.

"Because the planets go up and down in the ecliptic, just like the sun goes up and down. The effect depends on what planets---how many are involved----how tight the alignments are----which constellation they originate from, and how agitated the sun is to begin with," Peter replied lifting his hands up and down.

The bottle of Southern Comfort was now empty, so Peter opened the Jack Daniels. He poured some in his glass, and also into the half empty glass in Dayton's hand.

"Ever hear of the Carrington Event of 1859?" Peter asked. He arranged Saturn, Mars, Venus and the Sun, with Mercury and Earth opposing. "Telegraph wires were transmitting----on their own. Auroras were seen in Florida and various electrical fires broke out all over, in late August and early September of 1859. NASA recently said if a similar event happened today----and they are being very truthful about this, it would take three years to repair the electrical grids on the planet. Most people didn't give that report a second thought." Peter rolled his eyes. "People are used to seeing movies where the earth gets cooked by solar flares or hit by asteroids. They don't understand the implications." He blew out the candle on the center of the plate then re-lit it with a match. "Prior to WW2, there were never more than a billion people or two on this planet. Imagine every circuit, every satellite, every car, boat and tractor trailer not working. No power. No electricity. No computers." Peter paused to take a gulp and then he stared at Dayton right in the eye. "We have almost seven billion now. Within a year, without sanitation, transportation or modern food production, we would be back down to WW2 population levels."

Dayton considered the implications and quickly finished the liquor in his glass. He picked up the bottle and poured himself another and also topped off Peter's glass. His head was swimming at this point, but he continued to listen.

"Remember Sumatra on December 26, 2004. Earth was on the end of a lever, and a Jupiter/Saturn square." He lined up Earth, Mercury, Venus, and Mars, and with his hand, simulated a square to Neptune. "Arrangements in the solar system, Dayton."

Dayton's speech was starting to slur. "You mean it wasn't a US nuke being set off in the ocean, or done by HAARP, like some conspiracy theorists say?" Dayton fixated on Peter's lips as they began to move.

"No, it wasn't. These things are predictable. And that is the sad part."

Peter proceeded to arrange the shot glasses and coins around the plate, indicating dates and types of events. The evidence was undeniable, even for someone heavily intoxicated.

"The planets act as both magnets and magnifying glasses," Peter said. "When the earth is caught between two big outer planets, watch out for volcanism to increase. When it aligns tightly with Mercury and Uranus, or Neptune and Venus, look for those major twister outbreaks, especially if the alignment falls on, or to the west of tornado alley." Dayton looked over at the bottle of Jack. It was already half empty.

"So what is going to happen?" Dayton asked.

Peter tipped his head and caught himself from falling over. "The solar minimum we have been experiencing since January of 2008 will start to fade this month," said Peter, pointing at the calendar on the wall. "October 2009. Activity will increase slowly, and there should be some good size flares. We should be in maximum after Jupiter passes Uranus, sometime late next year, or early 2011. And like the last cycle, it will extend a few years."

In very slurred speech, Dayton asked as he laughed, "So will the world end on December 21, 2012?"

"No," replied Peter. "The Mayans knew their astronomy. So did a lot of other people on the planet. It's why Stonehenge was built. There are many observatories like Stonehenge around the world." Peter shook his head. "There is an ice core specialist, named Lonnie Thompson. He measured trapped gasses in ice cores. Well, about 5,200 years ago, according to core samples, there was a brief and very bad climate period. 5,200 years, Dayton. That is the Mayan sun period. But our 2012 might not be the Mayan 2012. And why did they call it a sun period? I am not quite sure myself."

Dayton felt his cheeks sagging. "What was the cause?"

"Best he could determine, something happened with the Sun. And if the Mayans and others are right, this stuff is cyclical. Not the end of the world, or some new age ascension bullshit. Just shifts. And I think the bastards who believe they own this world, know about it, and are using their knowledge to capitalize on it. They always have. I learned this from your dad."

"So the world won't end in 2012?" Dayton asked.

"No. But around December 21, 2012, Saturn, Mars and Mercury will align with the sun causing a large solar eruption. About a week later, the sunspots caused from the eruption will face earth. This, in combination with some other strong alignments in March and August of 2013 could cause some severe problems."

"How severe?" Dayton slurred.

"At best---there will be numerous localized communication and power outages."

"At worst?" Dayton prodded.

"All the communication satellites, power grids and anything with a computer circuit will fail on the entire planet----in 2013. If not in 2013, there are other opportunities between then and 2018."

Dayton poured out the last of the Jack Daniels into their glasses and drank it down. Dayton estimated it was well into the night, but he couldn't see straight enough to tell the time. He struggled to get up and nearly had his legs give way. He managed to get into

Peter's bathroom. He leaned himself against the wall and urinated into the bathtub. He wiped himself off with a towel and returned to the couch.

Peter had gotten up to get a beer out of the fridge, only to find his new young friend had passed out, with his head resting on the arm of the couch. He picked up his guitar and played it quietly.

Dayton awoke the next morning with his head throbbing like it was being hit by a jackhammer. He smelled eggs and bacon being cooked.

"What time is it?" Dayton asked.

"Hmmm, 'bout half past eleven," replied Peter.

Dayton sat up and nearly fell over. "Oh shit!" Dayton said. "I have to be in Boston in four hours."

"Don't worry about it. You are about twenty minutes or so from exit three of the Mass Turnpike. From there, it shouldn't take you more than two hours," Peter explained. Dayton was amazed how well Peter was doing, considering last night's alcohol consumption.

"I found that box you wanted. It was right under the bed. I stubbed my toe on it this morning."

Peter started humming as he continued preparing breakfast. "You look like crap, Dayton." Dayton was holding the sides of his head with both hands. He walked out to his Jeep to fetch his belongings.

Two men, dressed in camouflage, were hunched at the base of a thick area of trees and brush. One was communicating via earphone, while the other trained his rifle on Dayton. "We have the target in sight. Orders?" whispered the spotter.

From the other end of the communicator, a voice spoke. "Just observe the target. When he moves, follow and observe. Call with updates."

"Yes sir," the spotter replied. He then grabbed his neck and felt a small dart that had penetrated his vein. As he looked at his shooter, he noticed he was unconscious. Then he blacked out and fell to the ground.

Dayton re-entered Peter's abode and put the suitcase on the couch and pulled out the clothes. Holding his head, he stumbled as he walked into the bathroom. "Man, this shower smells like piss," he thought. "Uhhhh." His head and whole body ached. Worse yet, there was no hot water. As the cold water hit his torso, his stomach twisted.

He got dressed slowly; still feeling wobbly. Dayton went and sat at the kitchen table, while Peter brought over the eggs and bacon. "Just the bacon, Peter. And some toast if you have it."

"Coming right up Mick----I mean Dayton. Sorry."

The two ate with little conversation because of Dayton's aching head. "I had fun last night. You got to come up and visit again," said Peter, smiling.

Dayton moaned, "Next time, one bottle. And do you have any aspirin?"

"No problem." Peter laughed, then his tone became serious. "Please remember what I told you last night," Peter said, handing Dayton two pills. "Especially Carrington. Remember to look at events, especially big weather ones and study the patterns of the solar system. You'll find some interesting relationships." Peter slipped a sheet of paper in Dayton's black binder. "Alignments and squares. Just as the moon controls the tides, the sun's moons control the tides of the lake of fire."

Dayton got up from the table and collected his things. He put the small package into his camera bag then placed it in the Jeep. He trudged back into the house and thanked Peter for his hospitality, and told him that he would return someday. He gave him his email and address in Virginia. Dayton smiled thinking about how much his friend Mark would get a kick out of Peter and exhaled a short laugh, which sent shooting pain up to his temples.

"Mass Pike. Twenty minutes," he whispered as he turned the key in the ignition. He looked in the rear view mirror. "I hope Steve doesn't notice that I'm paler than he is."

He looked around the wooded lot through the windshield and listened to the motor idle. Peter certainly was an interesting man and seeing him put Dayton's thoughts back on his father. As his head pounded, he asked himself again what the hell his dad was into, but more importantly, what type of investigation was he getting himself involved in. He shook his head and put the Jeep in reverse. As his head throbbed, he knew it was going to be a long day.

Dayton was thankful Massachusetts was a small state; noticing the exits off the Pike were fairly close together. About ten minutes outside Palmer, his stomach started to turn, and he knew there was little time. Just up ahead was the Charlton Service Plaza and he knew he had to stop. He felt his stomach gurgle and he started to gag.

The Cherokee door flew open. Dayton knew he wouldn't make it inside to the restroom, so he made a bee-line run for the grassy area on the far edge of the parking lot. He covered his mouth with his hands as he ran between parked cars; barely making it to the grass.

His stomach growled like an angry lion and he could no longer hold back. He bent over, making his face perfectly perpendicular to the grass below. His stomach erupted; projecting milky-brown fluid intermixed with small pieces of undigested bread and bacon. Dayton looked at the freshly stained grass then turned when he heard the voice of a small child.

"Look dad. Barfin'," the child said, pointing over at Dayton. The father saw him, and quickly rushed his wife and child away from the scene, trying to refrain from using obscenities.

Dayton doubled over again, projecting more brown fluid into the grass. When he was done, he took a napkin out of his pocket and wiped the residue off his face, then proceeded to walk toward the service area's food court. While inside, he purchased a coke, a bottled water, and some French fries. He hoped this would settle his stomach and prevent any more embarrassing outbreaks, especially in front of the young and impressionable.

The rest of the drive to Boston was uneventful. Dayton pulled in to the parking lot of his hotel and checked in. He took a shower and changed his clothes so he wouldn't smell like a Sunday morning after praying in front of the porcelain. Dayton frowned as he looked at his camera bag; knowing there wouldn't be time to take the photos of Boston he wanted. He placed the bag, suitcase and laptop in the closet, then walked down to his Jeep. From there, he drove to the Barnes and Noble on 111 Huntington Ave.

"Peter lived in Huntington. I am going to the Huntington Ave Barnes and Noble. Synchronicity," he thought.

As he pulled into the parking lot, he noticed a pale red-head pacing nervously at the front door. Dayton looked in the mirror. His head still hurt but his skin color was starting to return. "I was beginning to worry. We're almost ready to begin," quipped Steve. He placed his hand over Dayton's shoulder and noticed his pale skin coloring. "Are you feeling all right?"

"I had to make a pit stop on the Pike. I think my breakfast didn't agree with me," Dayton fibbed. "The food here is different than in Virginia."

☙

Dayton struggled to get through his introduction. His head was beginning to ache again and his stomach was starting to turn. The fluorescent lights were hurting his eyes. He was relieved to see Steve stand up and hoped he'd shorten the session.

"Hasn't this been wonderful?" Steve said, addressing the crowd. "We have time for a few questions," he said looking back at Dayton with an irritated look on his face. "But, only a few."

"Mr. McCormick." A middle-aged man stood up, wearing blue jeans and a striped golf shirt. "I watched a segment of an interview with Aaron Russo. Are you familiar with him?" he asked.

"Yes. He produced from <u>Freedom to Fascism</u>."

"Good. Well he said in an interview with Alex Jones, that a Rockefeller told him that there would be an event in September of 2001, followed by a War on Terror, where we would attack Iraq, Afghanistan and Venezuela. And this was part of a larger goal to microchip the population. What are your thoughts on that?"

Dayton responded. "I enjoy listening or watching Alex Jones. He is quite animated." Dayton paused to take a sip of water and rub his forehead. "But the segment you were talking about was made after the September 11th attacks. I would give the interview more significance if it occurred before hand. No one that I know of has interviewed the Rockefeller in question, so Mr. Russo's statements are hearsay. Also, we haven't attacked Venezuela yet." Dayton paused and took a deep breath. "As far as chipping goes, the fear about that goes back to both a Peter Lalonde book from the 1990's and also the more recent and popular <u>Left Behind Series</u>." Dayton was starting to sweat and feel dizzy. "And the FDA's approval of the Verichip to be implanted in humans hasn't helped matters." He rubbed his forehead and then looked at the crowd. "Let's look at this realistically. I'd like to ask everyone in the crown the big question. By a show of hands," Dayton looked from left to right surveying the crowd, "How many of you would allow yourselves to be forcibly implanted with an RFID chip?"

Dayton and the questioner looked at the crowd. There wasn't a single hand in the air. "I don't think that's going to happen. Don't get me wrong, I am sure there are people who'd want to force it on people. Some may want it for their kids, especially those with young teenage daughters. But I don't think they'd get too far. Besides, what would happen to the effectiveness of all those chips if the power ever went out?" Dayton stopped for a moment and realized what he just blurted out.

"What did you mean by that, Mr. McCormick?"

"Just an passing thought. Sorry," Dayton responded.

A stern-faced blonde woman in her mid-forties stood up. "Mr. McCormick."

"Yes," Dayton replied.

She addressed the young detective and the crowd. "You say in your book to get to the root where most conspiracy theories begin. Could you elaborate on that?"

Dayton put his hand on his stomach as it began to gurgle. "That's exactly what I meant. Many conspiracy theories of today are attributed to some great plot launched many years ago by the likes of Albert Pike, Madame Blavatsky or Aleister Crowley, or someone before that, like Adam Weishempaut of the Bavarian Illuminati." He clutched his stomach a little tighter as he continued his reply. "When you really look at these groups, there really isn't anything to them. Just people, trying to find some answers to unanswerable questions. Yeats, the famous poet, used to hang out with people like this, and when he got disillusioned, he joined the Society of the Golden Dawn. People like belonging to groups." His stomach started twisting. "You'll have to excuse me for a few moments."

"Are you ok, Mr. McCormick?" the woman asked. Dayton, clutching his stomach, ran to the nearest restroom, followed closely behind by Steve after he asked the crowd for a minute. He threw open the stall door, lifted the seat of the toilet, and began throwing up.

"This is completely unacceptable, Dayton. That smells like liquor," Steve quipped from a few feet behind. Dayton put up his index finger as he heaved one last time.

"It's not liquor Steve. I think it is food poisoning," lied Dayton. "I wasn't feeling well, so I took some medication." He took a paper towel and wiped a trail of puke off his lip. "I think I took too much on an upset stomach."

Steve wasn't completely buying Dayton's lie. In a softer tone, he asked him if he would be able to do the signings. Dayton nodded his head and asked Steve if he had any breath mints or gum. Steve pulled some mints from his pocket and handed one to Dayton. "Thanks," he replied gratefully.

After the book signing was over, Dayton went back to his hotel, took a few more aspirins with water and laid down in bed. He couldn't wait until he returned home, so he could see his grandmother, Mark and Sarah. And he was really looking forward to sleeping in his own bed for a few nights before he got on a plane. As he began to fall asleep, he whispered, "I'm never drinking like that again."

He fell deep asleep and had a myriad of dreams. In the last dream he sat on the grass on the edge of a field of wildflowers. In the center of the field, he saw a woman standing. She turned to look at him and began to scream.

Dayton awoke to the sound of the hotel's courtesy call. His stomach was growling from lack of food, so he reached into his suitcase and grabbed a blue ball cap and placed it on his head. He exited the room and walked down to the hotel's commissary and restaurant, where he bought a small orange juice and a package of brown-sugar cinnamon Pop Tarts. He returned to his room, opened a napkin and placed it on the bed, next to his black binder.

He began to sketch out New York Bay, along with the numerical and astrological information he could remember from his visit with Peter the day before. In the middle of sketching, he got up and grabbed the remote off the desk and turned on the television, located on one of the room's dressers. Looking for a news channel, he stumbled across New England Cable News on channel 7. After watching the end of the weather forecast, which called for partially cloudy skies with a chance of precipitation, he opened his package of Pop Tarts and began eating. He had just about finished his sketch when the television began to report the "Breaking News."

"A sleepy Western New England hill-town awoke this morning to a tragic incident, " reported Chuck Taylor, the anchorman. "Authorities and residents in the hill town of Huntington were shocked this morning by a domestic incident which resulted in the death of four people. We're going live to State Police Spokesman Kevin Suprenaut."

The Pop Tart cracked in Dayton's hand, which resulted in both chunks and crumbs of the breakfast food overshooting the napkin below, covering the hotel sheets and his notebook with the sketch.

"Police and fire arrived early this morning to 1272 James Morrison Road, where a fire had broken out which completely consumed the small home before fire trucks could make it down the driveway. From what we can determine, it was a domestic incident, leaving three men and one woman dead. The woman has been identified as Shirley Devine, based on the license we found in an automobile registered to her. Her estranged husband, Peter Devine, was also found dead. Both suffered what appeared to be gunshot wounds. The other two men, both deceased, also suffered gunshot wounds. The fire was most likely the result of a struggle in which lit kerosene lamps and candles overturned and set the home ablaze. Fire investigators and police personnel are continuing the investigation at this time, and we will update the public if anything is found."

Stunned, Dayton shut off the TV. "My god!" he thought. "First my dad, then Hartman and now Peter." His mind began to race, wondering if someone had been following or tracking him. He got off the bed and walked over to the closet and reached for his camera bag. He brought the bag over to the bed and removed the small sealed box Peter had given him the morning before. After taking his knife and slitting the sealing tape, he carefully reached in to remove the carefully packaged contents.

"Two 35mm film canisters and a Canonet GIII QL." Dayton said, inspecting the camera. The leatherette was intact and looked overall, to be in fine condition. "Wait a second!" Dayton exclaimed. "This was my dad's camera." Dayton remembered the last time he saw it. He was on Liberty Island with his father the day before he died. He was about to open the camera by pulling up the take-up wheel when he remembered it was a mechanical camera and didn't have an automatic re-winder, and that he would expose any film if he opened it. He turned the take-up wheel and noticed there was tension. The camera had film in it. He turned the camera over and depressed the clutch button on the bottom, then rewound the film until he could feel no tension on the take-up. His fingers pulled up on the take-up wheel and the rear door popped open; revealing a canister of Kodak Film.

He placed both camera and film down on the dresser, and picked up the two film canisters. Upon opening, he stuck his finger in each, carefully removing the wound up black and white film and a small piece of paper, inter-wound inside one of the rolls.

The negatives were lifted into the light, revealing photos of ships at port, along with Asian temples and what looked to be stacked boxes. On the paper wound inside the second spool, he found the following words, written in what Dayton recognized as his Father's handwriting.

THERE WAS A TRAITOR AMONG US.

Dayton carefully wrapped up the old film and note and placed them back into the canisters. He again started thinking about the deaths of his father, Christopher Hartman, and now Peter Devine. If there was a traitor, he thought, it would have to be John Windwalker, Henry Hutchinson, or----Richard Mussen, the professor. Both Hartman and Devine were killed just after he met with them. Yet Mussen, after two visits, was still alive. His father had only left him a Bible, something which could be acquired anywhere. So maybe his father suspected him? Maybe professor Mussen was the traitor!

Dayton decided he had to stop in and see him again on his drive back to Richmond. He also knew it was time to hold his cards closer to his chest. He thought back to the previous day with Peter. "Study Carrington." Dayton shook his head. "We discussed so much. I wish I didn't get so drunk. It is going to be hard remembering everything he told me."

Dayton finished his sketch and studied it. "New York. Giza. Washington. Symbols. Arms shipments. A Traitor. Virgo and Gemini. Where were you going with all this dad?"

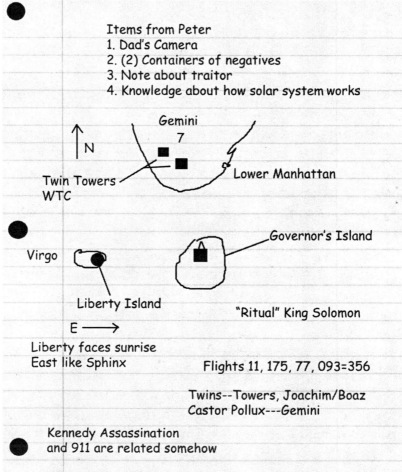

Items from Peter
1. Dad's Camera
2. (2) Containers of negatives
3. Note about traitor
4. Knowledge about how solar system works

Gemini
7
N
Twin Towers
WTC
Lower Manhattan

Governor's Island
Virgo
Liberty Island
"Ritual" King Solomon
E ⟶
Liberty faces sunrise
East like Sphinx
Flights 11, 175, 77, 093=356

Twins--Towers, Joachim/Boaz
Castor Pollux---Gemini

Kennedy Assassination
and 911 are related somehow

Chapter 12
The Outer Puzzle Pieces

"Professor Mussen," Dayton said aloud as he knocked on his front door. He could hear faint noises coming from inside the house. Within a minute Mussen emerged, wearing old pants and a shirt spotted with paint. In his left hand he was carrying a paint brush.

"Young McCormick. What a nice surprise," he said with a smile which elevated his glasses. "Please, come in."

"I'm sorry I didn't call first. My cell battery is dead----and I don't have your phone number," said Dayton.

"Wouldn't matter. I don't have a phone. All they do is disturb a man's peace and quiet," he replied. "And at my age, the only people calling are those with something to sell or those seeking my money for charity."

"I hope I am not bothering you?"

Mussen replied, "Certainly not. As you can see, I was just painting the kitchen. Paint is a wonderful tool to cover up the evils of many years of dirt and grime."

Dayton's back was turned to him. He raised one eyebrow as he looked about the living room. "That is an interesting way to put it, Professor. Well-worded."

"My dear young McCormick. A man must always choose his words wisely because his success or failure in life depends on it. Just let me put this down." He brought the brush into the kitchen. Dayton spotted his book sitting on an end table next to a lamp. He walked over to it; remembering the book he gave Hartman that disappeared. As he lifted the front cover, Mussen re-entered the living room.

"You can see I bought your book. I wanted something to read. I am about half way through it," Mussen lightly boasted.

Dayton opened his book and discovered the inside was blank. A feeling of relief came over him. "Would you like me to sign it?"

"Of course. I would be honored. Not only do I have a book written by the son of an old friend, but the very budding author is signing his book in my living room." Mussen reached into a drawer for a pen and handed it to Dayton, who promptly signed his John Hancock two inches below the upper right on the inside page.

"What would you like me to write in it besides my name?" Dayton asked.

Mussen responded, "How about questio verum in totus res?"

"What does that mean?"

"It means seeking truth in all things. That is the English translation from Latin," Mussen explained.

"Sounds good. Could you help me spell it?"

"Certainly," Mussen replied. He then told Dayton how to spell the Latin phrase. Mussen looked up at the young man. "Did you find Peter?"

Dayton shook his head. "No. I went to the address I had for him in Lee, Massachusetts. The only person I found was his irate ex-wife, who didn't know where he was."

Mussen's tone changed. He looked down at the floor and avoided eye contact with Dayton. "I am sorry to hear about that. Maybe you'll find him----another time." Mussen turned and looked out the window. "Sometimes people are not what they seem, young McCormick. Peter was an alcoholic, but was also a brilliant man." He turned and faced him. "And it never ceases to amaze me how things turn out in the end. And sometimes they are unfortunate."

"That's true," replied Dayton, who wondered where he was going with his statement.

Mussen raised an eyebrow. "It is almost as if there is a grand design to things-----Wasn't it Shakespeare that said all the world is a stage---and we are only players?"

Dayton stared at Mussen as he replied. "Sort of like there is a grand plan, we just don't recognize what it is?" Mussen shook his head in agreement and limped into the kitchen. He filled two glasses of water and returned to the living room; handing one of the glasses to the young detective. Dayton was suspicious, so he stealthily checked it to see if there was anything put into it when Mussen wasn't looking.

"Everything is tied together somehow." He pointed at Dayton's book on the table. "People look at a few facts and begin drawing their own conclusions. And they have been doing it since day one. Their assumptions are mostly due to a lack of knowledge."

"What do you mean?" questioned Dayton.

Mussen smirked. "We make the same mistakes over and over again. I believe it was Einstein who once said that doing the same thing repeatedly and expecting a different result was the definition of insanity." He began to laugh. "And yet, history repeats itself constantly. Do you remember when I wrote the word snowflake next to the Star of David during one of our last discussions?"

"Yes."

"Nature's design. It takes the right conditions----and then they form. Slightly different of course----but always with six sides. Civilizations aren't any different." He took a sip of his water. "They form and process in a similar fashion. When conditions are right, the influences cause the same or similar effects."

"Like the full moon bringing out all the crazies," Dayton responded.

"Yes, like that." Mussen tipped his head to the younger man. "Do you ever just know when you are going to have a bad day----on the job?"

"Yes."

"There are signs all around us, young McCormick. Sometimes we see them consciously. Other times with our subconscious. Their significance can only be determined under long and careful reflection and association."

Dayton was beginning to become ancy. He knew the professor was holding back something and he wished the windbag would just spit it out. As he studied the older man, something inside told him to be careful.

Mussen changed the topic of conversation. "Well. If you do get to meet Peter, please share with me what your father sent him." Dayton nodded. "And anything from John Windwalker too."

Dayton realized Mussen was looking for something. He looked at his watch. "I have to go, but I would like to come back and talk with you some more. I have to go out west for the second leg of the signing tour. But when I get back, I'd like to come see you again if you don't mind."

"Not at all, young McCormick. Have a safe ride back home and I'll see you when you return." The two shook hands and Mussen walked Dayton to the door.

Dayton began to think to himself, "Is Mussen the traitor? Can I trust him? What does he know that he is not telling? And why does he always get so philosophical?" He inserted the key into the ignition. It was time to return to Richmond.

Dayton caught something in his peripheral vision. He looked over to the passenger window and saw Mussen standing there. Dayton pressed the window button and lowered it. Mussen poked his head in.

"A man chooses his words carefully, especially when others may hear them." His eyes shifted to the left, which Dayton took as a cue to look behind his vehicle. A few houses away, sat a white van parked on the side of the street and Dayton noticed through his rear-view mirror, the driver wearing sunglasses. "Good day, young McCormick," he said as he pulled his head slowly out of the window. "Come again."

Dayton pulled on to the highway, heading south for Richmond. As the cars and trucks passed him, he asked himself whether the van was really watching them, as Mussen had indicated. If it was, was it Mussen being observed or himself? He couldn't be sure. But he was sure of one thing. He was determined to find his father's killer.

ℙ

The smell of fresh-baked chocolate chip cookies permeated the air in the McCormick house. Dayton, with his suitcase, camera bag and laptop walked into the kitchen to greet his grandmother, who was removing another batch from the oven. "Dayton, you're home," she said as her eyes widened with delight. She wrapped her arms around him and gave him a kiss on the cheek. "How were your book signings?"

"They went well," he replied. He walked up stairs and put his suitcase and camera bag in the study. "Grandma, I have to go check my Jeep."

She raised an eyebrow. "Is something wrong with it?"

"I don't think so," Dayton replied, "But after a long trip I want to make sure everything is ok." He gave her another hug, then walked out to the shed to get the wheeled dolly his grandfather used to work underneath cars in the driveway. Before going under, he carefully inspected the interior for anything being out of place. He pressed his hands throughout the upholstered interior and looked under both the seats and the dash. "Nothing," he muttered.

He laid down on top of the dolly and using his feet, rolled under the vehicle with a flashlight in his hand. The light moved methodically back and forth, covering every square inch of the bottom of the vehicle. "Nothing." He moved underneath to both the front and rear bumpers and used his hands to investigate the areas he couldn't see. "Nothing," he repeated.

He stood up and reached inside the interior to pop the hood. With a keen investigators eye, he inspected the engine compartment and found nothing. He unlatched the air filter housing and inspected it as well. Dayton remembered something he read about satellites being able to track automobiles through uplink devices then shook his head. "What would the government want to do with me?" After returning the dolly to the shed, he went back in the house, washed his hands and sat with Martha at the kitchen table.

"Sorry about that, Grandma. How has everything been here?" he said as he stared at the plate of fresh cookies in the center of the table.

"Oh, just fine---besides missing you. Mark has been over a few times to check on me and I had a delightful time most of last week with Sarah." She smiled. "She is almost like the daughter I never had. We went to lunch. We had girl talk. We ran errands. She even went with me on one of my walks." Dayton looked at his grandmother and knew she'd never get over George's death. But he was happy she was trying. Martha looked at Dayton with a funny expression. "I do have a question. What is all that stuff on the table in the study? Sarah spent considerable time looking over it for a few nights."

"Nothing much," he lied. "Just some of Dad's stuff." Trying to change the subject, Dayton began rubbing his eyes. "Gram----the past few weeks----doing the book signings----My mind really isn't on them a hundred percent."

"Why?"

Dayton was hoping she wouldn't ask that. But he knew he couldn't keep anything from her. Some of his best investigative techniques he learned from carefully observing his grandmother and she wasn't going to let him leave the table without answering truthfully. She never did, even when he was a teenager.

"I was afraid you'd ask that." They sat down at the table and Dayton explained some of what had transpired. He watched as his Grandmother's face went from happy, to concerned.

"I never really had closure when you're father died. George sent you downstairs and then told me to bring you back to the house that night. I never got to see him. Not the way George did. I think the only thing that saved him----was you," she explained. "I hope that wherever this investigation leads you, that the angels in heaven look out for your safety."

Dayton nodded his head and placed his hand on his Grandmother's shoulder. "I am not sure why my father---your son, was killed. I haven't discovered what he knew that was worth killing for." Dayton struggled trying to rationalize it. "Every day, I see things on the streets that make me sick. Someone knifing someone over a dollar or breaking into a house to steal someone's stuff to be able to pay for a quick drug fix. But those I can rationalize because I see them all the time. But there is something my dad knew. Something big. And I think, in time, I'll figure it out. But this is unlike any investigation I have ever worked on."

The old woman pushed her lips together then looked deeply into her grandson's eyes. "I'm sure you will." Then she frowned. "But don't lose yourself. Don't let it consume you." She got up and grabbed the phone and handed it to Dayton. "I believe you promised someone you'd see her tonight."

Dayton's shoulders slumped and he exhaled deeply; remembering he had promised Sarah he'd take her out.

"When I met your grandfather George, I knew I had something special. She is a nice girl Dayton and you'd be foolish to let all this eat at you and let a true prize pass you by."

He picked up the phone and punched in her number. "Hi Sarah. Sorry about today."

"That's ok. I got called in to work. There was another hit and run," she replied.

"Are you free tomorrow?" Dayton asked.

"I can make myself free at lunch."

"Perfect. I'll see you then."

༄

Dayton awoke the next morning at sunrise. He picked up the film roll from his father's camera and the two containers of negatives. He removed the "traitor" note from one of the canisters, made a copy, put in the safe and then placed the note on the table in the study. Martha was already downstairs sitting at the kitchen table sipping her orange juice and catching steam from the hot bowl of oatmeal set before her.

"Where are you going so early?" she asked.

"I have a few things to do down at the station before lunch. I want to get them done before lunch because Sarah is coming over."

"Well, I'll plan my walk for noon then."

"You don't have to do that Grandma. You could join us," Dayton responded as he watched the steam rise from her morning oats.

Martha smiled. "Maybe you two need some time alone. Besides, it is a little cool out this morning and it should be a much better temperature for walking a little later."

Dayton arrived at the police station around 7:30 AM. He was hoping to go in unnoticed. He placed his badge on his hip and walked down to the forensics department. He didn't own a film scanner, so he figured the next best thing, considering the potential sensitivity of the materials, was to use the department's equipment. As he began scanning, a familiar face peaked through the door, followed by the rest of his large exterior.

"McCormick. What are you doing here? Don't you still have a month or so of play time left?" he said in a sarcastic tone.

"Hello Chief. Good morning," Dayton replied, barely looking up.

Chief Paul Stankeiwicz stood to the side of the computer desk where Dayton was working. He was a large man at about six foot three, and about as wide as he was tall. He had straight grey hair, parted to the side, and was sporting a large pair of bifocals.

"You still didn't answer my question."

"I missed this place," Dayton said, finally making full eye contact. "After my grandfather died, I came across some old film and figured I'd come down here and scan it----for the family archives."

"Hmmm," the Chief replied. "Just checking. I thought you might be putting personal time into something else----like the 10-56 a few weeks ago."

"That's not my case. And from what I hear, it isn't Detective Tilenda's either," referring to his friend Mark.

Stankeiwicz smirked. "You know, I have been in law enforcement for a long time. Entered right after my tour in Vietnam. I have heard stories about jurisdictional difficulties, but until it happened to me----never gave it much thought. I had to sign papers, not to discuss the matter---under penalty of arrest." He looked down and gave Dayton a stern look. "I am going to retire in a few years. I would much prefer being on a boat enjoying my retirement with my wife instead of wearing a numbered outfit and getting an hour of recreation time each day in a federal prison."

"I assure you Chief, I am not working on any 10-56's. Just personal business."

"I know you, Dayton. You're the best investigator in the department. Bar none. And part of that is because you can't let things go." His smirk disappeared and his face dropped. His eyes began to pierce Dayton. "But if you can't let this one go, don't go through normal channels," the Chief said, sliding his finger across his neck, "Or I'll see to it you go back to being a beat cop for the rest of your career."

Dayton rolled his eyes, then put a confused look on his face. "What case are you referring to again?"

Stankeiwicz closed his eyes and moved his head up and down. "Very good. Enjoy the rest of your book tour----but hurry up about it. I need you back here."

Dayton smiled as the Chief walked out the door. He had never called him the best investigator in the department before. And Stankeiwicz seemed friendly, which was out of character for him.

Dayton scanned all the negatives. He burned two CD's of the pictures and then erased the scans from the hard drives on the department's computers. He placed one of the CD's back in to the computer and began viewing them with the trained eyes of an investigator. His father's photos were very clear and sharp. He observed multiple pictures of two shipping boats, and on a hunch, wrote down the numbers on the ship's port side. He then viewed photos of temples, temple interiors and stacked boxes. He zoomed up on the boxes and the writing on them.

7.62x39mm TULA U.S.S.R

Other boxes had writing in Russian or Chinese for what Dayton recognized were armaments. There were a few photos with open crates; displaying the contents inside, which verified the exterior writing. He quickly viewed more of the photos on the computer screen until he came across a negative with a group of shipping crates. This particular one had a packing slip on it. He zoomed on to the slip, which read: Baxter-Cudman Shipping, USA.

"I wonder?" Dayton whispered, as he put his hand on his chin.

The last photo was of his father and the five team members. It was the same as the one given to him by Hartman. Dayton ejected the CD and placed it in a case. He looked at his watch. It was 10:30AM. He had just enough time, he estimated, to run one more errand, pick up take-out, and join Sarah for lunch back at his Grandmother's house.

He stopped at the Picture Perfect photo center and went inside. He explained to the girl at the counter that the negatives he wanted processes were very old. She replied that as long as they were stored properly, that she should be able to get viewable images. Dayton asked her not to make prints, but only to make a high resolution archival CD.

"We can do that. But the scanner is down right now and we don't have a repair tech coming until tomorrow. I should have them by Friday, if that is ok?" she said.

Dayton was leaving Wednesday on the second part of his book signing tour. He was disappointed because he wanted to view the what could be the last photos of him and his father. His disappointment was hard to contain. "I won't be around for a week or so. Just do a good job," he replied quietly.

He exited the photo center and called for Chinese take-out on his cell. If he timed his jaunt right, he would be home with hot food minutes before Sarah arrived. He looked at the CD's sitting on his passenger seat. "I think the pieces are starting to come together."

His timing was perfect. The table was set with the good dishes. Two candles burned in the center. The napkins were folded properly. He was just dishing up when she walked through the door.

"This looks nice," she said. Sarah walked over to the table and Dayton pulled back her chair like a proper gentleman. She looked over to the counter and noticed the empty take-out containers from Wong's.

"Where's Martha?"

"She decided to take her walk a little later today," Dayton replied, "so that you and I could have a private lunch."

Sarah smiled. "She didn't have to do that. I like your grandmother very much." She paused. "I spent some time here last week. Well, a lot of time. I hope you don't mind?"

"Actually," Dayton replied, "I was pretty pleased about that. Being away on my book signings, I was worried about her. She told me last night that, with you here, it was almost like having the daughter she never had." Dayton scrunched up his face. "Kind of made me feel jealous, but in a good way."

Sarah was relieved. She was worried that he'd be upset. Mark had come over to mow the lawn and check on her. But unless he was doing something big, he never stayed long. Sarah, had stayed overnight.

As the two began to eat, Dayton opened up. "I was actually nervous that when you found out I moved back in with her, our long term relationship might end," he said jokingly. "Most women, when they hear you live with your grandparents, politely decline another date."

"Well, I'm not like most women."

Dayton smiled after her response. "When I was a kid, George and Martha were my whole world. When I went off to college, I didn't see them but once or twice a month." He paused to take a spoonful of fried rice. "When I graduated the academy and landed the job in the police department, I was hesitant about staying here because I was fearful some perpetrator would come after them. I was also ashamed, because every time I had a date, the topic of where I lived would eventually come up. Living with your grandparents ends relationships pretty quickly." He picked up a chicken finger and dipped it into the duck sauce, then took a bite. "But what I realized was that those women really weren't worth my time. I would give everything just to have a little more time with my grandfather."

Sarah took her turn with a chicken finger in the duck sauce. She twirled it around twice, took a bite, then repeated the action until it was consumed. "Most men aren't any different you know."

"I know. Believe it or not, Mark is a really nice guy. He just picks the wrong women. I was the best man at his second wedding. I told his wife during the toast to run for the hills. Only problem was, I wasn't kidding." Dayton took another bite. "He didn't call me until he was divorced six months later." Dayton looked down, then burst into laughter. "He really needs a loud, self-assured, nerdy chick who works in a bio lab."

"I told you Leslie and Mark make a good match. Do you know what it is like working a case and having him blab about her all the time?"

"Uh, actually I do. It is nice to see he hasn't changed. And I already promised him we'd double again."

Sarah looked Dayton right in the eyes. "So I guess that means our long-term relationship is continuing?"

Dayton arose from his chair and walked over to Sarah. His hands started to move toward her chest. She closed her eyes; expecting him to caress her breasts. "Piece of chicken finger," he said as he picked a medium-sized piece of breading off Sarah's shirt.

Sarah exhaled and burst out laughing uncontrollably.

"What's so funny?" Dayton asked.

"She looked straight at him and in a sarcastic voice said, "You know, you're known as the best detective on the police force. Didn't you see that I thought you were going to grab my breasts."

Dayton was taken aback. "I thought you closed your eyes because you were embarrassed that I found breading on your blouse."

Sarah took matters into her own hands. She stood up, grabbed him by the lapels and pressed her face against his.

"O, wat's wat u er tinkin," Dayton said in a mumbling voice as their tongues twisted in passion. When the kiss ended, Dayton wrapped his arms around her.

"You are a strange man, Dayton McCormick," Sarah said. "I have to go. My shift starts in an hour."

"You think I'm strange?" Dayton inquired. "Ask Mark if you two can come over tomorrow morning a few hours before shift and I'll show you strange."

"Does it have to do with your father's investigation?" Sarah asked. "I wrote the passages down that corresponded to the codes you know," Sarah said. "Have you figured out the other two?"

Dayton nodded his head. "Yes. I saw them upstairs. Thanks. The other two," Dayton replied, "were the numbers of two ships. I'd like to get your opinions on the other information I have found. Three heads are better than one."

"I'd be happy to come," Sarah replied. "So what am I going to get helping you with this personal investigation of yours?"

Dayton pressed his lips against hers, then squeezed her lower lip between his lips and slowly pulled back.

"Hmm? I think my services are worth a little more than that."

Dayton went in for another, but Sarah put her finger out to stop him.

"I really have to go or I am going to be late," she said. "What time is your flight Wednesday?"

"I have a red-eye. My plane leaves at 1:30AM for Chicago," he replied.

"My shift ends at eleven. I could swing by here and bring you to the airport?" she said raising her eyebrows while waiting for him to say yes.

"You just want another kiss."

Sarah turned around and headed for the door. She swung her head around and smiled at Dayton. "I'll see you tomorrow morning with Mark."

As Sarah was walking out the door, Martha was returning from her walk. She gave Martha a hug and told her she'd see her in the morning.

"Dayton," Martha said as she sat down at the table. "How did your lunch go?"

Dayton sat at the table with a happy look on his face while staring off toward the window. "Grandma," he said, "What was it about Grandpa that drew you too him?"

Martha was pleased lunch went well. "I met George in High School. He was a fine looking young man. And he had a brain. I first noticed him junior year. I was walking by a classroom, when I heard his voice." She smiled. "I stopped in the doorway and watched him while he debated. He noticed me. Social Security was the topic, if I recall. I heard later, he lost the debate, but the next day he asked me if I wanted to go out."

"Did you feel anything? Butterflies? Headache?"

"Dayton, I knew that day, that I was going to marry George someday. I loved the way he smelled. Don't tell anyone, but I haven't thrown out his pillow. Every night I put my head on it and I can still smell him." Martha's eyes swelled up and a solitary tear rolled down her cheek.

"I wasn't trying to make you cry, Grandma. I'm sorry. I know you miss him."

She picked up her head and smiled at Dayton. "We had fifty-nine good years. Who could ask for more?" She sniffled, then cleared her throat. "So, what did you feel the first day you met Sarah?"

"Same. She smelled nice."

"Well----she's welcome here anytime." Martha stood up. "I am going to go upstairs and lie down for a while with his pillow."

Dayton watched as his grandmother climbed the stairs. He went up a few minutes afterward, only to find her asleep, with a damp pillow under her head. He felt guilty about having her think of grandpa. This was the first time she broke down since the funeral. He understood she had to get it out.

Dayton walked down the hall and sat down on the chair in the study and starred at all the items on the table. The Bible and book. The codes and the black binder. The photograph and the aerial pictures. He recalled the images he scanned at the station of the boxes, temples and boats. He took his index finger and put it on the aerial of Giza. "Three pyramids without capstones," he whispered. "Three lengths of 1776," he thought as he touched Washington. "Capitoline Hill, three deities, one being Jupiter. Three cornerstone references, from the Bible, in the codes." Remembering what both Mussen and Peter said about symbolism, Leslie's quip about square circles and looking at Giza he said, "Three stars or----planets."

He looked again at the Bible passages and re-read Ecclesiastes 24:24. "A woman." His eyes darted to New York Bay. "A Woman with a torch. Spica. Virgo and Leo." He sat in deep thought. "A trinity involving three planets in Virgo. But which planets? And where in Virgo?" he pondered. "Why a crown? The crown is at the head," he whispered. "The sphinx is the head of a woman with a lion's bottom." The he looked at Washington again. "Three capstones each with a base of 1776. The Washington Monument is an Eye. The Grant Memorial is an Eye. The fountain on the West side of the Capitol is an Eye." He looked at three capstones laid out in D.C., from small to large. He again glanced at Giza which also had three pyramids from small to large. Then he remembered that Washington was formed from Virginia and Maryland. "The womb, of the Virgin Mary."

"Was my father trying to find out when the second coming was going to occur? When Christ was going to return?" He sat in the chair; thinking for over an hour. Then, he caught himself. "I don't believe I'm thinking this." Dayton shook his head. "I now understand why people buy into conspiracy theories. My father wasn't looking for Christ's return. How could he? He would have known better, being a student of history. The pyramids were built long before Jesus was born." He put his hand to his chin. "And why would Freemasons, who hated Catholics, especially at the time Washington's construction began, build a city into a shrine depicting Jesus' return? Was it to mock the Church of Rome, especially considering many believed Washington D.C. was the "New Rome?" But why so many references to the old Rome, like Capitoline Hill, or the Tiber creek, or the architectural styling of the buildings?"

Dayton felt a warm hand touch his shoulder. "Dayton," said Martha. It is almost 7PM. I think it is time to eat and stop thinking so much."

"You're right," he replied; shaking his head in agreement. "You're right."

"The soup I started an hour ago is almost ready. Let's go eat," she said.

After eating, Dayton spent the evening researching anything he could based on his findings. He felt he needed to be better prepared for when Mark and Sarah came over in the morning. "These are all tied together. Symbolically. And if I am looking at this correctly, the Statue of Liberty is the modern-day Sphinx. Interesting."

ɢ

Mark and Sarah arrived at the McCormick house and followed Dayton upstairs to the study. They began talking, with the evidence laid before them on the desk.

"Maybe your father was trying to find the Second Coming?" Mark asked.

Dayton replied, "I don't think so. But I'm not sure."

"Well, how about the coming of another Jesus?" Mark said.

"I'm not sure Jesus was his intent, or the intent of those who built these structures," said Dayton, pointing his fingers at the three aerials. "Giza is older."

Sarah popped in, "You said it yourself. D.C. was carved from the womb of the Virgin Mary. And when you look at the Sphinx, it is a woman and lion. Wasn't Jesus born of Mary, the virgin? And did he not come from the root and stock of David." Sarah paused. "The root and stock of David is Juda. Juda is the Lion," she added, "His father Jacob called him that."

"But Giza was built before Jesus," Dayton insisted. "And the men who designed D.C. were Freemasons who hated the Roman Church. And Washington was a deist. He believed in a supreme being. A Grand Architect of the universe." He smiled at Sarah, then turned his head to look at Mark. "I think what we are looking at here is older."

"I always thought the Sphinx had a man's face," Mark said. "Didn't they find a beard? Unless he was a bearded lady----"

Dayton interrupted, "But if it had a beard and fell off the chin, how come there is no damage to the chin?"

"Good point," Mark replied. "But then why is David's star in the streets above the Capitol?" as he pointed to the aerial photo of Washington.

Dayton looked at it. "This symbol, according to Mussen, is also symbolic of the conjunctions of Saturn, Jupiter and the sun. If you draw lines between the conjunctions, you get a star." Dayton took a moment to illustrate what he told them. "From what I got from Mussen and Peter Devine is that all symbols have their origins in astronomy." Dayton hit his head with his palm. "Peter had a whole bookcase of astronomy books." He looked at Mark. "And you would have liked him. I have never seen a man drink so much and still be able to function. I think he kept drinking beers long after I passed out."

"I'd like him huh? After your signings, can I go see him with you?" Mark asked.

"Unfortunately no. He's dead."

"Oh my God!" Sarah exclaimed.

Dayton looked at Mark. "Remember Hartman?"

"Not a suicide again?"

"Yes, but this time it involved his wife and two unknown people. I woke up to the news on N.E.C.N. the morning after my signing."

"Why didn't you go back and tell the cops what you thought was going on?" said Mark.

Sarah spoke before Dayton could answer. "Because he would be arrested. He'd be a suspect."

"Precisely," Dayton agreed. "But I am going to find out who did it. Chances are good, the same people that killed Hartman and Peter, killed my father."

Mark was concerned. "Do you think they followed you?"

Dayton looked out the bedroom window again to see if there were any unusual cars in the neighborhood. "I am not sure. I thought somebody may have bugged my Jeep, but I went over it yesterday with a fine tooth comb. Nobody knew where I was going. The address I had for Peter was wrong. His ex-wife, who hired and investigator to find him, gave me his address." Dayton showed Mark and Sarah the paper.

"Bastard huh?" said Mark.

"More like an eccentric hippie who drank like a fish. But he was smart as hell. He showed me theories about how the solar system worked. And he proved them repeatedly, as I recall. Some of it is pretty sketchy in my head because I was pretty drunk."

"So what did he tell you?" asked Sarah.

"Well, he told me the world would still be here on December 21, 2012. He said we were going to have a long and powerful solar maximum and the bulk of the potential damaging solar activity would commence when the outer five planets formed a pentagon around the sun in late 2012 through 2013."

Mark interrupted, "Like this one?"

"Yes." Dayton's heart felt like it had stopped. He grabbed a pencil and wrote in "2012,2013" and drew a line with an arrow toward the Pentagon. "When the outer five form the Pentagon, the sun was going to become really active. Then he talked about----"

"What?" said Sarah, who was thoroughly captivated by the discussion.

"He talked about an ice core specialist. Thompson----I think was his name, who said that 5200 years ago the earth went through a difficult climatic period based on his analysis of the gasses present in the ice cores from the period. Short and hard----Peter told me."

"But doesn't that coincide with the Mayan Calendar and their Sun Period?" asked Sarah. "He mentioned 2012."

Dayton looked over at Sarah. He thought to himself, "Peter's friend Ralph was right." He shook his head. "Yes."

Sarah continued for Mark's benefit. "The Mayan's had a time period they called a sun period. It was around 5,200 years. The divided it up in thirteen pieces called "Baktuns" of 396 years each."

"Yes," Dayton interrupted. "And 20 cycles of earth, Jupiter and Saturn conjuncts are 396 years, which is slightly less than fifty earth, Venus and the sun conjunction cycles of eight years each." Dayton described to his friends Peter's theories about alignments as he recalled them and how man's ancestors kept track of the heavenly bodies with the works they built.

Mark opened up. "So you're telling me that ancient peoples, like those who built Stonehenge and the Pyramids, knew that the positions of the planets and their interactions affect the sun and the climate on the earth?"

Dayton nodded his head. "That would be about right. As soon as I can remember the rest, I'll look into it a little more," Dayton responded.

Mark opined, "Well that makes sense."

Sarah piped in, "And five of those Mayan Sun Periods equals 25,920 years, or one complete solar procession through the Houses of the Zodiac."

"Correct." Dayton closed his eyes. "But there is something else my father was researching. The last two codes on the sheet I got from Hartman are not Bible passages. They are the numbers on two ships. This is what else I got from my visit with Peter," Dayton said as he held up the Canonet. "This was my father's camera. I dropped off the film to get processed and scanned. I think it was from the day before my father was killed when we were at Liberty Island." Then he held up two film containers. "And these are negatives that I scanned at the department yesterday morning. They contain photos of the ships, as well as temples and what I think are the insides of temples, filled with ammunition and other military hardware of mostly Russian origin." Dayton displayed the photos on his laptop. "I think my father, besides all this symbolic stuff," Dayton said while putting his hands on his laptop, "found traitors within the government and business during the Vietnam War. I just don't have any paperwork tying the photos and the shipments together. But there was one curious thing," he said, stopping at one photo and zooming in on a packing slip, "Baxter-Cudman shipping was involved."

"You mean Senator Philip Cudman?" Sarah asked.

"I am not sure he personally was involved, but I think this shipping slip was something somebody forgot to remove." Dayton paused and grabbed one of the film containers and opened it; removing a small slip of paper. "And my father figured out there was a traitor on his team," he said while holding the paper so both Mark and Sarah could read it. Then he picked up the photo of the soldiers with his father. "Hartman and Peter are dead. Both occurred right after I met them. Mussen is still alive and I have seen him three times. My father only gave him a Bible. So he is a prime suspect. Hutchinson I have yet to meet. So he is also a prime suspect. Then there is John Windwalker. Even though my dad, Peter and him were friends, I think he could also be a suspect."

A small voice came from the doorway of the study. "Dayton. Dayton. It wouldn't be John," said Martha from the doorway. She looked at Sarah in a manner in which she knew it was time to take Mark and leave.

"Mark," Sarah said looking at her watch, "We have to go on shift."

Martha looked at Sarah and thanked her with her eyes. They left Dayton alone with her in the study. She pulled a spare chair in the study and placed it up next to him. "Sit down Dayton. There are a few things I have been meaning to tell you for many years. Please don't be mad at me," she said, as she put her hands over his.

"I'd never be mad at you Grandma," Dayton replied.

She looked down and pushed her lips together. "When your father was a little boy, he had a friend that lived just a few houses down. His name was Jeremy Higgins. He was more than a friend. He was your father's best friend. They went everywhere and did everything together. They even dated a set of twins in high school."

She smiled and took a breath. "When they graduated, they both went into the military. Mickey went into the Army, like your grandfather. Jeremy, enlisted in the Marines. But they called each other. They sent letters. When your father went to intelligence school, Jeremy went to Vietnam. Then your father went over there." Her hand squeezed Dayton's tight.

"It's ok Grandma. Continue."

"Your father said he found things over there. Things that made him angry. He said there were traitors among us. John and the others came home because of their wounds. Mickey stayed because he had a job to finish. One day, he came across a list of dead soldiers returning home. His friend Jeremy was on that list. Killed-in-action. So your father, like you, tried to finish his investigation. He was so close. He told me he gave his commander what he had and a few days later, the Army discharged him and sent him home. You can imagine how he felt."

Dayton looked at Martha and she looked at him with the saddest eyes he had ever seen.

"Mickey was a very angry young man when he came back. He fought all the time with your grandfather, who wanted him to go to college and get an education. One day, in the middle of the night, he left." A tear started to roll down Martha's face. "And that was the last we heard or saw of him for a few years. He went out to Arizona, to live with John and Peter. John got a hold of our phone number and would call us to let us know he was ok. If Mickey had known, he would have been furious. This hurt your grandfather and I very much. Our only son had left us."

Dayton stared at his grandmother in shock. He never knew this about his dad. Martha continued. "He met a girl out there. She was your mother."

"Did you ever meet her?"

"No. Her name was Jan." Dayton nodded his head. His father had told him his mother's name. "When you were just in diapers, she died in a car accident. They say she was drunk. Your father had you. He also had no money. And John was angry at him. You see, Jan was John's cousin. Her last name was Windwalker. John blamed your father for her death----I never knew why. But he gave your father the money to come home. And one day in 1977, you both appeared on our doorstep. The rest----you know."

"Were my mother and father ever married?" Dayton asked.

"No." She touched his face softly. "One day a few years later John showed up at our door. He and Mickey settled their differences and began to talk again."

"Did my father have any contact with anyone else?"

"Yes. For a few years, when you were small, and after he had just finished college, he would make trips up to Baltimore. That was all. He never told us much. He never got any phone calls."

Dayton believed his father had to be visiting Richard Mussen.

"I am so sorry I never told you this before. George and I were so afraid you'd leave to go find out where your mother came from and not come back. You're all we had Dayton. And I am sorry I kept this from you."

Dayton gave his grandmother a big hug. "Grandma, it's ok. I am not mad at all. And you still have me. You always will."

She wiped a tear that was falling down her cheek and stood up. "I know you have to pack, but could we go for a walk first? I won't see you for a week or so."

Dayton nodded and put on his shoes.

Dayton had moved his luggage to the first floor to get ready for Sarah's arrival. He looked at the bags on the floor, then the tender old woman sitting on the couch. He thought, "I'm coming back Gram, don't worry."

She pulled up into the driveway, then came to the door. "Come in Sarah," Dayton said. She looked at the luggage and then walked over to Martha and gave her a hug.

"Don't worry. He will have a safe ride to the airport and I'll come for lunch tomorrow." Hearing this pleased Dayton. He walked over to Martha and also told her not to worry. He had his cell and charger and would call every day. He picked up his luggage and made one trip to Sarah's car. As the two sat in the front seats, Sarah said softly, "I'll look after her while you're gone." Dayton leaned forward and pressed his lips against hers.

"Thanks," he replied. "And I'll call you every day too."

The darkness and the contrasting headlights, along with a lack of sleep, put Dayton in an almost trance-like state. Sarah looked over at him. "Are you ok?"

Dayton shook his head. "I'll be fine. The past month or so has taken a toll on me. My Grandma told me this afternoon all about my father's life and what happened to my mother." He smiled. "Thanks for driving me to the airport. I haven't slept well lately."

"It's not a problem. You're growing on me." She put her hand on his leg. "And this is the last time I will be able to see you for over a week," she replied.

Dayton changed the subject. "How is it going in detective land?"

"It's ok. The usual. Some drug dealer shoots another. Some druggie robs a house to fence the stuff and buy a fix. Protect and serve." She laughed. "It is nowhere near as interesting as the stuff your father was researching. It's pretty cool."

Dayton gave her a half smirk. "Yeah, but I think that is what got him killed."

"Sorry. I didn't mean it like that."

"I know." Dayton wiggled in his seat. "I wasn't trying to upset you by saying that. It just seems like the only explanation that fits."

"So where do you think he was going with all his research? If it isn't about Christ's return?" Sarah asked.

"From the codes, dad was telling me to look at the sky for a sign. It would be at the head of Virgo. Three objects, or planets will be involved, and I figure they'll form a triangle in the sky. From the symbolism in the cities, one must be Jupiter." He took a breath. "I haven't figured out what the eye is yet on the dollar. But something troubles me?" Dayton said.

"What?"

"When I was with Peter, he told me September 11th was a ceremony and not a terror attack. He said those poor bastards got in the middle of someone's ritual. Then he described the World Trade Center as a modern depiction of the Temple of Solomon. The temple destroyed by the Babylonians first, and then the Romans."

"Interesting," Sarah replied. "Sick, but interesting."

"I told you and Mark that he also talked about how planetary lineups cause our weather and how certain ones cause natural disasters. I am wondering if the information my dad was studying involved a sign in the sky and a coming disaster of some sort. Whether before, during or after, I can only guess."

"Would you mind if I looked at the stuff while you were gone?" Sarah asked.

"Knock yourself out." Dayton smiled. "Copies of it are in the safe. Grandma has the combination and the override key."

Sarah pulled into the drop off zone at the airport and parked by the curb. "And when you get back, why don't you come over and I'll make you dinner?" She stared deep into his brown eyes.

"You make me dinner and I'll cook you breakfast." He put his hand on her chin and was about to kiss her, when out of his peripheral vision, he noticed a man approaching, topped with red hair.

"Oh shit! It's Steve, the publisher's promoter." He gave her a quick kiss and unbuckled his seatbelt. "He is a pain in the ass, but he is good at what he does." Dayton arose from his seat and opened the door. He swung to the back of the car and removed his luggage from it.

"Dayton, I thought that was you. Uh, I'll meet you inside at the baggage check in." He clearly looked uncomfortable.

"Okay," Dayton acknowledged as Steve went into the airport. He got back into the car and told Sarah, "I got to go. But I almost forgot something." He placed his hand below her chin and gave her a passionate kiss. He opened his eyes and noticed hers were staring back. There was a bond forming here. He was hoping it would be one like his grandparent's had. He forced himself to pull away from her. "Steve's waiting. I'll see you when I get back."

"Well, let me know when your plane is coming in. Otherwise, it is a long walk home," Sarah said sarcastically.

Dayton's mind was so busy thinking about her and everything that had transpired that he forgot his Jeep was at home. He smiled. "Right."

Dayton sat down, taking the window seat, while his red-headed companion took the aisle. Dayton looked over at Steve. He spotted a large white head on the right side of Steve's neck near his jawbone. He fixated on it, almost like he was a tourist in Tokyo with a camera. Steve noticed Dayton staring at him out of the corner of his eye and turned to face him. "What is it Dayton?"

Dayton didn't want to embarrass Steve or himself, so he had to come up with something quick. "Are you married Steve?"

"No."

"Engaged?"

"No."

Dayton paused. He was trying to think up something else to ask Steve that wouldn't sound stupid as he remained fixated; wondering if Mt. Fuji was going to blow in his direction.

Steve looked irritated. "And no, I am not gay." Dayton was caught off guard, which showed in his facial expression. "You know, my parents don't understand why I am not married or dating anyone. I tell them that in this economy, you have to put in 200% to keep your job and get ahead," he stated while pointing his fingers at Dayton. "After your signings I might get promoted in the company. Triple E books is always looking to promote those with talent and drive from the inside."

Dayton rolled his eyes. "Just explain to your parents that you are ambitious. There is nothing wrong with that."

Steve replied, "I have. My father tells me that by my age, he was married, had children and was working in his chosen profession."

Dayton began to think of his father, and the mother he never knew. "This kid doesn't realize how good he has it," he thought to himself. "Well Steve, I didn't mean to pry," said Dayton apologetically. "I think I am going try and get some sleep. Wake me up when we're about at O'Hare. Ok?"

Dayton closed his eyes and faced forward. He deliberately turned his head toward Steve pretending he was sleeping. He opened his left eye just a little, hoping Steve wouldn't notice. "It is still there," Dayton thought to himself while looking at the giant whitehead. "And it is looking at me." He didn't understand why he got these fixations. Maybe his intuition was trying to tell him something. He took his hand and began feeling the side of his own neck to make sure he didn't have a big pimple himself. He then put the blemish out of his mind and started to dose off.

While sleeping, Dayton dreamed he was a little boy again, but instead of being in Virginia, he was sitting on bricks of some sort in an ancient city. It was night, and his eyes were fixed on the stars in the sky, while his hands played with a single twisted strand of black hair coming down the side of his head. He heard footsteps, so he turned. Standing in front of him was his father wearing odd clothing. He put an amulet around his neck and told him to protect it with his life. His father then walked back into what appeared to be an ancient palace. Dayton followed and walked up to the window. As he looked inside, he noticed two other men had surrounded his father, with swords drawn. Dayton's father saw his son's frightened face looking through the window.

"Where is it?" one of the men asked.

"I don't have it," he responded. He again looked over at Dayton, mouthing the word "run." The two men plunged their swords deep into his torso and blood sprayed everywhere. Dayton looked on in horror, unable to scream as he watched his father drop to the floor. One of the men saw Dayton's face in the window. Dayton turned and ran.

At that moment, he awoke. The rear wheels of the passenger jet had just hit the runway in Chicago.

Chapter 13
Finding Hutchinson

Steve stuck to Dayton like glue. From O'Hare, to the hotel and throughout the city, Dayton couldn't go anywhere without being escorted. He understood that after the episode in Boston, the pale, red-head would most likely be babysitting him and keeping him away from anything that could stymie his rise in the publishing industry.

He got out his camera and began to photograph Buckingham Fountain, one of the most famous landmarks in Chicago. After he was finished, he put his camera back in the bag. Dayton wanted to spend a lot more time with his camera in the Windy City, but he conceded that it would only occur after he was done with his little brother and his book signings. "You mind if I go back to my room Steve? I think I'll just get some rest before the signing."

Steve escorted him back to his hotel room. "I'll stop by in two hours to pick you up."

❧

The signing at the Barnes and Noble at State and Elm in Chicago was a success. It had the largest gathering of all the book signings thus far, with over fifty people in attendance. A full table of books emptied and it took almost an hour to sign well wishes to the readers who had come to buy his book and listen to him answer the additional questions in line, which were not asked during the official Q&A.

Dayton was silent walking back to his hotel room, while his companion jibber-jabbered about how well things were going and how there was talk of promotion for him. He bid Dayton farewell after making sure he arrived without incident at his room.

He put his feet up on his bed, going over all the questions from his signing in his mind, as he laid with his hands crossed behind his head. Tonight had run through the gamut of topics spanning from New World Order conspiracies, 911, Kennedy, Oklahoma City, Waco, the North American Union and Secret Societies. But one question had caught the young detective off guard. It concerned the recent prediction by Russian Igor Panarin about the potential break-up of the United States, most likely around July of 2010. He told the audience that America was the world's essential country and although it was possible that at some point in the future America might endure large problems, the absorption of sections of the nation under the protection and rulership of various European, Russian, Chinese and Mexican governments was highly unlikely. It was even more unlikely that it would occur in the next nine months. Although America had taken a sucker punch from the economy, Dayton believed a total imminent collapse was out of the question, unless there was some kind of cataclysmic natural disaster or war. He did admit to the young man who asked the question that a Russian economist did predict 911 a few months prior to its occurrence, but that she specifically stated in an interview, which Dayton had listened to, that she didn't think the 911 event was going to be a terror attack. She said it would be economic. As he closed his eyes, he reviewed the signing in his head, using a visualization technique he used in trying to solve crimes.

Dayton visualized himself at the focal point of the crowd, completing the answer to the young man's question. He watched his own lips move as he heard himself speak. "Dr. Tatyana Koryagina is on record telling Pravda that there was some shadow group with an estimated value in total assets of three-hundred trillion dollars that was trying to legitimize their power into a world government of their design and control. Is this true? I don't know," he answered. "Three-hundred trillion is a lot of money. Six times the GDP of the entire planet for one year. Certainly if such a group exists it might be possible. And there were cases of airline insider trading just prior to September 11th. So somebody knew something." He also watched himself talk about an electronic run on the banks on September 11th 2008 in which 550 billion dollars was taken from US money markets. Dayton observed as he put his finger up in the air. "We don't need a wealthy shadow group to destroy the world economy. Derivatives and hedge funds can do that. So can everybody withdrawing their money from the banks in a panic, because of the fractional reserve practices. Look around. People are afraid to spend money. And that is just going to amplify the economic problems we have now." He fell out of his trance-like state when his cell phone vibrated in his pocket.

"Hi Dayton," Sarah said. "How did your Chicago signing go?"

He pinched himself; clearing his head from his self-induced trance. "Hi Sarah," he replied. "It went fine, except I had a baby-sitter."

"The red-headed guy?"

"Yes. He's like the little brother I never wanted." Sarah laughed on the other end. "He followed me around everywhere. I got a few photos of Buckingham Fountain, but had to come back to my hotel room for some peace, quiet and privacy."

"I know you're probably tired, so I'll let you go. Everything is fine back here in Richmond. I just wanted to let you know that. And I miss you."

Dayton smiled. "I miss you too. Goodnight." Dayton closed his phone and kicked off his shoes. "I really like her," he said aloud. He tucked into his pillow and hugged it; pretending it was Sarah. "Tomorrow, I'll be in Denver."

Dayton stood next the mural at the Denver International Airport. He'd only seen it in pictures. It truly was visually disturbing. He shook his head as he had a funny thought. He remembered the conversation he had earlier with Steve about not being gay. He laughed silently, thinking that anyone watching them, and noticing how close Steve was to him, might think they were lovers.

Dayton got out his camera and began taking photos of the mural.

"What are you doing?" inquired Steve.

Dayton replied. "This mural is a hot topic in conspiracy circles. I thought having my own pictures of it could be of use."

"Oh," Steve replied. He began to jibber-jabber about their schedule for the day. He told Dayton that after the airport they would check into the hotel. Then they would go to lunch and spend the afternoon at the Downtown Aquarium. Dinner was to be early at the Buckhorn Exchange and then the duo was to go right to the Glendale Barnes and Noble and set up.

Ignoring him, Dayton snapped a wide shot, along with many close-ups of the mural, including those of the alleged anti-Christ and the boy beating swords into plowshares. Steve motioned that it was time to go. Dayton kept his camera strapped around his neck, knowing that once they got into the rental car that Steve was going to stick to his strict schedule.

As the two drove away from the airport, Dayton snapped more photographs of the airport exterior.

"Looks almost like the Rocky Mountains from the outside," Steve said.

Dayton frowned as he took a few more snapshots.

"I'm really enjoying our time together Dayton," Steve continued, as Dayton packed up his camera. "Unfortunately, the publisher wants me to remain here in Denver a day longer to wrap up sales and do paperwork." Steve gave Dayton a look of disappointment. "So you'll be in Bozeman a day ahead of me. Just please try and be at the Gallatin Mall two hours early. For my sake?"

"I hit pay dirt!" Dayton screamed inside his head. He looked down at the freshly cleaned carpet of the rental car and faked a look of disappointment. "I must look pathetic," he thought to himself. "Steve. It has been great so far. You're a really nice guy." Dayton winked. "I'll be there two hours early. Don't worry." Inside though, Dayton felt as if his heart was going to leap out of his chest and stick to the windshield. Bozeman didn't have the symbolic landmarks of Chicago or Denver, but it did have a scenic Montana background to photograph. He also remembered that his unsupervised time would give him the opportunity to try and locate Henry Arnold Hutchinson.

❧

Dayton, Steve and the Barnes and Noble representatives sat around the table drinking water and eating popcorn at the Buckhorn, while waiting for their meals to arrive.

Kyle Jonston, the store manager, had told the two that sales of Dayton's book had been mediocre; but that he was hopeful a lively signing tonight could bolster sales. He told them a number of people had called ahead to make sure there was adequate seating. Jonston felt that perhaps customers were waiting to purchase Dayton's book after personally meeting the author.

The waitress brought the group their meals and sales talk diminished as the four began to eat. Tamara Weston, B&N's marketing director, commented that she had read Dayton's book and was quite impressed at the research he had put into it. "It runs the gamut across a whole spectrum of conspiracies. Where did you find the time?" she asked.

"I actually started the research a number of years ago," Dayton replied. "A few months after 911----to be exact."

Jonston piped in, "Kennedy and 911 are thought to be the biggest conspiracies of all time." He looked at Dayton and asked, "You really don't believe in a New World Order scenario do you?"

Dayton shook his head. "No, I don't. The main reason," Dayton continued, as he chewed, "911. Everybody points fingers at everybody else. I have seen people blame the Bushes, the Freemasons, the Government, the Israelis----Some even think the Vatican was behind it."

"But didn't the government know about a potential attack before hand?" Jonston asked. "I've read something about that."

"I believe so," Dayton responded. "But not knowing the exact day or method the terrorists were plotting to use----was the government supposed to shut down all air flights or travel in the US for months? On intelligence which might have been wrong?"

"Of course not," Tamara said. "That would collapse the economy."

Steve put up his finger and began to speak. "Preci----," then nothing. The other three around the table waited patiently for Steve to finish. He started waving his arms in panic as his face turned blue. Dayton stood up. He realized Steve was choking on his hamburger.

He told Steve to remain calm and walked behind him. "He's a twit---but he doesn't deserve to die," Dayton thought to himself as he made a fist and put his arms around him. With a quick thrust, Dayton pulled Steve back. He could feel the remaining air exit his lungs as a large chunk of meat propelled over the head of Kyle Jonston and nearly parted his hair. It landed in the center of a plate of food being eaten by an elderly gentleman at the table behind them.

"What the hell is this?" the old man said holding up and inspecting the meat through his bifocals. Steve was hunched over. He was starting to breathe. To an onlooker, he must have appeared as if he was laughing. He saw the old man glare at him. "You think this is funny, you little bastard?" He pulled back his arm and flung the meat at Steve. It landed square in the middle of his freshly ironed white shirt and made a large brown stain.

Kyle and Tamara stood up and motioned the waiter as he walked by. "Can we get this to go?"

Dayton sat with Steve and calmed him down. "It's ok. It's over."

"I am so sorry Dayton," said Steve, still catching his breath. "Thanks for saving my life." He looked down at the big brown stain. "I have to go buy a new shirt," he said. "I'll meet you back here in front of the restaurant in about twenty minutes."

Dayton watched as Steve walked out of the eatery. Back at the table, he estimated the trajectories of the meat from both Steve's expulsion and the return throw from the elderly gentleman. It was nowhere near his own plate. Dayton was still hungry, so he shook his head and sat down to finish his dinner.

The crowd was mulling around inside the Glendale B&N. Dayton's book was featured prominently around the store with signs that read: Meet the author, 7PM. Dayton and Steve walked by Tamara and Kyle and exchanged uncomfortable glances because of the embarrassing incident earlier at the restaurant.

At 6:50 PM, Dayton picked up a bottle of water and walked toward his chair, which was located at the focal point of a parabola of double-rowed chairs set to accommodate fifty guests. Dozens of patrons eager to hear him speak quickly took their seats.

Dayton walked over to his chair. "Hello everyone," Dayton spoke aloud. "It is good to be here. My name is Dayton McCormick and I am the author of the book: <u>Conspiracy Theory, Conspiracy Fact: Means, Motive and Opportunity</u>. I am not here to dispel all conspiracies, but only to examine them in a rational manner. As a police officer, I am called on to gather evidence to convict people in court. I wrote my book to help people understand that what is out there in books and on the internet is largely inadmissible evidence." Dayton took a sip of his water and continued. "If evidence at all. Rather than read passages, I would prefer to take questions and hopefully get a dialog going." A middle-aged man in the front row raised his hand. "Go ahead sir."

"Is there anything to the mural at Denver International?"

"Sir. I walked past that mural today. It was quite disturbing looking at it up close. But I don't see anything sinister in it. Leo Tanguma, the artist, didn't intend it to be anything more than a portrayal of the evils of man----especially in the Twentieth Century," Dayton replied.

"But isn't it anti-Christian?" the man asked.

Dayton replied. "How so?"

"The mural is horrifying. I don't even like going into that airport." The gentleman continued. "It makes me feel so uncomfortable."

"Doesn't do anything for me either," Dayton replied. "Art is a funny thing. One man's masterpiece----you know what they say about junk and treasure." He looked out and embraced the whole crowd. "It's called, <u>The Children of the World Dream Peace</u>. I don't believe it is some crazy depiction of a New World Order Globalist's dream. Like most art, it does evoke strong emotional reactions." Dayton sipped his water. "But I don't see anything in it suggesting the worship of Satan."

"But what about the secret codes in the floor at the airport?" asked someone in the crowd.

"Do you mean, Cochetopa or Dzit Dit Gaii?" Dayton responded.

"Yes. I have heard they are Satanic," said a young blonde woman.

"Ma'am, those are Navaho terms for geographic locations in Colorado. I don't think the Navajos ever worshipped the devil."

"Yes," he said, looking at a young man with his hand up.

"Are there underground tunnels and aliens living under the airport?"

"I can't say for sure. The baggage handler at the airport could of been a reptilian under his skin." The audience let out a light laugh. "In all seriousness though, the whole tunnel and alien thing comes from a man named Alex Christopher, who said he was employed digging the tunnels during construction of Denver International."

"But is he right?"

Dayton smiled. "I've never seen an alien, so I'm pretty skeptical. I think what the American people should be worried about is how the government has spent their money. Stapleton, I hear, was a perfectly good airport, and I think the cost of the Denver airport was double of what it was projected." Dayton took a sip from his water. "Could the government have a communications array and set up Denver International as a hub for travel in a crisis scenario----sure. They certainly laid down a lot of fiber for communications and they have the ability to produce alternative energy on site. So I think there might be something behind its construction, other than just funneling taxpayer dollars to a Congressional district. But I don't think it is a secret alien base tied together with an underground tunnel system to other underground alien bases. This brings up another issue," Dayton continued, "Are there bolt-holes, or emergency underground facilities for use in a nuclear war or major catastrophes by our government?" Dayton exhaled. "Absolutely, and without a doubt. Mt. Weather, Greenbrier and NORAD---just to name a few. But I don't think there are ET's in them. Just people. I think the whole alien angle is a distraction meant to keep people from looking at what the government is doing."

"Yes," Dayton said pointing to a young blonde woman at the right end of the group.

"So Denver Airport wasn't built as some sort of a center for a Masonic New World Order Plot against humanity?" she asked.

Dayton smiled. "I get the Masonic question a lot. Everyone seems to have their favorite dog to kick. For some, it is the Freemasons. For others it is the mythical Illuminati, the Jews or the Jesuits. I think the finger pointing at groups tends to be based on someone's political or religious beliefs and not on reality." Dayton paused to take a sip of water. "In 1991, Pat Robertson wrote a book called <u>The New World Order</u>, from his Christian perspective. Over the years, many people have also written about this conspiracy. But always ask what is their frame of reference. Eustace Mullins wrote a book in 1952, at the bequest of Ezra Pound, about the evils of the Federal Reserve. Yes, I admit, the Fed is not federal or a reserve. But just because a Jew or a Freemason might be involved in high finance, or on Wall Street, doesn't make a conspiracy theory into a real conspiracy. Chances are good, someone donated big bucks to a congressman and then won lucrative construction contracts in the building of Denver's airport. And yes, the Freemasons did lay a cornerstone at the airport, as they also have for the White House, Capitol Hill, the Statue of Liberty and hundreds of other important and historic locations in the United States. But I don't believe there is a conspiracy against humanity here in Denver----or for that matter, anywhere else."

"So the pentagram above the White House is not satanic either?" The young blonde inquired as a follow-up.

"George Washington, Ellicott and L'Enfant laid out the Capital. There is no record anywhere of Devil worship by any of those men." Dayton smiled.

"What about Baphomet?"

Dayton recalled the sculpture of a seated Washington by Greensbough that sat in the Smithsonian, and was posed in a similar fashion to the creature Baphomet. He was amused. "What about him? Secret societies are known for performing rituals which look strange to those unfamiliar with them. From studying the creature you mention, I believe it is nothing more than a compilation of astronomical data morphed into a strange looking beast."

"How can you assume that?"

Dayton replied, "On his forehead is the pentagram----similar to the one above the White House." Dayton then explained the eight year conjunction cycle where the earth, Venus and the sun line up five times. "If you look at the other characteristics of Baphomet, you will find other astronomical elements as well, I assure you." The young woman sat down. "Any more questions? Yes," Dayton said pointing at an elderly gentleman.

"So you don't believe in conspiracies at all, Detective---"

"Actually I do," Dayton interrupted. "I do believe there are people working against freedom. I also believe there are ambitious people who want to rule the world. They have always been there. I just don't believe there is a Masonic, Zionist or Jesuit plot."

"But hasn't our Constitution been compromised over the years?" the elderly man continued.

"Absolutely," Dayton replied. "I think most of the Constitutional guarantees which have been compromised over the years are due to a unfortunate belief that the Constitution is a living document. In other words, anything can be enacted into law if the times require it, or for the general welfare through the Commerce Clause." Dayton smiled. "I don't think that was the intent of James Madison. And there is a legitimate procedure for change. It is called the amendment process. But that is difficult. And anyone who studies American history realizes it was designed that way on purpose."

Steven stood up and looked at the crowd. "Okay, we have time for one more question before Mr. McCormick gets to signing your books." Steven looked over the many hands which were raised in the crowd. "Yes," Steven said after recognizing a brown-haired young man in the crowd. "Go ahead."

"Detective McCormick. If the President or the Governor of your State ordered you to do something which you believed was clearly a violation of the Constitution, would you follow orders?"

Dayton stood up and looked the young man square in the eye. "No. I took an oath defend the Constitution. I know things were handled improperly at Ruby Ridge and Waco. I know," Dayton continued, "that federal law enforcement and even the 82 Airborne were present after Katrina doing things they probably should have refused to do. But these were all unfortunate and isolated incidents. And steps have been taken both privately and politically to curb similar abuses from occurring in the future." He added, "No matter what someone tells you, it is not us cops against you citizens as many conspiracy peddlers would like you to believe. We're here to help protect the public and not enslave it. Thank you for your question."

Dayton walked over to his chair by the table stacked with books. He grabbed his pen and began inscribing a short note followed by his signature. When the young man who asked the question lifted the cover of his book, Dayton smiled. "What made you ask that question?"

"I'm joining the army after I graduate high school. I had second thoughts because of some of the things I read about that happened in Waco or after hurricane Katrina."

Dayton responded. "Katrina was more complicated than people know. I know a few ATF agents who went there. Because of the destruction of the storm, they were picking guns right up off the street. Most people, if they didn't see the destruction themselves, don't realize the area looked like a war-zone and had no public safety, therefore how could Posse Comitatus apply? In regards to the confiscation from law-abiding citizens that went on, that was ordered by officials who forgot what country we live in. And many states have reminded them by passing Katrina Bills." Dayton clicked his pen. "Remember, for every one bad cop or soldier, there will be ten of you. What is your name?"

"Ben," he responded. Dayton smiled and then wrote "Good luck in the future---Regards, Dayton," on the inside cover of his book.

"Pleasure meeting you, Ben."

Dayton walked toward the door after the signing and noticed Ben clutching his book, while perusing the titles of others. He was glad to see many younger people who were concerned about freedom. "Freedom only dies when people stop caring about it," Dayton thought to himself. He pushed open the door and walked into the night.

Dayton felt the wheels touch down on the small jet, as they meshed with the runway at Gallatin Field in Bozeman, Montana. Looking outside the window of the airplane, he couldn't help but stare at nature's beauty.

As he walked to his rental car, Dayton wondered if a local conspiracy theorist would show up at his signing this evening.

Bozeman was the home of Steve Quayle, who had his own conspiracy radio show and website. Mr. Quayle had been on the scene for decades warning everyone about impending doom. He had a large following and was often a guest on other conspiracy and paranormal programs; such as Coast to Coast AM. Dayton liked his website and found much of the information to be first-rate. However, he found a lot of really questionable things intermixed in with it. "Got to take the good with the bad I guess," Dayton muttered.

But his thoughts soon turned to another man, as he reached in his pocket and pulled out the address list: Henry Arnold Hutchinson. He turned the key in the ignition of the rental car and wondered if Mr. Hutchinson was still alive and in Montana.

Dayton remembered what Steve, the babysitter had said. "Be at the Mall two hours prior." He looked through the windshield at the Gallatin Mall as he drove down West Main Street, then turned his head to glance at his watch. "No problem," he said aloud. Hutchinson's address on Big Sky road was only 10 minutes away to the south, according to the map.

The house he pulled up to was typical of old farmhouses which started out small and then had additions put on them as the family grew. In a way, it was out of place on this street because he noticed large custom homes with long driveways, most likely to help keep them private, from even the longest telephoto lenses of the paparazzi.

He stepped out of the car and proceeded to walk up to the front door. He then knocked. Dayton determined it must have been made of solid wood because of the lack of an echo.

Dayton held his breath as he saw what appeared to be man of about the right age approach the door. The door opened.

"Can I help you son?" the man asked.

"My name is Dayton McCormick----"

The man interrupted, "You're not selling anything are you?"

Dayton replied, "No sir."

The man gave Dayton a once-over and then scoped out Dayton's rental car. He looked back at Dayton and asked, "You ain't one of those Jehovah's Witnesses are you? Cause I don't think I need savin'."

Dayton smirked, "No sir, I am not."

"Then what are you doing at my house at 10:30 in the morning on a Friday. Do you have a job?"

"Yes, I do. I am a police detective in Richmond, Virginia."

The older man squinted. "Well ain't you a little bit far from home?"

Dayton exhaled. "Yes. I wrote a book and I am having a book signing tonight at the Barnes and Noble at the Gallatin Mall."

The man gave Dayton a look of bewilderment. "If yer advertising yer book, couldn't you just drop a flyer in the post box?" he said while pointing to the mailbox at the end of the driveway.

Dayton shook his head. "I'm looking for a Henry Hutchinson. He was a friend of my father's during Vietnam." Dayton looked at the man and noticed he didn't have a large facial scar, but was hoping maybe this was Hutchinson's brother or some other blood relative. "Are you his brother or a friend of his?"

"Sorry son. No one by that name here. Lived here all my life. Never heard of no Henry Hutchinson." The man paused. "In fact, I don't think there are any Hutchinson's in Bozeman." A worried look came over the older man's face. "I am not in trouble am I?"

Dayton shook his head. "No. None at all. Sorry to bother you." He turned around defeated and walked back to the rental car and placed his hands in his pockets.

"Hey!" yelled the man. "Sorry I couldn't help ya." The man waved his hand at Dayton then closed the door. He peeked out the window as he walked over to his phone to dial it. After he saw the young detective drive away, he dialed the phone. Someone picked up on the other end and said "hello" in a mellow voice. "Member you said to call you if anyone came here looking for a Hutchinson? Well, someone just did."

"Thank you," a voice replied. "I'll be sure to compensate you promptly."

"Dead end!" Dayton said aloud, as he slammed his hands against the steering wheel and caused the car horn to sound.

He drove back to the center of Bozeman and entered a drugstore. "Do you have a phonebook?" he asked the clerk. The clerk nodded and handed it to him. He scrolled to the "H" section looking for anyone named Hutchinson who may be living in the area. He didn't find a single one. "No Hutchinson's. Well----I guess I'll have lunch and spend the day photographing the scenery," he said to himself while trying to contain his disappointment. He knew the list of addresses was dated, but because he had found others, he didn't anticipate a total dead end.

"Welcome to Montana, Dayton," he muttered to himself.

❧

Steve looked at the small crowd gathering and counted heads with his fingers. "Twenty-two," he said, with a pleased look on his face. "Could we all gather around and have a seat? Detective McCormick is about to begin."

Everyone settled in and placed their books and coffees in front of them on the tables. Dayton walked to his seat and sat down. He was amazed at the wide variety of people who had come to hear him pitch his book. Some were dressed for a night on the town while others donned hunting camouflage or farm attire. After giving a brief introduction, he opened up the Q&A session.

"Yes," Dayton said, pointing at a well-dressed man with his leather jacket folded on his lap.

"What do you think of Planet X, and do you think Bozeman is a safe place to ride it out?" he asked.

Dayton rolled his tongue inside his mouth. "What a stupid question! Where do people come up with this manure!" he thought to himself. Not wanting to turn away a potential book buyer, he responded calmly. "I have a chapter in my book on the end of the world. This topic is very popular in conspiracy circles." He began to fidget while he maintained eye contact with the group. "Planet X is one of the things I covered." He began to explain the origins of Planet X from the research of Sumerian cuneiform by Sitchin, and from the book, World's in Collision, by Velikovsky. "And it didn't help matters when NASA announced in newspapers that the IRAS Satellite discovered something in our solar system in 1983 and then reneged. Is there a Planet X, or some extra-solar body with a 3,600 year orbit? Or perhaps some large spaceship piloted by aliens?" He shook his head. "I don't think so." He further elaborated on scientific findings showing that there has been ice core, tree ring and geological evidence which indicates that earth has undergone catastrophic climatic upheaval in the past, and that this vaguely supported theories like a Planet X scenario. "But an extra-solar body might not be the cause. It might be something else----perhaps a random asteroid hit----or something that is cyclical that we don't know about." Dayton paused to sip his water. "But I don't subscribe to the rantings of a woman who says she is channeling aliens and tells people to kill their pets, like Nancy Lieder, a Planet X proponent," he stated.

"But would a place like Bozeman be safe if something did happen?" the gentleman kindly asked again.

"I am not a survivalist. Honestly, I don't think anywhere is safe. And with the Yellowstone caldera a short distance away---I would say no. But again, I am not an expert," Dayton replied. "Most of those people I have come across are just making money off scaring people. If you'll notice, they always have something to sell you to help you survive the upcoming catastrophe, which no one seems to know when it will occur."

Steve looked over at Dayton. "Maybe that is a good topic for another book, Dayton?"

"Maybe," smiled Dayton, "But I would have to do a lot more research. And to be honest, I don't know if I would want to live in a world without powdered donuts." He looked back at the seated group. "Yes," he said looking over at a smart-dressed, middle aged blonde.

"Why does NASA seem to be involved in a number of conspiracy theories?" she asked.

"N.A.S.A. has always had people taking second looks at it. The main reason is many of the scientists in the rocket program were expatriated NAZI scientists. They were brought here through a program called "Operation Paperclip" after World War Two. The Russians grabbed some of those scientists too. It is what countries do, because everybody wants the upper hand in the next conflict. I don't see a conspiracy against the people here. There are some people who believe the government blew up the Challenger shuttle." Dayton rolled his eyes. "What I ask is, for what purpose? Unlike insider trading on Wall Street, no one benefitted from it. There has to be a motive," Dayton said. "It is one of the reasons I wrote my book on conspiracy theories. There has to be a motive."

The questions and answers rolled on for about a half hour. Then Steve stood up and made his usual announcement. "We have time for one more question.

An older gentleman was picked. He looked across the table at Dayton and asked, "So when is the government going to take away our guns?"

Dayton replied, "This is one of the biggest fears a large portion of the American people have. It is a huge component in conspiracy theories." Dayton looked at the questioner. "When are you going to give them up?"

"Over my dead body," he replied.

"I feel the same way," smirked Dayton. "And I am from the government," he replied as he pointed at himself. "We have the Second Amendment in this country. Could there be small-scale confiscation attempts? That's happened already. But for the government to take away everyone's guns? That is highly unlikely and I don't believe it will be attempted. Since Barak Obama was elected President, enough guns and ammunition have been sold to outfit the armies of both China and India. And the politicians know this. I don't think they want to lose their jobs in the next election, like the Democrats did in 1994 after narrowly passing the Assault Weapons Ban." Dayton looked down, closed his eyes and lifted his head and smiled at the crowd. "And most rank and file members of law enforcement want nothing to do with gun confiscation. If law-abiding citizens can't be trusted, then it wouldn't be a country by the people and for the people anymore----would it?"

"So when are you moving to Montana and running for office?" the man joked?

Dayton smiled. "Although I have a strong interest in politics, I think I'll just stay being a police detective. Thank you all for coming. If you don't mind," Dayton said as he stood up and stretched, "Why don't you all stay seated and I'll walk around and sign your books."

After the signing was over, Dayton walked around the store. He picked up a copy of Virgil's, <u>The Aeneid,</u> and paid for it at the register. "Looks like something to read on the plane," he said to himself. As he flipped through the index, he noticed the structure of the work. "Twelve chapters. Hmm? Twelve Constellations. Jupiter's orbit is about twelve years. Maybe there is something more to this." He shook his head. "Annuit Coeptis."

Dayton laid down in his hotel room bed. He was going to start reading <u>The Aeneid</u>, but instead, he put it down and reached into the drawer where a Bible was kept. "I still have to finish reading the Books of the Law," he said to himself. "Twelve Tribes."

He completed his reading of the books attributed to Moses, then retired for the evening after calling both Sarah and his grandmother.

Sarah answered the phone. "I just thought I'd call and say hello. This afternoon, I photographed a few cool sights in Seattle, like the Space Needle. I am standing outside the Barnes and Noble now."

"You dog," Sarah replied, "I wish I was there."

"I wish you were here too," Dayton replied. "And I am looking forward to dinner when I get back. My plane leaves at 7AM, Seattle time. So I should be arriving sometime around 3:30 because I have to switch planes at O'Hare."

"Alright. When your plane is about to leave Chicago, give me a call," Sarah replied.

"I'll do that. I----I----can't wait to see you. It has been a long week," Dayton said.

"Well, your grandmother just beat me at cards, so I owe her a lunch."

"I'm glad to hear you two are having fun. I have to let you go," Dayton replied, looking over at Steve. He whispered, "The red-headed terrorist is telling me I only have five minutes until show time."

"I'll see you tomorrow, Dayton. Bye."

Dayton entered the Seattle bookstore through the front door. "The second leg of my book tour is almost done," he said with relief. He grabbed his traditional bottle of water and sat down in a chair in front of a mid-sized group of interested book buyers.

After introducing himself and presenting the crowd with his views on conspiracy theories, he stood up and asked if anyone the crowd wished to engage in a dialogue.

"I'd like to ask some questions," said a man wearing blue jeans and an oxford-style shirt. "Officer McCormick, you are familiar with OnStar?"

"Yes. Great for people who lock their keys in the car," Dayton replied.

The gentleman contorted his face and showed his displeasure with Dayton's reply. "Well, I just saw an ad on television showing that the On-Star people could disable a car's engine via satellite, if a vehicle was stolen. Could such a thing be used against the American people?"

The man stood unwavering as he awaited an answer. Dayton replied, "Doubtful. And let me tell you why. If the Government ordered On-Star to disable vehicles other than those being stolen or used in a crime, the public would be outraged and would demand such devices be removed from their vehicles. Likewise, there is a health debate going on right now, where people are fear mongering "Death Commissions" being set up for the elderly if a government health plan were to be enacted." Dayton paused to sip his water. "I think that every member of A.A.R.P. would be marching on the Mall in Washington if such a thing were to occur.

There is only so much people will put up with, and the politicians know this."

The man continued standing. "I have a follow-up, if you don't mind?"

"Go ahead."

"Couldn't the same type of technology been used to fly those planes into the Twin Towers and the Pentagon?"

This was the first time Dayton had been asked this during his signings. He knew it was a touchy thing to discuss, but seeing as this scenario was covered in his book, he felt it needed to be addressed if this man was ever going to sit down.

"The straight answer is yes. The question is----was it, and by whom?" Dayton took a deep breath and looked square in the eyes of the standing man. "Andreas von Buelow, a minister for technology in Germany has discussed this matter with Alex Jones----saying Boeing 757's and 767's have a type of "Home Run" technology tied into the flight computers of these planes, which could remotely direct their FCMS, or flight management computer systems and over-ride the pilot. It is an anti-hijacking technology. In order for this to have occurred on 911 though, someone would have had to steal the technology from Boeing, infiltrated the FAA or NORAD, or bolted some device on the planes utilized that day. All possibilities, for sure. But there is no evidence that this took place. I can't imagine our own military doing it, but that is my opinion, not evidence." The man continued to stand, waiting for further comment. "What we need to also ask, however, is would this technology have been needed at all to accomplish what occurred?"

"Well----I heard those hijackers couldn't fly well?"

"Sir, with auto pilot, would they have had too? The reason why I mention this, is that after takeoff, once those planes climbed over one thousand feet, the autopilot could be engaged. They didn't have to be great pilots. The height, of the Towers were 1,360 feet. If they let the autopilot fly toward New York City, all they would have to do is disengage the auto-pilot, and ram them into the tallest buildings in Lower Manhattan, once visual contact was made."

"Oh," replied the man. "But what about those whacky air maneuvers?"

"We can only theorize what happened concerning that, because the transponders were turned off," Dayton responded. "I'm not sure investigators could tell which planes did what with all the blips on the radar screens."

"Can I have one more question?" the man asked.

Dayton looked around at the crowd. The faces seemed more interested in hearing this man's questions answered, than not. "Go ahead, but only if you buy two books," Dayton said smiling. The crowd laughed.

"I'll buy three of them if you answer this one," he said.

"I'll hold you to that." Dayton looked over at Steve, who was muttering "I sure hope he does," to himself. "Go ahead."

"Weren't there a number of exercises going on that day, including one which simulated hijacked planes being used against skyscrapers as flying bombs?"

Dayton looked at the man with admiration. "This guy should have been a prosecutor," Dayton thought to himself. "I feel like a defense attorney for the government right now," Dayton joked. "Yes, there were a number of exercises going on that day, including the scenario you mentioned. It is one of the reasons why there was so much confusion on 911 because air controllers didn't know if it real or an exercise. It is one of the reasons why so many mistakes were made. There was Vigilant Guardian, which did what you mentioned. There was also Global Guardian. Operation Northern Vigilance was also being held in the northwest United States because of a Russian exercise with their 37th Air Division. You also had Tripod 2, involving Mayor Giuliani and F.E.M.A., although that was to be held on September 12th. There was a lot going on," Dayton emphasized. "Those who committed 911 couldn't have picked a better day. Yes, there are coincidences, and no, anyone from government who says they never imagined planes being used as weapons, is only misleading the public, because obviously they were training for it. Not to mention the government knew about the failed "Operation Bojinka" from 1995, where terrorists were going to blow up twelve airliners coming from Asia." The man finally sat down. "I am not saying that what you are questioning is not technically possible. It is just unlikely. And I can get all sorts of information on the Internet as to when government is going to run exercises and of what type. They plan these things long in advance. I am sure the terrorists knew about them and used it to their advantage."

"Thank you for your answers, Detective McCormick," the man said from his seat. "It is just hard to trust the government when things smell fishy."

"That's ok," Dayton responded. "A healthy distrust of government isn't a bad thing. George Washington called government a poor servant and a fearful master. People like yourself should ask questions. The problem is, for one reason or another, the government doesn't like to answer your questions. So instead of settling a matter, it just gives more fuel to the fire in driving these conspiracy theories."

"And I just have a hard time believing our government is so incompetent," the gentleman added.

"I wouldn't say incompetent. Just not perfect," Dayton replied. "I think we have all come to expect too much from government."

〜

Dayton relaxed on the bed in his hotel room and kicked off his shoes. He was relieved that this part of his book signing tour had come to a close, although he was still disappointed by not finding Hutchinson in Bozeman. But he hoped all was not lost, and that both the keys to his father's death and his research would be found with the last man, John Windwalker, in Tucson. Dayton reached into his suitcase and pulled out his laptop. In all the excitement, he had forgotten to look for what he had mentioned to Sarah and Mark. "Three planets closely aligned at the head of Virgo."

"Well, at least they're not putting me up in a cheap hotel," Dayton muttered while looking at the sign for wireless internet access next to the television. He booted up his laptop. The keys felt flat against his fingertips as he typed and searched for an accurate solar system simulator, which would display the arrangement and the right ascension and declination figures for the planets, according to a set date and time. He found a site which originated in Europe and bookmarked it for later use.

"The Statue of Liberty. What can she represent other than Virgo with the sun in Leo?" Dayton questioned. "She is made of copper." He remembered historically that each of the planets had a representative metal compound in alchemy. "Gold is the sun. Silver is the moon. Venus. Copper is for Venus," he muttered. He researched Liberty and recorded all sorts of fact and figures. "She had the moon under her feet at some point before her restorations. Maybe the moon is involved." Then he came across a cutaway of her structure on a history website and noticed two helical staircases. "Caduceus----." His eyes lit up. "The Planet Mercury. Mercury carries a caduceus." Dayton realized that a combination of Venus, Jupiter and Mercury made sense. "Mercury dimes---liberty halves and quarters. Like the dollar, the clues have been on American paper and metal currency." He stared at his laptop. "Currency. Frequency. Synonyms for cycles."

"But did this alignment occur in the recent past?" he mused. He looked in solar system simulator and found that Jupiter was in Virgo in 2004 and 1992, but the other planets he suspected, Mercury and Venus, didn't both line up at the area specified in the sky on those dates. The next potential date for Jupiter in Virgo, was in 2016, so he entered the data in the search fields.

He found that Jupiter would be at the head of Virgo sometime in late August through October of 2016. "I wonder," he thought to himself, thinking about the Statue of Liberty and the number of an infamous plane flight on 911 that crashed in Pennsylvania. He typed in the date and pressed enter. As he scrolled over to where the Lion met the Virgin, his eyes opened wide.

"Holy shit!" he exclaimed, almost falling backward in his chair. Jupiter, Venus and Mercury had formed a perfect triangle at the head of Virgo. But something wasn't quite right. "Where is the eye?" As he stared at his computer screen, he noticed it was there when he looked carefully. Then it hit him. "What time, exactly?" He sat there, thinking for a moment, then felt shivers rolling from his neck down to his spine. He typed in the most obvious time he knew. It was the one on the clock tower in Philadelphia on the hundred dollar bill. He typed it in and hit enter.

On the computer screen in front of Dayton was a small triangle with the All-Seeing Eye. The eye was the moon. The time was 2:22 UTC. "It looks almost like the capstone on the back of the dollar bill," he whispered to himself. "If you draw lines between the planets."

While Dayton was making his discovery, Sarah was making one of her own. She took a few things off the desk in the study at Martha's house and brought them to her apartment. She was on Google Earth looking at an aerial of Washington D.C. and reading the book <u>Picturesque Washington</u>. As she closed the book, she saw the writing on the inside front cover.

1m=36.525

She stared at it for a moment. "I wonder," she said to herself. She looked in the tool bar and found the measure function. "What if 1m= 1 meter. If 1 meter = 36.525----Wait a second! 36.525 is one tenth of a year of 365.25 days. One year----the base on 23rd is in miles, but the Meridian is in meters." So she took the start point from the measure tool, after setting the scale to meters, and clicked her mouse on what she estimated was the Meridian Line from the Zero Milestone. Then she measured up the Mall eastward. Just outside the perimeter of the base of the Washington Monument measured slightly under 130 meters, then to the outside, about eighty more. She minimized the window for Google Earth and typed in <u>Washington's Presidency</u> in the Google search engine.

"He was President from 1789-1797," she said aloud. "About eight years. And July 4, 1776 to 1789 is thirteen years."

She sat back in her chair in disbelief. "The Washington Monument reflects in time, through measurement, the presidency of George Washington. Wow!" Then she measured up some more, and did the mathematical conversion of meters to years. "The middle of third street is November 22, of 1963----Kennedy." Then she measured further toward Capitol Hill. Due to 3D rendering of the building and grounds she couldn't be one hundred percent accurate, but the Dome's center coordinated to sometime in late August or early September of 2016.

"I don't believe this," she said. "I think the Mall of the United States Capital is a timeline." She then measured west of the Meridian and went 290 meters past the seat of Lincoln in the Lincoln Memorial. "1620----when the pilgrims crossed the Atlantic."

She couldn't believe what she was seeing, so she looked up other important dates in American history and plotted their dates from the measurements corresponding with the equation from the book.

Just below Capitol Hill, but above the Peace and Garfield Memorials, she found it: 9-11-2001. "Wait until Dayton sees all this."

❧

He saw her standing there, waiting for him at the airport terminal. He remembered the first time he saw her waiting for him was at the hospital on the last day of his grandfather's life. "It's weird how things are connected----terminal," he thought to himself. And how guilty he felt for noticing how she looked that day, while his grandmother was upstairs holding the hand of a dying man who he loved like a father. But that was in the past and he hoped the woman in front of him, who was very happy to see him, would fill the void in his heart that he had closed off to all those he felt undeserving of his affection.

As he got closer, her eyes met his. She couldn't wait to bring him home. But she also had the look on her face that she wanted to tell or show him something.

"How was your trip?" Sarah asked as Dayton stopped in front of her with his luggage in tow and camera bag around his neck.

"It went pretty well," Dayton replied, "but I am glad to be back home." His eyes stared deeply into hers. He was so glad to be back in Richmond and looking at her. He slung the camera bag to the right side of his torso and extended his left hand downward, which was promptly joined by her right. It felt nice and warm holding her hand.

The two walked out of Richmond International and over to the parking lot where Sarah had left Dayton's Jeep. "Whoa. Where is your car?" Sarah gave him the "again" look, indicating that it was at the auto repair shop.

Dayton loaded in his luggage and walked over to the driver's door. "I don't think so," Sarah said. She dangled the keys in front of his face. "You're not getting the keys from me."

Dayton smirked and dutifully walked around the Cherokee and opened the passenger door. He sat and fastened his seatbelt.

As Sarah started driving, Dayton asked, "So what is for dinner? I didn't have time for lunch, so I'm extra hungry."

"Oh----I made something special," Sarah said, making eyes at Dayton. "I am cooking my world famous liver and onions with cauliflower and Brussels sprouts," she said proudly.

The reaction was immediate. Dayton had to look out the passenger window, because his face was mimicking the look of a child being force to eat something dreadful. Sarah laughed at his childish antics. "Hey, I was just kidding." Dayton looked relieved and exhaled. If he and Sarah continued their long-term relationship, the thought of eating liver with a smile wasn't going to sit too well. "I don't even like liver," she said.

"So what did you make?" Dayton asked sheepishly.

"Beef stew. Been slow-cooking it all day."

"Meat and potatoes are a man's best friend," thought Dayton, who had previously pictured himself signing divorce papers over irreconcilable differences at the dinner table, before he was even married.

"So? Who asked the best questions at your signings?"

Dayton looked at her. "You want to know the truth?" he said. "The best questions I was asked, were in Bozeman, when I was looking for Hutchinson. I didn't find him, but the man who lived in the house asked if I had a job, or if I was a Jehovah's Witness."

Sarah laughed so hard she nearly ran off the road. As she regained her composure, she poked fun at Dayton. "Were you wearing a suit?"

"No!" Dayton replied, making a funny face at her. They both started laughing. "So how is Grandma?"

"She's fine. Besides, you called her every night. If she wasn't, she'd tell you." Sarah rolled her eyes. "And I have been seeing her just about every day."

Dayton looked forward through the windshield. He was uncomfortable being in the passenger seat in his own vehicle. Then he looked over at Sarah, smiled and realized she was the only person to ever drive his Jeep, besides himself.

They pulled in to the parking lot of Sarah's apartment complex. Dayton unloaded his luggage while Sarah carefully brought his camera bag inside. It was a small apartment, with an eat-in kitchen, bathroom, bedroom, living room and one large closet in the hallway. But it was cozy and had a pleasant decor. He noticed that everything was neat and tidy as if it were recently cleaned. And the vacuum was still plugged in to the wall socket. He looked over at the desk, and next to the computer were copies of his father's aerials and the Picturesque Washington book.

Sarah noticed him looking at the desk. "I hope you don't mind?"

Dayton replied, "Not at all." He walked over to her and gave her a kiss, then noticed a freshly baked and frosted chocolate cake, in a pedestal style server with a clear top, on the counter. He looked around the apartment as if he were searching for some king or foreign dignitary. Then he realized Sarah prepared it all for him. He walked over to the window and used his hand to move the curtain aside. His eyes darted back and forth and checked the parking lot for any unusual vehicles.

"You ok?" Sarah asked in a concerned voice.

He walked away from the front of the window. "I'm fine," Dayton replied. "Just checking out the area. You know. Detective." Sarah rolled her eyes.

Dayton sat down at the table as Sarah retrieved two large bowls from the cupboards. He felt a furry lump jump on to his lap as Sarah was turned toward the stove and dishing up the beef stew. The lump purred and Dayton complied by stroking its soft fur. The warm lump and the vibration of friendship made him feel right at home.

Sarah placed a full bowl of stew in front of him and waited for a sign of gratitude. Dayton looked up and smiled as he reached for his spoon and promptly shoved it into the stew.

"If you see my cat Sausha, don't touch her," Sarah warned. She is not too fond of strangers and she bites. Mark tried to pet her one day and found out the hard way." Dayton smiled as he silently continued eating his stew. Sarah looked at him. "I didn't know you were left handed?"

"I'm not," Dayton replied; smiling like a Cheshire cat.

"Well----why are you eating with your left hand?"

"Meow," Dayton responded. Sarah got up from her chair and squatted below the table.

"I don't believe this," she said, looking under the tablecloth. "She bites everybody."

Sarah and Dayton continued with small talk throughout dinner and looked at each other as if they were teenagers. Dayton acted like he hadn't eaten in days; eating bowl after bowl of stew until the pot was empty and his stomach was ready to explode. "That was fantastic," he said as he washed the last spoonful down with some ice water. Then a horrified look came over his face. Looking at his empty bowl he said, "Sarah, I forgot to call my grandmother and let her know I was home safe, and that I wouldn't be going back to her house until tomorrow." Dayton arose from the table, sending Sausha airborne. He walked over to the phone and quickly dialed Martha.

Sarah stared at him as he began his conversation. "Hi Gram, I'm home----well, I'll be home tomorrow. Sarah dropped me at Mark's and the guys are taking me out. So I am going to crash at his place tonight." Sarah continued staring at him. She rolled her eyes and folded her arms.

Martha replied, "Now Dayton, I hope you had a nice dinner over Sarah's. She told me she was making you beef stew."

Dayton looked over at Sarah and had a feeling his grandmother knew he was telling a little white lie. However, he continued with his deceit. "The stew was fantastic Gram," Dayton replied. "But me and the guys are going bowling now." Sarah started tapping her feet.

"Well say hi to her for me. She is a lovely girl. And please bring me a bowl of that stew on your way home tomorrow."

Dayton looked over at the pot on the stove which contained only a thin layer of beef broth and a few small pieces of carrots and celery. Sarah was now starting to clear her throat. "I'll see you tomorrow. Love you Gram."

"I love you too Dayton. Please give my best to Sarah. And please try and save me a piece of the chocolate cake she made, especially if you finished off the stew."

Sarah looked over at Dayton, mouthing the words "BUSTED."

Dayton shrugged his shoulders after he hung up the phone. "Duh," Sarah said sarcastically. "Mark had to bring me to Martha's to get your Jeep. I told her I was making you beef stew and chocolate cake." Sarah paused. "And that you would be staying with me tonight."

"Oh," replied Dayton, as his face turned white.

"She is a grown woman, Dayton. She is not stupid."

Dayton immediately changed the subject. "So what was it you found that you wanted to show me?"

Sarah knew what he was doing, but played along anyway. "I'll show you mine if you show me yours?" she responded.

Dayton felt like pulling his pants down, but his full belly would probably not react well to intimate contact. Not to mention that Sarah looked like she was a little pissed off. So he waddled over to her computer and turned it on. "I think you'll find this interesting." He typed in the website of the solar system simulator he found in Seattle, then the date and time. "Wait until you see this. The clues my father left me show the arrangement of the capstone with the eye you see on the back of the one dollar bill."

Sarah walked over to the computer. Dayton continued. "Not only are there three planets in the sky; Jupiter, Venus and Mercury, forming a triangle, but the moon enters the inside of the triangle forming the eye, just like on the back of the dollar. And it does this at the head of the Virgo Constellation." He smiled at her with a twinkle in his eye. "I give you September 3, 2016 at precisely 2:22AM, Universal Time Code."

Sarah's eyes' lit up. "I'll be damned. It is a date and a time."

"That's right. The only problem is, I don't think most people will see it in the sky"

"Why?" she asked.

"Because it occurs during the day. However, astronomers will know it will be there, along with a few others who will see part of it form before it happens. On September 1st, 2016, there is an annular eclipse which should block out the sun enough to see it on part of the earth. One of the locations it should be visible is in Giza."

"But how do you know people won't see it?" Sarah asked. "In the Bible, there are all sorts of unexplained occurrences and phenomenon. Like the sun standing still for three days----for example."

"Which could only occur if the earth stopped rotating," Dayton added, "and there are tales of the sun standing still, while on the other side of the planet, ancient peoples have described a long night lasting three days."

"But how do you know people world-wide won't see this arrangement in the sky in 2016?" Sarah prodded again.

"Truthfully," Dayton responded, "I don't."

"I think you might want to see this. Please---" Sarah said, motioning Dayton to let her sit down. She went to Google Earth and brought up Washington D.C. "When was George Washington President?"

"It was from 1789 to 1797. He was president for eight years," Dayton responded.

"Exactly." She pointed to the Washington Meridian. "What if this was a date too----let's say July 4th, 1776?"

"That would make sense. It runs parallel from the White House to the Jefferson Memorial. And Jefferson wrote the Declaration. And on the tablet, in the left hand of the Statue of Liberty, is the date of July 4th."

She reached over and picked up the book <u>Picturesque Washington</u> and opened the front cover. "1m=36.525. Or one meter equals 36.525 days. This would make ten meters equaling one year." She took the measuring tool and started at the Meridian line and measured up east slightly less than 130 meters, stopping at the edge of the Washington Monument. "130 Meters or thirteen years. 1776 plus thirteen, is 1789----when Washington became president."

Dayton's eyes opened wide. "It's a timeline. Whoa!"

She looked at him. "It gets better. Watch this." She measured from the Meridian up to the center of the Capitol Dome, which has the Statue of Freedom atop. "A hair above 2.4 kilometers or 240 years. The center of the Dome corresponds to around August or September of 2016."

"This makes total sense. Look," he said, pointing to the Lincoln Memorial. "It is on 23rd street. But the Capitol is on the Capitol Line--twenty four streets. That is one tenth of 240." Then he looked at the White House. "Do you know where this is?"

"Easy----1600 Pennsylvania Avenue," Sarah responded. "Everybody knows that."

"Yes, but do you realize it intersects with 16th Street? Two sixteen's, Sarah, or 2016. Everything points to 2016." He pointed his finger to the Dome then followed it to Union Station where there is a statue of Christopher Columbus. "Columbus. District of Columbia." Dayton shook his head. "I can understand why Columbia Pictures uses a woman carrying a torch. Columbia is the Statue of Liberty. It is a play on the word Columbus."

"Columbus did come over on three ships."

"That's right," Dayton said. "The Nina, the Pinta and the Santa Maria."

"Not exactly." Sarah said. Dayton looked confused. "The Nina was really the Santa Clara."

Dayton thought for a moment. "Virgin Mary. The Santa Maria is Mary or in this case, the Virgo Constellation with Mercury and Venus---- My Spanish is bad, but if I am not mistaken, Pinta is Spanish for "Spotted One."

"And that would be Jupiter," Sarah said, putting her hand on his shoulder. "Let's look up Santa Clara."

The two searched the web and found information on St. Claire, who was made famous by saving children from wolves at night. "The Moon. The Moon----Sarah. Wolves howl at the moon. When the wolves saw her, they howled, allowing the children to escape." Dayton was as excited as a little boy at Christmas. "That is why Columbus was used. It was his three boats, representing planets, which would form an arrangement in the sky."

Sarah rubbed Dayton's shoulders and gave him a kiss on the side of his neck. "You have any room for cake?"

He got up and sat on the couch as Sarah walked into the kitchen. "How about just a small piece, with two forks on one plate?"

"Sounds romantic." After cutting the cake, Sarah walked over to Dayton and sat next to him on the couch. The two grabbed their forks and proceeded to feed each other. A small piece of cake dropped off Dayton's fork and landed on Sarah's shirt. He put down the fork and picked it up between his two fingers and then placed it in her mouth.

"Cake huh?" Sarah laughed.

Dayton, while chewing his own piece of cake responded, "Yah, cake." After he finished chewing he started to speak again. "You know Sarah, we have to ask ourselves what this all means? And even though we discovered this, because all this was built in to the design of both New York and Washington----that must mean the people who designed and built them, up through the respective changes and additions, did it on purpose---and they know what this all means."

"Or maybe things just work out this way. Like snowflakes." Sarah responded. "Some sort of cosmic influence. I don't know."

"Snowflakes." Dayton was skeptical about it being by chance. "Perhaps. But all these symbols and measurements were made deliberately by the people who designed and built them." He stopped briefly, taking time to look over the three aerials. "Is there a relationship between the people that built Giza, or other structures in the world, and the people who designed and built what is in D.C. and New York?"

"I don't know?" replied Sarah. "Maybe some of it is on purpose, and some by some sort of influence." She made eyes at him. "Could be both."

Dayton stood up and continued. He told Sarah about his purchase of the Aeneid. "That sign on the dollar has to be of some great significance, or why go through all this trouble----and the building of all this," Dayton responded, waving his hand across the aerial of D.C. "Is something going to happen? Does it occur before the sign? Or, when it occurs. Or is it an omen----either positive or negative of some future event? The only logical explanation is that whatever this signifies," he said pointing at the pyramid roundel on the back of the dollar, "has happened before and someone or some group has knowledge of it---or perhaps---the knowledge was lost in time, but someone figured it out from the clues left behind."

"Like Giza. There has always been a lot of interest in it. Even Napoleon went to see it," Sarah said.

"People always wondered what treasures were in those pyramids. Maybe there was no gold or silver----but knowledge of something." Dayton pointed again to the reverse of a one dollar bill. "Novus Ordo Seclorum, means New Order of the Ages." He walked to his suitcase and removed the <u>Aeneid</u>. "Annuit Coeptis was part of a poem to the god Jupiter---. The book was written by Virgil----very similar in spelling to the word Virgin."

"And D.C. was partially designed by L'Enfant---infant," Sarah interrupted. "The infant, of the virgin, which Christians know of as Jesus."

Dayton wasn't comfortable where this was going. He remembered his research into the possible birthdates of Jesus and the purported signs in the sky. Most were conjunctions of Jupiter and Venus. "I'm not so sure that is the meaning, although I must admit the similarities."

"Didn't the wise men follow Jesus' sign in the sky?" Sarah asked. "Three planets closely aligned, forming a triangle if you drew lines between them, and with the Moon inside? Maybe that was it."

"But that sign was after his birth." He felt bad because he seemed to be dismissing most of her theories. "Look. Maybe you are right." He looked down. "I have been reading the Bible. The Prophets of the Old Testament foretold his coming----and the prophets might have lived around the time the pyramids were being built."

"Thank you," Sarah responded sarcastically.

Dayton smiled. "Wait a second. In late August of 2016, Jupiter and Venus will closely conjunct. I think they'll only be off by fourteen seconds of measurement. Very small. Maybe all those Greek tales, and those of other peoples were about planetary interactions---- and they personified them for memory purposes, as well as what effects they caused on earth or on the sun. In my meeting with Peter, he explained how both earth's climate and the solar cycle was affected by the arrangement of the planets in the solar system."

"Maybe the timeline of the Washington D.C. Mall keeps track of these events?" Sarah asked. "With the Washington Meridian being a fixed point in time we can measure from."

"That is my suspicion too, although I am not ruling out Christ's return." Dayton turned and looked at a copy of the sketch he made that Sarah had taken from his grandmother's study. He picked it up. At first, he looked curiously at it. His look of curiosity turned to disbelief.

Noticing his pale expression, Sarah said, "I hope you don't mind that I wrote on that?"

"No, no I don't mind. I just don't believe what I am seeing."

"What? What is it you see?"

Dayton sat back down on the couch and took a deep breath. He turned the paper over so Sarah could see it. Then he pointed to the middle of 3rd Street in

Washington. "November 22, 1963." Then he pointed just below the Capitol area. "September 11th, 2001."

"I don't understand," Sarah said in a questioning manner.

"In my father's Bible I got from professor Mussen, there was an Aztec artwork. It depicted four men killing one at the top of a truncated pyramid, as two men below blew into horn-like instruments." Dayton continued, "If you look closely at where these events occurred, they are both at, or near, the top of a truncation." Dayton traced his fingers to illustrate to Sarah what he meant.

"Are you saying 911 and the Kennedy Assassination were done because of where those dates fell on this timeline?"

"I am not sure, but Peter told me that the people who were killed on September 11th were the victims of a symbolic ceremony----like a sacrifice." Sarah's eyes opened wide. "And see this," Dayton said, pointing to the Grant Memorial. "You list it as September 1983. I am willing to bet it is September 11, 1983."

"Go on," Sarah replied.

"Well, we have the sign on September 3rd, 2016. That is Nine-three or Ninety-three. The Statue of Liberty is 93 meters from torch tip to her base. The earth is 93 million miles from the sun------eighteen years after September 11, 1983 is September 11th, 2001. Take the eighteen out of 1983 and you get Ninety-three. And the first attempt to take down the World Trade Towers was in late February 1993."

"And Flight 093 crashed in Shanksville, Pennsylvania on September 11th," Sarah added. Sarah noticed Dayton was visibly disturbed. "Why don't we put this away for tonight. It is very interesting, but it is very creepy." She took the paper out of Dayton's hands and put it back on her computer desk. "You had a long week," she said as she put her hands on his face. "Why don't you go take a hot shower and relax for a while? Then we can watch some TV."

Dayton put his hands over hers. "You're right. I am sorry about all this. You made a great dinner and the cake was excellent." He laughed and tried to brush off the seriousness of what the two had seen. "I can actually move now and not be uncomfortable. I really did eat too much. Dinner was great." He stood up and looked at her. "A shower would be the best thing for me right now. You don't mind?"

"Nope," Sarah said, pointing to her bathroom. "It's all yours."

Dayton walked into the bathroom and shut the door. As he looked in the mirror, he thought to himself, "What the hell are you doing? You are alone with a beautiful women you really like." He looked in his own eyes. "And what do you do? You talk about conspiracy theories and human sacrifices. You're going to scare this one away, Dayton McCormick. Stop being a dope."

Dayton undressed himself and walked over to the shower. He turned the handle to start the flow of water and set the proper temperature, then got in and slid the shower curtain to keep the streaming water from going on the floor. As he stood in the shower, he put his head against the wall and felt the hot water rolling over his head. For a moment, he lost all feeling of time and space. Dayton let the water wash away his troubled thoughts.

He didn't flinch when a pair of warm hands gently touched his shoulders. He was used to his grandmother sneaking up on him all those years growing up. But these hands were different, and desired a different kind of love. He was so out of it, that he hadn't heard Sarah walk into the bathroom, drop her white bathrobe on the floor and climb in behind him. Her hands moved down from his shoulders to embrace him around his chest. He felt her warm torso against his, while a pair of hardening nipples pressed against his back. Down below, he became aroused. Not saying a word, she removed one hand from the embrace, and picked up the soap on the side of the tub. Then Sarah gently washed his shoulders and back. She wiped some soap on her left hand and reached around to grab and stroke him. He could feel his heart begin to beat faster as he breathed deeper with pleasure. She turned him around and made eye contact as the water poured over them both. He moved his head forward and pressed his lips against hers, while his hands fondled her breasts. After a minute of passionate kissing, she secured herself with her hands on his sides as she knelt in the accumulating water. She looked up, almost asking for permission with her eyes, but she also knew what the answer would be. She placed one hand around the back end of his shaft and opened her lips to take him in. As her head moved back and forth in a rhythmic motion, Dayton became more excited, almost to the point of losing his balance. But he held firm until he felt the release and the throbbing while her mouth continued its passionate motion.

He turned off the shower and removed two towels from the closet. Dayton gently dried her over every inch of her body, admiring her curves, and she returned the favor. He then took her by the hand and led her to the bedroom. Dayton sat Sarah in front of him, and straddled his legs around her lower back. His lips gently kissed her neck and his left hand caressed her breast while his thumb and index finger gently pulled on her hardening nipple. His right hand made its way down to her lower region and began to explore her soft, warm flesh. The tip of his finger found its target and he gently rubbed it back and forth. Sarah began moaning. Her breathing deepened and her lower region moistened as Dayton's fingers played her like a fine musical instrument.

She begged him to take her. Sarah then crawled on her back towards the headboard and he obliged her demand. As he pressed his chest against hers, she reached down and guided him inside. He felt her warm and wet orifice tighten around him as he penetrated her. The nails from her hands began to scrape his back as they danced in horizontal rhythm. He licked her neck like a ravenous animal as the bed creaked harmoniously back and forth.

Her head swam in sexual pleasure as her body reached heights she had never before achieved with any other man. Then Dayton released his tension inside her. He felt her internal muscles throb and grip, as the warm fluid of love lubricated her canal. Her nails gripped his back even more tightly, as she pushed him inside as far as he would go.

After many rounds of lovemaking, Dayton and Sarah passed out in each other's arms.

Dayton awoke the next morning first. He opened his eyes and looked at the woman lying in bed next to him. She appeared peaceful as she slept, and her fair complexion and auburn hair reminded him of an angel he once saw in a toy store as a child. He gently kissed her on the forehead and slowly climbed out of bed so he wouldn't disturb her.

He wasn't used to sleeping naked or walking around that way. After a few moments, he overcame feeling uncomfortable and actually began to enjoy it. "So this is what it is like to be a nudist," Dayton whispered to himself. He removed some items from the fridge and cupboard to make pancakes, then whisked the ingredients up in a bowl. He paused as he noticed the large chocolate cake on the counter and he wedged off a small piece for himself.

Sausha made an attempt to stick her head in the pancake batter while he was diverted. He picked her up, just in time, with one hand and placed her on the floor. The batter went into the refrigerator.

While the batter thickened in the refrigerator, Dayton walked into the bathroom to take a shower. When he was finished, Sarah enter the bathroom resembling Eve from the garden. "You could have waited," she said as she raised her eyebrows. "Water conservation is important."

"Yes, but you have to go to work today----and I promised you breakfast," he said with a smile. "If I got back in the shower with you, you'd have to call in sick."

"I could, you know," Sarah joked. "But you really need to spend some time with Martha today. She really misses you when you aren't around." Putting her index finger on her lower lip she asked, "What's for breakfast?"

"Pancakes. I have the batter brewing in the refrigerator. After I get dressed, I'll start cooking."

Sarah lunged forward at him, wrapping her arms around him tightly. "Thanks for last night," she said as she pressed her face against his chest. "It was wonderful." She then looked up at him and asked, "Our long-term relationship is going to continue, isn't it?"

He looked down at her and replied, "I think our relationship is pointing in the right direction." Sarah noticed Dayton was starting to become aroused. She laughed. "I get the point."

Dayton placed the fry pan on the stove then added more milk to the mixture. "So is that the secret of great pancakes?" Sarah asked.

"Mix it up, let it congeal in the fridge for about fifteen minutes, then add more milk and stir. Learned it from my dad," Dayton proudly responded.

"There is some bacon in the fridge if you want to cook it?"

Dayton closed his eyes as he remembered his last meal with his father. "That's ok. Just pancakes this morning----if you don't mind."

The two started eating their pancakes. Sarah stated that they were the best she ever had, but commented that Dayton should use less butter on them because it was bad for his heart. Dayton simply smirked and placed another pat in between the steaming cakes. Everyone in his family loved butter, he told her, and no one has ever had a cholesterol problem. "We're not even married and she's watching what I eat," Dayton thought to himself.

"I hope I didn't freak you out last night?" he asked.

"About what?"

"You know---the whole Kennedy Assassination, 911, measurement of DC and the sacrificial stuff at the top of the truncated pyramid thing," Dayton stated uncomfortably.

"Not at all. We should research this more thoroughly and sell it to the History Channel. People would find it fascinating."

After breakfast, Sarah secured her gun and badge to her waist. "So you bringing me to work?" she asked. He looked outside the window; remembering she had brought him back to her place in his Jeep. In his silliest Southern drawl, he replied, "Yes Miss Daisy, I'd be happy to drive you anywhere you want today." The two laughed.

Dayton pulled into the parking lot at police headquarters right next to Mark's truck. Mark was standing there looking at his watch and waiting for his partner Sarah so they could go on duty. Sarah leaned over and gave Dayton a kiss and Mark promptly saluted. She quickly exited the vehicle and ran into headquarters to punch in.

"Well," Mark smiled, "You two look like an old married couple."

"Ha. Ha. Very funny," Dayton replied. "She's already watching my cholesterol."

"No, I'm serious. She is a good fit for you." Mark raised his eyebrows up and down a few times. "Speaking of fit, how'd you do last night?"

"Mark. She made me dinner and we spent time researching my father's work."

Mark looked as Dayton skeptically. "Buddy, I think you did a lot more than that. More like bio research," Mark said, elbowing Dayton thought the Jeep window. "Don't play stupid with me pal. You have that guy got laid look. It's all over your face."

"That apparent huh?" Dayton replied.

"Uh yah. And you might want to think of something else before you go see your grandmother." He looked in the back seat. "Oooooh, what is this?" Mark withdrew his pocket knife and reached over to unlock Dayton's rear door. He picked up the cake pan and cut himself a piece.

"Hey. Just leave some for my grandmother," Dayton said.

"No problemo," Mark responded while chewing cake. "Hey, you and your wife got time this week to do a double? Leslie wants a repeat of dinner and pool."

"I think we can do that. I actually got a week before my last run of signings. The flight leaves Saturday for L.A.----then on to Tucson for a few days and then I finish in Dallas."

"Thursday night then. Thursday, Sarah and I got day shift, so we'll plan on dinner at 6PM, then pool afterwards." Mark began to walk away as Sarah exited headquarters. "Bring some money, Leslie's taking bets.----Oh, and I'll have Sarah home before midnight. You two really are picture perfect." Mark said as he pretended to take Dayton's photo. "Say hi to Martha for me too."

Dayton looked in his rear view mirror so he could look at his face. "Guy got laid look, huh?" he thought to himself. He glanced over at Mark and Sarah as they got into their official unmarked Ford. "Picture perfect.----- Pictures----Oh God, I almost forgot dad's photos were being scanned at the photo processor."

He entered the photo processing retailer with high anticipation. "My father's last photos. I hope they came out," he thought to himself. Dayton handed the clerk his slip and she returned with the negatives sleeved and a CD of the scans.

"These came out well, Mr. McCormick. I remember you saying the film hadn't been processed and that the camera had sat for years. There was no light leakage. Whoever had it, stored it well. We don't get a lot of that type of Kodak film anymore----or for that matter, film."

He thanked the clerk and paid for the processing. As Dayton walked to the car, he slipped out the thumbnail sheet and began studying the images. They were quite good, not only for their age, but the camera and technique used by his father had produced pictures of excellent quality. He could make out things easily, even though the images were small. He put the sheet back in with the CD and put them both with the negatives on the front seat. "I can't wait to show these to grandma," he thought.

As he drove down the road to his grandmother's, he noticed her out on her walk. He slowed the Jeep and pulled up alongside her. "Hey, want a ride?"

Her eyes lit up. "Dayton, you're home!" He opened the passenger door and removed the negatives and CD from the seat. She got in and gave him a big hug and kiss. "I missed you so much." Then she looked in the back seat and noticed the cake. "Well. I am glad you at least saved me some of that," she said laughing. "Are you ok?"

"Fine gram, why?"

"You just have a different look on your face today. I haven't seen it in quite a while. Kind of, happy-looking. Can't quite put my finger on it?"

"Oh God! Mark was right. I do have that guy got laid look on my face," Dayton thought.

"And how is Sarah? She has been very good to me you know. She has visited quite often. I like her very much."

"She does know," Dayton thought. "She is just being polite about it." Then he replied, "I like her a lot gram."

"Do you think you'll get married to her?" Martha asked.

Dayton nearly choked on his spit. After regaining his composure he replied, "Gram, I do like her very much. Don't you think I should date her a little longer before I pop any big questions?"

In a voice only a mother could appreciate, Martha replied, "Well, you are not getting any younger. You are thirty-three and single. A man your age should be starting a family." Then she smiled and pursed her lips together and made the statement, "And I want to be a great grandmother while I am still young enough to enjoy it."

Dayton slapped his forehead with his hand. "Sarah watches what I eat and grandma wants to marry me off. Geeze!" he thought. Dayton pulled into the driveway and shut off the Cherokee. "What if she says no?"

"You'll never know unless you ask," she replied.

"Before you have me married to Sarah and having five children, there is something I want to show you," Dayton said, holding up the CD. "These are photos from the day before dad died. They are the ones he took when we went to Liberty Island in 1987."

"Really? Where did you get them Dayton?"

"I visited a friend of his up in Massachusetts on my way to the Boston book signing. He gave me dad's old camera. And there was still this film in it. So I had the film processed, scanned and put onto this CD."

"Technology is in one of man's triumphs, Dayton. I'd love to see them."

The two entered the house. Dayton put his suitcase and camera bag in the study after removing the dirty laundry and bringing it to the wash area. He booted up his laptop and waited until it was finished. Then, he inserted the CD in the drive and copied it onto the computer's desktop for easy access. Dayton also made a back up CD, which he placed into the safe.

"Hey Gram. Come take a look."

Martha came into the study and pulled up a chair, and Dayton started going through the pictures. A tear dropped down her cheek as she saw Dayton as an eleven-year-old boy having the time of his life with her son Mickey, who was dead the following day. "He was so full of life, your father was. Mickey, ever since he was in high school carried a damn camera around everywhere he went." She noticed Dayton's camera bag next to the safe. "Like father, like son," she said. "But Mickey was far more annoying with it than you are. He always used to get in my face with it. He kept telling me to act like a model and work with the camera. I think if he didn't go in the army, he would have gone to work for Playboy Magazine." She dried her tears and began to laugh as she got up from her chair. "I am going downstairs to make lunch. Why don't you join me in a few minutes?"

Dayton studied the photos. He noticed his father got Lady Liberty from every angle he could, almost like a police photographer would. Then came the photo of him looking away from the camera, followed by one of him looking toward his father. Something caught his eye. "Wait a second," he whispered. The reflection from the sunglasses had made him look away. "What is that?" As he studied the screen, he zoomed in on the man wearing the mirror shades and noticed a large red scar, on his smiling face.

"Holy Shit!" Dayton thought, as he continued zooming tighter on the face. He remembered Peter's comment about a scar so large only a mother could love it. "Hutchinson. Hutchinson was on Liberty Island with me and my father. He must have been following us."

Dayton looked at the schedule he had received from the faculty secretary at Georgetown, with Mussen's class schedule. He then printed a normal copy of the photo, followed by one of an enlarged section of Hutchinson's face on his printer.

"Gram. Is there anything you need done around the house tomorrow?"

"Well, there is always something to do. Why do you ask?" she replied.

"I think I have to run up to Washington tomorrow. I hope you don't mind." Dayton stared off at the clock. "There is someone I have to see." He stared at the photo with the enlarged section as he walked up stairs to the study, then whispered, "I have to confirm this is him."

After the news, Dayton tucked his grandmother in to bed. "Don't be up too late dear," she said, before turning her head on her pillow.

"I won't be. Good night," replied Dayton. He walked into the study, where he had laid everything out on the desk. He looked at the dollar bill's reverse side. "Annuit Coeptis," he muttered. He looked over at his new purchase: <u>The Aeneid</u>. "That quote is from Virgil. It was a poem to the god Jupiter." Dayton suddenly remembered what his grandmother said earlier about technology. "A Triumph." He scrolled through some online Roman history. "A triumph is what someone erected after a foreign war. Caesar, after a loss in battle stated that Jupiter had not favored him." He inserted the CD of the photos he had taken in Baltimore and stopped at the Washington Monument in that city. "That's a triumph," he whispered, "but for Washington." The words and symbolism of all this began to run through his mind. He glanced over at the Aztec sacrifice photo, with the man being killed at the top of the truncated pyramid. "Annuit Coeptis----He favors our undertaking. But what? Jupiter favors what?" On a hunch, he went to his solar system simulator on the World Wide Web; keeping in mind the measurements and dates he discussed last night with Sarah. "Both the Kennedy Assassination and September 11th were ceremonies----at the top of truncated pyramids---- like they are in Washington D.C." Dayton typed in the date and time for the Kennedy Assassination. "November 22, 1963, at 18:30 UTC." What he saw, astounded him. He traced the lines from planet to planet. "Jupiter was in Pisces, above the top of a truncated pyramid formed by the other planets." He did the same in the simulator for 911. "September 11th, 2001, at 13:47 UTC." Dayton again traced the lines from planet to planet. Jupiter was again located above the top of a truncated pyramid. This time, it was in the center of the Gemini Constellation.

Dayton took a piece of paper and sketched out the planetary alignments. "Jupiter, on high. Jupiter above! I don't believe what I am seeing," he muttered to himself. "They are related in some way."

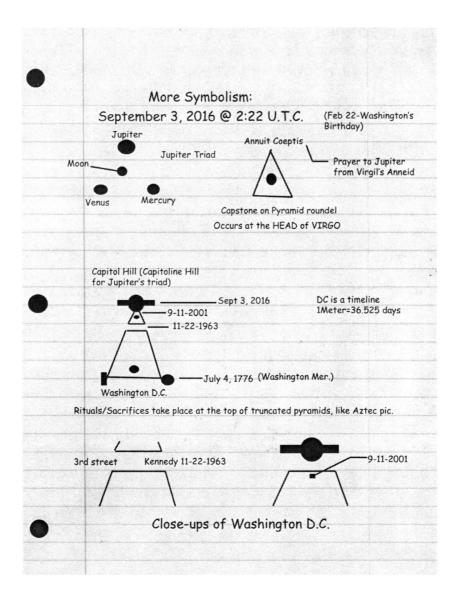

Chapter 14
Traitor?

Dayton walked briskly across Copley Lawn. He had gotten stuck in heavy traffic and feared that Mussen would not be at his bench feeding the pigeons. But as he approached, he caught a glimpse of the hat and tweed jacket through the trees, which was the signature attire of choice for a certain theology professor.

"Professor Mussen."

His hat bent upwards, showing his bushy eyebrows, as his hands continued feeding the hungry city doves. "Young McCormick. What a pleasure to see you. Beautiful day, isn't it?"

"Yes it is." Dayton said. He let out a sigh. "I was hoping to apologize to you----and ask you a few questions."

"Apologize?" He looked at him inquisitively. "What for?"

Dayton responded, "Last time I saw you, you asked if I had found Peter Devine." Dayton looked at the ground. "I lied and told you no."

Mussen lifted his left eyebrow. "Go on."

"I did find him----and he gave me some things that Hartman had sent him from my father." Dayton looked down again, reached into his pocket, pulled out a small slip of paper and then handed it to Mussen."

"Traitor? Interesting." Mussen frowned.

"I thought it was you, and that is why I didn't tell you the truth."

Mussen smiled. "How do you know I'm not?"

"Well, the day before my father was killed, he took me to Liberty Island." Dayton reached in his pocket again; pulling out the photograph of him looking away

237

from the camera. He handed it to Mussen and pointed to the man in the mirrored sunglasses. "Do you recognize this man?"

Mussen squinted. "I am sorry young McCormick, but my old eyes aren't what they used to be."

"That's okay. I blew up the man's face," Dayton replied, handing him the other photo.

"Well, the hair and scar are the same. So is the smile. That's Henry." Mussen handed both photos back to Dayton. "He hated when I called him that. He much preferred the nickname Hutch. Sounded more manly."

"He must have been following my father. And the only reason I can think of, is that he was the traitor and my father knew it."

Mussen's face took on a serious look. "Young McCormick. Let me tell you a story. But as I always say----" Mussen took a second to look around, "that a man must choose his words carefully."

"Okay."

"Your father was a good and honorable man. And when something didn't sit right, he'd---try to make it right. During war, there are people on all sides of a conflict that see it as a means to make a handsome profit." Mussen let out a small belly laugh. "Well, if you look at the highest levels, what you will find is that there is a certain family relationship. Sometimes it's very clear. Other times, well, they can all trace back their lineage to a common ancestor. Both Bush, and Gore, for example, can trace their ancestry back to Charlemagne."

"Continue," Dayton prodded.

"There was a company which specialized in the transport of---items of use."

"Like Bax---"

Mussen immediately interrupted, holding his finger to Dayton's mouth. "Yes. And come to find out, Henry's mother had a sister who married the half owner of a certain distribution firm. What else was in the possession of Mr. Devine?"

"Negatives of---other things. And a few----catalog sheets." Dayton used his words carefully, for Mussen didn't raise a finger.

He looked up at Dayton with his bushy eyebrows and sad eyes. "Not enough," he said. "Not yet. You know----doing right, isn't always right. And doing wrong, isn't always wrong. But there are some bills which need to be paid." Mussen paused to clear his throat. "I want you to trust me, young McCormick. And anything else of import in this manner, I hope you will share it. I know you want closure, but the process through normal channels will never happen." Mussen coughed. "And I don't want the son to walk in his father's footsteps," he said as he raised his eyebrows. "Your father used to visit me after he moved back to Richmond. We had great discussions and shared similar interests. In that regard, it is ok for history to repeat itself. But out in the open, with all this surrounding beauty, the poetry of the man with well-chosen words----."

"Understood," Dayton replied.

Mussen looked up. "Did I ever tell you about my brother, Jacob?"

"You mentioning he was killed in Vietnam."

"Hmm," Mussen frowned. "My brother was a tunnel rat." Dayton looked at him curiously and Mussen nodded. "We Mussen's aren't very big people. A tunnel rat was a soldier who crawled into tunnels looking for the Vietcong----or munitions. They used to store all their arms in those damn tunnels. They even lived in them."

"Go on."

"One day, my brother went into a tunnel on the command of his CO. He never emerged. Missing-In-Action."

"I'm sorry, Professor."

Mussen stood up and looked at his watch. "I have to go teach now. Maybe I'll make my way down to Richmond, when my duty of molding young minds subsides."

"I hope to see you again soon Professor," Dayton said with an outstretched hand. Mussen took it and pulled himself off the bench.

"Likewise young McCormick. Likewise." He smiled and waved goodbye.

Mussen started walking over to the lecture hall. Dayton watched him limp, as the professor labored his way slowly across the lawn and to the entrance. Dayton turned and slowly walked back to his Cherokee to drive back to Richmond. He knew Mussen was still holding back, and he wasn't sure he could totally trust him. But he wasn't the traitor his father mentioned on the slip of paper he got from Peter.

Mussen continued up the stairs to his classroom on the second floor. As he entered the room, he addressed his students. "I am very sorry. Something has come up today in my personal life that I must take care off. Class will resume on Thursday afternoon."

Mussen supported himself on the desk in the front of the classroom. After the last student left, he walked over to the door and locked it shut. He pulled out his wallet, put it on the desk and sat down. He placed his hat on the corner of the lectern top and opened his wallet. A tear started to run down his face as he pulled an old wrinkled photograph from a flexible plastic sheath.

As he stared into the eyes of a young marine in uniform, more tears began to form. Mussen blinked, then continued to gaze upon the marine's face.

"My dear, Jacob. It has been thirty-eight years since I last saw your face. May you look out for a young man down below and keep him safe. For if he is successful----there will be justice."

வு

Martha looked up from her game of solitaire as Dayton entered the house. "I didn't expect you home so soon. I just put the meatloaf in the oven."

Dayton walked over to her and put his hand on her shoulder. "It was just a quick trip, and I got on the highway before the exodus of government employees." He looked at the cards. "I never understood why you liked solitaire so much."

"It is a great way to pass the time," she said. "Besides, you never know if you are going to win or lose. Fifty-two cards in random order. Most of the time you lose, but on occasion, things line up just right."

Dayton smirked. "Have you given any thought about Thanksgiving?"

"Well, there is me and you, and Mark usually comes over."

"What about Sarah?" Dayton asked.

Martha looked up at Dayton and smiled. "I think she'll come if you ask."

"Can Mark bring a date too?"

"Dayton," Martha responded, "You can ask anyone you want. You know your friends are always welcome in our home."

Dayton looked over at the folder on the corner of the table. It was from Triple E Publishing. "Who dropped that off?"

"About an hour after you left, a strange red-headed young man came over." Martha made a funny face. "I think he is one of those attention deficit people."

"Steve?"

"Yes, that was his name. He said the plane tickets for the last batch of signings were in it. Strange boy. He wanted to use the bathroom. When he started to go upstairs, I told him the upstairs bathroom was broken, and that he would have to use the one down here."

"Why?"

"I figured that with all the work you have been doing in the study, it would be best if he didn't go up there. People tend to snoop around you know. And besides----I was by myself. These days, you can't be too careful."

Dayton gave her a kiss on the forehead. "I understand grandma. You did the right thing," Dayton replied. "I don't know what to think of him, other than he is always trying to make sure I am on time for the book signings. He's like a nanny." Dayton wiggled his nose. "I am going to go upstairs."

As he walked toward the stairs he asked, "Would you mind if I go out with Sarah later?"

"Of course not. You don't need my permission."

"Good. I'll give her a call. I was going to go down to Bev's for some ice cream."

Martha gave Dayton a sad puppy dog look and stuck out her bottom lip.

"I'll bring you home a sundae with hot fudge," he said with a touch of guilt in his voice. Martha turned around to resume her game of solitaire as Dayton dialed Sarah on his cell phone. "I can't believe that face still works on me," Dayton whispered.

"Always will," Martha said as Dayton walked upstairs.

Dayton looked at all the evidence sprawled across the desk in the study. "Dad. I'll find your killer and figure out all this stuff. I just need a little more time to kick back and put some balance in my life," Dayton whispered to himself. He looked over at the aerial of Washington D.C. "Hmm, a timeline."

✍

"Had a long day?" Dayton asked Sarah, who was seated in the booth across from him.

"Yes, but if I wasn't called in early on a car-jacking, I'd still be on duty. Bev's is only open until 9:30PM."

Dayton clanked his spoon against the side of the metal dish while scooping up some ice cream. "I'd like to apologize to you, Sarah."

Confused, she replied, "What for?"

"Well," Dayton said, "ever since we met, it seems everything has been all about me. My family. My book. The signings. The research. You have always been there to help, even before we started our long-term relationship." Dayton smiled. "What about you? Tell me about Sarah Geare?"

"Oh. There's not much to talk about," she said, blowing off the inquiry.

"No, I mean it. What about you?"

"Dayton. I am a thirty-two year old cop who lives in her apartment with her cat and has a broken car in the repair shop."

He stared at her, wanting to know more. "What about hobbies--- or family?"

Sarah began to look uncomfortable. "I like just about everything." She paused. "I find your research fascinating." She looked down. "I like this sundae," she said, holding out her spoon and sticking it in his mouth.

"I'm not trying to pry. I just want to know you better."

Sarah looked uncomfortable. "Did Martha talk to you about anything?"

"About what?" Dayton responded, looking confused.

"I talked to her while you were gone. Ok?"

"Ok," he responded.

"I don't have a family anymore."

"Did you eat them?" Dayton jabbed.

"No. They disowned me after I arrested my uncle for beating up his wife. I walked away from my family, Dayton. I couldn't take all the hypocrisy. My uncle was a minister who preached peace, love and tolerance." She paused. "All the things he wasn't."

"Ok."

"I was afraid to tell you because I really like you a lot." She reached for a napkin and wiped off the small drip of chocolate sauce on his chin. "I didn't want you to run from me, because I have a dis-functional family."

Dayton reached his hand across the table to hold hers. He looked at her and said, "I am Dayton George McCormick. My father was killed when I was eleven. I never knew my mother. I was raised by my grandparents. I am a detective and author and I live in my grandmother's house. How dysfunctional is that?" He paused. "And you know what? You are really pretty when you are trying to hide something from me."

Sarah blushed and held his hands tight. Dayton leaned forward.

"Your family----screw them." Dayton paused. "So, would you like to come over to my grandmother's house for Thanksgiving?"

"I was hoping you would ask."

"You can bring Sausha too."

Sarah burst out laughing. "Do you know what a hungry cat does when it smells turkey?"

"No, but I'll find out," he smiled. "Mark usually comes too. His parents are divorced. His mother lives in Florida, and his father----well, we never know where he is. It'll be nice. Maybe he'll bring Leslie and she can analyze the chemical make-up of the gravy." Sarah couldn't stop laughing thinking about Leslie in a lab coat sitting across from her at the table, taking a sample and placing it in a Petri dish.

"Remind me before I bring you home to get a sundae for my grandmother. She gave me the sad face when she realized where we were going." Dayton smiled. "And if Sausha behaves, you can bring her over at Christmas too."

Sarah held his hands and stared into his eyes; getting lost for a brief moment in time. "This guy is serious," she thought to herself. "So why hasn't a nice girl scooped you up sooner, Dayton?"

He looked her square in the eye and smiled. "Because I am dis-functional." He crossed his eyes at her. They both laughed. "Hey, if you have time before we do a double date with Mark and Leslie, why don't you come over and practice your pool skills. There is a table in the basement, and if we're going to play couples, I plan on winning."

"I'll come over in the morning," she replied.

❧

Dayton placed the sundae into the freezer then crept up the stairs into the study. His grandmother was asleep in her bedroom and he didn't want to wake her up. He stared at the table full of evidence. Then he remembered the sheet Peter tucked into his black notebook, and he retrieved it from the suitcase. He pulled it out and began to read it.

1 solar procession = 25,920 years

1/5 of procession is 5,184 years--True Mayan Sun period.

1/12th is 2,160--Spring Equinox, change of sign.

400 (396) year cycle Jupiter-Saturn 20 conjuncts, earth Venus sun- 8 years, 5 times, 584 day periods, 50 conjuncts.

Alignments and squares between outer and inner planets cause sharp weather-solar flare/cme. Dependent on which planets, how many, how tight alignment, and constellation origination. Pluto-Venus or Neptune with Venus or Mercury potent. Also when outer planets oppose or square sun. Study Carrington event of 1859 and other solar storms. As the moon is to the Earth, the planets are to the sun. Make a list of the major solar outbreaks, earthquakes and storms on earth and look for alignments, oppositions and squares.

When outer 5 planets form pentagon--watch out. Look for solar max to start late in 2010, but major issues early 2013, especially January to March. Then really bad in August. Should last until late 2015. December 21, 2015 could be what people expect in 2012. Communications and power grids will be affected. 2017?

Jupiter-Neptune bring cooler and wetter--cold winter 2009/2010

365x396/260=555+ 47x11.83=555+ Mayan.

Dayton put the paper down on the desk and shook his head. "I wish I wasn't so drunk that night," he thought to himself. He went on to Google Earth and began to re-measure Washington DC. He found that from a statue in Lincoln Park, to the Lincoln Memorial was 5.184 kilometers. "Amazing. Mayan Sun period, which is one fifth of the Zodiac procession. D.C. is filled with zodiacs."

He took the Capitol Dome as the starting point for another measurement. "3.56 to 3.58 kilometers to 23rd Street. 3,600 years?" He switched from metric measurement to standard measurement. "Or is it 2.22 miles----time----and George Washington's birthday---February 22nd." Then he measured from the Lincoln Memorial to the center of the Pentagon. "1.3 miles. Added to 2.22 and we get 3.52 miles total. Or does it mean three and a half years?" Dayton considered that perhaps Washington D.C. contained a multi-timeline, where both the metric and standard measurements were important, but for different scales of time. "Metric is long and medium term. Standard, could be a measurement for short term."

He looked at Arlington on the map. "That would put the center of the Pentagon at around late 2012 to March of 2013, if the center of the Capitol Dome is September of 2016. It is just like Peter said." He went to the solar system simulator on the web and typed in January 2, 2013. "The outer planets Jupiter, Saturn, Uranus, Neptune and Pluto form a pentagon around the sun if you draw lines between them. I'll be damned. The symbolism in the city coincides perfectly with the arrangement of the planets in the heavens."

In all his excitement, he lost track of time and realized it was well after 2AM. "I better get some sleep. Sarah's coming over in the morning," he said to himself. He looked over at his notes and thought about the significance of what he was finding. "Incredible."

The next morning, Dayton awoke and had breakfast with his grandmother. After breakfast, he got his camera out of his bag and placed it atop a tripod in front of the house. It was another beautiful warm day, and much milder than normal for early November, even for Virginia. Mark drove up in his truck with Sarah in the passenger seat. As Mark rolled down the window, he said, "What's this I hear that pool tonight is couple on couple----and not men against ladies?"

"You heard right," Dayton replied with a smile.

"Traitor."

"Ah come on, Mark. Besides you'll have Leslie the pool shark on your side."

"That's true, so you better plan on losing." He winked at Sarah. "What if we make a friendly bet and the losers pay?"

"Better plan on paying then," Dayton replied.

Sarah sighed, "I'm caught between testosterone." She got out of the truck and thanked Mark for the ride. "What are you doing with the camera in the front yard, Dayton?"

Dayton looked at it and then back at Sarah. "Well, it is a beautiful day and I thought it would be an ideal time to take some photos."

"Of what? The trees?" Sarah asked.

"No. Us." He took Sarah by the hand and brought her over next to the tree. He looked through the viewfinder and zoomed out enough so that he could fit in next to her and fill the frame. He focused and set the self timer for ten seconds, then ran over next to her and put his arm around her. "In about five seconds, smile." The camera displayed a red blinking light; indicating the timer was about to expire and take the photo. Click. Dayton ran back to the camera and looked in the LCD screen. "Perfect," he said. "That's nice. Image 3877." He broke down the camera and tripod, then walked with Sarah back toward the house. He brought the equipment upstairs and downloaded the image into his computer.

Looking at Sarah, Dayton asked, "So what do you think?"

"I wish I knew you were doing this today. I didn't put any make-up on."

"You look great without it," Dayton replied. He placed a piece of photo paper into the printer, then printed out two copies: his and hers. "When I'm on my signing this week, I'll at least have a photo of you to look it."

Sarah was flattered. "Is this one for me?"

"Yes, sure is. Give you something to complain about," Dayton said before he stuck out his tongue. Sarah elbowed him in the chest and shook her head. "Now, let's go down to the basement and play some pool."

The basement was well lit with low ceilings. Years earlier, Dayton's grandfather George had installed a drop ceiling, complete with fluorescent lighting. Around the area of the pool table, flags from various countries and time periods hung on the wall.

"Who did all this?" Sarah asked.

"It was my dad," Dayton responded, pointing to the various flags. "He was a history buff and loved flags for some reason." The first flag was the "don't tread on me" flag from the revolution, along with various adaptations of Old Glory, up to present day. His father had also collected flags from Nazi Germany, Imperial Japan, Great Britain, France, Mexico and Canada.

Dayton lifted two cue sticks from off the wall and handed one to Sarah. "If we're going to beat them, we'd better practice." He racked the balls in the pyramid holder and began staring at them. The black eight ball looked like an eye, sitting on a background of green felt. Sarah caught him staring off.

"Triangle with the eye, huh?"

Dayton immediately came to after hearing her comment. "I'm sorry."

"Don't be," Sarah replied. "I am starting to know how you think." She put down her cue stick. "Fifteen balls." She pulled out a dollar from her pocketbook, turning it to the obverse side. "Fifteen. Three rows of five in a triangle. 555, in feet, like the Washington Monument."

Dayton smiled. "And a background of green. Just like the Statue of Liberty.

Sarah walked over to him, giving him a kiss on the cheek. "You're not dysfunctional. You're just thinking too much."

He smiled at her and motioned her to break. The clanking of the breaking billiard balls snapped Dayton totally away from thinking about his research. He noticed on Sarah's second shot, after breaking and sinking a low ball, that she was standing too high to accurately place her next shot on the three-ball. He came behind her and pressed against her shoulder. "You're too high," he said. "You need to get a little closer to the table." Then he put his arm around her, showing her proper form and release of the stroke. "It is all in the rhythm and getting close to the table." He breathed warm air on her face, then kissed her gently on the neck.

"Hey, I don't think that rhythm is going to win us the game tonight," she said as she dipped her shoulder. Sarah pressed her lips against his and inserted her tongue in Dayton's mouth. She pushed her body up against his and pinned him to the table. Her eyes closed as she kissed him passionately. When the kiss ended, she slowly withdrew. "If we're going to win tonight, I think we'd better get back to playing pool. Tell you what. Every time either one of us makes a shot, the other gives a kiss tonight."

"I'm game," Dayton smiled. The two continued practicing for hours while trading compliments and kisses. "I think we got a good chance of winning tonight," Dayton said happily.

"We're just going to have to psyche Leslie out," Sarah responded.

$\wp$

"Okay, here's the tiebreaker," Mark said. "Whoever loses this one, pays the bill." Leslie winked at Mark, trying to build up his confidence for a win. Mark broke without sinking a single ball and Dayton capitalized putting in three. Sarah came over to him and kissed him three times.

Leslie sent three high balls into the corner pockets. Mark walked up to her and gave her three kisses. "Give me a few more of those, and maybe I'll sink them all," she said to Mark. On her forth shot, she missed.

"I guess the kisses only work for us," Dayton said sarcastically. Sarah bent down low to the table and placed two more low balls in the pockets, and she was dutifully rewarded by Dayton.

Mark took a swig of his beer and walked over to Leslie. "Oh yeah," he said. Then he bent Leslie over and gave her a big kiss. He then lined up his shot and missed. He looked over at Dayton, "It ain't over yet."

Dayton took two shots and sank them both. But he missed the eight ball. Leslie held Mark off from kissing her. She meant business. Nine. Eleven. Fifteen. Thirteen. Only the eight ball was left against the bumper. She sized up the shot. With a gentle stroke she sent the eight ball rolling toward the corner pocket. But it stopped just shy of going in. "Shit!" she exclaimed.

Sarah got low to the table. She pointed the cue toward the bottom of the ball and shot. The cue ball hit the eight into the pocket and backed up to mid-table. "Nice shot," said Leslie.

"You win this time----bud----but when you're done with your book tour, I want a rematch," Mark said, pointing his finger at both Dayton and Sarah.

"Tell you what," replied Dayton. "You two come over for Thanksgiving and we'll do a re-match in my grandmother's basement. Loser does dishes."

Mark steamed, "That's right. You got a pool table in your house. That's why Sarah went over yesterday morning. You guys practiced all day yesterday. Didn't you?"

Sarah looked down and pretended to ignore the charge while Dayton took the cash from Mark's hand to pay the bill.

"Is Thanksgiving at the McCormick's ok Leslie?" Mark asked.

"I was going to go to my brother's, but I think I'd have more fun with you guys. Okay."

"Then it is settled. Thanksgiving at the McCormick's," Dayton said. He turned to Sarah and changed the subject. "How's your car?"

"The mechanic said the transmission is dead," she replied. "He said it would cost more to fix it than clean up Hiroshima after the A-Bomb"

"All right. Give me a minute. I have to hit the men's room." Dayton walked into the bathroom and unzipped his jeans in front of the wall mounted urinal and relieved himself. He shook his head. "Hiroshima." He washed his hands and returned to Mark and Leslie and gave his Jeep keys to Sarah. "I have to be at the airport at 7AM. If you'll take me, you can have the Jeep while I'm gone." He put his arms around her and said, "When I get back, we can go car shopping."

"Does this mean I'm driving you home tonight?"

Dayton nodded his head in acknowledgement; realizing he had drunk a few too many beers and it would be safer for her to drive.

Sarah brought Dayton home and kissed him goodnight by the front door of Martha's house. As she drove away in his Jeep, Dayton looked up into the sky and whispered, "God------Thanks."

Dayton walked happily into the house. "Did you have a good time, dear?"

He smiled. "Grandma, I had a great time. My only regret is I have to leave tomorrow morning."

Martha got up from the couch and walked upstairs to bed. Dayton walked into the study and sat on the chair. "Hiroshima," he said to himself. He put his feelings for Sarah aside as he began to remember more of what Peter had told him. "Trinity." He surfed the net and read up on both the Hiroshima and Nagasaki bombings. "The Enola Gay was escorted by two other B-29's. A trinity of bombers," he laughed. A chill went down his spine when he read about the Enola Gay's numbering. Prior to August 1, 1945, it was twelve. "Jupiter's orbit in years." Then he read her assigned number after August 1st. "82, just like adding flight 77 to the Pentagon. Kennedy 1963. 19+63 equals 82." On a hunch, Dayton wrote down in his notebook .82 miles and converted it to feet. "Pretty close to 4,333 feet. Jupiter goes around the sun once in 4,333 days."

He continued his research, this time about Nagasaki and the plane called Bockscar. "Number 77," he whispered. "Kennedy was supposed to drive up Route 77 to go to the World Trade Mart." He looked at a photo of the tail section of the Bockscar. "N in a triangle." He paused. "N is the fourteenth letter. Thirteen levels and one for the top-----fourteen----like the thirteen step truncated pyramid with the triangle above it on the back of the one dollar bill." He put his hands over his face. "Synchronicity," he said. He looked up to finish reading the article "And look----the Bockscar is on display at the Air Force Museum----In Dayton, Ohio." He shook his head. "Manhattan Project, Kennedy, and 911. Synchronicity." He shut off the computer and the light in the study. "Is all of this a coincidence? Or is there something more to this?" he asked himself as he walked to his bedroom. "This can't be a conspiracy. It is way too complicated."

He laid down on his bed and placed his head on his pillow. As he looked out in the darkness before falling asleep, he whispered, "Little boy and Fat man. Hmm? Dropped on the Land of the Rising Sun. There is something to all this. It must be symbolic."

Chapter 15
Truth

His red-headed driver was clearly upset. Dayton had deliberately told him to take the wrong turn, in order to fulfill his own agenda.

"Steve----All I am asking for is five lousy minutes. Five!" Dayton stated emphatically.

"But we're going to be late to the Westside Pavilion Mall. We're supposed to have a late lunch at 2:30 at the Westside tavern and be meeting with the B&N reps," Steve argued as he zipped through traffic.

"Look----I didn't realize you guys booked me into a double signing. I thought I'd have a few hours to take some photos," Dayton whined.

"This is LA. Everything's bigger. Trust me----you'll have three days in Tucson and only one signing to go to after that. Can't you take your photos then?"

"I only got to photograph the fountain in Chicago and the Mural and the Airport in Denver. This is LA. City Hall guy! What self respecting cop and photographer wouldn't at least want to get City Hall? Didn't you ever watch <u>Dragnet</u> or <u>Adam 12</u>?" Dayton looked over at Steve. From the blank look on his face, he clearly didn't even know what <u>Dragnet</u> was. "You know----Joe Friday----just give me the facts Ma'am." Then Dayton realized even most thirty-three year-olds never watched those TV shows. He had forgotten that most people his age didn't grow up watching old programs on cable TV with their grandparents. "<u>Star Trek</u>?"

"I just saw that. Loved the Romulans." Steve broke down. "How far is the mall from City Hall?" Steve said begrudgingly, rolling his eyes. "I hope I don't get in trouble for this. But I owe you one."

"Look. We're almost there," Dayton said pointing up. "Just drop me off right in front and I'll take my photos while you drive around the block once. Come pick me up. Then we're on our way. According to the GPS, it is less than twenty minutes to West Pico from here. And it is only two o-clock," Dayton replied excitedly.

Steve pulled over across the street from LA City Hall and Dayton leaped out of the car with his camera bag. He put the wide-angle lens on the 20D and began to shoot the iconic building, which was emblazoned on the badge. He walked briskly to get a few different angles. Dayton placed his digital camera back in the bag and removed his father's Canonet G3. A few days earlier, he had bought a roll of film for this trip because he wanted to try it out, after painstakingly replacing the camera light seals, on his grandmother's kitchen table. The cut on his finger reminded him to be more careful with an Exacto knife. The camera required a non-available mercury battery, and because he couldn't locate a replacement in time, he set the exposures manually, based on the previous settings he remembered from his digital camera exposures. He also tried the sunny 16 rule and set the camera to F16 at 100 ISO. On the fifth shot, he noticed Steve pulling into the parking lot to pick him up, so he quickly brought the split images together and pressed the shutter. He forwarded the film once more and aimed it at Steve. He brought the twin images of his red-head together then clicked.

"Come on Dayton. We have to go!" Steve yelled. Dayton placed his father's camera into his camera bag and opened the door of the rental car.

"Thanks guy. You don't know how much that meant to me," Dayton said while looking at Steve.

Steve looked back at Dayton, before pulling out of the parking lot. "I have never seen a camera like that before. What is it?"

He opened the bag and showed it to Steve. "Oh, this old thing. I found it----at my grandmother's house. It was my father's old Canonet 35mm rangefinder."

"Looks almost new," Steve replied.

"My dad took good care of his stuff. And he loved taking photos. Looks like that passion passed down to me. I replaced the seals this past week," showing Steve the cut on his finger, "because after I opened it, most of the old sealing material gunked up the camera door. I actually saved an old roll he still had in it, and got it processed. They were from a trip to the Statue of Liberty when I was a kid." Dayton smiled. "I was a lot younger then."

A curious look came over Steve's face. "Your dad was a photographer?" His face became devoid of emotion. "I hate most photos of me. Every time I see one of myself, my red hair looks bright and my----fair complexion turns white. You can also see the veins in my forehead. I look terrible in photos."

Dayton shook his head. "Digital can be cruel when improperly exposed. Try taking photos of dead people."

"I can only imagine," Steve smiled as his face began to show emotion again. "How far are we away on the GPS?"

"According to the route, we should see the mall once you take your next left." Dayton opened his bag. "Did I take the lens cap off?" He lifted up the Canonet and saw that it had its lens cap missing. He felt his pockets and located the missing cap. "You have to be careful with rangefinders. Unlike an SLR, you don't see through the lens. So if you leave the cap on----no picture." Steve nodded his head in acknowledgement. Then, Dayton lifted the un-zipped cover on the bag and placed the Canonet carefully inside, so it wouldn't crease another bit of photographic importance. Dayton smiled when he looked at the photo of himself and Sarah.

᠀

Dayton nodded at Steve. "I'd like to thank everyone for coming, and I would also like to thank the good folks at Barnes and Noble for hosting this event." He looked over at the crowd, and it was just as large as the one at the late afternoon signing. It was now clear to Dayton why the publisher wanted a double header in L.A.

"My name is Dayton McCormick. I have always had an interest in conspiracy theories. However, I am also a cop, and in order to bring criminals to justice I need to secure evidence to be used in a court of law. Much of what you read today on conspiracies is un-provable in a court room. A lot of people make a lot of interesting connections, but without hard evidence, the accused go free. Believe me, if there was any truth to some of the accusations, I would be the first one to want to bring those who conspire to justice." Dayton paused briefly. "But what makes a good conspiracy is that the evidence necessary for conviction is not there, but it seems plausible." Dayton looked at the crowd and took a sip from his water. "Do any of you fine people have any questions?"

A young man from the crowd stood up. "Go ahead," Dayton responded.

"Detective McCormick. My name is Jason Wh--."

Dayton interrupted him and put up his index finger. "Just first names, Jason. Someone from the government could be watching." The crowd laughed.

Smirking, Jason continued. "Uh yes.----I managed to skim through your book a little bit and I noticed in Chapter 14, on electronics and the internet,----it was pretty frightening. Could you elaborate a little bit?"

Dayton was pleased someone actually looked in the book prior to asking a question. It was the sign of a good investigator and it made him smile. "Chapter 14----Yes. You are all being watched and monitored. Let me tell you a story. I paid cash in a Costco's a year ago for a package of toothbrushes. There was an electric brush with the package as a bonus. Worked great, actually. But six months after my purchase, I received a letter from Costco saying there had been a recall on the free electric brush, and that if used improperly, it could be a choking hazard." Dayton paused to sip his water. "Why am I telling you this? Because everything you buy that has a number, or anytime you use any form of electronic communication, it is being monitored. Every credit card purchase you make. Every cell or landline call. Every fax. Every email. Everything you post on an on-line chat room or website. And I mean everything. If there is a computer involved, that information is being stored. Now I don't want to scare any of you because computers are tools. But guns are tools too. And if in the wrong hands, terrible things can happen. As a police officer, I can obtain all sorts of information on people. Some of it with ease, while other information requires a warrant. Most people today freely give out information about themselves. It isn't like it was in the days of our grandparents. If this information is used to catch the bad guys, it is a tool. Of course many criminals are stupid, like those who post videos of a beating on Youtube. But the things average people post can also be used in negative ways. So be careful what you post on-line." Dayton paused again to take a sip from his water bottle. "How many of you have posted anything on a personal site, or have used email?" Nearly everyone in the audience raised their hands. "How do you think a website can offer you free email or a web page?"

"Advertising," an anonymous crowd member responded.

"Yes. That's part of it. But they also sell your information to other companies for data gathering."

"But isn't that against the law?" the same person asked.

"Read the fine print when you sign up with these sites. And not just the free ones either. Also the ones you pay for. I won't name the companies, we'll just say most of them, sell your email and personal information to the US Government." Dayton saw the horrified looks on some of the people in the crowd. "That's right, and I won't give specific names, but your tax dollars are being used to collect information about you. Of course, some information is given freely because of the communications licensure requirements."

Someone in the crowd asked, "Does that have to do with Total Information Awareness, or D.A.R.P.A.?"

"Somewhat," Dayton replied. "What people don't realize is that even if a project gets rejected by Congress in one law or another, there is another law which authorizes and funds its existence. Nothing government creates ever really goes away. The A.T.F. used to be the alcohol and tobacco tax collection department. When Prohibition ended, the Agency had little to do. Then Congress enacted the National Firearms Act, or N.F.A. of 1934. The tobacco and booze tax department now regulated firearms." Dayton had to stop and laugh, thinking about how government saved or created jobs. "So think carefully about who you elect and what they stand for. Guaranteed, while you're not paying attention, they are creating more government jobs." He looked up at the lights in the room. "Pretty soon, there will be more government jobs than private sector ones. Everybody needs a job----so someone might as well get paid to watch everything you do."

"So is there any privacy in electronic communication?"

Dayton looked at the questioner and sipped his water. "Sorry I went off on a tangent." He put his water bottle down and put his hands in the air. In a very serious tone, he continued, "You don't have any privacy in electronic communications. Zero. This does not mean that the government is watching everything you do. I am sure they don't care about your email on bread recipes to your aunt in Iowa. But say a word like "bomb" or something else considered threatening, via Boolean search, your conversation is being recorded somewhere. Make a threat against President Obama on a personal website, and you might get a visit from the Feds----even if you aren't serious."

After Dayton answered a few more questions, Steve stood up and told the crowd the Q&A was over and to bring the books to the table area where Dayton would be ready and willing to sign their copies.

On the way out, Steve told Dayton, "You did well on this double signing. The B&N rep said today they sold over four hundred copies of your book today. Incredible! That is the best sales from one store that Triple E books has ever had in a single day."

Dayton nursed his sore wrist from signing books for over hour. "That's great Steve. Hey, I want to thank you again for letting me take the photo of City Hall."

"No problem Dayton." Steve put his hand on his shoulder. "I am also sorry." Dayton looked at him curiously. "I never thanked you properly in Seattle for saving me from choking to death. I hope you never regret doing it."

"Ah, don't worry about that," Dayton replied. "You've been a good book promoter."

"You'll probably be pleased to know that your signing in Tucson is tomorrow evening, and after it, you'll have two full days before you have to fly to Dallas, for the last signing. Plenty of time for photos." Steve sighed. "Unfortunately, I won't be with you in Tucson or Dallas." He smiled. "The company has promoted me. Julie will be your new promotions assistant. She'll meet you at the airport in Tucson."

Dayton's eyes opened wide as he slapped Steve on the side of his shoulder. "A promotion. That's fantastic!"

"Thanks," replied Steve. "I am going to miss you though. It has been interesting." The two shook hands. "I'm sure I'll see you again. Here are the keys to the rental car and the hotel. Good luck with your last two signings."

Dayton thanked Steve again. He could only hope that Julie was a little less constraining and uptight. "Two more to go," he thought. Then he could spend more time with his grandmother, Mark and Sarah, in between arresting bad guys in Richmond. Things were looking up.

As he walked away from Steve, he thought about his remark about saving his life. "Hope you don't regret it?" Dayton muttered. He turned his head and watched Steve as he walked out of the bookstore. "Only a real dick would say that," Dayton thought to himself, shaking his head.

As the door closed behind Steve, Dayton remembered what was in his pocket. "John." He reached into his wallet and removed a slip of paper with his name and address:

John Windwalker
14 Sunrise Pl.
Tucson, Arizona

"Well Mr. Windwalker. Here I come," Dayton whispered as he walked out the door of the giant bookseller.

Starring out the window seat of the Boeing 757 was soothing. He really hated flying, but looking down at the clouds and listening to the hum of the plane's turbines put him in a state of relaxation. As he closed his eyes, his thoughts turned to the disturbing measurements he made in Washington D.C. in the previous days and weeks, along with the sacrificial picture from his father's Bible.

"There is no way George Washington and the others who completed D.C. were planning out the execution of 3,000 innocent Americans on September 11th, or the 35th president of the United States in November of 1963," he thought to himself. "This is just way out of bounds, even for conspiracy theories."

He racked his brain trying to figure out what the heck was going on. "Maybe----the measurements were for something else? Maybe some other group capitalized on some weird cosmic alignment or something? Maybe the way life happens or is structured, just made it happen that way, like a snowflake? Maybe, it really was just a nut job lone gunman or a group of angry fundamentalists."

Earlier, he had removed the photo of Sarah from his camera bag, which he used as his carry on. He looked in her eyes and quickly forgot about the disturbing symbolic connections in architecture and history. His muscles relaxed, and he drifted off to sleep while holding the picture in his hands.

In a dream state, he saw himself and Sarah walking past the Washington Monument; hand in hand. They walked all the way up the National Mall to the Peace and Garfield Memorials. Sarah pointed at the bronze plate under the statue of President Garfield. She turned to him and said, "It's here."

He awoke as the landing gear touched the runway.

Dayton unbuckled his safety harness and removed his camera bag from the overhead storage compartment, then placed the photo in the bag. "The first symbol in my dream was the Washington Monument." He removed a pen and a piece of paper from his camera bag. He recalled what Peter had written on a sheet in his black binder, which was in his luggage. He wrote down 365, for the days of the year and the Mayan Haab, then multiplied it by 396, for the Mayan Baktun period in years. Then he divided it by 260, the Mayan Tzokin. "555 and change. The height of the Washington Monument," he muttered quietly.

365x396/260=555+ Mayan.

"The Monument is 169 meters high. Or thirteen, thirteen's." A smile came across his face. "Thirteen conjunctions of Saturn---Kronos--the time keeper---and Jupiter, is 260 years. Twenty of those conjuncts is 396 years. And thirteen of them is 5,200 years." He wiped his eyes. "The Galactic Center, via Sagittarius A is 26,000 light years away from earth. The solar procession through the Zodiac is 26,000 years." He wrote down the number 260. "And Spica, the brightest star in Virgo is 260 light years away." He made a small sketch of the Washington Monument obelisk. Putting his finger on it, he said to himself, "It is a sundial. A sundial keeps time." His eyes opened wide. "The measurements concern keeping galactic time---they are timing something cosmic----Is it the triangle and eye of 2016?"

Dayton looked up at the stewardess looking down at him. "Sir, are you going to exit the plane? We're in

Tucson." He looked around and noticed that all the other passengers had left.

"Sorry," he said as he put everything back into his camera bag and arose from his seat. "This is weird," he said to himself, recalling what he just discovered. "But what was Sarah pointing at?"

He exited the aircraft and walked into the airport. A rather large woman was holding a sign with the word "McCormick" on it. As he approached, he saw the triangular symbol with three E's inside. He figured it must be Julie from the publishing company.

Dayton smiled. "You must be Julie."

"Sure 'am. Follow me." Dayton walked with Julie to the baggage pickup, where he picked up his luggage. "This is the key to your rental car, which is a blue PT cruiser in the Avis lot. And here is the pass card to your hotel room. I have to go get everything set up at the bookstore, so I'll meet you there around---6PM?"

Dayton was thrilled. Not only was she nice, professional and bubbly, but she wasn't going to babysit him like Steve did. He thanked her profusely and walked over to the Avis car rental lot.

After packing his luggage in the car, he pulled out his cell and called Mark.

"Hey Dayton. How's it hanging?"

"Pretty good. I'm here in Tucson getting ready to go to the hotel." He remembered his thoughts on the plane, and knew he would get a rational response from his best friend, so he asked, "What kind of person, or people would plan things based on numbers, symbols or astronomy?"

"Oh come on Dayton? Only crazy people do that. Don't you remember your first case as detective. The Birthday Killer?"

"Yes."

"Well only a fruit loop would feel compelled to do something based on that stuff. Got to kill someone today. It's Tuesday, February 2nd. Two-Two. You know the types. It's a ritual for them. They go off on it----feel their success depends on it. You know, candle burning, triangle praying types. Wackos."

"World's full of them," Dayton replied softly.

"Sure is. Some people are nuttier than a fruitcake." Mark changed the subject. "Hey, I saw Martha today. She looks good." Mark dropped his phone and picked it up. "Oh, I'm just about at check out at the grocery store. Got let you go. See you when you get home."

"Take care Mark," Dayton said, ending the phone call.

As Dayton drove, he recalled his first murder case. The other detectives were racking their brains trying to figure out who would want to kill four single woman in the Richmond area; all of which had no ties to any criminal activity. Dayton noticed the first woman's birthday was on January 1st. The second was on February 2nd---and so on. It was mid-April, so he believed the next one would be on May 5th. So he compiled the records of all single women above age eighteen in the Richmond area, and he got lucky.

It turned out that a male employee who worked for the Social Security Administration was the culprit. He was someone who had access to people's birth records and marital status. He pictured the sociopath's appearance. "Nice looking man in his mid-thirties. Used on-line dating sites to attract his prey." He also remembered the look on that man's face as he charged at him with a chef's knife, and how he pulled the trigger and put four rounds in his chest, before he collapsed. It was the first and only man Dayton had ever killed. He didn't regret killing him. He just wished he broke through the door sooner to save the woman whose birthday was on May 5th. He found her in the living room, surrounded by burning candles. She was killed by multiple stab wounds.

He considered using that case as the basis for a first book, but decided not to because it was too personal. He laughed as he opened the PT's door and whacked his head in the door jam. "Too personal," he thought. "What the hell am I doing now?"

He looked up at the hotel he was staying at for the evening. As he pulled his suitcase and camera bag from the hatch, he muttered to himself, "Wacko's, huh Mark. We'll guess what? I now have a club membership." He looked down at the pavement. "Rituals."

Dayton set up his laptop on the hotel room desk. There was something he had to know. He typed in the solar system simulator into the web address bar. "Lincoln," he muttered. He typed in April 14, 1865. The computer screen flickered and the planetary arrangement for Lincoln's assassination came into view. Dayton's eyes lit up. It wasn't as pronounced a pyramid or triangle with Jupiter atop. But it was so very close. "I'll be damned," he said.

He sat and contemplated what he had seen, in conjunction with the arrangements of both 911 and the Kennedy Assassination dates, and arrangements of the solar system in front of him. It was pretty undeniable. "All these events changed history."

He began to list the possibilities. "One: People, or some group plan events based on planetary positioning, for some benefit or purpose or ritual. Two: People may not plan it, but they are aware of what it can do. Three: The cycles and positioning in the solar system of the planets and Constellations have effect or cause actions on people, similar to what they do to the climate or weather." He counted his fingers. "Three possibilities." He put up another finger. "Four: It is all a coincidence."

He shook his head and put the forth finger back down. "I don't believe it can be just coincidence. Not after what I have seen." Dayton pulled out a dollar bill from his wallet and placed it on the table with the back-side facing up. He looked at the pyramid with 1776 in Roman numerals at the base, and the triangle atop with the eye. "Annuit Coeptis. Jupiter favors. Prayer to Jupiter. Jupiter atop the Pyramid. Triumph." He placed his hand on his chin. "I'll have to analyze this some more."

Dayton shut down his laptop. He gazed at the complimentary clock in the hotel room. It was time to get ready for his book signing.

∾

Dayton walked to the front door. Julie was waiting for him outside the Barnes and Noble on East Broadway. She greeted him with a smile that lit up a room, and then led him in. Dayton picked up his customary bottled water and walked around for a few minutes to peruse the titles of the books for sale.

The area was set up in a similar fashion to most of the others. Dayton's chair was in the middle of a parabola of chairs encircling the outside. There was a small poster of Dayton holding his book just outside the perimeter.

"Julie," Dayton said. This is all great. Thank you. But I have something else in mind for Dallas."

"What do you have in mind?" she asked.

"Well, for the Dallas signing, could you get me a whiteboard and markers. Because it's my last one, and because it is in Dallas, I was hoping to draw out the Kennedy crime scene for everyone, and really focus on the Kennedy Conspiracy. I know I would basically be giving away the whole second chapter of my book, but I think it would be a really cool thing to wet the appetite of the readers."

"You know, that sounds great!" she replied. "I am sure I can get you what you need," she bellowed cheerfully. "You almost ready to start?" Dayton nodded and walked over to the chair at the focal point of the audience.

Dayton gave his usual introduction. At this point, his delivery of the perspective in which the book was written was flawless, and there were no more butterflies in his stomach. He sat down and asked the onlookers if they had any questions. "Means, motive and opportunity---and a few ritualistic nutcases," Dayton thought to himself, before the questions began.

"Go ahead," Dayton said as he pointed at a member of the crowd.

A woman of about thirty years of age stood up. "I noticed you have a chapter on chemtrails and food production in your book. Are chemtrails real?"

Dayton smiled and stood up. "Is the government spraying us with deadly chemicals? This often comes up when people mention population control. My grandfather told me once that men in army trucks used to go around his neighborhood in the 50's, spraying some unknown mist. Turns out, after he inquired about it, they were spraying for mosquitoes and nothing more. We really have to ask ourselves if airline pilots or military personnel would knowingly spray their fellow citizens with toxic chemicals. Or maybe, especially here in the Southwest, ask ourselves whether or not they are trying to seed clouds to produce rain. The Chinese, for example, have been spraying for rain quite a bit lately. If all these planes were really spewing off all these harsh agents, why aren't people dropping dead in mass?" The crowd listened intently. Dayton put his finger in the air. "That isn't to say governments----

including our own, haven't done many deplorable things in the past. But if chemtrailing was meant to reduce the size of the population, it's not working very well."

Another hand went up. "Go ahead," Dayton responded.

"To follow her up on that question," said a young man wearing a shabby tee-shirt, "Are large food conglomerates poisoning us?"

Dayton smiled. "This is a common belief in conspiracy circles. I had the fortune to be at a friend's wedding a few years back. I sat at a table with a gentleman who was in quality control for a large equipment manufacturer. The equipment he sold and serviced made sure that when you bought a can of soup, or a condiment, that it would taste the same regardless of what farm the tomatoes or coco came from. I don't know if it is healthy for you. Maybe it isn't. But consumers spend their dollars based on the consistency and taste of a food product." He put his hands to his side. "This gentleman didn't raise any red flags with me. I didn't see any 666's on his forehead." The crowd laughed. "My best advice if you are worried about the healthiness of your food is to grow it yourself, or----buy locally from a food co-op or farmer. But I don't see any conspiracy in large food corporations to deliberately make people sick. They want to make a profit. They can't do that if they kill their customers off." Dayton looked over at all the raised hands. He was amazed. He pointed to a gentleman in the middle.

"Is H.A.A.R.P. a mind control weapon?"

Dayton responded. "There is a real installation in Alaska with a transmitter array. It is part of the H.A.A.R.P. project. Because we human beings operate with certain electrical frequencies in our brains, I supposed, like any tool, HAARP could be configured to be used improperly. I am not sure." Dayton took a sip from his water bottle. "I think what it was designed to do, was keep communications working if there was a nuclear exchange, as well as heat the ionosphere to extend electronic communications on the globe, and, also be used as a research tool. I noticed that H.A.A.R.P. tends to react when the sun emits solar flares, which can cause communications disruptions." Dayton paused again to sip his water. "Is the case closed on HAARP or other government projects? No. But once again, I have to ask everybody----is there some big plot by everyone----Corporations, the wealthy and the US Government, against the people? And for what purpose? As a cop, I have seen a lot of senseless stuff. People kill over a TV, or few dollars. Some say H.A.A.R.P. was used during the Second Gulf War on Iraqi soldiers to scare them into surrender. I can't verify or deny that claim. But if I was an untrained, underfed man with inferior weapons, facing a well-equipped and trained army----I'd consider surrendering too." He looked around at the crowd. "If it is being used to control minds, how come we're all here now questioning everything?" More heads nodded in agreement in the crowd. "If it can control minds, what are they----the infamous powers that be, waiting for?" Dayton sat down in his chair. "Want to hear a real conspiracy?" The crowd nodded their heads. "In 1977, the Department of Energy was tasked to lessen our dependency on foreign oil. That was their main, if not only, goal. Today, thirty-two years later, with a twenty-four billion dollar annual budget, have they done that?" He took another sip of his water. "When the trains run on time----heck if Amtrak could turn a profit, I might worry a bit." The crowd laughed lightly, catching Dayton's reference to the efficient use of trains in Nazi Germany. "There are two conspiracies in government I can see easily. They are called incompetence and corruption."

"Next. Shoot," Dayton said, pointing at another person in the crowd.

"So, there are no evil cabals running things from behind the scenes? No hidden hand?"

"I'm not sure. Everybody in the conspiracy world has their scapegoat. It is the Rockefellers or the Rothschild's, the Vatican or the Zionists. If not them----it's Skull and Bones or those 33rd degree Masons. And if it isn't them----it is the Communists, the Capitalists, or how about the Muslim fundamentalists? I think we have just charged 6.7 billion people for the commission of partaking in a conspiracy. Chances are good, there are groups of people who plan things. Maybe some are tied by blood, or greed, or political views. But I am not sure how powerful they really are. People have vivid imaginations and tend to believe what they want to believe. It is what makes conspiracies go."

Julie stood up in front of the crowd. "Hasn't this been wonderful?" The crowd responded by clapping. "Before we get to the signing, we have time for one more question." She looked to the back of the room where she saw a hand raised, then looked at Dayton, who nodded. "Final question. You, in the back."

"Mr. McCormick. Do you think there is any relationship to the September 11th attacks, the attacks which occurred later, and the flight numbers and dates chosen by the terrorists? I see a lot of sevens and elevens----don't you?"

Dayton nearly choked on his water. "I didn't cover this topic in my book, but I have thought about it, especially lately. It is no secret that the terrorists attacked the World Trade and Pentagon for their symbolic value, on 911. After all, there was a perfectly good nuclear reactor, Indian Point, they could have hit just north of New York City. But they attacked symbols. Why?" Dayton continued eye contact with the questioner. "You make a good point about all those sevens and elevens. But some of them could just be coincidence. The plane numbers, for example. How could they have hand-picked them based on the symbolic value of their flight numbers? The terrorists didn't work for the airlines." He paused briefly to collect his thoughts. "Maybe there is just some cosmic connection to all these numbers. Maybe----there is a subtle influence that caused these coincidences we just don't understand. Strange things do happen. For example, both Kennedy and Lincoln had Vice Presidents named Johnson."

As the signing line trickled down, Dayton noticed the young man who had asked the final question. "What is your name, guy?" Dayton asked as the young man passed Dayton his book.

"Pete," he responded.

"Well Pete. Keep asking those questions," Dayton replied. Then he wrote in his book, "questio verum in totus res. With respect, Dayton."

"What does that mean, Mr. McCormick?"

"It means seeking the truth in all things. It's Latin." The young man smiled, tucked his book under his arm and walked away.

The last gentleman in line introduced himself. "Hi, I'm Gary."

Dayton looked up and noticed his uniform and Border Patrol patch on his sleeve. "Have you seen any Russian or Chinese troops at the border in White UN Vehicles?" Dayton asked.

"No," he laughed. "Only Mexicans."

Dayton signed his book. Gary spoke. "Dayton. It is nice to see someone in law enforcement writing a book like this." He patted the book with his hand. "Lot of people out there think we're all the enemy and in cahoots with some evil group."

Dayton cracked a smile. "How do you know I'm not?"

Gary took a moment to size him up, then started laughing. "You're not the type."

"You sure?" Dayton taunted.

"Yes I'm sure," Gary replied, offering to shake Dayton's hand. "One, your nose doesn't have shit on it." He bent down and looked Dayton straight in the eyes. "And your eyes tell the rest of the story."

Dayton shook his hand and took the book back. He opened the back cover and wrote down his personal email. "Contact me anytime, Gary," Dayton said, pointing to his email. "And, in case you see any trainloads full of UN vehicles and foreign troops---?"

"You'll be the first to know," replied Gary. Dayton felt a tingle go down his spine as the Border Patrol agent walked away carrying his book.

"I hate when that happens," Dayton whispered, after the tingle left.

❧

Dayton stared at an image of Stonehenge on his laptop. "That is a pretty elaborate setup to build for people wearing goatskins," he said aloud. He remembered what Peter had told him on his visit before his death. "They used the stones to keep track of where the planets were. They were timing something---or many things. Ancient people were gathering evidence to how the arrangement of the planets affected the earth and sun, like a detective gathers evidence for a case," Dayton whispered. He looked over at the sheet Peter had written. "Cold Winter 2009. If someone knew the winter would be cold, they would invest in heating oil or natural gas." His eyes lit up. "They'd make a lot of money in fuel speculation. Like insider trading in the stock market. Information like this, could make a man, or a group rich." He pondered other possibilities. "It could also keep them safe from big storms or other disasters if they knew about when and where they would occur." However, one question kept entering Dayton's mind. "Why build it all out of stone? It must have been a lot of work for people trying to survive without modern conveniences."

He sat in quiet contemplation for a few minutes. "They must have been timing something of great importance. Something big." He twisted his head and studied Stonehenge's arrangement. "Maybe they had the information, but something happened, changing the timing---and they were using Stonehenge to re-establish where they were in time. They must have understood the root cause and effects of the arrangements in the Solar System. They may have been trying to determine when certain large events would occur again."

Dayton got up to go to the bathroom. As he relieved himself, he couldn't stop thinking about how mind-blowing all this was. "But what about the planetary effect on human behavior?" he said as he thought about 911 and the Presidential assassinations. "Do the arrangements of planets affect human actions? Or do they just represent up in space what occurs below on earth. He recalled part of the Lord's prayer: "Thy will be done, on earth as it is in heaven. Interesting. My only question is, does what occur in heaven control or influence man's actions----or do men plan their actions based on what occurs in heaven?" Dayton couldn't decide.

Dayton walked over to his laptop and shut it down for the evening. He sat in the middle of the floor, breathing in and out slowly to help clear his mind. "I've got someone to see tomorrow," he thought to himself. "Maybe if I find John, he'll have the evidence I'm looking for."

As he slept, Dayton once again found himself sitting on a strange stone walkway, looking up at the stars at night. He heard soft footsteps and he turned to see who was approaching. A man dressed in colorful robes walked right up to him and stopped. He looked down. As Dayton looked up, he saw the face of his father. He looked down at him. "Anu, are you not supposed to be sleeping?"

Dayton answered immediately. "Father. Why do we watch the stars?"

His father smiled. "We watch the stars for Pharaoh, so he may make sound judgments."

"What advice could you give Pharaoh by watching points of light?"

"These are not just points of light, my son. As the world turns, these lights tell the story of life on earth. The sky contains houses," he said, pointing up in the air. "And each house tells part of the story. Especially, the house of white, where the harvest virgin resides."

"What story does she tell?"

"She gives birth. After the sign. To Amun Ra."

"Who is Amun Ra, father?"

"He is the other bright light who spreads his wings and sings. All the world will hear him. All will be on bent knee in front of him."

"I thought Amun was---"

His father interrupted him. He placed the amulet around his neck. "I give this to you, my son. Protect it. The others in the temple are not to know when this is to happen. This amulet tells you when."

Dayton watched as his father walked back into the palace. He got up and followed after he saw his father clear the doorway. Through the window, he saw his father standing there, with men armed with swords questioning him. "Where is it?" they said. Dayton again witnessed his father mouth the word "run," and the unknown men plunge their swords into his torso. Unable to scream, he stood their helplessly as his father collapsed to the ground. One of the men noticed his face looking through the window.

He turned and ran as fast as he could. When he made it to the canal, he crawled aboard a merchant vessel and hid himself under a blanket that covered fruit. He heard the men in the distance calling out for him, but he remained silent. Water started sloshing from the sides of the boat, indicating it was moving. The voices became faint. The boy passed out.

Chapter 16
The Petroglyphs

Dayton awoke in a pool of sweat. "Why do I keep having this dream?" He pushed himself out of bed and got in the shower. "Am I going crazy?" he questioned, as the water ran over his body. He shook his head. "No. There has to be a reason for this." Dayton finished his shower, got dressed and ate. He pushed himself and cleared his mind, because there was an important task to complete. He had about two days in Tucson before he had to catch the flight to Dallas. Two days to find John Windwalker. This might be his only chance.

He packed his luggage into the small blue Pt Cruiser, and set out for 14 Sunrise Place. After about twenty minutes, he saw the street sign and turned right. Slowly, he scoped the houses. Two. Four. Ten. Fourteen. Only it wasn't house. It was a bright yellow automotive repair shop with a single gas pump in front. He read the sign on top of the building: Windwalker's Arrowhead Garage.

He pulled into a parking space in the front and got out. "Windwalker's Arrowhead Garage. Makes sense. He is an Indian," he whispered to himself. He opened the front door of the establishment and walked in.

Sitting alone at the counter was an older Indian woman. She had long black hair streaked with grey, and light wrinkles mapped out across her entire face. She smiled at Dayton. The smile looked permanent, almost like on a statue. Dayton thought for a moment about going up to her and pinching her to see if she was stuffed, but decided against it.

"Hello," said Dayton. He bent forward to get a better look at her. "I hope someone's in there," he thought.

"Um, is John Windwalker here?" Dayton said slowly. The old Indian woman continued smiling at him. Dayton repeated the inquiry more slowly, wondering if the woman understood English. "Is John----Wind--Walker----here?" She continued to smile, as she lifted her hand and pressed the buzzer to let him in the shop area. Dayton heard the buzzer and grabbed the doorknob. He entered the work area; looking back to catch another glimpse of the catatonic woman.

He walked over to a truck that had a wide pair of short legs sticking out from under it. They were meaty in appearance, almost like sausage links.

He cleared his throat. "Excuse me sir. Um----I'm looking for a John Windwalker."

Both shoes at the end of the wide legs put their soles to the floor and slid the man out from under the truck. He had long black hair with streaks of grey, like the woman at the counter. His head was square in shape, more Aztec in appearance than any American Indian Dayton was familiar with.

"What for?"

Dayton replied. "I just wanted to ask him a couple questions?"

"What if he doesn't want to answer?" the man replied.

"He doesn't have to, I guess. I am just looking for him. Do you know where he is?"

"Yes." The Indian tucked his head down and pushed himself back under the truck.

"Sir, could you tell me where he is?" Dayton asked quietly.

A hand came out from underneath the truck. "Could you hand me a 5/8ths inch box wrench first?" Dayton walked over to the tool chest and found it. He walked it over and placed it in the Indian's hand. He slid back out from under the truck. "I'm him. Seeing as you gave me the right wrench, you can't be too much of a knucklehead." He stood up and grabbed a towel to wipe the grease off his hands. He was about as wide as he was tall; standing at about five feet, six inches. Dayton looked down at him.

"You're John Windwalker?" Dayton asked.

The Indian stared at him, for asking such a dumb question, with the facial expression to prove it. "What do you want?"

Dayton exhaled. "You served with my dad. Mickey McCormick in---."

John interrupted. "Cambodia and Laos." He inspected Dayton up and down and grabbed him by the shoulders with his huge hands. "Last time I saw you, you were about knee high. The time before that, you were shitting in your pants." He smiled, which relaxed Dayton. "Are you hungry?"

Dayton didn't have to think about that question. "Sure."

"Good," John replied. "We'll go to my house and eat an early lunch. Burritos ok?"

"Sure," Dayton replied, nodding his head. They walked out of the work area and into the office, where the old Indian woman sat and was still smiling.

"Come home in a few minutes," John said to her.

"Okay, John. Just let me finish some paperwork," she replied in perfect English.

As they exited the garage, John looked at Dayton. "Did she stare at you and smile, pretending not to know what you were saying?"

Dayton nodded his head in acknowledgement.

"Ahh, she just likes fucking with the minds of you white people. My wife is a funny lady."

"That's your wife?" Dayton questioned.

"Thirty-three years," John proclaimed proudly. They walked over to the tow truck. "Get in."

Dayton complied with the request. "How far are we going?"

"Long journey," John replied. He started the tow truck and backed it into the road. "Long journey," John repeated. He drove forward about twenty feet, then took a left into a driveway. "We're here. 10 Sunrise Terrace. My home." Just then, he began laughing so hard it began to shake the truck. He looked over at Dayton with tears of laughter rolling down his face. "I always wanted to do that. Saw it in a movie once. He, he, he. Ha, ha, ha. You better go get your shit out of your car and bring it over, before somebody steals it."

Dayton walked back toward the repair shop to the Cruiser, and removed his camera bag and luggage. John's wife hung a sign outside the front door that read "Back After Lunch," and she escorted Dayton back to their home and struck up a conversation with him in perfect, unbroken English.

Dayton placed his belongings in the living room, but removed his black binder and brought it into the kitchen where John was seated. He looked around the kitchen. It was neatly arranged, with a cross of colorful decorative artwork and pottery; both Mexican and Southwest Indian in design. He pulled out the photograph of the servicemen to show John. "Yup, I was a lot skinnier then." John looked over at his wife who was preparing lunch. "I hope you don't like beans. Hate the fuckers myself."

Dayton looked surprised and relieved. He wasn't a fan of refried beans either, but if they were offered, he didn't want to offend. "Not everyone here likes them, you know," John replied. "It is good to see you cousin----as an adult." Dayton smiled.

He opened up, and began explaining to John what had happened over the past few months. "Looks like you are in some shit," said John.

"Up to my eyeballs," replied Dayton.

John looked Dayton square in the eye. "I liked your father Mickey. Good man. Didn't treat me like a dumb Indian grunt." He smiled. "I am first generation legal. My father came here illegally. Minded his own business and started the garage. Would fix some of the local's cars for free, to keep them quiet. Didn't want to go back to Mexico." John exhaled, then began talking about the war. "When we were over there, we saw some awful shit. Your father found out some company was shipping arms to the enemy. Lot of people never came back because of it." Dayton continued listening. "When I was all shot up in the chopper, your father calmed me down and kept me from bleeding to death. I was very thankful. Until he came to live with me, a few years later." He laughed. "Him and Peter were real bastards for a while, picking up local girls looking for men in uniform." Mrs. Windwalker put two burritos on plates and placed them in front of Dayton and her husband. "Would you like some?" John asked, lifting up some hot salsa. "Be a man." Dayton placed some on top of his burrito and began eating. John caught the expression on his face as his mouth turned into a blast furnace and tears rolled down his cheeks. "Looks like you're getting the cold sweats." He held up the jar and handed it to his wife. "Give me some of the mild stuff, dear." As John laughed, Dayton scraped off the rest of the hot salsa and replaced it with mild. "Sorry about that," John said as he laughed some more.

"No you're not. I can understand why my dad liked you. You have quite a sense of humor," Dayton said sarcastically.

"Oh, this is just the beginning," John replied with a smile.

The two finished their lunch and continued talking. "Your father knocked up my cousin, Jan. She had you. I wish she was here to see you."

"My grandmother told me she died from driving drunk."

John shook his head. "No," John explained. "When she met your father, she drank a lot. When she found out she was pregnant, she stopped. She was run off the road by a couple of intelligence people. She was gathering information for your father. At first, I blamed him, but after seeing how heartbroken he was, I was sorry for doing so." John looked at the floor. "He was going to marry her----ring and everything. My advice to you is-----whatever you're into, keep those you love out of it." He pointed over to his wife and to pictures on the wall of his children and grandchildren. "They wouldn't be here if I didn't tell your father to go home. He had no money, so I bought him some train tickets. You in diapers, and him. I put you two on the train and waved goodbye."

Dayton nodded his head in acknowledgement. "But you visited him a few years later."

"We let bygones be bygones. I was a dumb Indian with nothing, so I joined the service, like a lot of other dumb Indians. Your father kept me alive, and he treated me like one of the guys. I was trained to be a tunnel rat, because I was shorter than most guys. Your father never made me stick my head in one god-damn tunnel. Kid I grew up with lost his face to a hand grenade. His life too. Your father was a kind officer."

Dayton cracked a half smile. "I never knew my dad was an officer," he thought to himself. The stories told by John were interesting, but Dayton changed the subject and got down to business. "Did you ever receive a package from Christopher Hartman?" Dayton inquired.

John nodded his head and understood the real purpose behind the visit by the young detective. "I'll get it before you go. But I think there are things you need to see first." John got up and grabbed two backpacks out of the closet. He then took a key out of his pocket and unlocked a drawer, revealing a .45 automatic and a Ruger GP 100 in .357. He handed the revolver to Dayton, with a spare speed loader of ammunition. He placed his gun in the backpack and instructed Dayton to follow suit. After placing a few provisions in both packs he said, "follow me." They walked outside to the garage on the side of the house. John lifted the door and revealed two motorcycles: both older Suzuki dual-sport 650's, outfitted with oversize desert tanks and side bags. "Do you know how to ride?" John asked.

"It has been a few years." Dayton wondered where John was going with all this.

"Hmm. Take a few laps around the block to get used to it," John said, handing a helmet and an ignition key to Dayton. "Because after we leave here, if you go too slow, I'll turn around and come kick your ass."

"I'll be right back." Dayton walked up to the house into the living room and removed his father's Canonet. He wrapped it in a towel and placed it in the backpack. He rejoined John and put the key into the ignition and turned it to the run position. He got up on the bike and thrust his right foot on the kick starter. The engine roared to life. He let it run for a few minute to let the air-cooled engine warm up properly. Then, he took two laps around the block to familiarize himself with the controls.

John, helmet in hand, waved to Dayton to come over. He looked at the younger man with a serious expression. "There are a few things you need to see. Let's go."

"Where are we going?" Dayton inquired, his voice muffled by the helmet.

"First things first. You need to go pay your respects."

Dayton followed John's lead as they rode through Tucson. "This place really is just dirt and scrub," Dayton thought to himself as he looked around at the landscape through his motocross goggles. They traveled about twenty minutes southeast and turned on to East Old Spanish Trail. Just up ahead, Dayton read the sign for All Faiths Memorial Park. A sinking feeling came over him. "This must be where my mother is buried."

The two dismounted their bikes and took off their helmets. "Follow me," John said. They walked over to the far corner of the lot. "Here it is," John said, pointing down at the marker, which Dayton read. Chiseled in stone was the name Jan Windwalker and the dates February 1, 1953 to May 12, 1977. "She was your mother and my cousin." He breathed in and out, trying to remain calm and not show emotion. "I grew up with her and her brother, who is a year older. Good people. Bad time."

"I never knew my mother," Dayton replied as he put his hand on John's shoulder. He looked down at the small marker stone, then knelt. Dayton took his right hand and brushed the dust of it. "Hmm, I wonder if she had lived, would life have been different?"

"We can't go back or do what we should have done, Day. All we can do is move forward. Fact of life. Like it or not," John replied.

He looked up at John. "This question might sound strange, but if she was your cousin, how did your dad get the name Windwalker. I thought he was Mexican?"

"When my father married my mother, he took her last name."

"That's unusual."

"Not if you were an illegal in the 1940's. My father came here when he was fourteen."

"So what was his last name----his real one?" Dayton asked.

"He never said, and my mother would never tell me. He preferred to leave that part of his life back in Mexico."

John slapped Dayton on the back. "Come on, Lone Ranger. Two more things you need to see." He walked back toward the motorcycles as Dayton stared at his mother's marker. "Hey, let's go. We're going to run out of daylight if we don't get moving."

Dayton took one last look at the gravestone and walked back over to John. The two mounted their bikes and headed down Rt.10.

"Dirt, dirt and more dirt," Dayton thought. "The temperature is great, but who would want to live here?" He gave the cycle more throttle, so he could catch up to John; not wanting him to turn around and try and kick his ass. The two rode down Rt. 10 for a few more miles, then turned on to RT 90. Dayton could see more hills and mountains coming ahead.

John pulled his bike into a gas station and Dayton followed, shortly after arriving in Whetstone. "We need to gas up. Even with the bigger tanks," he said as he tapped the gas tank, "we don't want to run low on fuel down here." The two filled up the bikes and continued through Whetstone, then through Huachuca City. They road for a few more miles, until they stopped in front of the sign for Fort Huachuca.

John pointed over to the sign and pulled off his helmet. "We can't go in," he said as he pointed to Dayton's pack. "They'll arrest you on the spot." Dayton pressed the kill switch on the handlebars, silencing the engine. He removed his helmet and pushed up the kickstand on the bike.

"Ft. Huachuca," he said. "So this is where my father received his military training." He looked at the insignia designs of the units housed at the base.

"Intel Center," said John, looking at the blue diamond. It had a grey outline with a yellow half-sun on the bottom, and a yellow torch tip atop.

Dayton whispered, "Sun in Leo."

John looked over at him frowning. "Your father used to say that shit. All these," John said waiving his arm across them, "have a hidden meaning, he'd say. And most of the people that wear them have no clue as to what they mean."

"Army Intelligence. Always out front," Dayton replied, while looking at the Sphinx in gold, crossed by a key and lightning bolt. "Head of a woman with the body of a lion. Is this on purpose, or by influence?"

"Beats me, Day. Your father knew. He'd always tell me that someday in the future all this would make sense. He said the two conjoin at the crown of Virgo, then a third would form the triangle." Dayton knew exactly what John meant. "A short time would pass, about forty weeks, then there would be two eyes in the sky." John shook his head. "Your father would say fear or love. He didn't know which. He was hoping for the latter." As he listened, Dayton recalled the research he had done up to this point. "I would tell him to start a TV show, like that Nimoy fellow," John laughed.

"In Search of," Dayton replied with a wide smile. "My father and I would watch that show when I was a kid."

John replied, taking his fingers and making points on top of his ears, "I liked him better as Spock."

Dayton squinted at the sign. "The Ninth Signal Command and the Eleventh Signal Brigade." He smiled. "Boy, conspiracy theorists would have a field day with this one."

John smiled, scrunching his square Meso-Indian face. "They fly the predator drones."

"Yah," Dayton replied, shaking his head. "And look at the symbol for the Eleventh," he said, pointing at the sign. "The black eagle with the lightning bolts coming out of its central red eye. Maybe that is for Scorpio? It was once known as the Eagle Constellation, representative of St. John."

"John, huh? Day, the eagle can also represent the phoenix: The bird that rises from its own ashes. The bird that comes from the sun. Your father told me that the day before we were extracted that the Cambodian man showed him drawings from inside the temple. He also took him and Mussen somewhere else. Your father told me that morning, we are all the same. Christian, Jew, Indian, Cambodian. All the same. No difference. Only the stories we tell are a little different." John sighed. "Your father----he was a smart man. Most cultures use birds as symbols or messengers. You understand?"

Dayton pulled his father's Canonet out of the backpack and estimated the exposure. He focused the camera, using the small lever on the left side of the lens, and took a few photographs of the symbols around the perimeter of the military base. "Airplanes are birds," Dayton whispered, thinking about the World Trade Center.

John noticed a small military convoy coming down the base entry road. "We'd better get going. Maybe were attracting the wrong attention." The two started the bikes, put their helmets back on and then continued riding down Rt. 90, Past Sierra Vista, until they connected with Rt. 92.

They rode that for a few more miles until they were a stone's throw from the Mexican border. Up to this point, Dayton had wondered why they simply hadn't traveled by car. Then John leaned hard to the left and took the less traveled path. Dayton stood up; allowing himself to better navigate the motorcycle and absorb the bumpy ride. He leaned to the left, then to the right, to avoid the large rocks jutting up like icebergs in the path of reddish orange soil. John slowed down, because he noticed Dayton lagging behind. He realized this was no trail for any rider, especially an inexperienced rider, to speed on.

After about a half an hour of hard riding, Dayton noticed John come to a halt and park his bike. Dayton followed suit. He watched curiously as John looked around for something. He saw him lift a rock, then pull what appeared to be a large tan parachute from a hole in the ground. He walked up to Dayton, dragging the chute.

"I'm glad it is still here," he said happily. "Carefully lay down the bike on its left side."

"Why left?"

"Because the oil cooler is on the right side, knucklehead. You don't want to break it." John and Dayton laid down the motorbikes on their left sides next to each other. He tightened both gas caps to prevent leaking. Then, John threw the parachute over them; covering them completely.

"Why did we do that?" Dayton asked. "There is nobody out here."

John pointed up. "Wanna bet, city boy? Planes and satellites can see these easily. But under a blanket, infrared sensors in satellites see these as large lizards, until the motor and pipes cool. And although this ain't California, some desperate Mexicans do attempt to cross the border, even with Huachuca over there." John shook his head. "No bikes, and it is a long walk home."

Dayton felt out of his element. He was used to life in the city, near people, with lots of trees and grass; not out in the hills with dirt, rocks and scrub bushes.

"And if you got a cell phone, turn it off and pull the battery," John added. "You can be tracked by your cell phone." Dayton smirked. He knew that, but wondered why John was so concerned about not being seen.

The two hiked up a large hill; carefully placing their feet on stable rock. There were no hospitals or emergency personnel around, so they understood they were on their own, and a minor injury out here could be deadly.

John unzipped his backpack, opened a metallic zipper bag and handed Dayton a coldcut sandwich. "Sorry about supper. Nothing around here----unless you want to cook a snake." The two ate quietly until the sandwiches were gone and they washed them down with some bottled water.

After their meals were finished, John began to speak. "I showed you Jan's grave and the fort your father was trained at. Now I show you the cave." The sun was beginning to set, so John pulled out a flashlight from each pack. He also told Dayton to put the .357 in his front jeans pocket, as he placed the .45, Mexican style, against the small of his back.

They hiked up the hill a little further. Dayton's legs and back ached from the long cycle ride and the steep climb. He was wondering how John, a man about twice his age and weight, had seemed to do so well.

Just up ahead, Dayton noticed a large opening in the rock. "My father left Mexico at fourteen. He crossed the border near here." John looked around. "It was just as dangerous and desolate then. He spotted some patrollers in the distance, so he looked for a place to hide so he wouldn't get caught. He found this cave."

John and Dayton switched on their flashlights and crawled inside the crevice. About twenty feet into the small cave, John asked Dayton to sit. He then swung his flashlight to the wall on his right.

Dayton couldn't believe what he saw. "Petroglyphs," he said. He arose from his seat and walked forward, then bumped his head on a rock above him.

John burst out laughing. "That's why I told you to sit." Dayton shook it off, but he knew it would hurt in the morning, hopefully not as bad as the hangover after visiting Peter Devine. "When I mentioned this place to your father, he had to come see it for himself. He heard of strange things in the Southwest. He told me he hadn't seen anything similar since Cambodia. He'd come here at least once a month. Sometimes he'd bring Peter. Sometimes Jan. I'd come too. And sometimes, he'd come alone to think."

Dayton looked at the wall. There was a triangle formation. On the left, was a bright green bird in flight. On the upper right, was a spotted red bird doing the same. Making the third part of the triangle, was and orange spiral. To the left of the trio, was a small white crescent. "Holy Shit!" Dayton exclaimed. To the right of them was a yellow circle.

John shined his light to the right of the glyphs. "Say it again." He pointed his flashlight to the right of the yellow circle. Dayton's eyes opened wide as he viewed a small red circle and a large orange circle slightly higher on the wall then the previous symbols. From both came what appeared to be lightning bolts. Under them were stick figures, which looked like people running. In a tone more serious than Dayton had ever heard, John repeated an earlier remark. "Like I said, your father was hoping for love in the future, not fear."

Dayton reached into his wallet and pulled out a one dollar bill. "Novus Ordo Seclorum."

"New Order of the Ages. Yes," John replied. "Your father explained to me that all over the world, there were things like Stonehenge." The words stung Dayton's ears as John said them, remembering his analysis of Stonehenge from the previous night. "We are told these things were used for sacrifices----or to tell when best to plant crops. He told me all of that was bullshit. My mother's people said when the kachinas danced in the sky, a great tragedy befell the earth. When the earth stabilized, the order in the sky had changed a little bit. Understand?"

"Completely."

"My mother told me our first teacher is the sky. It tells us when things are going to happen. But most people living now don't realize this."

"For signs and for seasons and for days and for years," Dayton whispered.

"You got that right, Day. Genesis One-fourteen." John winked and took a deep breath. "And from Abraham to David was fourteen generations, from David to Babylon were fourteen generations and from Babylon to Jesus was fourteen generations. Matthew, One-Seventeen." Dayton was surprised, which John found amusing. "What, you think an Indian doesn't read a Bible? While recovering from my wounds, I befriended an Army chaplain." He smiled. "I needed something to read." John displayed a big grin under the dim light. "Besides, the good book had a lot of begetting in it." John burst out laughing. "Closest thing I had to sex for about four months." Dayton shook his head and they laughed together.

He set his flashlight to illuminate the two circles with the lightning bolts and he asked John to use his to light up the triangle. He removed the Canonet from his pack and set the shutter for bulb and estimated the distance for focus. He held his hands as steady as he could;

making exposure after exposure, counting for seconds, until finishing the roll. "One of these are bound to come out." He pressed the clutch on the bottom plate and rewound the film, leaving it inside the camera for safe keeping. He then took a closer look at the two bright orbs: one smaller and reddish, the other orange and large. Dayton's thoughts turned to the twin nuclear bombings of World War Two. "Little Boy and Fat Man. Synchronicity. Rituals."

"What?" John asked.

"John. Did you ever think that everything in history happened because of some big plan. Like there is some order or control over what happens here on earth?"

"Between my mother and your father----yes----all the time. My mother said you will always know what will happen or has happened based on looking at what's happening."

"Interesting way of putting it." Dayton smiled.

The two talked for about an hour until the flashlight batteries began to fail. John removed small blankets from each pack and handed one to Dayton. "Time for some sleep, Day. This will be softer on your head than that rock."

"Thanks cousin," said Dayton.

John noticed Dayton looked troubled, even in the dim light. "No one knows what the future holds, Dayton. I could have been killed in that shithole almost forty years ago," he said, referring to Cambodia. "The future's uncertain."

They both shut off their flashlights. Dayton put his head on his makeshift pillow. The slight breeze coming in from the cave's entrance made his tired body feel as if it was slowly spinning. He breathed deeply and began falling into the darkness of sleep.

In the morning, a splinter of light entered through the cave's entrance; making its mark on Dayton's face. He awoke slowly and allowed his eyes to become accustomed to the low light. He walked carefully toward the entrance and exited, then began the trek down the hill. As he walked, he thought to himself, "This feels good. Now I know why grandma goes on her walks." After a few minutes, he stopped in his tracks and bent low to the ground after hearing someone hollering in Spanish. He looked over to where John had covered the motorcycles and saw five men pulling at the parachute. "Oh shit!" he thought to himself, as he turned around and made a bee-line for the cave.

Dayton took his hands and shook John, which interrupted his snoring. "Wake up Tanto," he said, "or we're going to be walking home."

John shook his head and opened his eyes. "Did you just call me Tanto?"

"Never mind," Dayton responded, "Just rack your .45. Some guys are down below and they found our bikes." Dayton pulled his .357 from his pocket, and placed the speed loader from his backpack into his back pocket.

The two exited the cave carrying their backpacks. When they reached the spot where Dayton saw the men, they crouched down. John looked at them through a small monocular he pulled from his pants pocket. "Bad news, man. Bad news. Banditos."

"We'll----we'd better go down there or we're walking home."

John smiled at Dayton. "I have an idea." He handed him his .45 and a spare loaded magazine. "I'll go down and distract them. Then you shoot them."

"You're going down unarmed?" Dayton whispered sarcastically.

"Look. With a rifle, I'm a good shot. Can't hit the side of a barn with a pistol. I'm old," he continued, and held up his hands which were knarled from years of working on cars, "arthritis has set in and I don't see as good as I used to." He placed his large hands on Dayton's shoulders. "Besides, you're a cop. You shoot people all the time right? Lone Ranger?"

Dayton frowned. He didn't like the idea. But John had already turned around and started walking down toward the men. "Fuck!"

John walked quietly toward the men, who were in the process of picking up the bikes and putting them upright. When he was about ten yards away he yelled, "Hey! Assholes. Get away from my motorcycles!" The men looked at John with a confused look. "I know you fuckers speak English. Don't give me none of that speak-a-no-English shit." One of the men turned to the other, said something in Spanish and drew a knife. Two of the others drew guns.

"I think we take your motorcycles half-breed," the knife holder said. "Get done on your knees and beg for mercy, you fat bastard," another said in heavily-accented Spanish.

Dayton moved quickly, but quietly toward the group. He saw John get on one knee, as the others trained their guns on him. "I think I'm just gonna slice you up, you fat bastard!" Dayton began to sprint, as the knife wielder got behind John, slowly bringing the blade down horizontally to his throat.

The .45 barked in Dayton's hand after he pulled the trigger, while pointing it at the head of the knife wielding bandito. He had just started pulling the knife across, and John caught the blade with the outside of his right hand. Blood sprayed all over John from above as the large caliber handgun round penetrated the knife holder's throat. Dayton squeezed again and again; training the front of the slide on each of the banditos. One round hit one man square in the chest, knocking him down, while another grazed another bandito's shoulder. Dayton saw one of the men raise his gun toward him, so he turned, exposing his backpack. He heard something shatter inside his pack after the flash and report, but continued toward the man, returning fire. Bam. Bam. One shot hit center of mass on the gun wielder, while the other caught him in the arm. He collapsed on the ground, writhing in pain.

The other bandito with a shoulder wound, along with another who was unscathed, ran away from the melee as fast as they could. Dayton pulled his pack off his back and tried pulling the body of the dead knife wielding bandito off John Windwalker. Before he could pull him off, the bandito wiggling in pain on the ground raised his gun and attempted to point it in the direction of the duo. Bam. Bam. Bam. The .45 barked in Dayton's hands, finishing the job it started.

"Get this asshole off me Dayton! He, he, he, ha, ha, ha," John laughed. "And I got cut, so bring me something to tie up my hand." Dayton pulled the dead man off John, then took his knife and cut off one of the sleeves of John's white shirt, then made a tourniquet out of it.

"You gonna cut off the other one too, and make me look like a real bad-looking biker dude?" John said sarcastically.

Dayton began to laugh and fell down to the ground. "I can't believe I just shot four people, killing three of them, and you're laughing about it."

John realized then that Dayton had never been a soldier or seen death in combat as he had. "Better them, than us amigo," John responded, tightening the shirt sleeve around his hand. "I was worried. I thought you got hit.

Dayton looked at the hole in the backpack, with small shards of glass sticking out of the bullet hole.

He reached inside and pulled out his father's camera, frowning at the shattered lens.

"You're just as fucking lucky as your father was!" John exclaimed. Dayton smiled as he remembered the story Peter told him about his father's camera having it's lens shot out in Cambodia. He looked at the hole, pulled at the rewind spool and opened the back.

"Luckier," he responded, examining the film canister. "It didn't hit the film." He placed the film canister into the zippered pocket in the front of the pack. He handed John the .45 and the .357 as he shook the shards of glass out of his backpack.

"We'll, the buzzards and dogs will eat good today," John said.

Dayton and John put on their helmets and started the motorcycles. They drove slowly down the treacherous trail back to RT. 92, then headed back straight to Tucson.

↊

Back at his house, John poured alcohol over his hand after washing the wound. "That was one hell of an adventure, McCormick!" He bandaged himself up and slapped Dayton on the back. "When you get time, you have to come back and see me. We'll go for another ride," he said smiling.

Dayton nodded his head and smiled. "I'll see what I can do. My father had interesting friends."

"Hey, we're more than friends, we're cousins."

Dayton looked at his watch with disappointment. "I have to get going soon. I have an early evening flight to Dallas."

"Wish you could stay," John said, looking disappointed.

"So do I," Dayton replied. "I had one hell of a time." Dayton paused, then remembered the reason he came to see John in the first place. "Do you have the package Hartman sent you from my dad?"

"Yep, right over here." John walked into to the kitchen and opened the freezer. "Nobody looks in here." He brought the box over to Dayton and popped it on his lap.

Dayton grabbed his pocket knife and opened it, slicing through two layers of tape. On top, was a key. He picked it up and examined it. "Strange."

"Put it in your wallet. You won't lose it that way."

Dayton followed John's suggestion. Then he examined the papers in the box on his lap. "These are shipping records for two boats owned by Baxter-Cudman Shipping, along with docking records. They span a period," he said flipping through them, "of over five years----1968-1974." At the bottom were three sheets, paper clipped together. "And these are duty records for a naval communicator named Phillip Cudman. In times. Out times. They correlate with some of these shipping records for the ships----at least for 1969-1971." Dayton looked over at John. "I have photos of those ships, along with photos of munitions and other military hardware in temples in Cambodia. There is even a photograph showing a shipping slip from that company on boxes inside one of those temples." Dayton sat in awe of the evidence his father had collected. "Senator Phillip Cudman was a damn traitor."

John's tone changed. "Tread lightly Dayton. Or you might end up like your father."

Dayton tried to contain his anger, breathing in and out as he sat on John's couch. He closed his eyes and remembered what Professor Mussen had said. "Not enough." "I think I know someone that can handle this John. I don't think something like this," he said, holding up the paperwork, "can be done through normal due process."

John shook his head in agreement, knowing Senator Cudman was a very powerful man. "Good luck cousin. If there is something I can do, let me know." He reached into his pocket and removed his monocular, then handed it to Dayton.

"What's this?"

"A present. You might use it in your police work." John smiled and gave Dayton a hug. "Helps with aging eyesight."

Dayton gathered his belongings and walked to the rental car. He looked back at John's house and saw him waving his bandaged hand out the window, with a big pouty look on his face. As he turned around to walk to the rental car, he heard John yell, "Hey cousin! One more thing!" Dayton turned to see John's face hanging out the window. "You know some red-haired guy?"

"Yes," Dayton replied; remembering Steven, his former promotions man and babysitter.

"Well, my wife said some red-haired guy stopped over here yesterday afternoon looking for you," John said.

"Did he have really white skin, and was his name Steve?"

John pulled his head out of the window to look at his wife. "Yah, he did----but he never said his name?"

"That's strange?" Dayton thought. "How the hell did he find me here? I thought he was supposed to be in L.A." Dayton yelled back to John. "Did she tell him where we were?"

John looked at his wife again, then put his head out the window. "Nope. She just smiled at him like she did with you. So he left." John laughed. "Hey----don't be a stranger. Come back and visit soon."

"I will," Dayton responded while waiving. He thought for a moment and looked at the rental car. "He couldn't have tracked me with the rental car. They wouldn't give him that info." He crawled under the car and looked for any electronic devices. "Clean." He shook his head and got into the Cruiser, then drove back to his hotel.

Dayton showered quickly. There was only two hours before his plane was to depart, and he knew sometimes security at the airport was slow. He put on some clean clothes and packed his belongings into the car: consisting of one suitcase and a camera bag he used as a carry on. He put the monocular in his pocket.

He dropped the car back with the rental agency, then entered the airport and checked in his luggage. "How can anyone find me?" he thought. "Strange."

He looked around the boarding area and he felt like someone was watching him. His eyes scanned all around the room until he looked just below him. There was a small child, cute as a button, with brown eyes staring at him while she clutched her teddy with one hand and her mother's leg with the other. "I must be going paranoid," he thought, while smiling back at the little girl.

"Now boarding American Airlines flight 052 for Dallas--Fort Worth," a voice announced over the intercom. "Gate C, Dallas Fort Worth." The line began to move, and Dayton followed. He couldn't take his eyes off the cute little girl ahead of him. Until, he felt the tap on his shoulder.

"Excuse me sir," the uniformed TSA agent said. "Are you Detective Dayton McCormick?"

Dayton came out of his daze. "Yes." He looked carefully at the officer and realized from the serious look on his face that this wasn't a social visit.

"Could you step out of the line and come with me sir?"

Dayton looked confused. "What for?"

"Just come with me sir. We need to ask you a few questions."

Dayton responded. "Couldn't you have done this earlier? I am going to miss my flight."

"I am sorry sir, but this is important."

Dayton was escorted by the agent down the hall to a security area. The agent passed a portable metal detector over his body, while another agent took his camera bag. "What is going on?"

"Are you Dayton McCormick?" As Dayton looked up, he saw the man who asked him the question. "My name is Matthew Broderick. I am head of Homeland Security, Southwest division. Could you please come with me?" He escorted Dayton down another hallway and into a small room with two chairs and a small table. Dayton was asked to sit.

"Could you tell me what all this is about?" Dayton asked.

Broderick sat down in a chair across the table from Dayton. "There was an incident earlier this morning down by the Mexican border."

Dayton tried to keep a straight face. He thought to himself, "Oh my god, they found the bodies!"

"Border Patrol found a Mexican National with a bleeding arm. He was questioned and detained. When asked who shot him, he pointed to a book one of our agents was reading. Your book----with your picture." Broderick paused. "Were you near the Mexican border this morning?"

"Yes."

"Were you alone?"

"No. I was out riding with my cousin on his motorcycles," Dayton replied calmly.

He held up a photo of the Mexican. "Did you shoot this man?" Dayton stared at the photo to get a better

look at him. "Please just answer the question----
detective."

"I might of. It all happened kind of fast." Dayton
wiped his hand across his face. "My cousin John and
I parked the bikes. When we came back, these guys
were trying to steal them. When we told them to get
lost, they drew guns and knives on us and tried to kill
us."

"Self defense then?" Broderick asked quietly.

"Yes," Dayton replied. "Of course, although he might
have been hit by one of his pals."

Broderick's tone changed. "Why didn't you report
it? You are a god-damn peace officer." Broderick was
clearly not amused.

"Because, it wasn't my gun. I was out of my jurist
diction. We didn't know if we were on American or
Mexican soil at the time. And they were bandits----
shooting wildly. What good would a report do besides
generate more paperwork?"

Broderick smiled. "I'll be right back."

About twenty-five miles away in the desert, two
men in a brown SUV were parked; smoking cigarettes
and speaking in Arabic. One pointed to the blinking
screen and his watch, so the other got out and opened
up the hatch in the rear. He pulled out a large box and
opened it. Inside, was a Stinger missile. He waited for
word from the other man to arm it.

Back at the airport, a gentleman wearing sunglasses
and sitting near Gate C, picked up his cell phone and
made a call. When there was acknowledgement on the
other end, he said softly, "Abort. Abort the mission."

The man in the front seat on the phone, watching
the moving blip, understood. He jumped out of the SUV
waving his hands, telling the man holding the missile

tube to stop. He took his finger off the arming pad and placed the Stinger back into the box.

A few minutes later, Flight 052 flew over the SUV, which had just turned on to the highway from a dirt road.

Broderick returned to the room and sat down in front of Dayton, holding some paperwork in his hand. "There is always paperwork in law enforcement, detective. And this is your lucky day. Turns out, the Mexican had a record----making his word carry less weight than yours." He placed the paperwork in front of Dayton and handed him a pen. "We need to keep good relations with our neighbors to the south. I am sure you understand." He presented Dayton with some papers.

"What is this?" Dayton asked.

"It is just a statement saying you were attacked without provocation and you responded appropriately. This is just a formality. When the Mexican National returns home, he will be dealt with by local authorities in Mexico."

Dayton looked over the statement carefully; searching for any legal or other content which might cause future problems. Finding none, he signed his name on the bottom line and dated it.

"You can go now, detective McCormick. Thank you for your cooperation. The TSA agents will walk you back to the ticketing area," Broderick said in a bureaucratic tone.

"What about my camera bag?"

"That will be returned as well," Broderick stated.

Dayton received his camera bag from the TSA agent, walked out to the ticketing area and looked for the next available flight to Dallas. He had to use another airline in order to get a flight on time for the Dallas signing, so he charged it on his Visa card.

As he sat, he inspected the contents of the camera bag. Everything was there, except the roll of film from the cave. At first he became upset, but then remembered that he might have left it in the backpack in John's house. "I'll call him when I am far from here," he thought to himself. He lifted his digital camera out of the bag and turned it on, to view the photos he took in Los Angeles. The screen stared back at him: NO IMAGE. "They formatted my card. All my pictures---- gone."

Broderick sat in his office holding the paperwork he had given to Dayton to sign. He smiled, stood up and walked over to the machine in the corner of his office. After turning on the power, he fed all the paperwork between the jaws of the shredder. "It never happened," he muttered under his breath.

Chapter 17
Dealey Plaza

"What do you mean it is not here?" Dayton asked the supervisor of baggage claims at American Airlines in an irritated tone.

"Sir. We're sorry. No luggage from flight 052 remained on the conveyor. We searched the plane. We searched the baggage transport." He felt bad for Dayton. "It's not here----anywhere."

Dayton looked at the ground as he turned to walk away. He thought to himself, "The final piece of evidence to bring my father's killers to justice is gone. Now all I have is----not enough."

He walked slowly, consoling himself with the fact that he still had his camera. He purchased a bottled water to quench his thirst, then walked outside and sat on a bench to call John Windwalker on his cell phone.

"John," Dayton said into the microphone on his cell phone. "My luggage is missing. And so are the papers."

"I'm sorry to hear about that cousin."

"Did anyone else come to see you?"

"No. Why?"

"Because I was detained at the airport in Tucson," Dayton replied.

"Hmm? Sounds like someone used you as a delivery boy. I don't know what to say." John's voice sounded disappointed. "Maybe something will turn up. Don't give up hope."

"I think I left my film in your backpack. Is it there?"

"I'll check." After a few minutes, John came back on the phone.

"Sorry Day. It is not in the pack. Maybe it fell out on the ride back from the border."

"Well----at least I have my memories," Dayton sighed.

"Yes you do. Again----I'm sorry. But don't forget me. And when you get a chance, you come see your cousin."

"I will John. Thanks for everything." He closed the flap on his phone and put his head in his hands. He didn't see her approach.

"Dayton? I have been looking all over for you."

He raised his head and saw Julie, his new promoter from the publishing company. "Hi Julie."

"Are you ok? I heard you missed your flight and I was worried," she said while having a genuine look of concern on her face.

"I was detained by Homeland Security."

"Nothing serious?" Julie asked.

"No. Just a few routine questions. Wrong place---- wrong time sort of thing."

"Oh thank goodness." She lifted up her hand. "I have your rental keys and your hotel pass card," she said, trying to cheer him up.

He looked up at her and smiled, "Thanks Julie. Thanks."

She handed him the keys and asked, "You are going to be at the signing at 6pm?"

"I'll see you there," Dayton responded. "Did you get the write-on board?"

"And multi-colored markers," she said proudly.

"You are one in a million. Can I ask you for one more favor?"

"Whatever you need," Julie replied. Dayton described to her what he wanted to do at the signing. "That sounds like a great idea. I'm sure I can arrange it. Laptop and projector. Anything else?"

"No. That would be fine. The signing is at 6PM. I'll be there an hour or so early to prep."

Dayton and Julie parted. He took the shuttle service to the car rental agency, where his mid-sized sedan was waiting for him. As he got in the car, an uneasy feeling came over him. "How did Steve find me? Why did he come looking?" He recalled how on his signing trips, Steve was always tied to the hip with him when he was in an area where none of his father's former army buddies resided. But when he was near a location where one lived, he always seemed to have something else important to do. Dayton thought back to the break-in at his condo when his grandfather died. Everything was trashed. Everything, but his laptop. "Why didn't the vandals smash it?" he asked himself. He considered that someone may have seen him and followed him when he met Christopher Hartman. But he drove himself to Peter Devine's house. And it wasn't even at the last known location on the sheet given to him by Hartman. And he had his laptop on his first series of signings up the East Coast. The Cherokee was clean. He checked it thoroughly.

He pulled out his phone. "The phone----maybe?" he thought to himself. "No, it couldn't have been the phone, because the battery died in New York," he said shaking his head. He had left the charger at home on the desk. "But someone could have followed me from that point." Then a thought crossed his mind. "If the luggage never arrived in the Dallas baggage claim, then someone must have taken it in Tucson, or scooped it off the plane in Texas. If the laptop had a tracking device, it would have been easy to find."

He flipped open his cell phone and called Sarah. "Hi Sarah. I'm in Dallas."

"That's great. I was getting worried. You hadn't called since you arrived in Tucson," she said in a concerned voice.

"I'm sorry about that. A lot of things have happened." Dayton paused to choose his words carefully. "I need a favor."

"Sure. Anything," she replied.

"Could you stay at my grandmother's tonight?"

"Sure. I'll drive over there when I get off duty. Is something wrong?"

"Please do this for me. I'll be arriving in Richmond around noon, the day after tomorrow."

Sarah in a worried tone persisted, "What's wrong?"

"I'll tell you when I get home. Not now. Tell my grandmother to keep Little Suzy Weston handy."

"Suzy who?"

"She'll understand," Dayton replied. "Just tell her that." Dayton hoped the message sunk in. "I miss you and I'll be home soon."

He didn't know if someone had tapped his phone, or his grandmother's. Giving Sarah the cryptic message was the most logical choice.

The drive to the hotel took about fifteen minutes. Dayton was tired and felt after all the events of the past few days, a good night's rest was in order. So he stripped himself naked and crawled in to bed.

Sarah got off duty and drove straight to Martha's house. Martha saw her pull in, driving Dayton's Jeep, so she came to the door.

"Sarah. What a pleasant surprise," she said, happy to have company.

"Dayton called about an hour ago," Sarah replied. "I'm really worried about him."

Martha gave Sarah a confused look. "Why?"

"He was being very cautious on the phone for some reason. He told me to tell you to keep a Suzy Weston handy."

Martha's expression changed and she raised her eyebrows. "Come in," she said as she took Sarah by the hand. She locked the front door behind them and asked Sarah to follow her upstairs into the study. "Wait right here for a minute," she asked Sarah, as she fetched a key from her bedroom, then returned. "I could never figure out this damn combination lock, so George gave me this key." She unlocked the safe and pulled out the 1917 S&W revolver in .45 caliber. She opened the cylinder, then reached in the safe and retrieved a loaded moon clip. She loaded it and held it in both hands; showing Sarah. "Suzy Weston. Smith and Wesson. It is a code word Dayton and George came up with. If someone Dayton arrested was out on parole, or there was a break-in nearby, Dayton would call and tell me to get out Suzy Weston."

Sarah smiled. "There is a lot I have to learn about this family."

Martha replied, "Oh, you're doing just fine. I'll bring Suzy down to my bedroom and keep her with me while I am at home."

"He wasn't worried about himself. He was worried about you."

Martha nodded her head. "Ever since he met one of my son's army friends, things have been a little different with him." Martha shrugged her shoulders. "Until he finds whatever he's looking for, I think I'll keep Suzy handy," she said patting the top of the gun. "Dayton is a lot like his father----always getting into something."

Martha walked down the hall to her bedroom to retire. Sarah sat in the chair looking at everything in the study. "If Martha's in danger, it might be because someone wants this stuff," she whispered while looking at the accumulated evidence on the desk. She found a empty box in the closet and placed all the items in it, except the Bible and the Washington book, walked the box down to the basement, then hid it under the pool table.

ↆ

The hotel phone rang. It was the courtesy wake-up call at 9AM coming from the front desk. Groggy, Dayton entered the shower. He wanted to get an early start, because he had a lot to accomplish in a short period of time.

First came the new clothes. Having your suitcase swiped meant Dayton didn't have any fresh clothes for the signing tonight. It was his last one, so he wanted to look sharp. He stopped at a Men's store in Dallas and purchased some dress pants, socks, underwear and a button-down dress shirt and tie. "Visa card, one-hundred thirty-four dollars and forty-two cents. Having new rags for your last book signing: Priceless," Dayton said and laughed as he left the store.

He stopped at a local drug store where he picked up another black binder, a pad of paper, a pen to take notes, and a toothbrush. "No laptop----we're going totally old school."

His last shopping stop was a department store at the mall to purchase a replacement suitcase.

Once all the shopping was done, he headed down toward Dealey Plaza; the infamous location of the J.F.K. Assassination. He parked the rental in the lot around the former School Book Depository, now known as the Dallas County Administrative Building. He walked to the Grassy Knoll, and surveyed the route taken by the President forty-six years earlier. "There is no way possible there was a shot from here," he muttered to himself. He walked northeast up Elm and looked up at the brick building; paying particular attention to the window on the sixth floor. "Best place," he said to himself, noting the distance to target couldn't have been more than a hundred yards. He looked across the street at the Dallas County Criminal Records building. "Nope." He shook his head. "Would have hit Jackie first." He wrote this all down on his notepad. He reached the same conclusion when he visited the site a year prior to authoring his book. But a good investigator always reviews the evidence again and again.

"I think I'm ready," he said to himself, as he walked away from the crime scene and back to the rental car.

Dayton returned to the hotel. He really missed his laptop, but the hotel had two computers in the lobby with free internet access. Even though he lost some of the evidence for one investigation, he still had his father's symbolic studies to research.

He sat down at the PC and worked from memory, for his black binder was also in his lost luggage. He recalled some of what Peter had told him concerning planetary alignments and that their effect was determined on the planets involved, degree of alignment and Constellation of origin. Then, he recalled the reverence shown to the Virgo constellation by the Masons, with their cornerstone ceremonies in D.C.

He Googled Virgo. "The virgin----Spica---260 Million light years----260, that is the same as the Mayan Tzolkin count. Spica was the brightest star in Virgo. But then he remembered the Virgin Mary symbol: The Virgo symbol with the crown. "The head," he whispered to himself. "What is so special about the head, besides it being where the planets form the triangle?" His interest peaked as he read that the head of Virgo had one of the highest concentrations of galaxies in the universe. Messier 87, was fifty-five million lights years away. "Fifty-five, the amount of signers of the Declaration," he thought. "And M87 has a strong output of radio and gamma waves. It even shoots forth a ray; one which astronomers have measured at over five-thousand light years long," he said quietly. "Interesting. I wonder if under the right circumstances, an outburst could reach our solar system. Radio waves could send a message," he thought. "But gamma rays could be bad. A focused ray, now that is interesting." He thought to himself and considered the possibilities. "What if one thing all these cultures long gone were timing, was some sort of an emission from the head of Virgo that gets amplified by the planets? Something they saw which they could remember it by." He pulled out his wallet and removed a dollar bill. "There are light rays coming from behind the triangular cornerstone with the eye. Could it be this energy from Virgo?" He wrote all the information down in his notepad.

"Sir, there are other guests who wish to use the internet," the man at the front desk told Dayton.

"No problem. I'm all set," he replied. Dayton got up and went back to his room. He placed the pad in his camera bag and proceeded to get ready in fresh clothes for his last signing at the Barnes and Noble, on 7700 West Northwest Highway. "Concentration. Conception. Head."

His hands adjusted his tie as he grinned in the mirror. "I can't wait until all this is over and I can get back to a normal life----if I can get back to a normal life." He walked over to his camera bag and removed the picture of him and Sarah standing in his Grandmother's front yard. "A normal life," he whispered. "What cop has a normal life anyway?"

Everything had been set up as Dayton had requested. The white board was to the left and a projector and laptop projected the cover of Dayton's book on a screen to the right.

"My name is Julie, and I am a representative from Triple E books. This evening we have a special guest, Dayton McCormick, who, instead of just talking about his book and answering a few questions, is going to make a presentation based on Chapter two of his work, <u>Means, Motive and Opportunity</u>. I would like to thank the generous folks here and Barnes and Noble for their hospitality----and without further ado, here's Dayton."

Dayton arose and addressed the crowd in his new outfit. "I don't wonder why people believe conspiracy theories. Hey, when the government seals records, like the one for the Kennedy Assassination until 2039, who is going to believe them?" He looked to his left and right at the crowd of about forty people. "Normally, I am just a cop. I need evidence to put criminals in jail. Without it, they walk. But tonight, were going to take a different walk. We're going to go through the conspiracies of J.F.K. Join me, and let's walk together down Elm Street, here in Dallas, on November 22nd, 1963."

Dayton projected a 3D image of Dealey Plaza on the screen. He looked at it for a second then asked the crowd to excuse him while he took away the screen and projected on the large write-on-whiteboard. "That's better," he remarked, "now I can draw on it."

He explained that Kennedy was on a fence mending and re-election tour. He traveled from Love Airfield. He addressed the crowd at his hotel. Then, because the weather turned nice, he had the top taken off the car and the bullet-proof side windows were rolled down. "In part, nice weather in combination with Kennedy's arrogance allowed his assassination to go forth----and I have no qualms about saying that."

"The '61 Lincoln, with agents Roy Kellerman and William Greer, took a right off Main street onto North Houston, then a left onto Elm." Dayton traced his hand along the path of the limo. "Sitting behind them were Governor John Connally and his wife, and the Kennedy's in the rear." Dayton pointed his fingers at a location before midpoint on Elm. "This is where he was shot." He minimized Google Earth and brought up the Zapruder film. "Here is the Zapruder film. If anyone is squeamish, please close your eyes. I'll let you know when it's over."

The crowd watched as the young president grasped his throat and Governor Connally leaned against his wife. "This is when the first bullet hit Kennedy in the back, sending a shard to his throat while the rest of the bullet exited and hit Governor Connally." A few seconds later, the crowd witnessed the right side of Kennedy's head explode open. "Although the first shot might have killed him----the second was a sure thing." He minimized the Zapruder film and maximized the 3D view of Dealey Plaza. "Look around folks. Based on the entry and exit points for the President's wounds," Dayton lowered his head, "the only place the shots could have come from was the Book Depository. And there were witnesses who saw a rifle hanging out of the sixth floor window." He walked back from the board. "If there was a shooter in the Grassy Knoll, he didn't hit the President. Only the shots from the Depository did that. Whether it was two, three or four shots, or maybe the possibility of more than one gunman, I can't be sure." Dayton turned around. "Some say Kennedy's murder was a Zionist conspiracy, or try to disprove the Zapruder film. After all, Zapruder was a Russian-born Jewish immigrant. But he was also a Kennedy supporter."

Dayton made a pair of X's on the spots where the limo was located and the hits occurred. "Did you know the limo was only going eleven miles per-hour. Eleven. After the first hit, Agent Greer, the driver, slowed down. After the second hit, Greer pushed down the gas pedal and sped off to Parkland. You know, there are some people who think the driver was involved. I don't believe that. Normal reaction----that's all. There are some that think a flechette was fired from the dash." Dayton brought up an image of the six sitting in the car. "Who could of fired it? And wouldn't it have hit Connally, and not Kennedy? Sure, it might have went through him first, but I think planning that would be more difficult than squeezing off two shots from a scoped rifle----at less than a hundred yards----at an open-topped limo."

Dayton walked up to the image of Dealey Plaza and pointed to Main Street. "Why did the motorcade turn on to North Houston then take a left on Elm? Why not just go up Main Street?" He walked over to a small table and picked up his water and took a sip. "Could it be that the fastest route up 35E, A.K.A. Route 77, to the World Trade Mart luncheon he was supposed to speak at, was to take the highway? If the agents drove straight down Main Street, the northbound entrance to the highway would have been inaccessible, and they would have had to double back to access the highway. Some say this route was planned last minute. Perhaps, but this change was most likely for speed of travel by accessing the highway, not necessarily for assassination purposes." Dayton pointed to the buildings surrounding the Plaza. "All of these are government buildings. No one had anticipated a sniper would be able to get inside."

Dayton maximized of photo of Lee Harvey Oswald. "Did he act alone? Not sure. He got the job at the depository shortly before Kennedy's visit. Fibers from his shirt were on the Carcano rifle." Dayton nodded his head. "He did have military training and was an alleged communist sympathizer. And eye witnesses saw him murder Officer Tibbits." Dayton's face appeared to scrutinize the crowd. "But he was only drinking a coke, right? It's interesting that there was plenty of Secret Service at the World Trade Mart, but nobody thought to secure the School Book Depository. If I was planning a motorcade, I am sure I wouldn't have overlooked the easiest sniper shot on route, although this is Monday morning quarterbacking. Oswald had means, motive and opportunity. My only question is, did he have an accomplice?" Dayton removed the photo of Oswald and projected other notable Kennedy Assassination conspiracies on the board. "But before I continue, the reason why I ask this is because in 1963, there was no instant news, like we have today. How did Oswald know Kennedy's limo would have the top down? Was it luck, or did someone call him on the phone?" Some people in the crowd looked like they had just been sucker punched, never hearing this suggestion before.

"Bay of Pigs and Cuban patriots. They had motive. Some say two of the Nixon plumbers from Watergate were there in Dallas. I find it hard to believe they would kill a President and not an old security guard at the Watergate."

"Nixon was not the friendliest of fellows. Was Jack Ruby, really Jack Rubenstein, a former aide to a then, Senator Nixon? Perhaps. But Ruby liked Kennedy and was disturbed by his death. His whole family testified about this."

Dayton took another sip. "What about George Herbert Walker Bush? Some say he was photographed at the

Book Depository. Bush was also the first to ask Nixon to resign because of Watergate. So could the former President have been the trigger man?" Dayton shook his head. "Doubtful. How about the mob? Probably not. Ahh I know who did it---." Dayton pulled up a photo of the Federal Reserve. "It was Alan Greenspan." Dayton smiled. "Just kidding. The Fed is a wealthy group. You think they could have purchased a better rifle than a Carcano, for an assassination? Sorry, that's here-say." He paused and mimicked Nixon's famous hand gesture. "The Federal Reserve conspiracy goes this way: that the Fed had Kennedy killed because of an Executive Order for the issuance of Silver certificates; thus by-passing the private central banking consortium. Only problem is it would have been easier to hire a lawyer to argue against said issuances in court. The President has no constitutional authority to coin money or assign value. That clearly rests with the Congress. They didn't need to hire an assassin."

Dayton shut off the projector. "Everybody killed J.F.K. folks---- according to conspiracy theorists. It was the mob, the plumbers, the Cubans, the Communists, the Fed, Nixon, Bush, Johnson, and if not them, the driver shot him. Could a conspiracy this large exist without anyone talking?"

A man stood up in the crowd. "So you mean to tell me, none of these conspiracies are provable and most likely are all false?"

"Yes, that is what I am saying. Want to hear something else? Life is full of coincidences. I find it interesting that one of the worst days in US history, the World Trade Center was destroyed, and on another miserable day in November of 1963, a President was assassinated on the way to the World Trade Mart. Sometimes things are just like that."

"Do you think Oswald was the shooter?" the man followed up.

"Yes. But as I stated, he may have had help," Dayton responded. "There are a lot of kooks out there. Was he working on someone's behalf? I don't know. But I would sure like to know how he got that job at the depository only days before the assassination. But that might not prove anything either. All these years, and nobody says a word. Nobody. Maybe there is a conspiracy here and maybe there isn't. One thing is for sure----On November 22, 1963, the stars were not aligned in John F. Kennedy's favor."

Dayton sat down at the table and the crowd began to line up with their books. A curious book buyer of about twenty years of age bent down and asked Dayton flat out, "even if you can't prove it and take it to court with evidence, who do you really think killed Kennedy and why?"

Dayton looked up at the young man. He had one of those faces; complete with a shit-eating grin. Dayton just had to respond. "Personally, I think he was killed simply because he was the President on November 22, 1963." He motioned the young man to come a little closer, than whispered in his ear. "But maybe a cult did it. A cult that follows astrology. But I can't bring Ur---anus or Jupiter into a courtroom."

The young man picked up his head and started laughing. "That is the best one I ever heard!" he exclaimed. Before he closed his book, Dayton sketched Dealey Plaza, and wrote the word "sacrifice," at the top, and below it, "Due to good weather."

After the last book buyer left, Julie walked over to Dayton, beaming a big smile. "That was fantastic Dayton. I wish this wasn't your last signing."

Dayton smiled. "It might not be. Maybe I'll write another book."

Julie's eyes lit up and her fat face glowed. "If you do, please ask for me for a promotions assistant. I'd love to work with you again," she replied, handing him her business card.

"Do we really get to choose our promotions assistants?" Dayton inquired.

"Oh yes. Usually authors get to meet all of us, and then they pick one of us who is available for when they are scheduled for their signings."

"So why did I get stuck with Steve? Not that he was a bad guy."

Julie looked puzzled. "I don't know. We're a small company which caters to budding authors." She took a second and continued. "Steve was hired right before your book was approved for publishing."

"Really," Dayton responded inquisitively. "What did he do before he came to Triple E books?"

"I think before he came to work for us, he did some time overseas on one of those relief efforts; helping out the poor in third world countries. I think that is what he told me."

Dayton smiled and thanked Julie profusely. "When I sit down to write again, I'll be thinking of you Julie."

He walked out of the Barnes and Noble in bewilderment. "Informant houses? Couriers? Relief efforts?" He questioned all of them in his mind. He shook his head as he got into his rental car. "I'm just glad it is over and I'm going home."

Chapter 18
Unfinished Business

Dayton stared out the window of the jet and watched the sun come up over the horizon. "A bright yellow ball----so precious to life on earth," he thought to himself.

He turned away from the window. "What a ride it has been over the past few months," he whispered softly. His thoughts turned to the mysterious friend of his father's, named Christopher Hartman, who turned his life upside-down by telling him his father had been murdered. Hartman's gift had gotten multiple investigations rolling for Dayton.

Then he met Mussen, who was another cohort of his father's. He was the paranoid intellectual who seemed to know more than he was willing to share, and there was something about him Dayton could not put his finger on.

Peter Devine was quite the character. He showed him how the planets interacted and their effects on both the sun and the earth. Dayton wished Peter was still alive, for he had countless questions that needed to be answered. Dayton realized the significance of the information Peter had presented to him, and he was determined to analyze more about how the solar system operated by following Peter's suggestions. "Thank god I made a copy of that sheet."

He found family in John Windwalker, as well as closure concerning the death of his mother. He also realized during the visit with John that, when necessary, he could kill with little or no thought. This bothered him.

And then, there was the cave. "Oh I wish I had those negatives," he thought to himself. Did the cave illustrate the potential effect which may occur sometime after the date for the sign in the sky that he and Sarah had found? A sign, which was incorporated into the geometric and symbolic structure of the Capital of the United States. But there was something he was missing. Something big. And he was determined to figure it out.

Dayton's thoughts turned to his stolen luggage. He felt angry because it contained the last needed information to bring to justice some of the people who were most likely behind his father's death. "I feel like I've failed. Now, I have nothing."

The plane taxied down the runway, and after a brief turn, accelerated to take-off speed. He felt his body become lighter as the nose of the plane lifted up and the rear wheels left the ground. "On eagle's wings," he thought, as he looked out the window at the aluminum arms which gave the aircraft its lift. "Or that of a Phoenix."

When the airplane leveled, he unbuckled his safety harness and reached up for his carry on. After he unzipped the top, he removed the photo of himself and Sarah and replaced the bag into the compartment above. His hands held it firmly as he looked at her face. It was a much more pleasant sight then the one he recalled in the cave discovered by John Windwalker's father, or the dead Mexicans laying on the ground near the border in the sand. His eyelids became heavy and his breathing deeper, as his thoughts floated away. Soon, he'd be home.

∾

Dayton stared at Sarah as she drove him back to Martha's house.

"What?" she asked, looking a little uncomfortable while he stared. "Are you ok?"

"I am so glad to be home. And I missed you." He gazed at her fair skin and her lightly freckled nose. Her hair was freshly washed and he noticed she recently had it styled. "I'd like to take you out tomorrow," he said.

"I'd like that," Sarah replied. "So. What are you going to do when you get home?"

"I think after I give grandma a big hug and get something to eat----I am going to go upstairs and crash. It's been a long couple of months. I didn't realize being an author was so much work." Dayton smiled. "I think my first book might be my last."

"Why is that?" Sarah asked. "You're a good writer."

"I don't know if I want to do this again," replied Dayton, shaking his head. "These signings took me away from the people I care about. And even though I get busy with the job, I still go home every day and sleep in my own bed."

"I hear you. And you don't lose your luggage." She paused for a minute. "Is that why you wanted me to have Martha get out Suzy Weston?"

Dayton smirked. "So you met Suzy, huh? She is long, cold and blue."

"Did you really think she was in danger?"

Dayton nodded his head. "Yes----and still is. I think I am too. And possibly you, so be careful. The loss of the luggage-----it was stolen----it was to keep me from putting evidence together that was very damning, because it proved treason against the United States during wartime. Without that evidence, I am not sure if trouble will come knocking. But I don't know if it is over," he explained.

"Well, I wouldn't worry about me. I'm a big girl."

Dayton replied, "You're worth worrying about, Sarah. And thanks for watching over my grandmother. She is the only other woman in my life."

"Only, other?" Sarah smiled. She then asked, "What about the other stuff? The symbolic stuff your father was researching? Did you find anything more about that?"

Dayton exhaled a small laugh. "That case is still ongoing. I just wish I could have showed you what I saw one night up in a cave in Arizona, with John Windwalker."

"Well, you could draw it out for me sometime. I'd love to see it."

"Maybe I'll just take you to Arizona and you could see it for yourself."

"A trip? Together?" Sarah replied in a happy tone.

"Yes. It was a real trip all right." Dayton yawned. Give me a night's sleep. I'll tell you all about everything that happened tomorrow."

Sarah pulled into the McCormick's driveway. She walked Dayton to the door and carried his camera bag as he towed his new luggage. A smile from inside the kitchen lit up the room. "Dayton, you're home!" He walked up to his grandmother and gave her a big hug.

"Good to see you Grandma," he said with a smile. "Let me walk Sarah---"

Martha interrupted. "Sarah, please take my car a few days until yours is fixed," she said, handing her the keys. "I'm sure Dayton wants his Jeep back."

"Are you sure, Martha?"

"Of course I am dear," she replied.

He walked Sarah out to Martha's car. Before she got into the driver's seat, he leaned forward and gave her a kiss. "Thanks for driving me home."

Sarah started the car. "I can't wait to hear all about your trip Dayton. Sorry I can't stay. I have to run some errands," she said. "But I'll come by later." Dayton gave her another kiss before she drove off. He walked back into the house and sat with his grandmother.

"Sarah made another batch of beef stew for me," Martha grinned. "Next time, don't be such a pig and save some for me."

"I'm sorry Grandma," Dayton replied.

She got up from the table and walked over to the stove. "I thought I would surprise you, with a nice brunch of pancakes and bacon." She poured some batter on the griddle and placed some bacon next to it. "How were your signings?" she asked.

Dayton sat thinking about whether or not he should tell her about everything that had happened. He decided not to. "They went well Grandma," he replied with a yawn. She looked over at him with a concerned glance.

"Is there something you're not telling me?" she asked as she filled two plates with food.

Dayton knew he couldn't avoid telling her everything, but he was going to try and stall. As she placed the plate in front of him, he raised his hand and put his finger and thumb close together. "I was this close," he said, "to having the evidence I needed to punish my father's killers. I had the evidence in my suitcase. And it was stolen."

Martha stopped walking as she held her plate of pancakes. She exhaled and looked at him with concern. "Dayton, let it go. Nothing can bring him back." She paused. "And you have a really nice girl and a good friend, which you need to spend some time with."

Dayton replied with his mouth full. "I know. I just---"

"It's ok," Martha interrupted. "He was your father. He was my only son. I understand the anger and the pain. But you need to move on. From what you have told me, Mickey had all this evidence and sent it away. Why?"

"To protect it," Dayton replied.

"But why didn't he use it?" Martha asked sternly.

Dayton stopped chewing. Her words had struck a chord in him.

❧

Sarah answered her cell phone. "Hey Sarah. Dayton home yet?" asked Mark.

"I just dropped him off," she replied. "He's really tired."

"Bummer for him. I'm my way over to the house, after I run a few errands. Should be there within an hour."

"He'll probably be sleeping," Sarah replied.

"Oh----he's such a Momma's----excuse me, Grandma's boy. Don't worry. I'm just going to pop in and pop out."

❧

After breakfast, Martha took the dishes and washed them in the sink. As she placed them in the draining board she asked, "Before you go lay down, I haven't picked up today's mail. I'm sure there are some bills----so I'm going to go upstairs and get my checkbook. Could you go out and get them from the mailbox?"

"No problem," he said.

Dayton walked out the front door and walked to the mailbox. He reached into the box and pulled out the mail. "Bills and junk mail," he whispered to himself. As he turned around, a large black SUV pulled into the driveway. He couldn't see the passenger, but he immediately recognized the driver. It was Steve from the publishing company.

As he got out of the SUV, Martha peaked out her bedroom window on the second floor.

"Hey Dayton. Good news. Sales have been terrific," he said grinning from ear to ear. He walked up to him and shook his hand. Steve was the last person Dayton expected, or wanted to see.

"That's great Steve. No offence, but I'm really tired from all the traveling. Can we meet some other time?"

Steve put up his finger. "Dayton. This won't take long. The division head of publishing is in the passenger seat. He wanted to meet you."

Dayton sighed.

"I'm so sorry I didn't call you first," Steve added.

"It's alright." Dayton looked inquisitively at Steve. "I thought you got promoted and Julie was my new contact person from the company."

"I did. But because I was your first handler, he requested I bring him."

Dayton thought for a minute. "Handler----that's an odd term," he thought to himself. Then he remembered John telling him that Steve had stopped by the Windwalkers looking for him.

"Is your grandmother home? I don't want to intrude."

"No," Dayton lied. "She wanted to get a jump on her Christmas shopping before Black Friday, so my girlfriend took her out in her car," he said while pointing to the empty spot in the driveway.

Steve motioned to the man sitting in the passenger seat to come out of the vehicle. The door opened and he walked around the front of the SUV, only showing his left profile.

"Mr. McCormick," he said. "I'd like to congratulate you on a great book." He turned and faced him. Dayton noticed right away the large scar on his face, but tried not to show it. "I know you know who I am," Hutchinson said. "So you don't have to play stupid." Martha stopped peeking through the window. She opened her nightstand drawer, walked over to the bedroom closet, got inside and pulled the clothes on hangers in front of her.

"You're Henry Hutchinson," Dayton said, eyeing him.

"Correct----and I work for Triple E Books. I couldn't pass up the opportunity to help out the son of an old comrade. Don't get me wrong, your book is very good. But in the publishing industry," Hutchinson emphasized, "connections are helpful." He handed Dayton the copy of his book, along with a pen. "I was hoping you could sign this for me."

Dayton accepted the book and pen. He opened the front cover to sign it, but stopped cold as he read the inside cover.

I was a friend of your dad's. He didn't commit suicide. He was murdered. Can we talk?

Any friend of my dad's deserves a free coffee and conversation. Wait outside. Respectfully, Dayton McCormick.

Dayton looked Hutchinson square in the eye. "You bastard!" He clenched his fist; getting ready to strike. Hutchinson waved his finger back and forth and pointed at Steven, who was holding a semi-automatic pistol at Dayton, from under his folded coat.

"Let's go inside. Any sudden moves----well----I think you get the point."

Dayton knew he had to play this one cool. His grandmother was inside. As he walked up the front steps, he closed his eyes and prayed that she would be ok. He hoped she would sneak out the back, or hide in a closet until it was over. As he breached the front door, he felt a cold metal needle pierce his neck, then felt his legs give way.

"I should have let you choke to death," Dayton slurred as his vision became blurry and his body hit the floor.

"You should have," Steve replied sarcastically as he kicked him in the stomach. Hutchinson and Steve stripped off his clothing in the living room. Dayton was powerless to do anything. They picked him up and dragged him upstairs to the bathroom.

"Your father gave us more of a fight," Hutchinson said. "I am disappointed in you." Steve laughed. They placed him in the bathtub and began running water. Steve went into the study to fetch the evidence Dayton had collected, but found the desk had been cleaned off.

"It's not here," Steve said. "Somebody took it."

"No matter. Come back in here," Hutchinson commanded. He looked down at Dayton as Steve came in and sat on the side of the tub, putting his back to the wall. Dayton tried to mutter something, but he was clearly incapacitated. "Do you have the suicide letter Steve?" Steve shook his head in acknowledgement. "After we kill him, we'll finish off Mussen and the Indian too. And without the paperwork we got from his luggage, the rest of the evidence will be inconsequential."

Hutchinson withdrew a straight razor and put it in the medicine cabinet. He then withdrew a brand new blade from his pocket. He looked at it, as the light from the vanity reflected off the blade. "Your father could have ruined everything for me and other associates of mine.

You see, wars are all about making money Dayton. I was placed on his team by someone important, to make sure he didn't find any evidence and bring it to light." Hutchinson smiled. "When you wrote your book, I saw it as an opportunity----to see if the evidence your father collected was complete and still existed. From tapping his phone, I realized he did. So I made a move." Hutchinson began to talk with an angry tone. "Only he had dispersed it out to the others first. I could have just gone out and killed them all. But I needed to know what they knew first." He approached Dayton lying helplessly in the bathtub. "If it wasn't for your father----and that Jew, Mussen, I would have never taken a bullet to the face in Cambodia." Hutchinson slowly rubbed his scar. "This wound runs deep----just as this razor will cutting into your veins."

He bent down to begin slicing Dayton's left wrist, but before the metal could touch skin, Hutchinson's right side erupted and blood splattered the vanity, milliseconds after her finger pulled back the trigger. He fell forward and jammed his right hand into the toilet. With a firm grasp, her hands guided Suzy Weston's barrel to the surprised, younger red-headed target. BAM. BAM. Steve collapsed straight down the outside of the bathtub, leaving blood splatter on the walls behind him, while red liquid oozed down his shirt, from two large holes in his chest. Hutchinson looked back at her, as he struggled on his knees to get up. His eyes were ablaze, like a wounded animal waiting to strike. "You killed my only son," Martha said coolly. "You won't get his." Without saying another word, she emptied the last three rounds into him. BAM. BAM. BAM.

Five minutes later, Mark arrived at the McCormick house. He reached for the doorknob and found it to be locked. "That's unusual. I thought Sarah said Dayton was home," he thought. He knocked on the door. "Dayton? Mrs. McCormick. Are you home?" He stopped knocking when he heard the voice of Martha McCormick crying for help. He reached into his pants pocket and pulled out a spare set of keys Dayton had given him. After entering the house, he withdrew his sidearm and quickly ran upstairs, finding Martha crying on the floor in front of the bathroom.

"Those bastards killed my son!" she said while clutching the revolver.

Mark ran into the bathroom and saw blood splattered everywhere, with two dead men on the floor and Dayton lying in the bathtub. He stepped over the men to check Dayton for a pulse. He was semi-conscious. "Thank god you're alive." He saw Dayton whispering something, so he bent down and put his ear to his Dayton's lips.

"Pictures," Dayton whispered.

"Pictures?" Mark asked.

"Get camera."

Mark walked out of the bathroom and checked on the shaken Mrs. McCormick, then dialed 911. "Officer down! Officer down! This is Detective Tylenda. Please send paramedics to 519 Cooper's Way. And hurry." He then dialed Sarah and she answered. In a broken voice, trying to keep calm, he said, "Sarah, you need to get back."

"Where? Mark, are you all right?"

"I'm at the McCormick's. Dayton's hurt."

"Oh my god!" she exclaimed, as her heart dropped into her stomach. "What happened?"

"There's been a shooting." Mark heard silence coming from the other end. "It wasn't Dayton, or Martha. I got two dead guys here and Dayton is barely conscious in the bathtub." Sarah dropped her phone and ran out of her apartment to Martha's car.

Mark fetched Dayton's camera out of the study and began to photograph the scene. He saw Dayton whisper again, so he bent down to listen.

"Hide card," Dayton said.

Mark put Dayton's camera away, took out the memory card and placed it in the top drawer of the dresser in Martha's bedroom.

Police, paramedics and Sarah all arrived in front of the McCormick house simultaneously. Sarah sprinted past the medics and the other cops and rushed upstairs. She found Mark comforting Martha. "He's in the bathroom."

She stepped over the bodies of the two other man and looked at Dayton lying naked and in a state of semi-consciousness. "Has he been shot?" she said while looking at the splattered blood throughout the bathroom. She breathed deeply to regain her composure.

"No. Just the other two," Mark frowned. "Martha got 'um."

Sarah looked over at Martha, who was still clutching the 1917 Smith and Wesson. She turned to look at Dayton and watched his lips move. Sarah bent down to listen, for his speech was still barely audible.

"Love you," Dayton slurred.

Sarah was taken aback. She kissed his forehead, then stood up. She then backed away from the bathtub so the paramedics could do their job.

"He should be ok Sarah," Mark said. He looked at one of the paramedics and said, after recalling what happened to Hartman, "I think they injected him with a combination of Flunitrazepam and Pancuronium." He gestured at the two dead men on the floor, then added, "Make sure they take a blood sample from Detective McCormick for analysis."

They brought in the gurney, hoisted him out of the bathtub and then rolled him outside to the ambulance.

Sarah followed in Martha's car as the ambulance drove off toward the hospital. Mark stayed to help Martha with her statements and keep her calm.

"He'll be ok, Martha. He's a strong guy."

Martha wrapped her arms around Mark. "Please take me to the hospital. I need to be with him."

Chapter 19
Recovery

"Sounds like she is a funny lady," Mark said in reference to Mrs. Windwalker.

Dayton sat up straight in his hospital bed. "They were both quite unique people," Dayton replied, laughing as he finished telling Mark, Sarah and his grandmother about the first time he met the Windwalkers, at the Arrowhead Garage in Tucson. He looked at Martha. She was barely cracking a smile. "Are you ok, Grandma?"

"I'll be fine," she replied. "It's nice to have some closure concerning Mickey's death." She stroked Dayton's hand. "When you said he'd been murdered, I didn't know what to think. I tried to hide my feelings." She closed her eyes and made an angry face. "I felt it would be easy killing the people who did it----and pulling the trigger was easy. Living with it afterwards is something else. I don't know how you police do it?"

"It feels horrible when you shoot someone Grandma. And even if you know it was in self-defense, or in defense of someone else, you still see their faces----and the faces they make when you pull the trigger," Dayton said as he pictured the four Mexicans near the US/Mexico border. "I can still see then."

"I'm just glad you're ok Dayton," Sarah said. "And that Martha had Suzy Weston." She winked at Martha. "And that she is a good shot."

Martha finally smiled. "After Dayton became a police officer, George would take me to the shooting range once a month. He said it would be a good idea to learn to shoot, because I might need to someday. George was right about so many things."

Mark stood up and looked at the time on his cell phone. "Sarah, we got to go on duty," he said reluctantly.

Sarah leaned over and gave Dayton a kiss. "Remember what you told me in the bathtub yesterday?"

He looked at her and put a puzzled look on his face. "I must have been pretty out of it. What did I say?" Sarah walked toward the door.

"I'm sure it will come back to you," she replied, as she walked out the door with Mark.

"That girl loves you Dayton," Martha said while poking him in the side with her finger. "Don't tease her."

Dayton smiled. "I know she does. And the feeling is mutual."

Both Dayton and Martha turned their heads toward the entrance of the hospital room after hearing a light knock. The large framed, be-speckled man entered the room with a less than pleased look about him.

"Hello Chief," Dayton said.

He looked at Martha. "Mrs. McCormick. I was wondering if I could have a few words in private, with Dayton? I feel rude for asking--- especially because of what you've been through."

She got up off her chair. "It is not a problem Chief Stankeiwicz."

"Are you ok, Ma'am?" he said with a nod.

"I'll be fine," she replied. As Martha walked out of the room, Stankeiwicz closed the door.

He walked over to the hospital bed and looked Dayton straight in the eye.

"Would you mind telling me what the hell you got yourself into?"

"Chief----it is a long story. Basically, my book publisher was really a former member of my father's army intelligence unit, who was really there to...."

Paul put up his hand and motioned Dayton to stop. "I am sure the rest of the story is very interesting. But you know what? This morning, for the second time in my career, Federal agents came into my police station, took bodies out of my morgue, and confiscated the rest of the evidence. And you know what else?" His face turned beat red. "I had to sign paperwork saying I couldn't talk about it, or I could be imprisoned. Do you remember what I said to you in the evidence lab?"

"Does this mean I am now patrolman McCormick?" Dayton asked.

The Chief leaned over and got right in his face. His red colored skin returned to normal and he began to smile. "No. You still are a detective, thanks to your cool-hand grandmother." He began to pace. "Thanksgiving is tomorrow. Your vacation time ends as of Monday. I suppose in between turkey and stuffing, you'll be cleaning and patching up your bathroom. But I expect you in my office Monday morning at 8AM. Detective."

"Thanks Chief. I am tickled by your concern."

Stankeiwicz smiled. "Couple more things. No case----means no deposition. Tell your grandmother to keep quiet about her shooting abilities." Dayton smiled. "I have her revolver in my desk. I had to haggle with the Feds for it. After all, if this didn't happen, then I could give an old lady her gun back." Stankeiwicz paused and smiled. "Oh, and you'll have a new partner as of Monday. Your partner Frank, after coming back for a few weeks after his gall bladder operation, decided that early retirement was for him. I'm envious. Your new partner's name is Nelson."

"Nelson?" Dayton repeated.

"You need your ears cleaned? That is what I said. I know you'll show him the ropes. He's green---but smart." Then Stankeiwicz pointed his index finger at

Dayton. "First thing I want you to teach him is not to get in over his head. Understand?"

"Yes Chief," Dayton acknowledged.

Stankeiwicz walked over to the door and turned the knob. "Have a nice Thanksgiving, McCormick. And stay out of trouble."

As the Chief left, Martha and the doctor entered the room. "Mr. McCormick. We just want to observe you for a couple more hours to be sure the effects of the drugs have worn off completely."

"Okay."

He pulled his glasses off and squinted to get a better look at the chart. "Looks like someone gave you a cocktail?" he said, raising his eyebrows. "Haven't seen anything like this since my days doing mission work in Central America."

"We're you in the military?" Dayton asked.

"No," the doctor replied, trying to brush off the inquiry. "Well regardless, you should be home before dinner time. Do you have someone to drive you?"

Dayton pointed at his grandmother. "Don't let her fool you. She's Mario Andretti and Annie Oakley, all wrapped up in to one."

"Very well then. Someone will be by in a few hours with your discharge paperwork." The doctor bid them well and went about seeing the other patients on the floor.

༄

Dayton and Martha stopped at the home center so Dayton could pick up the necessary items to fix up the bathroom. He picked up some new tile, and cleaning agents to give the bathroom a thorough scrubbing. Dayton piled the items in the shopping cart and went through the checkout line.

On the way back to the house, Dayton opened up. "I want to thank you Grandma for saving me----twice."

"What do you mean twice?"

"You saved me from those two men, who would have killed me, just like they did my dad and his friend Christopher. That was the second time. You saved me the first time after dad died. It wasn't easy growing up with just a father, but you and grandpa George were always there to help. And when dad was killed, you both loved me and raised me as your own."

"Well, why wouldn't we? You were our grandson."

"I know that. But it is still right to express my thanks. I don't know if I ever did before. I think these days, people take things for granted and I just wanted to let you know that I don't."

Martha smiled and glanced over at him quickly, then looked back at the road. "This is the first time I ever drove your Jeep. Now I know why you like it so much. You can see everything."

Dayton frowned. "Speaking of changing the subject, I know it is hard to sort through your feelings about what happened yesterday. Killing is never easy. When I was with John out in Arizona, I killed three men and wounded a forth. If I didn't, they would have killed us both."

"Dayton," she replied, "the feelings I told you about in the hospital----the ones I said I had a hard time dealing with----were feelings of joy. It felt good to shoot those bastards. It shouldn't feel good to kill anyone. After shooting them, my only regret was I didn't have more bullets in the gun."

"Whoa!," Dayton said as his eyelids smacked his forehead. After he regained his composure he said, "Gram, they took away your only son. Those feelings are natural. And we have both good and bad in us. The difference between us---and them----is we try and feed

337

the good parts of us and repress the bad ones. They don't. Although I see it all the time on the streets, those men you killed are far worse than most I have come into contact with as a police officer."

"I still wish I had more bullets." Dayton shook his head and laughed.

Martha pulled into her driveway. They both got out and carried the purchases from the home center into the house, and Dayton immediately walked upstairs and began to repair and clean the bathroom. Looking from the hallway, Martha said, "Watching you work brings back good memories. Your grandfather always loved using tools----and teaching you how to use them too." She smiled. "Obviously you paid attention to what he taught you."

Dayton pulled the tiles off the wall which had been shattered by gunfire. Sarah and Mark had cleaned the area up earlier, but there was still some residue, so he scrubbed the bathtub out, along with the tile and grout around the walls. The replacement tiles Dayton fitted were an exact match, for the McCormick's had just renovated the upstairs bathroom three years prior, and the style hadn't changed. After he finished, Dayton carefully inspected his work. "No one would ever believe two people were shot in here yesterday after lunch," he thought to himself. "Grandma, come check out the bathroom."

"I think I'll stay away from it for a few days, if you don't mind," she replied. Dayton frowned. He was barely conscious when the shooting took place, and he understood that she needed time to rationalize what had occurred.

"Give her time, Dayton," he said to himself.

"Mrs. McCormick," Mark said, holding his stomach with his left hand while using his right to sip his beer. "That was the best Thanksgiving meal I ever had."

"Well don't just thank me, Mark," she replied, looking at Dayton. "Dayton and Sarah both helped me prepare it. In fact, Sarah made the stuffing. It was her own recipe---and I noticed you had seconds," she said nodding her head. "Or was it thirds?"

"Fourths actually," Dayton quipped. "And he is going to have to work out for three days straight to keep this meal off his waist."

"Hey, I got watch my girlish figure," he replied.

Leslie laughed. "You are all too much. And thanks for inviting me, Mrs. McCormick. Dinner was terrific. I usually eat at my brother's house, and his wife usually dehydrates the turkey."

Sarah, Mark and Dayton laughed aloud. "There's a biochemist in the house," Sarah said. Leslie blushed. "I'm just busting you Leslie," Sarah replied, as she was making a small plate of turkey for her cat Sausha, who had to be locked in the basement as soon as the smell of turkey began emanating from the stove.

Everybody got up, cleaned their plates off and stacked them on the counter. Dayton started washing the dishes. "Can I help?" asked Sarah. Mark, Leslie and Martha went in to the living room to catch the football game. "Sorry I lost the pool game for us earlier."

"Sure." The two washed and dried the McCormick's fine china, and were careful not to break a single piece. Then Dayton and Sarah started stacking them in the cupboard. While moving about the kitchen, they nearly collided, as they both tried putting the dishes away. They stopped for a moment and looked in each others' eyes.

"You were supposed to come see me yesterday," she said looking at him. "I guess due to circumstances, I'll let it slide."

"I'll try not to have anyone try and kill me on days we have dates."

"You know I am just kidding."

"I know."

She placed the dishes she had in her hands into the cupboard then grabbed the dishes he held and did the same. Then, the two embraced. "I almost thought I had lost you the other day."

Dayton kissed her on the forehead. "The only way you'd lose me is if you kicked me out of your life. I meant what I said to you in the bathtub."

Sarah's eyes opened wide. "You told me you couldn't remember what you said." She put her hands up in the air, pretending to mimic Dayton. "What did you say----I was kind of out of it."

Dayton threw his arms around her and pressed his lips against hers. "I WUB U," he said as he kissed her." She smiled and continued kissing him.

After it was over, he looked at her. "A man needs to choose his words carefully. Well-placed----they can do great things. Mis-spoken, and they can lead to his undoing," Dayton said as he thought of Mussen. Sarah smiled at him. "I guess some of his cliché's are pretty good," he thought to himself.

Sarah then bit her bottom lip. "Well---you can tell me those words every day."

"Hey, would you two stop playing house in the kitchen," Mark yelled from the living room. "You're missing a great game. And Dayton, could you bring me another beer from the fridge?"

Dayton opened a cold beer, put it on a tray and entered the living room. "Yes Honey," Dayton responded snidely. "Coming right up dear. Could I get you anything else---darling?"

"Oh, knock it off Dayton," Mark replied. "But could you go back in the kitchen and fetch some beers for Leslie and Martha too?"

A UPS truck stopped in front of the McCormick house Saturday morning. Looking out the window, Dayton asked, "Did you order anything, Grandma?"

"No. Why?"

"There is a delivery truck out front. And now the driver is walking to the door with a package in his hand."

The driver, clad in brown, pressed the doorknob. Dayton opened the door.

"This is a package for a Dayton McCormick. Are you him?"

"Yes," Dayton replied cautiously, getting prepared to move quickly if this was a set up.

"Could you sign here," he said. Dayton signed the electronic signature reader and handed it back to the UPS man. "Have a nice weekend sir."

Dayton looked at the package in his hands. He shook it and felt something jostle inside. "So what is it, Dayton?" Martha asked.

"I don't know. But it is addressed to me." He brought it over to the kitchen table. "I can't read the return address----and it is marked "Auto parts" on the outside of the box."

Martha's curiosity got the best of her. "Are you going to open it?"

Dayton removed his pocketknife and sliced the sealing tape on the brown box. He removed the contents, which were heavily sealed. He carefully removed the bubble wrap around the object. "It's a JEEP-Willy's Overland manual from 1956. I didn't order this." He opened it up, to find a typed letter in the front of the binder.

Hey Day,
Your father taught me good. 1st Rule of intelligence--don't open the package. But if you do, follow rule #2----Make copies.
Cousin John,
P.S. when you get time, don't forget to come visit. I have your little friend here too. Don't say too much on phone--bad thing to do. People listen.

Dayton flipped through the manual. Behind all the electrical Jeep schematics was a copy of the Baxter-Cudman shipping records and the Naval records for a young communicator named Phillip Cudman.

"Oh my God! It ain't over yet."

"What isn't over?" Martha asked.

Dayton ran upstairs and removed the evidence from the Willy's binder. Although his laptop was gone, his printer copier was still in the study. He made copies and put them in the safe. After he shut the safe door, he ran down into the basement and fetched the other evidence Sarah told him she hid under the pool table. Holding it all in his hands, he returned upstairs to the kitchen table and sat down with Martha.

"I have to take another short trip to Baltimore. I'm leaving early in the morning." She looked at him and noticed a twinkle in his eye.

"What are you up too?" she asked him, as she would a curious child.

"Do we have any wrapping paper in the house?" Dayton asked.

"No. No, I don't think so."

Dayton got up from his chair. "I'll be back in a few hours. I have to do a little shopping."

Dayton got into his Jeep and headed for the mall. His first stop was the computer store to replace the laptop that was stolen with his luggage back in Tucson. He picked up ink cartridges for his printer, along with photo-grade paper. His last stop was the card store, where he purchased some fancy Chanukah wrapping paper.

He loaded his photo editing software into the new laptop, then hooked the USB cable up to his printer. He inserted the CD of the scans of the negatives he made down in the forensics room at the police station, then printed out 8x10 copies of each, sans the photo of his father's military team. He carefully packed the photos, shipping records and naval records into a black binder, then put it in an empty box he had laying around in the closet from his move to his Grandmother's house. On top in the binder, he placed a typed synopsis of the contents of the box and their relation to one another, which included the codes for the ships from his father's code page he had received from Hartman. Carefully wrapped and with a bow on top, Dayton knew the contents in the box were sure to please a certain Jewish professor.

The following morning, Dayton kissed his grandmother goodbye, and carried the wrapped gift to his Cherokee. "I should be back by late afternoon."

"Just be careful Dayton," Martha reminded him.

"I'll be fine. See you this afternoon." Dayton smiled. "If anyone asks where I am going----tell them I went shopping."

Chapter 20
The Scales of Justice

His knuckle tapped the door three times. "Professor, are you home?" Dayton looked through the window and watched the older gentleman limp to the door in his pajamas and sleeping cap.

"Oh," Dayton heard from coming behind the door. "Young McCormick. What a pleasant surprise." Mussen looked at the clock on the wall and noticed it was half past eight. "I'm sorry," he said as he looked at his sleeping attire. "I must have slept in late."

Dayton looked up at the older man. "I don't see any vans. Why don't we go out for breakfast. My treat."

A smile came over Mussen's face. "I'd be delighted. Just give me a few minutes to put on something more appropriate." Mussen walked up stairs and got dressed. He came down wearing his signature tweed jacket and hat.

"I'm sorry I came unannounced Professor," Dayton apologized, "but you really need to get a phone." Mussen raised one of his bushy grey eyebrows.

The two stopped at a restaurant offering a full brunch buffet. They filled their plates and sat in a remote corner of the establishment. "So what do I owe this honor, young McCormick?"

Dayton opened the binder he carried in with him and showed the professor the solar system arrangements of the dates for the Kennedy and Lincoln Assassinations and 911, followed by their corresponding symbolic locations when measured in the Mall in Washington. "Triangles or pyramids, with the Planet Jupiter, at the top. Like a Roman Triumph and the symbol on the back of the dollar bill."

"Roman?" Mussen questioned. "Are you sure?"

Dayton looked puzzled. "What do you mean?"

"I read your book," replied Mussen. "Very good---by the way. One thing about it struck my fancy." Mussen smiled, showing his teeth wrapped around his wrinkled mouth. "How did you put it? In order to find the truth, you must go back to the original source material for the conspiracy. Over time, stories grow legs."

"I'm not following you," Dayton said.

"Symbolism should be looked at the same way. Who came before the Romans? Or should I say----where did they get their knowledge from?" questioned Mussen.

"The Greeks, the Egyptians and the Babylonians," replied Dayton.

"Correct," smiled Mussen. "And where did they get their knowledge from?"

"Where are you going with this Professor?"

Mussen laughed as he picked up his fork. "Western civilization was formed by two things: The Bible, and those who started those early civilizations. The ones who came from an empire that was destroyed, where you are now living. The land of the flat-topped mountain of God."

"Atlantis?"

Mussen forked up some home fries. "You could call it that." Dayton and Mussen talked about the mythical early empire while eating. When their meals were finished, Dayton pulled out a dollar bill.

Pointing to the eye, Dayton told Mussen. "This is a date. The arrangement is representative of a sign in the sky." Mussen nodded his head. "September 3, 2016." Mussen nodded again. "Jupiter, Venus and Mercury forming a triangle with the moon in the middle as the eye." Again, Mussen nodded.

"Your father knew that." Mussen acknowledged. "That is why he studied New York, Giza and Washington D.C. The sign is the capstone."

"But what is the light behind it?" Dayton questioned.

"I am the mother of fair love and of fear and of---"

"Holy hope. Ecclesiastes 24," Dayton replied, finishing Mussen's statement. "The light of the Virgo Supercluster."

"You've done your homework. Very good."

"It's the Virgo super cluster." Dayton paused to drink some juice. "The light of Virgo. And when I was with Peter, I learned that there is cause and effect upstairs," Dayton pointed up, indicating the solar system. "Messier 87 projects a gamma ray. I was thinking maybe the arrangement on September 3rd somehow amplifies it. If it doesn't, then maybe it is just a sign for something that had occurred or will occur in the future----perhaps with our sun."

"So you've read Genesis too. Signs and seasons," Mussen laughed. "I know what you are thinking. Many people seem to think Jesus Christ was nothing more than the sun, personified. After all, Matthew, Mark, Luke and John are symbols for Aquarius, Leo, Taurus and Scorpio. The Seasons." Mussen paused. "I think they are mistaken." Mussen had Dayton's complete attention. "Yes, Jesus had twelve apostles, like there are twelve signs in the Zodiac. Yes, he had his four, like four seasons. But he is, and was, not the sun. Like a good conspiracy theory----that idea has misled many people."

Dayton considered what Mussen had said for about a minute. He looked up at Mussen. "I think this sign comes before," he said, pointing at the all-seeing eye, and remembering what he saw in the cave.

"Noah knew a hundred years before the flood was coming. And God left his sign in the sky afterward. The Magi found Jesus after he was born, by following a sign in which they understood the significance. Through careful Bible reading, however, King Herod did not. Nor did his advisors." Mussen elaborated further. "Signs can come both before, or after. But in this case," he stated while pointing at the dollar, "you may be right."

The two got up and Dayton paid for their breakfast. They returned to Mussen's house. At the door, Dayton said, "Wait a second. I forgot something." He returned from the Jeep carrying a box wrapped in Hanukah paper with a bow on top.

"For me?" inquired Mussen. The two entered the house and sat in the living room. Mussen placed the gift on the coffee table.

"I really enjoyed our breakfast today," stated Dayton.

"I did too, young McCormick."

Dayton motioned a hand toward the gift box. "Well. Are you going to open it?"

Mussen opened his gift. After he tore off the paper and opened the box, he found a black 3-ring binder similar to the one Dayton carried. He flipped through the photographs of the arms shipments, shipping tags for Baxter-Cudman, temples and boats. His eyes lit up when he saw the shipping records and the naval records for a young man, now Senator from Louisiana. "Where did you get these? I've seen the photos before, because I watched your father take some of them." He looked up. "But I didn't know your father had gotten the other records. He told me on one of his trips up here a year before he died that he had someone on the inside. A new person. The other one, he told me, died years before."

Dayton nodded his head. "The first one was my mother. I think she got the Naval records."

Mussen blinked his eyes. "I'm sorry, young McCormick----so sorry."

"I've been to her grave and looked at her headstone. I don't know how to feel, because I never met her." Dayton exhaled. "Not to change the subject, but I don't know what to do. As my Police Chief puts it---I'm out of my league---over my head. The kind of people that can steal my luggage from an airport and erase the airline records are beyond my reach." Mussen understood.

"I received these copies of the records in the mail from someone I had visited."

"John?"

"Yes," Dayton replied. "It is so hard to know who I can trust in all this."

Mussen frowned. "Bear in mind, young McCormick, there are two sides operating. Or perhaps, three. Some good----some bad. It is hard to tell them apart sometimes."

"Like the reporting house in Bozeman?" Mussen twitched his cheek. "Hutchinson never lived there."

"Intelligence is a interesting business." He flipped through the papers again. "I think I know someone who might be able to bring about some closure to this matter. It can't be through ordinary channels, because of the geopolitical implications. Not just because of Vietnam, but also Cambodia. You've heard of the killing fields?"

"Yes."

"Well," Mussen continued, "Collaborating with the enemy to the detriment of your own is one thing. Providing materials which led to the massacre of millions, is another. It would be a international scandal, which could open up a very large can of worms."

"So you'll take care of it?" asked Dayton, while raising an eyebrow.

Mussen frowned. "Did you make copies?"

"Rule number-two."

"Indeed. If something were to say, happen to this old codger, see to it that those copies make it to the papers. Understand?"

"Understood." Dayton got up off the couch. He looked at his watch and said, "I have to be going."

"Thank you, Dayton," Mussen replied as the younger man walked toward the door. "I had a nice time this morning." He held up the binder. "And for this."

Dayton was just about out the door when he remembered one question he had always meant to ask Mussen. "Professor," he said, turning around. "One last question today. The man in southeast Asia. What did he show you and my father?"

Mussen arose from his chair. He looked out a window and noticed a van parking a few doors down from his house. He looked at Dayton apologetically and exhaled. Dayton understood Mussen's concern, so he didn't press further and walked toward the door. "He took us spelunking, Dayton."

Dayton turned. "What was that again?"

"Spelunking," Mussen replied. "Thanks again for breakfast. Next time, it will be on me."

Dayton walked to his Jeep and got in. As he drove away, he muttered, "Spelunking. I'll have to look that up." As he continued driving, a funny thought came over him. "Was that the first time he called me by my first name? Hmm?."

Mussen reached into his coat pocket and pulled out his vibrating phone. A voice from the other end spoke. "Does he know?"

Mussen replied, "I'm not sure. But as of now----no."

"Make sure he doesn't."

Mussen closed his phone, then opened it. He called information, looking for the office number of Senator Phillip Cudman. He wrote it down from the recording then called. "Is the good Senator going to be around this week? I need to speak to him about an important matter."

The staff worker replied, "The Senator has left the Capital for Louisiana. He should be able to be reached through his offices there this weekend."

"Thank you," Mussen replied; closing his phone.

&

Dayton arrived back in Richmond and stopped at the police station. He walked into Stankeiwicz's office, where Chief Paul promptly got up and removed his mother's S&W revolver from his filing cabinet. "Nice gun," the chief commented.

Dayton picked it up and noticed there wasn't any powder residue. "I cleaned it for your grandmother," the Chief replied. "Now get it out of here and I'll see you tomorrow."

Dayton held up the gun. "Thanks Chief." He placed it in his coat pocket, walked out of the station to his Jeep and then drove home.

When Dayton entered the house, he was greeted by Martha. "You weren't gone long." She kissed the side of his face.

"Just had a short breakfast meeting," Dayton replied, "with an old friend of dad's." Martha nodded her head. Dayton walked upstairs and placed the gun back into the safe in the study.

When he came back down, Martha spoke. "Just to let you know, Mark is downstairs in the basement playing pool. He came to check up on me----and you."

"But where is his truck?" Dayton asked.

"He told me a friend of his is borrowing it to move some furniture this afternoon. He's right downstairs. You should go see him."

Dayton grabbed his new binder with his notes from the study, then walked down into the basement and silently watched his best friend leaning over the table to take a shot. "If you want to sneak up on someone, you'll have to learn to walk quieter," Mark announced. "I've been here for an hour and was wondering where the hell you were?"

"Spelunking," Dayton replied, remembering what Mussen had told him.

"You went caving?" replied Mark, confused.

Dayton smiled, realizing Mussen had chosen his words carefully due to being watched. "No. Just went to have breakfast with someone."

"Well, let's play some pool," said Mark. The two engaged in billiards for about an hour; both winning an equal amount of games.

"We'll play the tiebreaker in a minute. I want to show you something," Dayton remarked. He arranged the billiard balls in the same fashion as the solar system arrangements of the Kennedy and Lincoln Assassinations and 911. He asked Mark if he noticed anything.

"Seeing as this isn't a shell game, I would say the eight ball was always at the top."

"Correct," Dayton replied. "The eight ball is Jupiter. And actually it was always on top of a truncated pyramid, if you drew lines between the other balls."

"So?"

"The arrangements I made, were for Lincoln's Assassination, then Kennedy's. Then for 911." Dayton opened his folder and showed Mark his sketches, the sacrificial photo and pointed to the pyramid roundel on the dollar. "Symbolism, astronomical make-up and timing and the symbolism from a fixed point, when measuring from the Meridian in Washington D.C. They are all related."

Mark looked at Dayton puzzled. "So you are saying that either someone had planned these events based on the planetary arrangements----or that the solar system somehow influences events on earth."

Dayton looked pleased. "You have been thinking about it."

"Of course I have. It is pretty interesting," replied Mark. "I just don't know if I believe it." Dayton then arranged the balls to look like Stonehenge. "Ok," Mark replied. "What's that?"

"Stonehenge."

"Enlighten me," replied Mark, waving his hand.

"Ancient people built these because they were timing something."

Mark rolled his eyes. "What----like a global cataclysm? Like 2012?"

Dayton smiled, nodding his head. "Exactly, and other things too. But it isn't 2012---although I am not absolutely sure about anything yet."

"Dayton," Mark said, "We could be taken out anytime by a big meteor, or some star which shoots a gamma ray or goes nova. I just watched something on-line last night on a news site. Scary stuff."

"I'm not saying they couldn't happen Mark. But there is something important---something big---which happens cyclically. It is why people built these," Dayton said as he pointed at his makeshift Stonehenge of pool balls, "to find the timing. I just don't know what that big thing is. But my hunch is that it is not from outside this Solar System. Maybe it is with the sun----or something."

"Could be anything, Dayton. Remember a few years back when the department got all those calls from yahoos thinking there was a UFO in the sky?"

"Yes. And it was only Venus." Dayton recalled how bright Venus was. He knew that Venus goes through stages of various brightness as both the morning and evening star. But it was, as he recalled, abnormally bright. He stood silently, deep in thought. He considered that maybe the brightness of Venus could have been considered a sign, although not the one he was looking for. Then he remembered his research into the speculation of the sign in the sky around the time of the birth of Jesus. Most involved Venus and Jupiter. He looked at Mark. "You are a god-damn genius."

"I like to think so," boasted Mark. "And you are better than the Discovery Channel. Creepy----but better."

"I do have a big question," Mark stated. "You mentioned to me that the Statue of Liberty was a sign of the Trinity, and that it witnessed 911. If so," Mark continued, "and 911 and the Kennedy assassination are related----then where is the Trinity with Kennedy?"

Dayton thought for a moment. "On 911, the World Trade Center was destroyed. Liberty watched it occur. Kennedy was on his way to the World Trade Mart for a luncheon." Dayton stopped to tap his forehead with a finger. "Kennedy was shot at the truncation of a pyramid on Elm Street in Dallas, if you look carefully at the structure of Dealey Plaza. He was rushed to Parkland Hospital." A smile came over Dayton's face. "Huber. Father Oscar Huber."

"What?"

"Father Huber gave J.F.K. his last rites."

"Where are you going with this?" Mark asked.

Dayton smirked. "Father Huber was from the Holy Trinity Catholic Church in Dallas. He was the trinity witness."

Mark nodded his head. "That's deep."

"And this opens up a whole can of worms," Dayton said.

"How so?"

"I should have known," Dayton said with a smile, "when things are related."

"What do you mean?" Mark inquired.

"The Kennedy family was considered America's royal family. What some have perceived as their curse----their tragedies----perhaps had a hidden meaning or message behind them. For one family to be so successful----yet so unlucky. Why?"

Mark shook his head and grabbed his cue stick. "Bad things happen to a lot of high profile people. Let's rack these balls and play the tiebreaker. You can test your theories later----after I beat your ass at pool," replied Mark.

Dayton smiled. "Bring it on. I'll break."

❧

Dayton explained the timeline feature of Washington D.C. as they both sat in front of his new laptop. He showed Mark the middle of Third Street and demonstrated the relationship of meters to years in the Washington timeline.

"11-22-1963. Truncated pyramid," Mark said as he traced his finger on the streets of D.C. "Now I better understand what you meant downstairs with those triumph things and the roundel symbol on the dollar. But what about the Jupiter on top----in the city itself?"

Dayton pointed to Capitol Hill. "Capitoline Hill----for Jupiter----and his triad." Dayton measured from 3rd street to the center of the Grant Memorial. "This is September 11th of 1983----not 2001." He surfed to his favorite solar system simulator website and typed in that date.

"Oh my," Mark remarked, as he traced his finger between the planets. "It looks similar to the Capital layout----and with Jupiter in the middle----like the Washington Monument."

"That's right," Dayton answered. "And eighteen years later, planes hit the Twin Towers and the Pentagon." He looked at the date. "1983," he muttered, then wrote it down. "Eighteen years later." He scribbled over the one and eight in 1983. "No 93," Dayton said. "Flight 093 crashed in Shanksville, Pennsylvania."

"And the first attempt on those buildings was in February of 1993," Mark stated. "93. That's pretty interesting."

Dayton typed in September 3, 2016 into the simulator after he removed a dollar from his pocket. "This," Dayton said, pointing to the triangle with the eye, "Is a date." He switched the simulator into sky view mode, which portrays how the planets would look from the earth.

"I'll be damned," Mark replied. "September 3rd, 2016 at 2:22 UTC." He stared at screen on Dayton's laptop. "Hey. September 3rd. That's 9-3, Dayton. 93." He looked over at Dayton, who was smiling. "What does this mean!" Mark exclaimed.

"That is what I am trying to figure out," Dayton replied. "When I get a chance, I think I am going to take another walk down Pennsylvania Avenue and look around for some clues."

 و

"Are you almost ready?" Dayton asked Sarah on his cell phone.

"Come pick me up anytime," replied Sarah.

Dayton put his hand over the microphone on his cell. "Grandma," he yelled downstairs. "Sarah and I are going out to dinner."

"You don't have to yell," Martha said as she peeked out from her bedroom door. "I'm up here."

Dayton frowned. "You're so quiet that I never know where you are in this house." He thought about how she had recently saved his life due to her stealthy movements. "But that is a good thing," he said with a smile.

Martha knew exactly what he was thinking about. She smiled. "You two have a good time. Don't forget, you're going back to work tomorrow."

Dayton appreciated his Grandmother's reminders. She was always looking out for him. He took his finger off the microphone on his cell. "I'll be over in about fifteen minutes Sarah."

He walked upstairs and took a couple minutes to make a sketch of what he got from John Windwalker and put it in his new black evidence binder. "Everything is coming together." Dayton looked at his watch. "I got to go get Sarah."

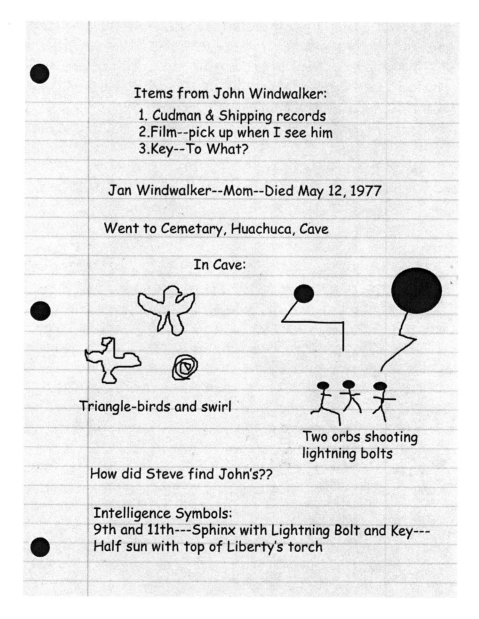

Items from John Windwalker:

1. Cudman & Shipping records
2. Film--pick up when I see him
3. Key--To What?

Jan Windwalker--Mom--Died May 12, 1977

Went to Cemetary, Huachuca, Cave

In Cave:

Triangle-birds and swirl

Two orbs shooting
lightning bolts

How did Steve find John's??

Intelligence Symbols:
9th and 11th---Sphinx with Lightning Bolt and Key---
Half sun with top of Liberty's torch

Dayton sized-up the younger detective, as he stood waiting in front of his desk. "You must be Nelson."

"Yes sir."

Dayton didn't look amused. He was only thirty-three, and not some old fart. "Call me Dayton----Nelson. Sir, is way too formal." Dayton thought about how young Nelson looked. "Did I look this young in my mid-twenties?" he wondered.

"Okay," replied Nelson. The two walked out together to their un-marked police car in the back lot. "So what crimes are we solving today?" inquired Nelson.

"Don't know yet. There is nothing on the docket." Dayton smiled as he handed the keys to his new partner. "You drive----and as far as cases go, we'll see what happens."

The two sat and ate donuts in the car while they watched over some mom and pop stores. As he chewed, Dayton pulled out the monocular John had given him and panned back and forth to look for anything unusual.

"That's not standard department issue, is it?" Nelson asked while pointing at the monocular.

"No----it is not. I like using my personal stuff," Dayton frowned while pulling his eye away from the eyepiece. "My camera is in the trunk, so make sure we keep the car locked when we're not in it."

Dayton stared at the younger man while he ate. Nelson had a fresh high and tight, and he looked more like a rookie patrolman than a detective. "You might want to grow your hair out a little. You're not covering a beat anymore." He put his monocular back to his eye and continued scanning the area. After a few minutes, he saw something he didn't like. "Oh shit! Jamal."

"Who's Jamal?" Nelson inquired.

With the monocular still pressed against his eye, Dayton responded. "Jamal is a low-level hood. He's very book smart. I wish he'd straighten himself out."

Dayton pulled his eye away from the viewer. "And he is the fastest motherfucker on two feet." He looked back through the lens. "And he just went into that store." Dayton exhaled. "Nelson, I want you to walk around the block and cross the street," Dayton pointed, "and get right near the front door of that convenience store, on the right hand side. I'm going to walk to the alley on the other side. Understand?"

Nelson shook his head. "Do you think something is going down?"

"Petty theft," Dayton nodded.

"Shouldn't we call for other cops?"

"See that store over there?" Dayton pointed.

"Yes."

"It is owned by the mob. We're trying to prevent a homicide."

The two detectives got out of the car and walked into position. Nelson took his position to the right of the store, while Dayton placed himself in the alley on the left. He picked up a top to a garbage can. "Old school," he muttered, "Should work fine." He looked down the street and motioned Nelson to be a little less visible.

Jamal darted quickly from the store with the owner shouting "thief" right behind him. Detective Nelson came from around the corner on the right and was spotted immediately by the young robber. Jamal turned in the other direction and began to run.

"Stop! Police!" shouted Nelson. He stood there amazed at how fast Jamal accelerated.

Dayton stood in the alley while swinging the can top with his wrist. "Three--two--one," Dayton whispered as he flicked his wrist and sent the garbage can top whirling in the air toward the sidewalk.

BAMMM. Jamal ran right into it and collapsed to the sidewalk. "What the---"

Dayton spread his legs over him, pulled Jamal's arms back and cuffed him. "Hi Jamal," Dayton smiled. "Miss me?"

"How do you know I'm Jamal?"

Dayton reached into his back pocket and removed his wallet. He pulled out the young man's ID and put it to his face. "It says Jamal, right?"

"Yo----you got me McCormick." Jamal put his nose down to the sidewalk.

Dayton's thumb was still in his wallet. He noticed a large stack of green bills. "Being a currier again, Jamal?" Nelson walked up and joined his partner.

"No. That's my benefit money," Jamal quipped. "Give it back."

"$893.00. That's a pretty big benefit. What did you take?" Dayton noticed a soda bottle was exploding in the road and there were a few mashed chocolate bars on the sidewalk. "You stole about five dollars worth of stuff, when you could have paid for it. Hmm?"

Dayton walked to the convenience store as Nelson watched Jamal. He handed the owner, who stood outside, a five dollar bill and then walked back to Nelson. "I just paid your bill. Nelson," Dayton motioned with his hand, "Pick him up and walk him over to the car."

When all three were in the car, Dayton turned around and faced Jamal. "We're going to take a ride."

"Are you bringing me to the police station?"

"No."

Jamal looked nervous. "So what are you going to do with me officer Dayton? And what about my wallet?"

Dayton whispered in Nelson's ear as he began driving.

After about five minutes, Nelson pulled into a parking lot at a different shopping area. Jamal looked confused and Dayton threw his wallet back at him with all the money inside.

"I'm going to let you out here, Jamal."

"Why here?" he asked.

"Because----you're still being a courier. And if you don't return that money in a timely manner, Detective Nelson and I will be putting a tag on your toe. We're dropping you here so anyone who watched your stupid maneuver at the store will think you got arrested."

Jamal looked confused.

Dayton continued. "I want a location and a time for when the next deal is going down. If you don't give it to me, I will bring you to the police department. The money will disappear. And when the judge releases you back on the street because it was only a petty crime, you'll disappear faster than your money did. Capishe? Now talk to me."

Jamal told Dayton about a deal that was going down later in the week and gave the address. "If this turns out to be bogus----next time I won't be so concerned about your welfare," Dayton said sternly. Nelson got out of the car and opened the back door. He unlocked Jamal's handcuffs and motioned for him to exit the car.

Dayton grabbed his arm and smiled as he spoke to the young hoodlum. "You are a smart kid Jamal. Turn yourself around. And no more stealing."

Jamal looked down and sighed. He walked away from Dayton and Nelson in silence. When Jamal was out of earshot, Nelson spoke. "That was a little un-orthodox, wasn't it?"

"Nelson," Dayton replied, while he pointed at Jamal's shrinking silhouette, "that boy could have had a full scholarship to college. He is a top notch runner. And he is smart too. It is not too late for him. I talked with him and his mother about this before I went on my book signings. Hopefully he'll think about what happened today and put his feet back in the right direction."

Dayton exhaled and looked at his new partner. "And I didn't want to see him dead. It is why I paid the convenience store owner with my own money."

"Why?" inquired Nelson.

"If you are money courier for a dope dealer----chances are good you are also working for the mob. If you then rob a store which is protected by the mob, you might as well kiss your stupid ass goodbye."

℞

The older man sat in his shiny new car within eyesight of the home of Senator Cudman. He looked down at his briefcase in the passenger seat which was covered by his tweed hat. With his arthritic fingers, he flipped open the phone and dialed.

"Hello," a woman answered.

"Hello Ma'am. My name is Andrew. I'm calling on behalf of the Veteran's Association. Is this Mrs. Cudman?"

"Yes."

"I was wondering if the veterans could count on you this year for a one-time pledge of one-hundred dollars?"

"No. I am sorry," she replied and hung up.

"Who was that?" Senator Cudman asked his wife.

She replied, "Just another beggar asking for money."

"Well----there are a lot of those. I see them all the time with their lobbyists," he replied. "Are you going shopping today, dear?"

"Yes," she replied while swinging her pocketbook over her shoulder. "I'm going out for some Christmas gifts and I need a few new pairs of shoes."

"Have fun," he said as he gave her a kiss on the cheek. He watched her walk out the door and stared at her long, slender legs. "Second one is always a charm," he said with a smile.

As he watched her drive off, Mussen started his car and proceeded to drive down the long windy driveway of the Cudman estate. After he put on his hat, he grabbed his briefcase, walked to the door and rang the doorbell.

"Would someone get that?" Cudman yelled. He remembered he had let his staff out early, so he got up and walked down the long polished wood floor, which led to the front door.

"Who are you?" he said, as he looked down with steely eyes at the man in the tweed jacket and hat, holding a briefcase with his two hands.

"Pardon the interruption, Senator. My name is Richard and I represent---shall we say---a loyal constituency," Mussen said as he patted his briefcase. "I'm sure you understand."

"Which one?"

"Insurance. Life and health."

Phillip smiled. "Come in." The two walked down the long polished floor through the elaborately decorated living room and into the Senator's home office. Mussen looked around at all the extravagance, including many pictures of Cudman's family on their vacations.

"Your home is very nice Senator. And you have a fine looking family," Mussen said pointing at the framed photos on the wall.

"They're my whole world," he replied, "well----besides the good people of Louisiana." His smile was bright and his demeanor pleasant. "So what of interest to me do you have in that briefcase?"

Mussen replied, "Oh, very important things----I'm sure you will find the contents to be---eye opening."

Cudman put his hands together and rubbed them back and forth. "Lobbyists get such a bad name. But you know, without them, the wheels of government wouldn't get greased. People just don't understand how things need to be done in government."

"Very true Senator." Mussen opened his briefcase and pulled out a manila folder.

"So----convince me what's best for the American people concerning this upcoming vote," Cudman said jokingly.

Mussen opened the folder and spread the photographs of the ships, arms shipments and temples on the desk.

"What the fuck is this!" Cudman exclaimed. Mussen pulled out his naval records, followed by the shipping records.

"You and your father were very bad boys," Mussen said. "This is evidence that your father's company shipped Russian and Chinese made arms through ports in Cambodia during Vietnam. You were the naval communicator who informed the ships when it would be safe to pass, so they wouldn't be boarded."

"That's bullshit!" Cudman yelled. "Get the fuck out of my house!"

Mussen reached into his coat and removed a small digital recorder. He began to play recorded naval messages of Phillip radioing the ships into port. "And this is your voice. For years, your father took money from the enemy. It was easier to bring the munitions through Cambodia to avoid having bombs dropped on them. From there, the munitions moved through the N.V.A.'s extensive system of tunnels. Of course, after his untimely death in 1972, you came home and continued the practice until war's end-----and then some."

"I'm a god-damn Senator! Do you know what committee I'm chair of?"

"Armed Services," Mussen responded as he watched Cudman's face turn red as an apple. "And this evidence, if brought forth, means you will lose your chairmanship and most likely be charged with treason."

"Fuck you! I'll call a plumber and it will all go away," Cudman stated.

"Like the plumbers you had in Virginia? Not very good----were they? No match for a granny with a gun."

Cudman settled down. "Okay Richard. How much would it take to put this under the rug?"

Mussen leaned down and his bushy eyebrows displayed extreme prejudice. "I don't think you fucking understand me, you bastard! I bring this forth and you'll be tried for treason and executed---that is if it gets that far. More than likely, the government will come in here, take your business, and or you, and some of your family members will meet an unfortunate end. There are a lot of top brass who lost friends and family in that war. Chances are good, you'll be talking to J.F.K. within the week. And I know there are others who would be more than happy to sacrifice you to keep their past shady dealings private."

Cudman sat in silence and looked straight at Mussen. "But I am a kind man, and I offer you an alternative." He reached into his jacket pocket and pulled out a small revolver, which he put on the desk and spun it by its grip. Cudman watched the barrel of the gun spin, with its muzzle going from him, to Mussen, and back.

Cudman slapped his hand down on the gun as Mussen turned to walk away. He pulled back the hammer and trained it on Mussen.

Recognizing the unmistakable sound of the hammer locking in to place, Mussen closed his eyes and began to speak. "There is only one bullet in that gun----Senator. You could shoot me, but then you would have to explain why you shot an Army Intelligence asset, in your home office. Furthermore, if you think that the only copies of this information are on your desk, then you are sadly mistaken." He opened his eyes and turned around to face Cudman. He took three steps toward him and watched the gun shake in his hands. Mussen placed the evidence in the manila folder and carefully tucked it back in his briefcase. "The choice is yours," Mussen said, as he turned around to walk out of Cudman's office. "Good day, Senator."

Mussen tipped his tweed hat and walked back down the hallway floor of finely polished hardwood. The echoing sound from his shoes reminded him of the sound of automatic gunfire in the jungles of southeast Asia. He pictured his brother's hand stretched through the top of a shallow tunnel and protruding the jungle floor as he cried for help, but received none. As he limped out the door, he remembered his own outstretched hand being pulled by the father of young police detective from Richmond.

He opened the car door and sat in the driver's seat. A muffled shot emanated from inside the house. He closed the door and started the car. "Justice," he mumbled. "Justice----Jacob----Justice." He looked in the rear view mirror and adjusted it, so he could gaze upon himself.

"Mickey. I hope you're watching over your boy. I'll do what I can."

Chapter 21
Normalcy?

Dayton sat quietly in the study as he read his father's Bible. His mind absorbed the text as he turned its yellowed and tattered pages. The previous night, he had finished the Old Testament. At this point, he had finished reading the Gospels.

"There is a lot in here. And there are a lot of repeating patterns," he said quietly to himself. "But there has to be something I missing, otherwise, why did my dad have it sent to Richard Mussen? An astute person could have figured out the codes eventually on the code sheet, even without this Bible as a clue. And is there another reason why the sacrifice picture was in his Bible?"

"Dayton," Martha yelled from downstairs. "Sarah's here."

"I'll be right down." He closed the Bible and placed in on the corner of the desk.

"Hi Dayton," Sarah said as she walked up to him and gave him a quick kiss.

"You ready to get going?" he asked. The two walked down the stairs and conversed with Martha.

"Where are you two going?" Martha inquired.

"We thought we just go for a nice long walk together." Dayton replied as he smiled and grabbed Sarah's hand. "We'll be back in a little while."

The two walked out the front door; hand in hand. Both wore tee-shirts and jeans, which was unusual for the second week of December. There was a mild breeze blowing, but it was in the high fifties outside. It was perfect outdoor weather for a couple to go for a walk.

"I hope it stays like this," Sarah remarked about the weather.

"It won't," Dayton replied. "I think we're going to have a cool, wet December. Might even get some snow?"

Sarah looked at him curiously. "How do you know that?"

"I'm slowly remembering what Peter told me about climatic effects of the planets. Remember this past summer? It was a little cooler and wetter----right?"

"I suppose. I just moved here. If you say so," Sarah replied.

Dayton smiled. "It was. Trust me. Every time Jupiter and Neptune align with the earth, the overall weather tends to be cooler and wetter. This alignment happened twice this summer, and it will happen again on December 17th. I went back and looked at weather records for about the past sixty years----and sure enough, this happened every time, only varying in degree."

Sarah cocked her head. "That's interesting."

"It's taking me a little time to recall what Peter showed me. I was quite drunk." Dayton crossed his eyes, which made Sarah laugh.

Sarah poked him in the side. "I'm surprised you remember anything at all. You did tell me you threw up at a rest stop off of the highway."

Dayton gripped her hand. "Don't remind me. Projectile vomit in front of a young couple with kids was pretty embarrassing."

"How's Nelson working out?" Sarah said, changing the subject.

"He's all right. Smart. He's green though. But he'll learn the ropes. I don't think he's used to my way of doing things yet." Dayton smiled as they continued walking. "He acts a little like Joe Friday?"

"Joe who?"

Dayton sighed. "I was raised by older people who liked to watch re-runs of old TV shows. Joe Friday was a detective on the show <u>Dragnet</u>. Grandma and I still catch it once in a while on TV Land at night."

The two walked a little farther, taking time to enjoy the warm sunshine and gaze at the flora.

"How are sales going of your book?" asked Sarah.

"Most of the signings were pretty well attended. I don't know what my commission check will be---if it ever arrives, considering one of the company's head publishers was shot dead by my grandma," Dayton laughed.

"That's not funny Dayton," Sarah replied; poking him in the ribs.

"Sorry. I got a letter from the accounting department at Triple E books apologizing for the check being late. They said the vice president of publishing, Mr. Hutchinson, had taken an extended vacation-----so they have to wait to get a hold of the owner, Manly P. Jacobs, to sign the check." Dayton laughed lightly some more. "Go figure? Anyway, I get a fifty cent commission for every book sold."

"That's it?" Sarah asked.

"First-time author." Dayton shrugged his shoulders. "The original deal was five thousand up front, all my expenses paid for the signings, and a commission check based on overall sales."

"That isn't too bad, I guess," Sarah remarked.

Dayton changed the subject. "Why don't we go look for a car for you after supper," smirked Dayton. "I can help you with the down payment."

Sarah looked upset. "Dayton, you don't have to do that."

Dayton stopped walking, pulled her in and gave her a big hug. "I know that. I want to. Besides, since I moved back in with Grandma, my expenses have been next to nothing. You don't have to accept it, but I want my Jeep back." Dayton began to tickle Sarah in the side, causing her to laugh and squirm.

"What am I going to do with you?" Sarah said, with a loving look in her eye.

"I don't know. I could think of a few things," he replied, and then raised his eyebrows a few times.

Sarah grabbed his hand. "Come on," she said rolling her own. "I think we should be getting back." She reached into her pocket and pulled out a dollar bill. "Did you ever find out what the eagle roundel stands for?"

"I was wondering when you would bring up the research." Dayton took the bill into his hand. "The official story about the eagle roundel---"

Sarah interrupted. "I know the official story."

"Sorry," replied Dayton. "At first, I thought it might have to do with the Scorpio Constellation. But now, I am pretty sure it doesn't."

"Why?"

Dayton exhaled. "Originally, that roundel was supposed to be on the left, not the right. But for some reason, President Roosevelt, in 1935, felt is should be on the right, and didn't approve the design until it was moved."

"Interesting."

"I think the eagle represents the Phoenix," Dayton continued. He pointed to the thirteen stars forming the Star of David above the eagle. "Thirteen is an important number Biblically. Although there were twelve original tribes of Hebrews, there was always one that was split in two, making thirteen." He walked away from Sarah and started looking around the ground.

"What are you doing?"

"Ah ha," Dayton said as he picked up a stick. "Let me show you." He took the stick and began to draw the area surrounding the White House in the dirt. "The area to the north of the White House----the five pointed star for Spica of Virgo, has a dual symbolic layer, like an onion." He drew out a bird in the outlying streets. "Do you see it?"

"Yes," Sarah replied. "That is amazing."

He looked up at her. "Washington D.C. is in some ways, like a modern version of the city of Heliopolis----complete with an obelisk called the Washington Monument. And what mythical bird lived in Heliopolis?"

Sarah frowned. "Let me guess. The Phoenix."

"You get an A+." Dayton tossed the stick. "The phoenix--"

Sarah interrupted, "Would burn into ashes at its death, and from its ashes, would rise again."

"Yes, the Phoenix would rise again. I believe it rises from an egg embalmed in Myrrh. The bird's perch was the Obelisk."

"Like the Washington Monument is connected to the White House by the Ellipse, which is the egg," replied Sarah. "This is incredible."

Dayton responded. "But there is more. Some of the early Church fathers used to use the symbol of the Phoenix for Jesus."

Sarah stopped walking and stared at Dayton. "And Jesus was brought gold, frankincense and myrrh from the Wise Men. I thought you said this had nothing to do with Jesus."

Dayton raised an eyebrow. "I said I wasn't sure. And I'm still not convinced. What I am sure of," Dayton said as he gripped Sarah's hand, "is I really enjoy your company." She smiled and starred at him, as the two walked up the steps of Martha's house.

"Did you two have a nice walk?" Martha asked.

"Yes." Dayton let go of Sarah's hand and walked over to his grandmother. "I figured I'd cook some hamburgers for the three of us."

"That sounds nice Dayton. Do we have cheese?"

"Bought some yesterday," Dayton responded. "And after supper, Sarah and I are going to look at cars. We've intended to go car shopping, but we ran into a few distractions lately."

Sarah rolled her eyes and shrugged her shoulders.

After he cooked the hamburgers, Dayton placed the patties on a separate roll on each plate and garnished them with a handful of potato chips and a dill spear. Martha sat up straight in her chair. She had an announcement to make.

"Dayton. When was the last time you saw me drive?" she asked.

Dayton thought about her question for a moment while he chewed on his cheeseburger. "You drove me home in my Jeep from the hospital."

"True. But when was the last time you saw me drive my own car?"

Dayton exhaled a deep breath. "The last time before the hospital was taking Grandpa George to the doctor when he was sick."

"Yes, before he got sick, he drove me everywhere. And in the past few months, either you, Mark or Sarah have taken me everywhere I've needed to go." Martha got up and picked her car keys off the hook on the side of the kitchen counter. She sat back down at the table and handed them to Sarah. "I'm seventy-six years old. And I really don't like driving. You've been so good to me."

Sarah sat in astonishment. "I can't accept these." She was all choked up. "Dayton offered to help buy me a car. I wasn't going to let him. Now you are offering me your car. I really can't accept it. I don't know what to say?"

Martha wrapped her hands around Sarah's. "You can say thank you, because I'm not going to be driving it."

"What about your card games with your friends?" Dayton asked.

Martha smiled. "They are only once a week. And they can come here. So please accept them Sarah. We can transfer the title to you at the registry sometime this week."

Sarah was speechless. "It is not a big deal. You have already been driving it," said Martha. Sarah got up from the table and walked over to Martha and gave her a big hug. "Besides, I like riding in the passenger seat. You're a good driver. You'll still take me to lunch, won't you?"

"I'd drive anywhere Martha," Sarah replied.

"I know you would." Martha got up and walked into the living room. "Why don't you two join me for the news?" She sat down in her chair and turned on the TV with the remote control. "Look Dayton---- Breaking News. I wonder if that golfer had another affair?" she said sarcastically.

Dayton and Sarah sat down on the couch together.

"This just in," said the announcer at CNN. "We've just learned, and it has been confirmed by police, that Senator Phillip Cudman, Chairman of the Senate Armed Services Committee, has committed suicide. Apparently, the fifty-nine year old Senator from Louisiana had shot himself in the head, in his home outside Baton Rouge. He was found late this afternoon by his wife, Eileen Cudman, after she had returned home. Police had found no signs of forced entry at the estate of the late Senator, nor do they believe foul play was involved. Sources say Mrs. Cudman is in the process of planning a small, private service for her husband.

Continue watching CNN for more up to date coverage and breaking news."

Dayton sat back into the couch and folded his arms behind his head.

"I never liked that man," Martha said.

Sarah looked at Dayton. "Is that----"

Dayton interrupted, putting his finger to her mouth. "Yes, he's the one. Baxter-Cudman Shipping."

After he removed his finger, Sarah asked in a soft voice, "Is there something you're not telling me with that smile on your face?"

Dayton looked straight at her and touched the tip of his nose against hers. "Sarah. Sometimes justice comes along wearing a tweed jacket and a hat."

Martha looked irritated. "Is there something you two aren't telling me?"

"He got what he deserved grandma," Dayton replied. "Although I think he got off a little too easy."

Dayton got up off the couch and motioned Sarah to follow him. They walked upstairs into the study. Dayton turned the combination lock on the safe, opened the door and removed copies of the materials concerning his father's investigation on arms smuggling into Cambodia by the Baxter-Cudman shipping firm.

Sarah looked at Dayton, "So this man was partly responsible for your father's murder?" Dayton nodded his head yes, then replied, "and potentially the deaths of thousands of Americans, not to mention countless millions of Vietnamese and Cambodians." He pointed to a cropped section of a photo he had. "This tag was left by accident by that company on an arms shipment stored in a Cambodian temple." He then pulled out the records sent to him by John Windwalker. "These are shipping records, along with the naval records of a young, Phillip Cudman."

"Does this mean the case is closed?"

Dayton smirked. "Yes. I think this one is. I'm still working on the other stuff."

"I'd help you all you want," offered Sarah. "The first case with Cudman was definitely a conspiracy," she quipped as she pushed his shoulder. "But what about the other stuff?"

Dayton paused a few seconds before he answered. "I don't think my father's other research involves a conspiracy. But the jury is still out on it. It all depends on where the rest of the evidence takes me."

"Well, I know where I'd like to go." she said, prior to kissing his neck.

"I'll tell grandma we're going out for a little while." As he walked to the living room, he stopped in the hallway. Dayton closed his eyes and remembered the wonderful day at Liberty Island with his father. "My last, happy memory of him." Dayton nodded his head and opened his eyes. "Justice has a name. It's Richard Mussen," he whispered. "I'll be damned. He did it."

❦

Dayton's new partner looked up at him. He paused for a second then began to speak. "So Dayton. I haven't read your book yet. Is there a secret Masonic plot to take over the world?"

Dayton rolled his eyes. He was asked this question so many times during his signings that answering it again was going to make his throat bleed. "Are you married, Nelson?"

"No."

Dayton laughed. "Did you ever think that men sometimes need to get away from their wives?"

"Sure," he answered.

"Whether it is the Masons or the Knights of Columbus, the vast majority are just guys that want to get away from their wives for one or two nights a month and run fundraisers for charity in between dinners, beers and games of pitch."

"Oh." Nelson looked down. "Then why do they have secret ceremonies and stuff?"

Dayton quipped, "So that their wives won't think they are drinking beers and playing cards." Nelson realized he couldn't force Dayton to give the answers he wanted to hear, so he decided to change the subject.

"Man," he said to Dayton," I just don't understand how a guy with everything----money, a beautiful wife, children and power can just go off on a nutty, put a gun in his mouth and then pull the trigger."

"Maybe Senator Cudman wasn't happy? Maybe he was sick in the head?" Dayton replied.

"Oh come on Dayton. He had everything," Nelson said sarcastically.

"So did Alexander the Great, and his own ambition led to his downfall," Dayton retorted.

"Was he the guy with the elephants?" Nelson asked.

"No. That was Hannibal," sighed Dayton. "Sometimes people when they are about to lose something they think is important, do something really stupid and forget what they still have," Dayton opined. As the two men sat in silence, Dayton thought to himself, "The schools must have gone really downhill since I was a kid."

"Could you turn on the heat? It getting chilly," Nelson asked. As Dayton reached for the heat controls on the dash panel of the Crown Victoria, the radio chirped.

"Hostage situation. 34 Pine Street. Man with gun. Unknown amount of hostages. Officers on scene."

Dayton picked up the microphone. "This is detective McCormick in car thirty-two. We are one point five miles from scene. Will proceed to provide assistance." He put the car in drive and drove to the scene without the sirens or flashing lights.

Upon arrival, Dayton and Nelson exited the vehicle and Dayton walked up to the officer in charge. "Hi Finney. Whatcha got here?"

Finney's real name was Sergeant Jeffrey Finnegan. He stood about six feet tall and had a pale white face, topped with thinning silver hair. He turned to Dayton. "We got a disturbed man----most likely in his early to mid-thirties, with a shotgun. I think he's holding his wife and children hostage. Don't know if he's sober." He pointed over at the roof across the street. "We got a police sniper getting into position up there. I hope this doesn't go like the one last month did."

"What happened?"

"Suicide by cop. Man ran out of his house and started shooting at us. It just seems things are getting tougher out here."

"Okay," Dayton replied. "Let's try and end this one better." He put his hand on his chin. "You mind if I try and talk to him Fin?"

"Be my guest----and hey, welcome back."

"Yah. Welcome back. This is the shit I didn't miss," he stated while staring blankly at the house.

Nelson waved his hand in front of Dayton's face. He didn't even blink. "You okay?" Nelson asked.

Dayton took out his service pistol and handed it to Nelson, then began to walk slowly toward the house with his hands in the air. He noticed the neighborhood had gone south since he was a kid. "Old houses once occupied by proud, hard-working families. What's happening," he thought.

"Excuse me sir," Dayton yelled.

"Got outta here! Leave us alone," the man yelled out the window of the brown two-family house.

"Um, sir. It's kind of cold out here. I was wondering if I could come ins--"

"No," interrupted the man. "Go away! I ain't ending up like that other guy a few blocks away!"

"Well, this is a good sign," Dayton thought himself. "At least he doesn't have a death wish." He walked toward the door and began to talk to the man in the house. "Sir, I--I can't do that. What I can do is come up to the door of your house. I'm not armed. Could we talk?" Dayton continued walking slowly toward the house.

Nelson looked at Finney. "I think my partner is a nutcase."

"Well if he is, you might be getting a new one soon," Finney whispered uncomfortably.

"What's it to you?" the man replied as he swung the shotgun in a haphazard manner and more toward the approaching detective.

"Well, I figured it might be harder to shoot a man if you know his name. And you have the gun. I'm going to ask you to please let me come in. I'm not here to hurt you," Dayton said calmly.

"Let me see that you don't have a gun."

"Okay." Dayton kept his hands in the air and rotated slowly 360 degrees. "See. No gun." Dayton continued to keep his cool.

"Pull up your pant legs! I've seen you cops hide a gun in ankle holsters."

Dayton slowly bent down and pulled up each leg of his pants. "I don't like ankle holsters because they are uncomfortable. I am going to come to the door. Um----instead of saying hey you, or something impersonal, what is your name?"

"Tom."

"Well Tom. It is nice to meet you." Dayton stopped short of continuing what he was going to say. He remembered the wise words from professor Mussen. "A man must choose his words carefully. Well spoken, he can succeed. If spoken poorly, it could be his demise." He slowly reached for the door handle with both hands. "See. Both hands, and nothing funny."

"Any quick moves and I'll defend myself," Tom replied.

Dayton pressed the button on the door with his thumb, while keeping his eyes trained on the man with the shotgun in front of him. He pulled it open, ever so slowly, and placed one foot into the abode. He then took both hands and slid them across the glass, so he could show his intentions and not spook the potential shooter. Dayton noticed an empty chair by the table. "Can I sit down, Tom?" The was a strong presence of liquor on Tom's breath.

Outside, the other police were behind their patrol cars with their guns extended over the hoods; pointing them at the brown two-family house.

Tom kept the gun's muzzle pointed near McCormick as he slowly walked to the chair and sat. "My hands are getting pretty tired. I was hoping to put them down on your table. And um, if I could, yell out the window to the other cops out there to put their guns away. Would that be okay, Tom?" He nodded his head in agreement. Dayton stared at an empty bottle of booze on the counter. "I'm going to tell them now. Okay?" Tom nodded again.

"Guys! Please put your guns away while I talk to Tom." Dayton looked out the window. His fellow officers still had their guns trained on the house. "Finney. Order everybody to stand down." He glanced out the window and saw the older sergeant motion the others to stand down. He slowly turned to face Tom and saw that the muzzle of the shotgun was only about a foot from his face. "Is that a Remington 870?" He noticed a glint of light coming through the muzzle.

Tom looked puzzled. He wasn't expecting that question. He turned the shotgun to its side to look at the manufacturer's name on the side plate. "Yes, it is."

Dayton smiled. When Tom was looking for the brand name of the shotgun, he had turned the muzzle away from Dayton enough so that the detective could see that the orange plug in the feed tube was showing. Dayton determined the gun wasn't loaded. He breathed a sigh of relief. "Tell me what happened here, Tom?" Dayton asked.

Tom put the gun down on the table. "I lost my job six months ago." He pointed to the empty Christmas tree in the living room. "I have no money for any god-damn presents. So I grabbed a bottle and my shotgun and started yellin', like I used to back in Arkansas years ago. And I think my neighbor----that bitch upstairs, called the cops on me."

Dayton gently rolled his hands, which encouraged him to continue.

"Next thing I know, I got you damn cops in my front yard, yelling at me to put my gun down. They are all out there freaking pointing guns at me and my family like I am some sort of murderer or something." A tear rolled down his face. "I sent my wife and kids down cellar in case I ended up like that other guy. My kids--"

"Tom," he interrupted, as he flipped his thumb toward the window, "Those guys out there don't know you. All they know is someone called the police saying there was an angry man wielding a gun in his kitchen. They want to go home tonight." Dayton looked at the shotgun. "And I know it's not loaded."

Tom looked down at the floor. "I've been selling everything I had to pay the bills. I was yelling because I was going to pawn this," he said as he pointed at the shotgun, "so I could buy my boys some trucks for Christmas. It was my father's."

Dayton put his lips together. "I have an idea," he said. "Do you play cards?" The detective pulled a deck of cards from his front pocket. He shuffled them and dealt Tom seven cards. "How about gin?"

Outside, the other police, including Nelson, were worried about Dayton's safety. Finney radioed the sniper. "Can you see what is going on in there?"

The sniper looked through his scope and did a double take. Finney prodded. "Can you see what's going on?"

"Fin. It looks like Detective McCormick and the suspect are playing cards."

"I don't believe this!" Finney exclaimed, as he waved the radio in his hands. Dayton slowly moved the curtain, because he knew making sudden movements could be dangerous.

"Finney. It's okay. Come in slow," yelled Dayton.

After cuffing Tom and removing him and the shotgun from the house, Dayton walked over to the cellar stairs and opened the door. "Ma'am. It's safe to come up now." As Tom's wife emerged, she held her twin boy's hands in each of hers. He walked with her over to the couch, as the other officers checked the children.

"I'm going to ask you this once," said Dayton. "Did he threaten you or the children?" She shook her head no. "Ok," Dayton responded. He looked at her sad face. "I'll put in a good word, Ma'am."

"He's a good man, you know," blurted Tom's wife. "Just been having a hard time," she replied with a tear rolling down her face.

Dayton nodded and walked out the door with Nelson back to the car. Finney walked over to the car too. "Dayton," Finney asked, "What happened here?"

"Some people reach a breaking point Fin. Tom reached his. I don't think he was going to hurt his family." Finney raised his eyebrows. "He thought we----us cops---- were going to come in with guns blazing, like you see in the movies." Dayton shook his head. "I guess you don't think too clearly when you are drunk, especially when you hear about other people being gunned down by cops nearby."

"Hmmm," replied Finney. A curious look came on his face. "Hey. What really happened last week up at your Grandmother's house with those guys? "

"Sorry Finney. I can't talk about it." Dayton frowned and pressed the button to roll up his window. As he drove away from the scene, he looked at Nelson. "The Chief is going to pissed off at me as it is."

"At least it ended well," replied Nelson. 'We're you scared?"

"Not after I realized the gun wasn't loaded," replied Dayton.

"But why do you look so upset?"

Dayton frowned. "During my book signings, I told a young guy that I would never take away guns from someone who wasn't a criminal. And I just did." Dayton pulled the car into the police parking lot and turned off the motor.

Nelson shook his head. "But this was different. We didn't know what was going on in the house. We could only go by what we were told."

Dayton bent down and put his head in his hands. "I realize that. But this guy just got into more trouble than he needs, because people made decisions based on false perceptions."

"You did what you had to do, Dayton. Sometimes situations arise that are beyond our control. Sometimes you just have to go with the flow," Nelson reminded him.

Dayton looked up at his partner. "I know. That's what bothers me. Mankind always goes with the flow."

"Sorry Dayton. That's just the way things are."

Dayton and Nelson stood together in front of Chief Stankeiwicz. He took a deep breath and let Dayton have it. "What were you thinking? The department negotiator was on his way."

Dayton looked up at his superior. "You did send me to H.R.T. training last spring----Chief."

Stankeiwicz stomped around his office and continued yelling at both men. He sat down, and after his face regained its normal color, he pointed his finger at Dayton's face. "Take the rest of the day off. Both of you. I want you out of this office. Now!"

Dayton walked with Nelson back to the parking lot where their personal vehicles were parked. After a long silence, Nelson asked, "Is he pissed at us, or what?"

Dayton shook his head. "His bark is worse than his bite, Nelson. He's just glad everything was settled before the media got there and that he didn't have to go on TV."

"Oh? How could you tell?"

Dayton smiled. "I'm still Detective McCormick. See you tomorrow, Nelson."

Mark stood at the door of his truck as he watched a steaming mad Sarah stomp toward her car. She so wanted to rip open the door and slam it as hard as she could. She so wanted to slam her hands against the steering wheel. But she couldn't. She took a deep breath and opened the door as calmly as she could, then sat in the seat; putting her face in her hands. The car was a big gift, which she felt that if she abused it, would be disrespectful.

As she stewed, she heard a light tapping coming from the passenger window. Mark had put his sensitive guy face on and motioned her to unlock the door of the 2004 Camry.

"God-damn him! What the hell was he thinking!" she exclaimed to her slightly startled partner. "He could have gotten killed!" Before Mark could open his mouth she yelled, "Is he stupid?"

Mark put his hands on her shoulders and turned her toward him. "He's a cop, Sarah. And so are you. We could get killed any day out here. Even a routine traffic stop---"

Sarah interrupted, "But did he have to enter a house with some guy pointing a damn shotgun at him?"

"It wasn't loaded, Sarah."

Tears began to roll down her face. "But it could have been." She put her face into his chest and sobbed.

"Come on Sarah. Don't cry. He's ok," Mark said softly. "Someone had to go in there and---Dayton knows how to handle stuff. When we were patrolmen, he was so good at talking people down. And he's always been lucky."

"This time."

"No---Look. Look at the past two months. Two men died after he visited them. He had to shoot four guys trying to rob and kill him in Arizona. He was detained by Homeland Security---and he didn't even get arrested."

"He what?" Sarah steamed. "He didn't tell me he shot four guys out in Arizona." The word "oops" was written all over Mark's face. "Yes, and he was nearly killed like his father in his grandmother's bathtub. If she wasn't there---"

Sarah sobbed more into Mark's chest. "But she was. And I was on my way too. Dayton's lucky. Always has been. I can't explain it. It's like he has some sort of guardian angel, or a sixth sense---or something like that. I catch him staring off. It's like he knows things." Sarah pulled her head away from his shirt, which was now soaked with tears.

"I'm still going right over there," Sarah said.

Mark opened the door of the Camry and got out. "He's ok Sarah. That's all that matters."

She wiped off her face and shook her head. Mark closed the passenger door. "Go easy on him." Sarah started the car and backed out slowly. She was determined to give him a piece of her mind.

ஒ

Sarah knocked on the door, which was quickly opened by Martha McCormick. Sniffling, she apologized. "I'm so sorry for coming over this late Martha."

Martha replied, "It is only 10:30PM Sarah. And to be quite frank, you're like family. I wouldn't bother me if you moved in here." She smiled at Sarah, but was concerned about her appearance. "Come in. Dayton is upstairs in the study."

It took Sarah a minute to realize what Martha had just said. As she hung up her coat on the back of the kitchen chair, she understood the magnitude of what Martha told her. Her emotional state mellowed as she walked up the stairs, but not completely. There was still a little anger brewing, which Dayton sensed before she even cleared the door of the study. He knew his best defense was to change the subject, and give what he thought was bothering her time to diffuse.

"Ever hear of the Carrington Event?" Dayton asked, while he stared at his computer screen.

"No," Sarah replied.

Dayton flipped his hand and asked to her to come closer. "Here, let me show you." Dayton pulled up a solar system simulator and typed in the date of August 28, 1859. "There was a period during late August through early September of 1859 where the sun went crazy." He pointed his hand to the screen and traced his finger's along the alignment of the planets. Saturn was aligned with Mars and Venus---right to the sun. Mercury, the Moon and the earth were on the opposing side. The lineup originated from the Constellation of Leo." He sketched it out on a piece of paper in his black evidence binder.

"The sun went crazy? In what way?" she asked.

"Gigantic solar flares and coronal mass ejections. They came right at earth and caused huge, bright auroras, as far down as the equator."

"I thought those only happened up at the poles?"

Dayton shook his head. "Most of the time yes, but not then. Telegraph systems all over the world failed. I read a report recently from N.A.S.A. They said if a similar event were to occur now, the electrical grids world-wide could be down for as long as three years."

"Three years?" Sarah said in disbelief. "I wouldn't want to be a cop if that happened. The world would be thrown into chaos."

"That's right. No cars. No electricity. No nothing," Dayton replied. "Imagine riding a horse to a crime scene?"

Dayton had Sarah's complete attention. "This is the stuff you learned from Peter?"

"Yes, and I am learning more and more every day. Check this out." Dayton pulled out a photo of the Star of David. "This is the motion path of the Saturn-Jupiter-Sun conjunctions and oppositions. Conjunctions are every twenty years, with oppositions at half. This is interesting, because the solar cycle, from minimum to maximum is averaged at eleven years, with polarity changes around every twenty-two. This is approximate, but as Jupiter and Saturn's positions change----so does the sunspot cycle. I've found other potential regulators--"

"Like what?" Sarah asked.

"The other planets. When Saturn and Uranus are in opposition---or Neptune, the sun goes into a minimum with fewer spots. This occurs approximately every thirty-six years. And this is what has happened, since December of 2007, until now."

"This isn't in any textbooks Dayton. Why?" she said as she put her hands on his shoulders.

"I don't know. If I can see the relationship easily, why can't trained scientists?" Dayton was giddy as a schoolboy. "And look at this." He handed her a chart of powerful solar flares and their dates of occurrence. "Look at the first one. You give me the date, and I'll type it into the solar system simulator."

"November 4, 2003. X28." Sarah read.

"The alignment was Pluto, Venus, Sun."

"April 2, 2001. X20."

"Neptune, Mercury, Sun."

"August 16th, 1989 X20."

"Pluto, Venus, Mercury, Sun."

"September 7th, 2005."

"Pluto, Venus, Sun."

She scrolled down the list, hoping to find something different. "December 6th, 2006."

"Pluto, Venus, Sun," Dayton replied. "Notice a pattern? Outer planets, particularly Saturn, Neptune or Pluto, aligning with Venus, Mercury or both, while aligning with the sun. The strength of the effect is dependent on how agitated the sun is, which is determined by Saturn and Jupiter, but also where the alignments originated from, the degree of the alignment, and which planets are involved."

"That's amazing," Sarah proclaimed.

Dayton had a sparkle in his eye. "And if I'm right, you'll see the weather somewhere on earth turn nasty a few days after Christmas, followed by some solar flares, sometime in mid-to-late January of 2010." Dayton got up off his chair. "More importantly though, I was hoping you could come shopping with me in the morning to go buy some presents for a pair of little boys."

"You change subjects faster than a woman," Sarah commented.

Dayton motioned to follow him downstairs. "Let's go watch a little TV together."

"One condition. No news," she said while squinting one eye.

"Done." He put his hand in hers and walked downstairs to the living room, where they sat on the couch. Dayton began flipping through the channels. He came across a Christmas concert.

"Hey, that looks good." The two began to listen to the soloists and groups as they played traditional Christmas songs. She sat close to him and leaned her head against his shoulder. About forty minutes later, they were both asleep and snoring lightly in unison. Martha had awakened upstairs and heard the TV, so she went down to shut it off. As she looked at Dayton and Sarah asleep together on the couch, she smiled, then made the sign of the cross. "They are already starting to sound and act like a married couple," she whispered to herself as she smiled.

After deciding to leave the TV on, she took the blanket she kept on the recliner, spread it across the two of them and then returned to bed.

Dayton awoke the next morning to sounds of Martha happily stirring in the kitchen. He felt a warm face against his shoulder, covered in auburn brown strands. She nuzzled her cheek against his as she opened her eyes. "Nice blanket," she said.

Martha walked in to the living room. "I hope French toast is ok?" Dayton curled his hand and pointed his finger at the blanket. "Well," Martha said, "I didn't want you two to be cold." She smiled a motherly smile, then returned to the kitchen.

After breakfast, Dayton and Sarah headed out shopping. "What are we shopping for again?" Sarah asked.

"Trucks. I need to go pick up some trucks for Christmas. I have two little boys to buy for," Dayton replied.

Sarah looked at him curiously from the driver's seat of the Camry. "Why are you buying toys for little kids? I didn't know you had any little cousins or other children in your family. Is there something you're not telling me?"

Dayton pointed his finger. "Take a right here. If you go down Route 6, about a mile or so, we should be only a few streets away from Toy's R Us."

Sarah kept looking from the road back to Dayton. "You still didn't answer my question. You mentioned trucks last night, but I didn't think anything of it, because you distracted me. Who are you buying them for?"

Dayton sank in his seat. "Just two kids. Twin brothers," he smiled.

"How do you know them?"

"Uh. Umm. Met them----yesterday. Nice kids. Always wanted to buy some toys, for kids. You know----"

Sarah remembered why she visited him last night in the first place. She was angry at him for becoming involved in a hostage situation. "Where did you meet them? Was it at some church or something?" Her voice elevated in volume. "Didn't you have a hostage crisis yesterday?"

Dayton sank in his seat and shrugged his shoulders. He couldn't avoid talking about it now. "Remember that situation yesterday? Well, the two boys are the sons of the guy with the shotgun."

"What!" Sarah yelled as she jerked the steering wheel to avoid a car that cut in front of her.

"Yesterday isn't what it seemed, Sarah. Perception is--"

Sarah interrupted. "Oh really?" she answered sarcastically. "Studying symbolism is one thing. But don't give me that shit concerning this."

Dayton shrugged. "Yesterday was about a father who lost his job. His unemployment was running out. He couldn't afford presents for his kids and pay his mortgage."

"That's no excuse, Dayton! And you are not a social worker!"

"Let me finish. He starting drinking and became angry. Unfortunately, he grabbed his shotgun. A neighbor heard him yelling and carrying his gun, so she called the cops. Cops show up with their guns drawn."

"Okay," Sarah replied, dropping her jaw.

"We'll----he never threatened his family. But he did hear about another guy who was killed by cops a month ago here in Richmond. So he told his wife to bring their kids in the basement, in case the cops----us, started firing." Sarah stared in disbelief. "Sarah. Some people are scared of us, and when someone is intoxicated, it makes matters worse. After Ruby Ridge and Waco, many people stopped trusting government and law enforcement. And when you have a bunch of politicians who are always trying to restrict people's freedoms, many assume we're the bad guys too. Why do you think people form militia groups? They're not afraid of a foreign country invading. They're afraid of their own government. It is one of the reasons I wrote my book. I wanted to----"

"Enough with the political diatribe, Dayton."

"Let me finish. Please," Dayton pleaded. "I was at a police academy graduation. It was for a friend of mine outside Virginia. The Lieutenant Governor addressed the cadets. He told them that they were to enforce the laws, regardless of whether they felt the law was right or Constitutional. Cops are supposed to blindly follow laws? We're here to protect and serve. Maybe I'm old school. I don't like all the military style equipment and practices that has become standard over the past twenty years. We're not supposed to be in the business of instilling fear in the public. The Nazi's did that." Dayton looked down at the floor mats in the car. "So now, a pair of young kids are probably going to have to watch their dad go to jail because of a misunderstanding. The least I can do is pick up a few presents for them."

"But you could have been killed."

"But I wasn't." Dayton motioned her to pull in the parking lot.

Sarah remained silent as she walked with him into the toy store. He walked up and down the aisles, looking for trucks the Collins boys would treasure.

391

Sarah broke her silence. "Dayton. How about these?" Sarah asked, finding two identical Tonka dump trucks.

He turned and wrapped his arms around her. "I'm sorry I scared you. And there is nobody on this earth I'd rather be shopping with right now." He picked up the two trucks as well as two smaller ones. "These are all perfect. After we pay for them, let's go home and wrap them up."

"What about wrapping paper?" Sarah asked.

"Good point. We'll stop and get some of that on the way home."

As they loaded the trucks into the trunk, Dayton looked up at Sarah. "You know. You never told me what you wanted for Christmas."

"Dayton," Sarah replied, as she put her soft, warm hand on his cheek. "I've already got it. But please, no more hostage situations before Christmas."

❧

"Mrs. Collins," Dayton said as he knocked on the door. He watched as she came slowly over to the door. She looked down at the floor, almost in shame.

"What is going to happen to Tom?" she asked.

Dayton signed. "Ma'am. At minimum, because he'll probably be charged with disturbing the peace and resisting arrest, but considering his record is clean----probation. At worst, he might see some time."

Mrs. Collins looked down at the floor and hoped for the former. Nelson took the four wrapped presents from the trunk of the car and brought them into the house.

"There are two presents each," Dayton said. "They're both identical. I hope they like them. And please tell them they're from Santa Claus." A tear began to roll down her face. "Ma'am." Dayton tipped his head and motioned Nelson to follow him.

The walk back to the car seemed to take forever. Dayton wondered how many times Tom Collins walked away from this house, looking for work since being laid off. And he imagined how it felt for him to walk back home without success.

Nelson looked at Dayton in the car. "I never did anything like that before."

"Me neither," Dayton responded.

"Could you turn on the heat, Dayton? It is starting to get really cold."

"Be thankful we're not in the center of the country, Nelson," Dayton responded. "It is supposed to go below zero tonight."

Nelson smiled. "I thank God we live in Virginia. Another thing. You might still be a detective, Dayton, but obviously the Chief is still pissed at you. Look, we have night duty on Christmas Eve," complained Nelson. "He's going to bust your balls every chance he gets, and in turn, bust mine."

Dayton smirked, "Crime doesn't take a vacation, and neither does the fury of the Stankeiwicz."

"But we're doing narcotics duty on Christmas Eve!" Nelson whined.

Dayton reached inside a wax paper bag and removed a donut. "Stick this somewhere Nelson," he teased.

As Nelson chewed his donut, he continued talking. "So, that lead by that kid Jamal turned up bogus."

"You win a few, you lose a few," said Dayton, shrugging his shoulders. "But I have a clear conscience."

Nelson pointed over to the street about forty yards away. "Speak of the Devil. Isn't that him?"

Dayton pulled out his monocular and studied the young man they stopped shoplifting a few weeks earlier.

He noticed Jamal walking solo, and a group of other young men approaching him. "Start the car Nelson."

"Huh," he replied, as he chewed his donut.

Three of the young men facing Jamal grabbed his shirt and pulled it over his head. "Start the fucking car now!" Nelson, spit out his donut and turned the key after he realized what was going down. As Dayton watched the men drag Jamal by his shirt, he grabbed the radio asking for assistance and an ambulance. The car jumped the curb with engine at full throttle, and sped its way toward the group. As Nelson hammered the brakes, Dayton witnesses a hand go back and forth while gripping a shiny object, and Jamal dropped straight down to the sidewalk. "Damn it!"

Both detectives broke out of the unmarked cruiser. Nelson drew his weapon and began pursuit, but Dayton yelled for him to stop. "Let them go!" Dayton commanded, as he held up Jamal's head with one hand and used the other to apply pressure to the two large puncture wounds oozing blood from the young man's lower torso. Jamal's breathing became labored as he screamed in pain.

"I'm going to die!" He began to scream primally, as he looked down at Dayton's hand which was covered in blood. As the blood oozed out to the rhythm of his beating heart, Dayton removed his hand from Jamal's head and used it to apply more pressure.

He looked straight into Jamal's eyes and yelled. "If you don't calm the hell down, you're going to bleed to death."

"But it hurts so bad! I can't feel my left leg," Jamal screamed. Dayton applied more even pressure to try and slow the flow of blood. "When is the god-damn ambulance going to get here? Nelson, get the roll of duct tape out of the car," Dayton yelled. Nelson quickly fetched the tape. "Tear me off two big pieces."

Dayton took the tape and pressed it against the wound. Nelson had already gone back to the car for the first aid kit. He removed a large gauze bandage and placed it over the taped area, then tore off two more pieces of tape. Jamal's two wounds finally stopped oozing blood.

The EMT's arrived about thirty seconds later. They started working on Jamal and put him into the ambulance. Dayton went back to the unmarked cruiser to get the wash kit to clean the blood off his hands. "Nelson," he said as he sprayed his hands.

"Yo."

"Take the car and follow the ambulance to the hospital. I'm going to ride with him." The EMT started Jamal on an I.V., then shut the rear door after Dayton crawled in.

"I'm so scared," Jamal said. "I feel cold."

Dayton gripped Jamal's hand in his. "You're going to be ok," he said compassionately. "But promise me you'll get off these streets and go to school." Dayton put his lips together, then spoke again. "The info you gave me, which I gave to the NARC unit, turned out wrong."

Jamal opened up. "I swear I told you the truth. Those were the guys making the deal," Jamal said as he winced in pain from his wounds. "You were supposed to arrest them."

"Maybe you were wrong about the location."

"I wasn't wrong. I swear," Jamal pleaded.

"Don't worry about that right now. Just remain calm," Dayton said. "Let's get you patched up first and then we'll talk."

Jamal closed his eyes. "If you don't get them Dayton, when I get out of the hospital, I am a dead man."

Dayton took a deep breath. He understood Jamal's dire predicament. He looked down at the youth and sighed. "I need their names, Jamal. And I need to know where they live."

Chapter 22
The Discovery

Dayton sat in the study in front of his computer; monitoring the weather reports after Christmas. Record cold had settled into the middle of the US, and heavy storms had started to pound Northern Europe. Heavy snow and ice had closed roads there and shut down the airports. He listened to the rain pound on the roof above, which was caused by a system that had developed rapidly in the Gulf.

"Incredible Peter," he whispered to himself as he shut off his computer and picked up the photograph of him and Sarah. Around the desk was a barrage of gift certificates to restaurants and stores he and Sarah exchanged with each other. They both had the same idea to buy each other them for Christmas, because it meant they could spend more quality time together.

Dayton began to hear a tapping noise, so he put down the photograph. "Grandma, do you hear that?" he said.

She walked into the study. "Yes. The rain is terrible. You would think we were in the tropics."

"That is not what I meant." He walked from room to room. "That," he said, as he pointed up toward the ceiling in the bathroom.

"I can't hear anything, Dayton. What is that?"

"A clicking," he responded. He looked up at the corner of the bathroom ceiling. It had started to look wet. "Grandma, come here," Dayton asked. The two watched as the spot became larger; expanding about an inch every minute. "I think there is a hole in the roof."

Martha shook her head. "It wouldn't surprise me one bit," she said with a frown. "Your grandfather George put some tar up on the roof in the early spring before his illness started to take over him. He said it should hopefully last a year or two, but the roof needed to be replaced."

"Oh Grandma. Why didn't you tell me? I would have done it, or hired someone to do it."

"We didn't want to bother you. And when George got sicker, it just wasn't a big concern." Martha shook her head. "There should be a brush and a can of tar in the basement."

Dayton ran down to the basement and located a one gallon can of black tar and a brush on a shelf. He grabbed the brush and can, along with a small ladder and went upstairs. "I'll try sealing it off in the attic." He set up the ladder and pulled open the attic access panel.

Once in the attic, he found the pull chain for the light, and he immediately noticed where the leak had been coming from. The water was entering the house through a nail hole; where it then ran down a beam and dripped over the bathroom ceiling. He sealed up the hole with a large glob of tar, which stopped the leak. Then he inspected the rest of the attic roof. Another nail hole had just begun to leak, so he plugged it with tar. He sat there for a few minutes and checked to see if any other leaks would pop up due to the torrential rain outside.

There were a few old boxes that had been stored over the ceiling of the study and forgotten long ago. Dayton crawled over to inspect them and made sure they hadn't gotten wet. He moved the boxes aside and found a small footlocker behind them. He looked at the side of the locker. Dayton read, in black spray-paint, the words, "McCormick US ARMY." He carefully pulled out the locker and brought it before him.

In the front, there was a shiny brass lock. "I wonder," he said to himself. He took his hand and felt his back pocket. "My wallet must be in my other pants."

He backed down the ladder and ran into his bedroom. The pants he wore yesterday were on the floor and his wallet was in the back pocket. He walked back to the ladder in the hallway. "Is everything ok, Dayton?" Martha asked.

"Yup. I'm just going back up in the attic for a while to check for more leaks," he responded.

He took the key he received from John and removed it from his wallet. It fit perfectly in the lock. As he turned it, the lock snapped open. Dayton opened the footlocker carefully. On the top, was his father's army uniform, complete with the Sphinx patch for Army Intelligence. Below it, was another uniform, without a name or markings of any kind. It was covered with dried blood stains. He held it up. "This must of been the uniform dad wore when he was being extracted from Cambodia."

Under the uniform was a box. Dayton opened it and found a reel-to-reel tape, marked US NAVY, along with a small cassette tape in a case. All the Baxter-Cudman shipping documents and naval records for Phillip Cudman were together in the same box. Underneath the records, were 8x10 black and white glossy photographs, made from the negatives he received from Peter Devine. "It was all here, all the time, right above my head. Dad must have brought this stuff over at some point close to his death."

Dayton sat quietly and wondered. "I never collected an audio recording from any of my father's friends. It truly is the final piece in the Cudman case." He looked at the reel, and the tape with it. "Did dad send it to Hutchinson? Or did he give it to Mussen?"

He looked back into the footlocker. There was another Bible. As Dayton flipped through it, the passages from the code sheet were highlighted in yellow. Every single one from the code sheet, sans the last two. But there was no Aztec sacrifice picture between its pages. "Mussen."

He found another box and opened it. Inside were copies of the aerial photos of New York, Washington D.C. and Giza. Along with them was a sketch of D.C., which he studied. Dayton was amazed how his father, in an age before easy access via computer, came to such similar conclusions as he did. The Kennedy Assassination was marked on the sketch for 3rd street. September 11th, was not, because his father died fourteen years before that event. But his father's sketch had some things his did not. Union Station was circled. Above it were the words "Crown of the Virgin," and below it, "Jupiter/Venus--Union." Mt. Vernon Square was also circled. Above it, were the words, "Virgin's Womb."

And there was something circled on the Aerial of New York Bay. It had Liberty Island circled. In caps, the words proclaimed: "Modern Sphinx." "I knew that one," Dayton muttered.

The last item in the box was a manila folder, which he opened. It contained two sheets of paper. The first was a coversheet. It was titled: <u>The Darkness Before Dawn: The Survivors Complete the Great Work of the Age</u>. "Interesting," Dayton whispered, as he looked on the to second sheet and began reading.

In the span of one hundred years, modern man has gone from black powder arms to the Atom Bomb; quite an incredible feat. In our quest for technical advancement though, we have forgotten ancient wisdom.

Man has been on earth for a very long time; far longer than most people realize. Over the ages, something has repeatedly kicked man backwards. Because of fossil records, along with the artifacts and structures left by ancient peoples, the only determining factor is something big happened long ago--and its cyclical.

In what we now call the United States, there was once a great empire. This empire, due to internal power struggles and the loss of unity among its peoples, erupted into Civil War. Prior to the outcome of this war, something interceded which utterly destroyed the empire through climatic means. Most people alive then had also forgotten wisdom and the use of their heart.

The survivors, both good and bad, sailed to other parts of the world and arrived in various places. The two largest contingents, arrived in Egypt and Babylon and intermingled with the local populations. They became the priest class which constructed the Pyramids and the Sphinx and carried with them their vast knowledge of the stars. Their symbols were that of the Phoenix and also that of the Eye of Providence, encapsulated in a triangle, above a truncated pyramid. We see this today on our one dollar bill.

Over the years, they constructed what we call Western Civilization. In the late 1,400's, the few that still had knowledge of their past, desired to rebuild what was lost so long ago, and America was re-born.

This is their story. But it doesn't stop there, because in about twenty to thirty years, their history and the groundwork they laid will reach an apex, because all history repeats itself due to the cycles of influence from above, unless the heart intervenes.

Let me take your hands and tell you this incredible tale and what you also need to know. For we are truly in the time, just prior to the rising of the second sun, and the darkness before the dawn of the new age.

Sincerely,
Mickey McCormick

A special thanks goes to my friend Richard Mussen for helping me with the research for this endeavor, for who, along with all who I love, I dedicate this book.

"I only wish I had the whole book to read," Dayton whispered, as he packed everything back into the box. He looked into the nearly empty small footlocker. It was almost empty, except for one small plastic bag. He opened the bag, which contained a note and a small box. Dayton opened the note.

Contained in this box is the wedding ring meant for my soul mate, Jan. I bought it for her the week before she died. My only regret is that I waited too long to put it on her hand.

Mom and Dad. If something happens to me and you find this, please give it to Dayton to give to the woman he chooses for his wife.

Dayton, my son. If you are the one to find this, don't wait to give it to the woman you love. For everything on this earth eventually goes to dust. Everything, except love.

Mickey

He opened the box. In it was a beautiful band of gold, with a single diamond mounted by six prongs. He watched it sparkle from the light given off by the incandescent lamp hanging from the ceiling. Dayton stared at it for a while, before he placed it back in the box, which he put in his pocket. The note and the bag, along with all the other items, were all neatly placed back into the footlocker, which was left unlocked.

"Dayton," Martha said. "What have you been doing up there? You've been up there for over an hour." He didn't reply.

Dayton closed the attic access, folded up the ladder and brought it downstairs. "Dayton. Are you all right?" Martha asked down the basement stairs.

He looked up at her and smiled, then walked up the stairs and stopped at the apex where she stood. He whispered in her ear. "Yes. I think so," Martha replied.

"When this rain clears, I need to make a trip to Baltimore," Dayton said. "I have a little unfinished business. There are a few questions I need answers to."

Chapter 23
Twin Pillars

Dayton awoke suddenly and sat straight up in his bed. He blinked his eyes and caught the start of the sunrise out his bedroom window. "Second sun?" he whispered. "Amun Ra? My strange dreams."

He walked down the hall to the study and sat down at the desk. His father's Bible sat on the top. "If my hunch is right, Mussen left the Aztec picture because there were pagans in the early church."

Dayton continued flipping through the Bible. "Patterns. Lots of patterns. The stories containing them repeat----but not exactly the same way." He flipped to the beginning of the Gospels. "The first three---- Matthew, Mark and Luke are the Synoptic Gospels. Some differences, but mostly the same. John's is different." Then it hit him. "The first three planes hit their intended symbolic targets on 911. Flight 093 didn't." He closed his eyes. "A ritual uses symbolism to re-enact an event of significance." He also recalled aspects of other notable terror attacks. The 2004 bombings in Madrid had four trains; three of them being blown up inside the train station. The London Bombings on July 7th 2005 involved three subway trains, and one bus. "Three the same----one different---like 911 and the Gospels," Dayton whispered.

He put down his father's Bible, opened up his black binder and pulled out both the sketch and the aerial of New York Bay. He put his finger down on Building 7. "Salomon Brothers. Solomon. Sol. Sun." Dayton shook his head. "Not the yellow sun. Solomon was the son of King David. David was from the line of Judah---- the Lion. Leo. Therefore, this is the sun of Virgo. He paused. "Not the sun, but the son of the sun. The second sun."

"The Twin Towers formed an eleven when you looked at them. But they were Tower 1 and Tower 2. Twelve. Jupiter's orbit is about twelve years." He looked through his research on Jupiter. "4,333 days or 11.83 years." He knew both towers were 110 stories high. "Wait a second!" Dayton wrote down the number 47, for the number of stories of Building 7. Then he multiplied it by 11.83, for the orbit of Jupiter. "556," he whispered. "Very close to 555----the height of the Washington Monument in feet. He then multiplied 110, for the height in stories of the towers, times 47, the height in stories of Building 7. "5170," Dayton said. "Very close to the Mayan Sun period, and only 14 meters shy of the length in meters from the Lincoln Memorial to the Emancipation Monument in Lincoln Park in Washington D.C."

A smile came across Dayton's face. "The World Trade Center was not a temple to the sun. It was a temple for Jupiter----Just like Capitoline Hill. Capitol Hill----Jupiter's temple. Baalbek, Heliopolis, Rome----They were built everywhere on earth! Little sun worshippers!"

Dayton now knew why the terrorists didn't hit Indian Point and instead went after symbolic targets. "In all rituals, there is symbolism." He closed his eyes, and pictured what he saw in the cave near the Mexican border with John Windwalker. "It is what people see," he said softly, "and how they interpret it." The unknown artist had used birds to convey what he saw in the sky. Dayton's eyes opened wide. "The terrorists used airplanes on 9-11-2001: modern metal birds that carried a message."

Dayton looked over at the Bible resting on his desk. "God used doves as messengers. Noah's dove told him when it was ok to come out of the ark. God also sent another when Jesus was being baptized in the river by John the Baptist." He put his finger in the air and pointed it as if there were real words on the wall in front of him. "Planets----Birds----Airplanes----Doves----Pigeons---Mussen----Messengers."

He picked up the dollar bill on the desk. "FDR made the Pyramid Roundel first, the Eagle second. Why?" He stared out at the still rising sun, through the window in the study, and then it came to him. "The first symbol, the triangle with the eye is the messenger. He is announcing something is coming. The Eagle Roundel," he thought, as he put his lips together and cleared his mind, "is the phoenix----a bird that lives normally, but on a regular basis, consumes itself in flames, dies and is then reborn from its own egg."

His thoughts turned back to 911. "If the terrorist attack was something more----let's say a message----then there has to be clues in the attack." He began to write down what happened, in sequential order, on that fateful September day. He wrote down how Tower 1 had been hit, then Tower 2. The Naval Intelligence office was hit at the Pentagon. Flight 093 crashed in Pennsylvania. Then Tower 2 collapsed. Then Tower 1. And at 5:20 EST, Building 7. He picked up the dollar again and held the edges of the bill between his two hands. Dayton then flipped it. "Wait a second," he whispered. "5:20. 2---1----7. Time, and order of the numbers of the buildings. 5-20 217." He remembered in his study of numerology that zeros were not used. "5-20-2017. Second, or main event? The Phoenix."

Dayton turned on his laptop and went to the Solar System simulator. He typed in the date and what he saw amazed him. "Jupiter on high; like on the pyramid roundel and during the Kennedy Assassination and 9-11-2001." He put his finger on the screen. "It's around Virgo's belly. Virgo's womb! And the whole layout looks

405

similar to Washington D.C, if you draw lines between the planets."

From the other room, Dayton heard his grandmother ask, "Why are you up so early, Dayton?"

"Sorry Grandma," Dayton replied. It was 6:45 AM on his clock. "I'll be quieter."

Dayton thought back to what he learned from Peter about the effects on both the earth and sun by planetary alignments, then applied them to his recent findings. He looked at the arrangement for the date he typed in the Solar System simulator. "But what if arrangements also effect other planets? Let's say---make one of them look brighter, like Venus did a few years ago?" He pictured in his mind the drawings from the cave in Arizona. "There were two lights in the sky," he whispered. "One was the Sun---Fat Man----Nagasaki. And the other one was the Little Boy----Hiroshima----the second sun." He switched off the light on top of the study table and walked back to his bedroom. He got dressed and whispered to himself. "There will be two suns. This is, in part, what the truncated pyramid with the triangle and eye above it stands for symbolically: the time when two suns will be in the sky."

Dayton sat down on his bed and put on his shoes. "This is incredible," he whispered. "Stories of old---- events in history. History and man's actions have been messages and clues for the timing and characteristics of a major celestial event. Only our perception of these events has prevented us from seeing them for what they truly are. Is this coincidence----or has this all been planned?"

Dayton parked his Jeep and threw a few quarters into the parking meter. He walked briskly up Pennsylvania Avenue. Although he had already reviewed his own photographs of the monuments, he wanted to get up close and touch them again with his own hands. "Twin Towers---Twin monuments," he said to himself as he walked.

He looked upon the white stone of the Peace Monument, which was erected by the US Navy. On top were two women. One held a tablet as the other cried over her shoulder. Just below, was the woman, holding the wreath, with a baby Mars and a Baby Neptune squaring her on the sides. "Earth, aligning with Venus, being squared by Mars and Neptune. It's here," he stated, looking at his diagram of the solar system. "Base of four points----like the base of a pyramid."

He walked the 17,760 centimeters to the Garfield Memorial and gazed at the light which reflected off the Botanical Gardens in the background. Dayton walked up to the monument of the slain President and found what he was looking for on the bronze plaque. "Two suns," he whispered. "And the base of this monument has three points. A Triangle. How incredible!" He smiled uncomfortably and thought about the arrangement of the World Trade Center prior to its destruction. "Building 7, with the two towers, making an eleven. The bases of these two monuments are four and three----seven. The two monuments making an eleven visually in front of the Capitol." Dayton placed his sketch and layout papers back into his pocket and walked back down Pennsylvania Avenue toward his vehicle. "Capitol Hill and the WTC are, or were, both temples to Jupiter---- whether intentionally by design, or influenced by some unknown power."

"It is time to go see the good professor."

Michael Dialessi

Chapter 24
Discussing Theology

"Professor Mussen," Dayton said as he knocked on his door. "It's Dayton McCormick."

Mussen limped over to the door and opened it for him. He scratched his head and looked at Dayton. "Hello, young McCormick. What can I do for you?"

Dayton entered the house and looked around the living room. He noticed many packed suitcases on the floor by the couch. "Are you going somewhere?" Dayton asked.

"I'm heading up to see my sister in New Jersey. I was planning on leaving within the hour," Mussen said.

"I won't be long," Dayton said, as he unfolded a news article on the suicide of Senator Cudman. "Did you have a nice Chanukah?" he asked with a smile.

"Quite," Mussen replied. "And thank you for the gift, by the way. I'll reciprocate before you leave. Please, sit."

The two sat on the couch. Dayton began to speak as he pulled out the sacrificial photo and handed it to Mussen. "My father never believed in putting all his eggs in one basket," Dayton said smiling, "but he always made sure he also had a full basket." He stared Mussen in the eye. "And I thought I would return this to its rightful owner." Mussen graciously took it. He placed the sacrifice picture on the table and shrugged his shoulders.

"Could you indulge me in a theology discussion for a few minutes?" Dayton asked.

Mussen raised an eyebrow. "Certainly."

"I finished reading the Bible, Professor. It seems there are many repeating patterns in it that are very

409

similar to----" Dayton continued, as he pointed his finger up in the air. "Upstairs. Forty days of rain. Forty nights in the desert. That sort of stuff."

Mussen put his lips together. "Hmm. And----about how Joseph, the eleventh son of Israel, was called by Pharaoh, the savior of Egypt at age thirty. And how Jesus has been called the Savior of Mankind, and he started his ministry at age thirty. Both were sold out for pieces of silver, by a Judah," Mussen laughed. "If you do the math, young McCormick, from Adam to Abraham is twenty generations which equals 1,948 years----plus or minus a year. In 1947 and 1948, in the 20th century, the nation of Israel was re-established." Dayton reacted with curiosity.

Mussen continued. "You know, we have a President, who lived with his step father in a foreign land, then returned to become a community activist. He ran against McCain, which means son of Cain." Mussen laughed some more. "And, McCain compared him to Moses, a messianic character, in a TV advertisement."

"Yes," Dayton interrupted. "I saw that ad on Youtube."

"Well. Moses was raised by Egyptians. He had a wooden staff. Egyptian mysteries, of course, had a staff of Ra. The Sun staff-----being the chief, or God staff for them." Mussen stood up and walked over to his luggage.

"And Obama has a Chief of Staff, named Rahm Emmanuel. Staff of Ra," Dayton interrupted. "A play on words."

"You're very bright, young McCormick," Mussen replied with a smile as he bent over slightly to arrange his luggage. "But if all you noticed were patterns in the Bible, then you missed out on a whole multitude of more important things. Like morality from the Law-givers. Or God, punishing iniquity. Or human nature, which if you look at it today is little different from what it was in biblical times. Or the messages of Jesus."

"Very true," Dayton smiled. "And that being one of God's chosen people, means you get screwed. Or that events today, are influenced by what happens up in space----just like they always have been."

Mussen nodded his head in agreement. "History does repeat itself. How did Shakespeare put it? All the world is a stage. The only problem is, people don't understand why this is the case. They have forgotten to look up at the sky and recognize the planets all move in the same direction around the sun. And this motion repeats, as does human history."

"A lot of people think the world is going to end," stated Dayton as he stared at Mussen.

Mussen sighed deeply. "Mankind has been trying to find out when that will happen for a long time. I have even looked at it myself. But nobody knows the day or the hour. How could they?"

"Not even you?" Dayton asked.

"Not even me," Mussen replied. "Not Newton, Einstein or ----Washington knew either. Nobody knows that. But that doesn't mean they didn't know how things worked." Dayton turned and looked out the window. He watched a white van pull up near the curb next to Mussen's neighbor's house.

Dayton stood up. "Interesting. I don't want to keep you Professor. But by Jove, you are a very interesting man." Mussen raised his bushy eyebrows, as he caught Dayton's careful use of words. "I am sure you want to get going---and we can continue our theology discussion another time."

"Yes we will." Mussen gave Dayton a funny look. He walked into the kitchen, then returned with an envelope and handed it to Dayton. "Merry Christmas."

Dayton looked at the elder man in front of him. He watched his lips move----silently telling him to open it when he got home. He folded the envelope and placed it into his jacket pocket. Dayton then extended his hand. "Be safe on your trip, Professor."

"I always am. You too," he replied as he shook his hand. Dayton walked out of Mussen's house and got into his Cherokee. He could see the man in the white van was watching him.

"I hope he doesn't end up like Peter, Christopher or my father," Dayton thought to himself as he drove away.

Mussen watched the young man pull out, then he felt his pocket vibrate. He removed his cell phone and answered it. "Yes."

From the other end of the phone, a man spoke. "We see you have been spending some time with him."

"Yes."

"Does he know the date of the sign?"

"Possibly."

"Does he know the date of the other?"

Mussen paused. "No," he responded. "I don't believe he does."

"Don't let your feelings for his father get in the way Richard. Understand?"

"I understand completely."

"But you will keep an eye on him? And you will inform us if he figures it out?"

"Of course," Mussen replied before closing his phone. With the phone clasped in his hands, he muttered, "By Jove," then thought to himself, "I think he knows when, but not the magnitude of what."

Mussen watched the van pull away. When it was out of sight, he loaded up his car with his luggage.

Chapter 25
Annuit Coeptis

Dayton arrived home to an empty house. There was a note on the table from his grandmother. She and Sarah had gone shopping.

He walked upstairs into the study. "Something is missing," he said to himself. He walked down the hallway into the bedroom and pulled the box out from under his bed, then dragged it into the study. Dayton pulled the electric piano out of the box and set it up on a portable stand against the wall. He plugged it in and tested the keys. All of them worked, so he smiled. "Maybe I'll finally sit down and learn to play," he said to himself.

As he stood there and looked at the piano, he placed his hands in his jacket pockets. In the left pocket, he pulled out the envelope he received from Mussen during his meeting with him earlier in the day. "Merry Christmas," Dayton said to himself. He began opening the letter as he sat down in the study chair.

His eyes opened wide as he pulled out two checks and a note. One of the checks was for $9,031 dollars for the sales of his books. The other, was for $20,000, with a memo stating "retainer." "What the hell is this?" he questioned. Both checks were from Triple E books. Both checks were signed by Manly P. Jacobs. "Mussen. That son-of-a bitch!"

His hand carefully opened the note, which Dayton had anticipated would provide some answers to his questions.

Dear Young McCormick,

You are now aware I am the absentee owner of a certain book publishing company. Actually, it is a front for an intelligence agency, for which I will not disclose the name.

I am sure you have many questions. Therefore, I want you to meet me at Patrick Henry's Church in Richmond. You know the one. Look for the place which has the best view. I will be there on March 1st, at noon. Come alone.

I will no longer be at the house in Baltimore and I have resigned my position at Georgetown.

The retainer check is for you. I want you to write another book based on the information you have most certainly discovered. You can make it fictional, if you fancy that. Do not use a computer connected to the internet to write it, or they will find you and kill you.

One more thing: There is another man who is responsible for the death of your father. I will help you find him.

Annuit Coeptis, young McCormick. Look deeper for meaning.

Sincerely Yours,

Richard A. Mussen

P.S. My niece Julie wants to work with you after you finish your next book.

Dayton sat stunned in the chair. "He was holding back----but is he what he seems?" he said aloud. Dayton thought for a moment. "Annuit Coeptis." The professor was always careful about the words he used. They often lead to clues.

He opened his new laptop and turned it on. His fingers typed away as he looked for a Latin to English translator. Upon finding one, he typed in "Annuit

Coeptis." "He approves our undertaking" appeared in the translation box. "Jupiter approves our undertaking?" Dayton questioned, as he also looked at the inscription above the pyramid on the one dollar bill. He thought for a moment. "What if I translate the words separately? Annuit?" Dayton typed in the first half of the phrase and pressed enter. "Oh my God!" Dayton exclaimed in the empty house, as his voice echoed off the walls. "Annuit means to destroy, or annihilate!"

Dayton closed his eyes. "Stop it Dayton. Your father believed in hope. To annihilate also means----to end. Coeptis means----begin."

Dayton opened his eyes. He shut down his computer and folded up the note from Mussen, then placed it among the copies he made in the safe. He smiled. "A beginning and an ending of a cycle----represented by the astronomical birth of Jupiter in Virgo."

Dayton recalled the code which represented the verse from Ecclesiastes. "I am the mother of fair love and of fear and of knowledge and of holy hope. Hope." He put his hand on his father's Bible on the desk, paused and then walked downstairs to make himself something to eat. "So this happens every 5,200 years."

❧

His hand scribbled a few ideas on the notepad, as he sat and waited at the kitchen table. He looked toward the window and noticed a pair of friendly headlights turn into the driveway.

Sarah and Martha entered the doorway carrying shopping bags and was greeted by his smile. "Did you two have a nice time shopping?" Dayton asked.

"You could have come with us if you were home, instead of going up to Baltimore," Martha replied.

"Well----I won't be going up there anymore."

Sarah walked over to him and put her hand on his shoulder. "What are you writing?"

Dayton smiled. "I'm trying to come up with a title for my next book."

Sarah looked puzzled. "I thought you said you were done writing books, Dayton."

"I was, until I got a letter from the owner of the publishing company. I mentioned to him when we talked, that I had an idea for another book, and he agreed. He retained me as an author."

"That's great, Dayton," Sarah said. "I didn't believe you'd stop writing." She looked down on his sheet, which was marred by erasures and pencil scratches. "I like this one."

"Washington's Child. I like that one myself," Dayton replied.

"What is it about?" she inquired. Before he could answer, she asked, "And why are you doing it in longhand?"

"I thought I would do this one old school. I'll type it out when I'm done."

Sarah sat down next to him. "George Washington never had any children of his own. He helped raise Martha's."

Dayton gave Sarah a kiss on the cheek. "I know that. Raising children is a great work. So is being President and designing a city."

"Does this mean you are done with your father's research, or is this part of it? You haven't mentioned it since our last walk."

"Yes----in part. Would you like me to show you everything I found and could I share a theory with you?"

"Sure. Let's go upstairs," she suggested.

"I can't do it there." He closed his eyes, exhaled and then opened them. "Tomorrow is going to be a nice day.

I thought you and I could go up to the Capital." Martha walked by the two of them and winked at Dayton, as she brought the last of the shopping bags upstairs.

"Is something going on?" Sarah asked. "Martha winked at you."

"No."

"Then I'd love to make a day of it tomorrow."

"You'd better get to bed early then. I'll come over around 5AM to pick you up," Dayton said.

"Why so early?"

"So we can enjoy the sunrise together with Mr. Lincoln." He pulled out a copy he made of the map of Washington D.C. from the <u>Picturesque Washington</u> book, and put it on the table. "It has been an amazing unfinished work-in-progress since the 1880's. But now, I think it's done."

"The city?" Sarah asked.

"No," Dayton replied. "The great work that caps the age."

Chapter 26
The Secret of Washington D.C.

"I learned a lot in the past four to five months," he said to Sarah as he drove her up to D.C. "I received a little information from everyone I met----including you." Sarah smiled. "Now, I can't prove in a Court of Law what I am going to show you today. And I don't quite understand the motive behind any of this. It is just a theory based on everything I have learned."

"Sounds like a conspiracy theory," Sarah replied.

Dayton smiled. "Perhaps. But I don't think this is one anyone has ever heard before." Sarah put a puzzled look on her face.

He parked the Jeep by a hotel near Pershing Park, which is close to the White House. After placing a few quarters into the parking meter, he walked Sarah down to the Wall.

Dayton pulled out a pencil and a piece of tracing paper from his black binder. "I need to find a friend of my father's who died in the war."

"You're going to do a rubbing?" Sarah replied. "What was his name?"

"Jeremy Higgins. I believe he died around 1970." The two scanned the Wall.

Sarah put her finger on the black granite. "Here he is." Dayton placed the tracing paper over the name and did the rubbing with the side of the pencil.

"I'm going to put this in my dad's footlocker up in the attic," he said, as he folded it and put it back into the binder.

Sarah grabbed his hand and the two walked down to the Lincoln Memorial. "I think he'd appreciate that," she said.

The two hiked up the white steps of the monument dedicated to the 16th President, then sat on the top step. "The timeline you discovered really opened up all of this for me. Thank you."

Sarah leaned her head against his shoulder. "You're welcome."

"But just as the timeline in the metric scale is for years----kind of like the long count the Mayans had, I believe the mile scale indicates a more short-term timeline." He explained that from the center of the Capitol Dome to Lincoln was 2.22 miles, and that from Lincoln to the center of the Pentagon was 1.3 miles. "3.52 Miles. Or three and a half years. If the Dome is September 3, 2016----then the center of the Pentagon is February 26, 2013---when the outer five planets form the pentagon in our solar system."

"So the world doesn't end in December of 2012?" Sarah mocked.

Dayton laughed. "No, it doesn't. That isn't to say this whole period won't be difficult, or that something won't happen in 2012. But the world won't end."

"Isn't February 26th the same day the Twin Towers were first attacked in 1993?" Sarah asked.

"Precisely. It is all tied together here and is cyclical," he said, as he swept his hand across the Mall. Dayton smiled. "This whole city is one giant observatory. Down over here," Dayton pointed to the Kennedy Center," is what used to be Foggy Bottom, where the first US Naval Observatory was located. Presidents used to observe the stars at night, before all the lights."

Dayton put his arms around her and pulled her close. "Every morning, Mr. Lincoln gets to watch the sunrise. Because the city is laid out from East to West, he always knows what time of day and what season of the year it is, depending on where the sunrise occurs and where the shadows of the Washington Monument are cast." He stood up with Sarah and pointed at Lincoln's seated figure. "Look at his face," Dayton said. "It is almost as if he's waiting to see something important."

"But what is Lincoln waiting to see?" Sarah prodded. Dayton removed a dollar bill from his wallet and pointed to the pyramid roundel. "The man who saved the Union, is waiting to see the union."

"I don't understand," Sarah replied.

"In the box Hartman gave me, there were three aerials. Just as on the code sheet, there were three references to capstones, or cornerstones. Giza, New York and D.C. are related."

"How so?"

"The three pyramids are indicative of three planets," Dayton answered.

"That form the triangle on Sept 3, 2016 in Virgo," Sarah added.

"Yes. And I believe that the eclipse the day or two before will allow someone standing West of the Pyramids of Giza to observe these planets complete them with capstones. It is why they were built at that location. I just don't know what spot you'd need to observe from."

Sarah responded, "So it is like Indian Jones using the staff and headpiece at a certain place and time in Raiders of the Lost Ark."

Dayton nodded. "Yes. The Sphinx, like D.C. and the Statue of Liberty, faces east, where the sun rises. In fact, you could say Lady Liberty is a modern version of the Sphinx and the pyramids because she faces east and indicates three planets in the heavens, in the head of the Virgo Constellation. And she wears a crown. It's a royal trinity."

"This is better than the Discovery Channel!" Sarah beamed.

"Mark tells me the same thing." Dayton gave her a big hug. "The solar system is divided up into declination and right ascension. It is its latitude and longitude." He pointed down the Mall, but about 15 degrees off center to the northeast. "One hour of right ascension means that one hour after sunrise, this trinity of planets will come over the horizon. If the Dome on Capitol Hill represents the sun, which domes and arches traditionally represent, then Union Station is where the trinity of planets will be located at dawn, from Lincoln's view."

"Lincoln preserved the Union. And now he's waiting to see the joining of Venus and Jupiter. This is incredible!" Sarah stated.

"Let's take a walk over to the White House," Dayton said. The two walked hand in hand down Lincoln's steps and past the Wall. They stopped briefly to walk around and look at the World War Two Memorial, then hiked northeast toward the White House.

They paused at the Zero Milestone. "You really can see a line between the White House and the Jefferson Memorial." Sarah turned and looked at the symbols on the stone. "This one is for Mercury," she said, "But why the sun symbol, and why the Fleur de Lys pointing at the White House?"

Dayton smiled. "There are a lot of zodiacs and symbols in Washington. The Fleur is a symbol for the Virgin Mary. It is only fitting, that the Virgin's house of the zodiac, should be white."

"Interesting," Sarah replied. "Virgo is the White House."

"And just behind the White House, is the outline in the streets of the five pointed star of Spica." Dayton paused. "But if you look carefully from above, there is another symbol there."

"What?"

"You forgot what I told you on our walk a few weeks ago. It is the Phoenix," Dayton replied. "There is a big bird there. The fountain in front of the White House is its eye. The glitch in Pennsylvania Ave. of the triangle, around the Treasury Building, isn't a glitch. It is the beak of the Phoenix. The star formation of the streets forms its wings."

Sarah looked at Dayton. "This just keeps getting more interesting, and I do remember our conversation. The Phoenix is the bird that burns itself up and is reborn." She looked toward the Washington Monument. "The Ellipse," she said pointing, "is it's egg." Sarah gave Dayton a strange look. "Didn't a Pope compare Jesus to the Phoenix?"

Dayton laughed. "Yes. Come on. It is almost 9AM. Capitol Hill tours are starting."

The two walked up Pennsylvania Avenue and crossed Third Street. "So on the timeline, this is the Kennedy Assassination," Sarah stated.

Dayton nodded his head in agreement. "A sacrifice at the top of a truncated pyramid." He explained how the solar system was arranged, with most of the planets forming a truncated pyramid with Jupiter at the top. "Annuit Coeptis. Jupiter above the truncated pyramid."

"That is whacked," replied Sarah.

They got their tickets and toured the Capitol Building. "Capitol Hill or Capitoline Hill----For Jupiter, Minerva and Juno."

Sarah looked at him. "Jupiter, Venus and Mercury." She looked up at the Apotheosis of Washington, under the Capitol Dome, and pointed at it. "A triangle shaped cloud formation. This is really, really interesting."

As they walked down the west side steps, Dayton asked Sarah to take a break around the fountain. The two gazed over the Grant Memorial, down the mall, past the Washington Monument and down to the Lincoln Memorial. Dayton turned Sarah toward him and gave her a kiss. "I hope this isn't creeping you out?"

"Are you kidding?" Sarah replied. "This is the most interesting day I have ever had."

"Hopefully it will get even better," Dayton said with a smile. "Let's go walk over to Union Station."

In front of Union Station, Sarah gazed at the large rendition of Christopher Columbus. She smiled. "Columbus. Three Ships. Columbia----the woman with the torch. The Statue of Liberty. The place of the Union."

"You catch on way too fast," replied Dayton. "And there is a walkway, which is like a ray that points to the center of the Capitol Dome." He pulled her hand. "Let's go down K Street."

The two conversed as they walked down to Mt. Vernon Square. Dayton stopped at the corner of 9th and K. He pointed at the main building with his index finger. "This used to be Liberty Square. We're at the corner of 9th and K streets. K is the eleventh letter. 911."

"I don't understand," Sarah replied.

Dayton pointed south. "About .82 miles, or about 4,333 ft, is the intersection of Virginia and Maryland Avenues." He turned to Mt. Vernon Square. "This is the womb of Virgo." Sarah looked confused. "Let's take a walk."

The two walked down 9th street and stopped in front of the National Archives, on the giant rendition of the planet earth. "This is neat," Sarah said. "I'm standing on the world."

"Yes you are," Dayton replied. "If you look at the Mall, as the Galactic Center, with the Peace and Garfield Monuments representing Gemini, then you are standing on where the earth will be in the solar system in May of 2017." He pointed. "Straight along here are the Sculpture Garden and the Hirshhorn Buildings. They represent Venus and Mercury. Because in mid-May of 2017, the earth will be aligned with them, and Jupiter," he said, pointing back at Mt. Vernon Square, "will be opposing."

Dayton pulled out a one dollar bill and turned it to its reverse. "Throughout history, God has been represented as living on the top of the mountain. Moses went up to the mountain top to receive the Ten Commandments and---"

Sarah interrupted, "Zeus lived on Mt. Olympus. So is that symbol in the Pyramid Roundel really a sign for God?"

"No," Dayton replied. "Annuit Coeptis is a prayer to Jupiter. Jupiter above the pyramid."

"Zeus was Jupiter."

"Yes he was," Dayton replied. "But he is not God." Dayton took Sarah's hand and walked her to the Garfield Memorial.

"On both 911 and November 22, 1963, the solar system formed a truncated pyramid from most of the planets. Except Jupiter, which was on top. Like it is symbolically on the one dollar bill."

"Okay," Sarah replied.

"It will do it again in 2015. But on May 20th, 2017, it will be perfect. Both Kennedy and 911 had symbolic natures to them. They were messengers telling of an important future event."

Sarah looked at the bronze plate on the Garfield Memorial. "Hmm," she thought. "Virgin Mary. Union. Womb. That is for a birth."

"Go on," prodded Dayton.

"Phoenix and Jesus," she continued. "I'm confused. With all the religious symbolism, it can only point to one thing----The Second Coming of Christ. The Magi were astrologers. That is why they knew what Jesus' star looked like, and Herod didn't." She put her hands on her hips. "But why are there two suns on this bronze plate?" Sarah tilted her head as she looked at Dayton. "And I thought you said this wasn't about Jesus."

"It is not about the world ending, or Jesus, Sarah. It is a play on words." He realized she was nervous, so he took her hand. "This is all astronomical----like I said." Dayton paused. "It is not about the second coming of the Son of God. It is about the coming of the second sun----Jupiter," Dayton replied.

"Jupiter is going to become a sun?"

"I can't prove it----but everything here points to it."

"For how long?" Sarah inquired.

"If 911 provides the clues, the collapse of the buildings, and the times, point to May 20th, 2017, for the end." He pointed to the date on the side of the Garfield Memorial. "May 12th, or there abouts, should be the beginning. About eight days." Dayton closed his eyes and visualized his mother's headstone. "It is also the same day my mother died. And the last code from my father, said eight days until circumcision. Luke 2:21."

"911 was bad, Dayton. Is something bad going to happen?"

Dayton gave her a big hug. "I don't know. The Mayans believed in cyclical time: A beginning and an end. But a circle has no end----so both points are the same. All cultures around the world have a woman and child in their symbolism. So this has happened before, and we are still here. The end of the world scenario is a western based interpretation, because of the Book of Revelations. This is the beginning and end of an age, marked by an astronomical event."

She looked up at him. "So that is why Virgo is the virgin constellation. People have seen this before, and because it is about forty weeks after the union, it was natural to give it the attributes of a woman and a woman's pregnancy."

"Precisely," responded Dayton. "Concepts come from your head. Virgo's head, therefore, is the place of conception. I don't think the world is going to end, Sarah. Only that a New Order of the Ages will begin. Just like life----with a birth."

Sarah smiled. "So, Jupiter is sort of like a brown dwarf? Like many solar systems, we too also have a system with a binary sun," Sarah said.

"That's my theory. That is why I will name my next book Washington's Child." Dayton waved his hand across the District. "The structure of this city was his baby, so to speak."

"So all this was on purpose?" Sarah asked.

"I think most of it. And once the foundations were laid for the city----the rest naturally fell into place, or someone in the know continued the design." Dayton put Sarah's hand in his. As they walked, Sarah asked about more of the symbolism involved in what Dayton researched.

"Your head is where knowledge is. Virgo is the sixth house of the Zodiac. The capstone sign, Jupiter, Venus and Mercury, occurs at the head. Kennedy was shot in the head from the sixth floor window of the book depository. A book depository is a storehouse of knowledge."

"A creepy ritual by somebody," Sarah said as she walked.

Dayton nodded. "Jupiter is known for sending birds as messengers. On 911, metal birds brought a message. It may not have been the message that the terrorists meant to send, but on inspection of the symbolism involved, it is the only one that makes sense----especially because Jupiter was between the twins of Gemini on 911, and also because the WTC represented King Solomon's Temple, which also symbolically represents Jupiter's temple, because Sol, is for sun, and he was the son of King David. David was also of the line of Judah the lion, or Leo. Therefore the ritual is for the sun of Virgo."

"From what you are saying, I get the impression you think that the stories in the Bible are only allegory. Astro-Theology," Sarah responded.

"Not at all," replied Dayton. "But I do think the pagans who worshipped Jupiter made sure the passages about Jesus which had similar astronomical attributes, made their way into the Biblical canon." Dayton smiled. He stopped in front of the Zodiac Fountain. "Let's stop here and rest for a minute."

"Another complete Zodiac," Sarah said as she walked around the fountain, looking at the twelve signs surrounding it. "I got to tell you Dayton, today has been more than interesting. There is a lot to look at here. And you have an interesting theory."

"It isn't over yet," Dayton responded as he sat down. "Hopefully, it gets even better."

Sarah looked overwhelmed. "You mean there is more?"

"Of course there is. I am writing a book you know. It is going to be fictional."

As she held his hand, she gazed into his eyes. He looked back at her and studied the facial features of the woman he had come to care for deeply. "What is the storyline?" she asked.

Dayton smiled and gripped her hands tight. "I thought I would try something original."

"Well, you've blown my mind all day with your theory. Why stop now?"

"I thought I would write a detective novel."

"About?"

"A young detective who writes a book questioning the validity of conspiracy theories." Sarah narrowed her eyes. "During his first signing, the main character meets a man who tells him his father was murdered, which starts him on the path of discovery, of both treasonous activities and an amazing secret contained in the architecture of America's Capital."

"That sounds oddly familiar," Sarah responded playfully.

"It will have a lot of great stuff in it," Dayton replied. "It will have suspense, action, intrigue and----I'll even throw in some romance."

"Really?" Sarah smiled as she nodded. "You sure this hasn't been written before?"

"No. I am pretty sure it hasn't," Dayton said confidently. "And I was hoping you'd help me write the ending."

"What?"

"Look around at this city, Sarah. It is all about astronomical unions, consummations and cycles."

"And a birth," she added. "Don't forget that."

Dayton reached down into his pocket and pulled out the box containing the ring. He opened it and handed the band to her. "So how does this story end, Sarah?"

She took a moment and stared at the diamond. For a minute, she felt as if she had gotten the wind knocked out of her. When she regained her ability to breathe, she placed it on her ring finger and embraced Dayton tightly. "Your first book was----ok." She pulled her head back, so she could look him straight in the eye. "But I think this one is going to be a best seller," she said, as small tears of joy flowed down her cheek.

"Would the future Mrs. McCormick like to get something to eat?"

After wiping her tears with her hand, Sarah replied, "Yes."

The two walked back to his Jeep in Pershing Park. He opened the door for her like a perfect gentleman and then climbed into his own seat. As they drove away, Dayton took one last look in his rear view mirror at the shrinking Washington Monument.

He looked at Sarah and studied the gentle curves in her face. He smelled her auburn hair discreetly. "I don't know what the future holds," he thought to himself. He turned his head to pay full attention to the road. Clouds were forming in the sky, indicating a storm was coming. But Dayton didn't care. Sarah had said yes.

"But I am still missing something?" Dayton thought to himself.

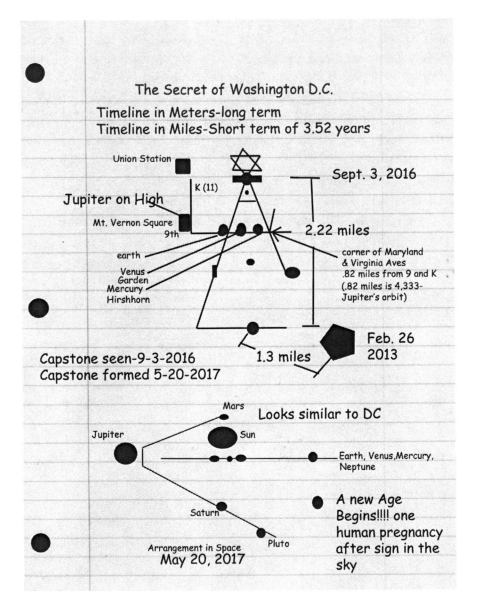

The Secret of Washington D.C.

Timeline in Meters-long term
Timeline in Miles-Short term of 3.52 years

Union Station

K (11)

Sept. 3, 2016

Jupiter on High

Mt. Vernon Square
9th

earth

Venus
Garden
Mercury
Hirshhorn

2.22 miles

corner of Maryland
& Virginia Aves
.82 miles from 9 and K
(.82 miles is 4,333-
Jupiter's orbit)

Capstone seen-9-3-2016
Capstone formed 5-20-2017

1.3 miles

Feb. 26
2013

Mars

Looks similar to DC

Jupiter

Sun

Earth, Venus,Mercury,
Neptune

Saturn

Pluto

Arrangement in Space
May 20, 2017

A new Age
Begins!!!! one
human pregnancy
after sign in the
sky

Chapter 27
The Wiseman

"Nelson, drop me off right here," Dayton commanded.

"Isn't this kind of unorthodox?" he inquired. "An informant, meeting you here?"

Dayton smiled. "Don't worry about it. Just go grab some lunch and pick me up here in a half an hour." Nelson did what he was asked. The unmarked car pulled up next to the red brick sidewalk surrounding St. John's Church, and Dayton got out.

He waited for the car to be out of eyesight before he began his search for Mussen. "Meet me at the place with the best view," Dayton whispered. "It would be a lot easier, if he just gave me a specific location."

He walked around the red-brick sidewalk surrounding the 270 year-old church; made famous by the conventions held during the Revolutionary War. The Second Virginia Convention was the most important. It was where and when Patrick Henry made his famous proclamation on liberty or death. Dayton looked carefully, trying to notice anyone on the grounds walking around with a limp. He saw none. As he walked to the front of the perimeter, he noticed the perfect view of the whole church. Across the street in Patrick Henry Park were a few benches that faced it. "A good view," Dayton muttered, as he noticed someone reading the newspaper.

He tried to sneak up on the man who was reading. As he approached the bench, a mesmerizing voice spoke. "You'll have to do better than that to sneak up on me." Dayton sat down next to Mussen, who then put down his paper.

"I almost didn't recognize you without the tweed jacket and hat," said Dayton. "You don't look like a professor in those clothes, Mr. Jacobs."

"I'm not a professor anymore. So you can call me Richard," Mussen replied.

"Well Richard. You can call me Dayton, instead of young McCormick," Dayton responded. "That name irritated me."

Mussen nodded his head.

"And you can tell me why you have been using me," Dayton stated in a quiet, but stern tone. "I know you had a falling out with my father. He wouldn't give you the Cudman information. Would he?"

"No."

"Why?"

"Because he was doing what I am doing now---- protecting your ass."

Dayton raised his eyebrows. "What is your point?"

Mussen looked straight at Dayton. "When you wrote your book, it raised red flags all over with various groups. You see, there are two which had a vested interest: A good one and a bad one."

Dayton nodded his head. "Continue."

"Mr. Hutchinson was brought in to finish what he thought was a dead case. Your father's information was damning for a number of powerful people, of which, a few more have been quietly disposed of."

"But didn't he work for you?"

"I was the absentee owner. He knew nothing until that red-headed twit figured it out."

Dayton smiled. "Steve. I didn't like him either."

Dayton mentioned the incident at his Grandmother's house. Mussen shook his head. "Hutchinson knew about how the phone system works. He talked, but deliberately gave the wrong date for his arrival at your house. He wasn't supposed to be there until after Thanksgiving."

Dayton laughed. "Well I guess it is a good thing my grandmother was there."

"Quite," replied Mussen. He straightened himself up on the bench. "So, by now you have learned the dates, the real meaning behind the symbolism in the cities and on the currency. And the future we face?"

Dayton sighed. "The truncated pyramid with the triangle and eye represent a 5,200 year period, which begins and ends with the conception in Virgo's head, followed by a Jovian birth in the womb. D.C. is basically one big hieroglyph from above----telling the tale." He looked curiously at his elder. "I am not so sure about the future we face, other than to say it might be difficult." Dayton became irritated. "Why didn't you just tell me about everything that is going on in the beginning, when I first met you, instead of just giving me clue words in our conversations?"

Mussen laughed. "I didn't want to blow my cover, nor deprive you of what certainly must have been an incredible investigation. Your father is smiling now. I'm sure of it. But he also knows how serious this is."

"How serious is this?" Dayton asked.

Mussen explained his role of being caught between two opposing forces. One wants to utilize the upcoming events to their own advantage; the other, to help save people. "The problem is, Dayton, it is hard to tell them apart." Mussen sighed. "When certain events occur----especially at the end and beginning of ages----they can be very unpleasant. This is why ancient people studied the stars and had a reverence for Jupiter. This is why they used the oral and written traditions, as well as architecture, to preserve this knowledge for future generations. Unfortunately, languages change and books burn. Cities tend to last longer. George Washington understood this."

"So what is the name of the evil cult?" Dayton asked.

Mussen remained silent and didn't flinch. "Come on Richard, only a cult would kill a President and 3,000 innocent people utilizing rituals chock-full of astronomical symbolism," Dayton said.

"Jupiter has many names, Dayton. Zeus, Marduk, Amun and Baal. Those who occupy seats of power within the inner circles of evil are going to use the next few years to turn the people against one another and try to establish complete control for themselves."

"What is their name, Richard?" Dayton persisted.

Mussen closed his eyes and bowed his head. "They call themselves the Brotherhood of the Most High. And they have infiltrated every group of note on this planet. They structure their rituals to gain some kind of power from them. I---"

"So, there is a giant conspiracy going on?" Dayton interrupted.

"Yes." Mussen kept his head down. "As we get closer to 2016, we will all feel the noose tighten, and brother will be turned against brother."

"So where do we go from here?" Dayton asked.

Mussen put his hand on Dayton's shoulder. "Finish your book." Dayton nodded his head. "At the end of every age on this planet, there is a final battle between the forces of good and evil. Washington knew the timing for this and much more, and put the signs for it in his city. Over the years, those entrusted, completed the work." Mussen looked at Dayton with sad eyes. "Are you ready for this?"

Dayton responded, "I don't really have a choice, do I?"

Mussen shook his head and quietly replied, "No. This is something your father knew all too well."

Dayton put his hand on his chin. "What about the other man who killed my father?"

"I'm still looking for him. He is an Egyptian and I know he is still alive. Last I knew, he was working for the Brotherhood."

"When you find him, I want to go after him with you." Dayton noticed the grey unmarked cruiser coming down the street. He looked at his watch and stood up. "I've got to go."

"I'll be in touch," replied Mussen. "Change is coming, Dayton."

Dayton nodded his head and walked to the curb. He opened the door and sat down in the car next to Nelson. Dayton buckled his seatbelt and stared out the window.

"So how did your meeting go?" Nelson asked. Dayton sighed and turned to look at his younger partner.

"Change," replied Dayton.

"What's that mean?" Nelson asked.

"I have some change for some donuts," Dayton said as he reached into his pocket. "Let's go get some." He smiled at his partner. "Just remind me to save a powdered one for my grandmother."

Nelson noticed Dayton was troubled. "Are you ok?"

Dayton looked over at his new partner. "I'll explain it to you someday. Right now, let's go get those donuts."

ℓ

Dayton sat down on the chair in the study. He was overwhelmed after his meeting with Mussen. He shook his head as he looked at his desk. The evidence he had collected over the last seven months stared back at him; almost waiting for a reaction. "The Brotherhood of the Most High."

Using his pencil, he made on one page a series of sketches, with a list of incredible symbolic associations that he learned concerning the Kennedy Assassination. He put the final sheet in his binder and snapped the rings shut.

"Whatever cult did this----it looks like they may have planned out others too," he whispered. "But did they plan out every symbolic aspect of these events, or is there something else to all this? And what is this force or power they gain through their rituals?"

He picked up the pad and his pen. It was time to work on his next book.

TO BE CONTINUED

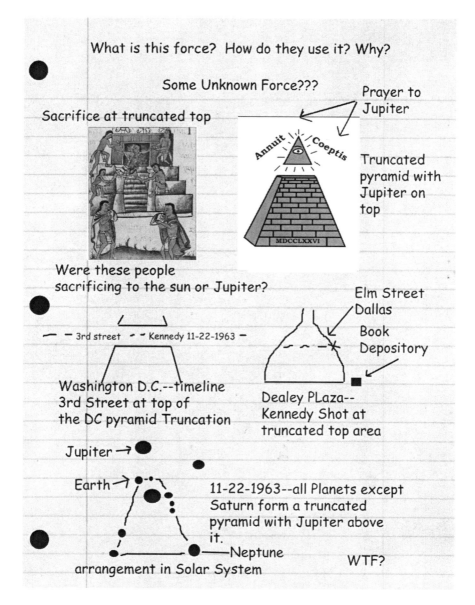

What is this force? How do they use it? Why?

Some Unknown Force???

Prayer to Jupiter

Sacrifice at truncated top

Truncated pyramid with Jupiter on top

Were these people sacrificing to the sun or Jupiter?

Elm Street Dallas

Book Depository

— — 3rd street - - Kennedy 11-22-1963 —

Washington D.C.--timeline 3rd Street at top of the DC pyramid Truncation

Dealey PLaza-- Kennedy Shot at truncated top area

Jupiter →

Earth →

11-22-1963--all Planets except Saturn form a truncated pyramid with Jupiter above it.

——Neptune

WTF?

arrangement in Solar System

437

LaVergne, TN USA
25 August 2010

194644LV00005B/11/P